RAGE AT EDEN

JAMES C WARNE

Matador
9 Priory Business Park,
Wistow Road, Kibworth Beauchamp,
Leicestershire. LE8 0RX
Tel: 0116 279 2299
Email: books@troubador.co.uk
Web: www.troubador.co.uk/matador
Twitter: @matadorbooks

ISBN 978 1800462 281

British Library Cataloguing in Publication Data.
A catalogue record for this book is available from the British Library.

Printed and bound in the UK by TJ Books Limited, Padstow, Cornwall
Typeset in 12pt Bembo by Troubador Publishing Ltd, Leicester, UK

Matador is an imprint of Troubador Publishing Ltd

For Emily

TIMELINE

2045   Global population hits ten billion

2047   World recession; Russia collapses into city states; South American civil wars

2048   Gulf States war; oil production capacity down seventy percent

2049   Global banking collapse; mass unemployment; governments struggle

2050   Africa experiences continent-wide famine and water wars as China withdraws

2051   China invades Taiwan after US abandons area; Israel-Arab war (non-nuclear)

2052   US adopts policy of isolationism; Scotland breaks away from England and Wales

2053   European countries bankrupt; Germany leaves EU

2054   Eastern European governments fall; dictators rise; international commerce collapses

2056   No medicine transport leads to worldwide plague in winter; US and China go quiet

2057   Thirty percent of population dies in just three months; food chain collapses

2057–2068   THE CHAOS

Six billion die worldwide

Records and systems break down; government is meaningless; mass graves are commonplace; cities are abandoned; families are devastated; local strongmen compete with others for resources; no communication from outside world

Civilisation falls

2069   Plague ends; people struggle to survive in near-mediaeval conditions

2072   Rise of warlords and roaming gangs; countries break down into small local areas

2076   World population bottoms out at four percent of highest level

2078   Population now low enough to be supported by local farming communities

2080   Minor wars between local groups all over England

2082   A form of feudal stability takes hold

2100   Old industry starts to reappear – steam, mining, solar, printing

2101   Jeremiah Bowles starts his company in Wilshire, buying and selling

2106   Kernow Collective rebuilds Cornish politics

2112   News from France for the first time in fifty years; Europe in the same position as England

2114   Bowles Mercantile formed, based at Somerton Manor

2124   Bowles Mercantile takes charge of south-west stability

2140   Trade opens with the Welsh valleys and the Middle-lands

2159   Present day

PROLOGUE

THIS TIME THERE WAS NO GREAT FLOOD, NO ANGRY SIGN FROM God that humanity had lost its way. It started slowly, building momentum with no one noticing. Events one day on one side of the planet led to others the next all across the globe, all while people concentrated too hard on their own troubles to notice what was going on. Some spoke out, trying to tell of what was happening to their world, but their voices were lost against the myriad noises of those with too much to lose.

It took just two decades for the civilisation we recognised as unending and complete to collapse.

It takes a century to start climbing out of the chaos it left behind.

PROLOGUE

ONE

Mary Howey sat with her back to those watching, operating the communications system in front of her. Josh Hestor peered over her shoulder at the console, thinking that even with his limited knowledge it appeared to be in good working order. He watched Mary's growing frustration, her head resting on one hand as the other played with the dials and screens running the machine.

Artur Haye glanced over at Josh, raising his bushy eyebrows before sighing and looking back at the table. Just as Josh was about to speak, Mary raised her hand for silence. As she adjusted a dial, they heard a female voice coming through the system, but too quietly to hear it clearly.

Josh leant in. 'Can you make it any louder?'

'I don't think it's our unit – it's turned up to maximum.' Mary glanced round. 'That's the best I can do with the signal that's coming through. I'm sorry but that's it.'

The three of them concentrated on the ethereal whisper. After listening for over a minute, Josh drew his breath in quickly and grabbed Art by the shoulder.

'That's sounds like Amelia, Amelia Bowles. I'm sure that's her!' Josh looked at both of them. Amelia had nothing to do with communications, so to hear her operating the unit at the other end was unusual to say the least.

'Really?' asked Artur. 'How can you tell?'

'It's the way she's talking, it just sounds like her, I'm sure of it. Are we transmitting as well, Mary?' Josh watched as Mary adjusted the systems in front of her.

'We are, but I'm not sure if it's getting through at all. Ours all seems fine. There must be something wrong with their end.' Mary went very quiet, listening carefully to the hushed voice speaking to them.

Josh turned and hurried round the side of the caravan. He looked around the camp to where Tom Bowles had been sitting when he left him. He'd moved in the last few minutes, over to some of the others sitting by the fire. Josh casually jogged over to Tom, beckoning him to come with him.

'What?' Tom said, stretching. 'I'm just getting comfy.'

'Art needs you at the comms.' He did his best to speak calmly, trying to keep the tension out of his voice.

Tom stiffly got to his feet. Before he could ask anything further, Josh ran back to Artur and Mary. Tom quickly followed.

In the few moments Tom had taken to reach the communications wagon, Mary had refined the reception a little further. There was less static coming through and the voice was slightly clearer, but it still sounded faint. Josh looked up, motioning his friend to come closer.

'What is it? What's wrong?' Tom asked.

'Listen. Tell me what you hear,' Josh urged.

Tom focused on the sound coming out of the receiver, but the signal had disappeared briefly. Suddenly, the voice started to talk again, quiet words coming through.

They were all concentrating when Tom shouted out: 'What on earth? That's Amelia talking! What the hell is she doing transmitting? What's she doing in there?'

'I don't know. Can you tell what she's saying? I can't make it out.' Josh let his concern show.

Tom closed his eyes to listen. All four of them sat there in absolute silence. As they did, Josh began to make out the odd word and then it became clearer.

'Tom? … Anyone, can you hear me? … Please, I need— Tom, help…'

Amelia was calling for help, that much was clear.

'Can we reply and ask her what's going on?' Tom asked Mary.

'It doesn't appear so,' Mary said, as she continued to adjust the settings in front of her. 'I've tried a few times, but I don't know if they're hearing it the other end. I'll keep trying, though.'

'Thanks, Mary.' Artur put a hand on Mary's shoulder. 'We need to know what's happened.'

They all stood there, staring at the receiver, the words fading away, until there was nothing coming through at all. They continued to remain quiet; Josh hoped it would burst into life again at any moment.

'Josh, that's a massive breach of procedure! We've got to go and find out what's going on and why Amelia's transmitting.' Tom's voice wavered. 'We're not that far from home – I'm going now. Are you coming?'

'Of course.' Josh took a breath. 'Art, I want you and three others to saddle up and ride with us. Something's not right, so let's go and find out what it is.'

'Absolutely. I'll go speak to Irv and let him know what's going on. Let's be ready to leave in five minutes. I'll take Nolan and Janner with us. They're outstanding rangers – it'll put us at ease having them with us.' Artur strode off to the camp.

'C'mon, let's go get ready.' Josh looked Tom in the eyes as he put his hands on his friend's shoulders, trying to calm him. 'I'm sure there's a good reason for all this, Tom. Let's go find out what it is.'

Josh hoped his reassurance would help. Nodding at the words, Tom thanked him before they both headed back to the campfire.

Josh watched Artur talking to Irving Thales. They looked animated. How concerned were they? He turned the events over in his mind. Amelia shouldn't have been in the communications area – the operators always kept that area secure – so why was she there? Something was very wrong here, and they needed to find out what.

The freshest horses were quickly made ready for the journey; they had been watered already and were felt to be best for the trip back. Although the horses had spent the day pulling wagons, they hadn't been pushed too hard.

With all the preparations complete, the riders started mounting up. Josh stood next to Irving as he gazed around the camp.

'Take a break for an hour or two, to give the rest of the horses a break. Then get everything packed away and load up the caravan, Irv.' Josh kept his voice low as he spoke. 'Head for home the planned way but go via the Sanderson Farm. I'll try and leave a message for you there if I can, just to update you.'

'Okay, be careful and good luck.' Irving matched his friend's tone, his hair flying around his face in the wind as it picked up. He smoothed it back before turning to walk towards the campfire, issuing instructions firmly to those who were staying behind. He started to take charge of the remaining group.

Josh climbed onto his horse, carefully getting his feet in the stirrups before making himself comfortable. He looked at the team he would be riding with and felt prepared for whatever they may find. They were good people, ones he was proud to have on his side. He glanced over at Tom – his silhouette against the skyline looking nervous and eager to move out – and wondered how well he would cope with the next few hours. Tom often allowed his emotions to rule his thoughts at the first sign of real trouble; Josh would keep an eye on him as they rode.

'Let's go, then,' he called out, gently nudging his horse forwards. They were on their way home. He made sure he led everyone out, knowing he needed to take control of the group for now. Although

Tom had been representing Bowles Mercantile at the trade mission up to this point, it was time for Josh to take the lead.

They started out at a gentle pace for the first ten minutes, slowly warming up the horses. The sun was still out; there was a good amount of light to travel with for another couple of hours. Josh planned to travel by the main highways as much as possible, at least until they hit the solar farms. Then they could cut through the countryside back to home, all easily done in four hours or so – at least that was the theory.

As they rode, he let his fellow riders know his proposed route, taking their assent by the nods and grunts that came his way. Few words were spoken.

Picking up the pace, the horses started moving well through the Wilshire countryside. They were riding through a quiet part of the country and could see only a few ancient houses dotted around. Some with lights on inside, others with fires throwing light through the windows. These households had been lived in for a very long time, having been built long before the Chaos. Josh envied their lifestyle, living and working on the land. Maybe one day he would have a family and settle down to a quieter way of living, he thought, just not yet.

As the daylight began to fade, they reached the crest of a hill. It afforded them a good view of the surrounding area. Josh called a halt, slowing the riders before gathering them together. The sounds of the horses panting filled the air around them as they came to a stop.

He glanced at the riders behind him, seeing them all waiting for him to speak. 'Right, if we head east now, we should be at the solar farm shortly, then we'll head home. I said I'd leave a message for Irv at the Sandersons' on the way to keep him updated. Should be home soon then.' He raised his voice for this last part, mainly for the benefit of Tom, who had been so quiet during the ride, but Josh couldn't blame him. He'd feel the same if it were his family in trouble.

'Yeah,' Tom murmured, pulling his hood up over his head.

'So, let's carry on, then. Come on.' Artur pulled on the reins, pushing his horse forwards with his heels. The horse shook his head at the command, whipping his mane from side to side, before reluctantly moving on.

The others followed, pushing on to the next leg of their journey home.

As the light faded further, the pace slowed. But they were still making good time in the twilight. The concentrating faces of the riders grew dark, with the dwindling sunlight directly behind them.

On they rode, past hamlets and farmsteads. All were now dark inside at this late hour, their inhabitants turned in for the night. Soon they came to the grassy banks of the algae basins below Somerton, which in turn surrounded the fishing lakes. They were nearly home. It was good to see familiar sights after their time away.

Suddenly, Josh raised his hand then called a stop to the riders. They all halted at the top of a small rise, watching him as he sat up in his saddle looking at something in the distance.

'What is it?' Tom called out. 'What do you see?'

The ground in front of them slowly sloped away over a mile or so to more dark countryside. The riders looked down onto the murky scene.

With the sun now disappeared, the moon cast its gentle light over the fields before them. It was possible to just make out the skyline in the distance, with the endless scattering of trees dotted around the landscape. It seemed exactly like the last few miles of countryside they had travelled through.

'Look,' Josh urged all of them, pointing over to somewhere on the horizon. 'What do you see?'

'Just fields, I guess.' One of the riders spoke from behind him. 'Nothing else.'

'Darkness!' Artur exclaimed. 'Damn. You're right, Josh.'

Josh turned around. 'There's no power on. You're looking at the Bowles' main solar farm in the territory. And there's no lectric or lights down there – there's always lectric on there.'

Tom looked over at Josh, his hood still covering most of his face. 'I can't think of a simple reason why there wouldn't be any power. I know that facility – even major maintenance can be done whilst keeping the rest of it running. Do you think this has something to do with what's happened at home?'

There were murmurs of agreement. 'Let's find out,' Josh said. 'We'll get a bit nearer, but let's be cautious and take it slowly.'

They rode down a slight incline for a mile, until they came to a lane which led directly to the solar facility centre. They paused, looking for any signs of what had occurred, but seeing nothing out of the ordinary they turned left onto the small track and headed onwards. They were still a short distance away, but already a small plume of white smoke could be seen coming from directly in front of them, highlighted against the night-time clouds. If there were any further proof needed that this wasn't an ordinary problem, that was it.

Artur called them all to a halt and gathered them together. 'Right, everyone tie up the horses. This is as far as we take them.' He spoke quietly as he issued his orders. 'We're going on foot now to find out what the hell is going on.'

Josh recognised the firm authority in Artur's voice, and like the others immediately complied.

Once dismounted, they led the horses to a nearby copse, tying them there with plenty of slack so they could relax and graze. The horses looked to be glad for the rest after a hard journey through the night.

'Art, I'll go with Tom and Nolan, you go with Janner. We'll go in about a hundred metres apart. Keep quiet and try and find out what's happened,' Josh said, keeping his voice low.

'Right,' Art answered, examining the scene in front of him. 'Let's try and fan round to meet up at the main station. It looks quiet, but everyone needs to be on alert. How many people normally work here, Tom?'

'Twenty, give or take. But it could be half of that if they haven't had any problems with the gear for a while.'

'Okay, keep a look out for them, then. They'll be around here somewhere.' Josh looked at them all, trying to reassure everyone. He pointed to the two going with him, beckoning them to follow.

TWO

Josh stepped forwards, attaching his sword to his belt after taking it from his horse's pack. 'Tom, Nolan, let's go and look.' They were doing the same with their own weapons as the trio set out towards the facility. Nolan was an outstanding ranger; his experience made Josh feel much more comfortable.

The three of them stayed within a few metres of each other as they moved quietly towards their destination, keeping low and behind cover where they could. The fields around the solar farm were well looked after, so the going was soft and simple.

After a short walk they came across the farm's perimeter, a small wooden fence meant mainly to keep the wildlife and curious people out. They climbed over and started making their way towards the solar farm centre. The solar panes were all laid out on their stands, neatly in order, row on row. At the first ones they reached, Tom stopped to give them a cursory check over.

'These seem fine to me. Everything looks normal. There's no disruption in this area at least,' Tom told the others, kneeling down to inspect the lectrics leading away from the panes.

Nolan looked around. 'How big is the farm in all, though?'

'About thirty acres or so. But it's not all covered in solar panes,' Tom answered, running his hands over the wires criss-crossing the area.

'So, let's move in towards the centre then.' Nolan drew his weapon, moving forwards half crouching.

Silently, the three of them made their way through the field of panes, wiring hanging haphazardly down from everything they passed, running down to the floor littered with boxes of lectrics. Trying to find their way through the solar panes, as well as looking out for any signs of trouble, was difficult. They could only see a few metres ahead of them at any one time. After walking through what appeared to be a small forest of glass, wire and metal, they paused as Josh raised his hand motioning for them to stop.

He looked around before moving on. With the moonlight fading under the approach of some fast-moving clouds, visibility was starting to decrease. They concentrated on the few sounds around them from the autumn night. Coming from not far away, a crackling noise could be heard. They made their way towards the sound until they were in a position to see what was making the noise.

About forty metres ahead of them was a group of buildings, with the central one on fire. Or rather it had been on fire some hours ago – now it was embers and the remaining glowing pieces of what it had once been.

Josh gave the signal to spread out, each to approach separately from different positions. As they did so, he saw a figure lying on the floor not far from the smouldering building. Josh rushed over to the body, kneeling down before it. The woman was dead, run through by a long blade. Looking around, horrified, he saw another body a short distance away. He got up and hurried towards it. He saw the man's throat had been cut before he even reached the prostrate body, the victim's tunic splashed in dark black liquid. From the feel of the drying blood, it had happened only hours ago.

Josh was on one knee next to this second body, revulsion filling his mind as he fought the compulsion to retch. He slowly rose to his feet, turning to see what Tom and Nolan were doing. He saw the other two standing still, a few metres apart. Then it struck him: they were seeing and feeling the same thing. There were bodies everywhere.

Standing there, looking around the area, with his eyes filling with tears, he could see the remains of what looked like a slaughterhouse. Part of him felt like throwing up, part of him wanted to cry out. He started to move around the sides of the building, kneeling at body after body to see if there was anyone left alive. There was not.

Josh walked sluggishly around the area; it was quiet save for the spitting embers.

Coming to what appeared to be an office building, he noticed the door was open. Calling out, he asked if anyone was inside, to no reply. He entered, carefully pushing the door wide open, and looked around the room. Desks and chairs with piles of paper on them, shelves filled with books and homemade manuals: everything looked normal. After a quick look, he left and headed on to the next building.

Josh opened the door, looking through the doorway, not bothering to go inside. The scene was the same as the previous one. Nothing had happened indoors, it seemed. Pots stacked neatly on tables, fruits and herbs hanging from the walls.

He continued his search. He reached a series of small outbuildings, storage areas by the look of it. The doors were locked and untouched, so he left them for now, before moving back the way he had come.

Tom and Nolan made their way towards him, from the other side of the relay station. As the three men came together, unable to speak, they heard a noise from behind them. As one, they turned and raised their swords, reacting without thinking.

'It's okay, it's us,' called out Artur, arriving through a small patch of trees with the moon behind them. 'We've just found…' He went quiet as he saw the scene in front of him.

'It's a bloodbath here, everyone's dead,' Josh told them. 'We've looked around and can't see anyone alive. Everyone, spread out and see if you can find out what happened here. I don't think that whoever did this is still around but be careful anyway.'

'I'll check out some more of the buildings – there's some still locked,' shouted Tom. 'Nolan, you come with me.'

Nolan followed him over to those buildings yet untouched, as the others fanned out and started to look around for themselves.

Josh stood there for a long time, trying to calm himself, his mind racing. Why would anyone want to attack the solar farm? He had to find out what had happened. He could barely believe the scene in front of him. Only a few hours ago he had been relaxing on the journey back from the successful trade mission for Bowles Mercantile; how unimportant that seemed right now.

He examined the ground, looking at the bodies. There had obviously been some form of surprise attack here. He tried to picture what had happened, but all he could see was death and blood. He knew he needed help understanding this. Artur would surely read what had happened here better than him.

Artur was kneeling down nearby, turning over one of the bodies. As Josh reached him, he stood slowly, looked around and slowly muttered something to himself.

Artur Haye had been Bowles Mercantile's head of security for almost ten years. He was twenty years older than Josh, and the presence he projected in any group indicated he was a man who knew how to take control. As usual, he wore his thick long coat. Well buttoned up, no matter what the season, that coat was always worn.

Josh didn't speak, allowing the much older man to take in the surroundings. He studied Artur as he thought, his face covered with a long, deep scar running from his right eye down to his lips. His short, thinning hair brushed forwards and parted on his left-hand side.

'Looks like a significant group. They came from an easterly direction, settled behind that copse for a while, watching and planning the attack. They then advanced from over there,' Artur said. 'It looks well organised, mind you. And of course, the people working here weren't experienced fighters. I don't think that many of them were even armed when they were attacked.'

Tom reached them. 'That building on fire, it's the main relay station. With that gone, the whole solar farm is useless and remaking those parts will take a lot of time and resources. It means the algae basins production line won't work either as a large part of the lectric produced here is directed over there. It completely stops the honey bars being made, and with winter not far away too. I know food supplies are better lately, but it could be a huge problem if it's a particularly harsh winter.'

'No other building touched?' asked Josh.

'Doesn't look like it at first look, no. All the flowpumps have been left alone and considering they would probably break down from a good, hard kick, it looks like they were purely after the lectrics.' Tom paused, rubbing his eyes. 'I think everyone here had started trying to put the fire out. There's a few buckets lying around on the floor.'

'So, they set the fire, waited for people to start trying to put it out, then attacked. Despicable, cowardly act,' Art ventured. 'Meaning everyone would be busy with the fire and not prepared for anything that was coming. Not that anyone could have expected this, mind you.'

'Dammit!' exclaimed Tom, putting his hands to his head. He raked back his hair before rubbing his forehead. 'Who the hell would do this? This'll take weeks to repair, if not longer. It's huge, taking out the main solar farm. This supplies the company most of its lectric.'

Josh shook his head. 'I don't know, but we need to finish up here and get back home. I'm worried this could be connected to the communications problems there.'

'What about the bodies? We can't just leave them like this,' Nolan said.

'They'll wait, lad,' Artur assured him. 'Right now we need to focus on getting back. This is a major attack on the company's capability. Let's get back home first. We can arrange for all this to be sorted tomorrow.'

Tom was getting agitated.

'Agreed,' Josh said. 'We need to get home quickly.'

Tom nodded.

'Let's go get the horses and get off home. We can be back there about sunrise.' Josh had a rising feeling that this was no indiscriminate attack, caused by random raiders or some disgruntled idiot. No, this had the feeling of a concentrated, organised attack on a hugely vital part of the company's economy. They were deep inside their own territory, nowhere near a border. Anyone who had planned and committed themselves to this act was serious about whatever it was they were up to.

When they reached the horses, they stood in silence for a few moments. Bowing their heads as Artur led them in a small prayer to the fallen. Finished, they readied themselves for the ride home. Hearts heavy and voices silent, everyone stowed their weapons.

They set off at a steady pace, keeping close together, alert for anything unusual around them. The dawn was a few hours away; the countryside around was quiet. The riders pulled their hoods up tight as they rode along, to keep out the night-time chill. It also shielded their faces from each other, hiding their revulsion at what they had seen.

Josh and Artur were at the front, taking them due east, so they could go via the Sandersons' farm. They were an old farming family whose ancestors had been around as long as anyone could remember. Josh had worked there for a number of summers when he was younger. He remembered happier times spent in the fields; the farm was an apple producer with orchards where he would spend his time pruning the trees after the fruit had been picked.

Because of his closeness to the whole family, Josh knew he could trust them with whatever sensitive information he told them. If he left instructions there for the rest of the travelling party when they arrived later, it would be relayed without question.

After the long ride, they found themselves approaching the farm. The full sunrise was still half an hour away, but the pre-dawn light was already beginning to make it easier to see. Riding up a long, dusty path, they saw someone sitting outside on the steps to the home. Josh knew it must be Ben, the owner of the farm; he was an old farmer who was always up before first light. Josh headed towards the surrounding timber fence, climbed down off his horse and approached the seated figure.

'Ben, is that you?' Josh called out from a few metres away, walking nearer.

The man looked up, seeing Josh. 'Josh? What on earth are you doing here at this time?'

'Trying to find out what's going on around here, Ben,' Josh replied, shaking Ben's hand firmly once the older man had risen to his feet.

'How do you mean?'

'We've just come from the solar farm. It's been burnt down and everyone there killed.' Josh's pain showed in his voice.

Ben's eyes went wide. 'What? When did this happen?'

'Not too sure. Yesterday some time, by the look of it.'

'Oh my God!' Ben exclaimed. 'What can I do to help?'

'Did you see any groups yesterday, passing through? Anything out of the ordinary?'

'No one, no. I've been up early the last few days and working out in the back fields, haven't seen anything unusual at all. But that explains the lectric loss we had. It went down yesterday afternoon. We just thought the lines had gone down somewhere – besides, we don't use much of it anyway. I've rigged up our small water wheel for now if we need any.'

'Well, we're heading back to Chilmark, to the company's office complex. There's more following this way, a few hours or so behind as they're bringing some wagons. Let them know what I've said and tell them to leave everything here and to come find us immediately. You can put the wagons in one of the barns, if that's okay? But tell them to be careful and keep an eye out for any problems. Is that okay with you, Ben?'

'Of course, Josh, no problem. If you need anything else, you just let me know, okay?'

Thanking his old friend, Josh started to put out his hand. Ben pushed it away, giving him a huge hug. Telling him to take care and to let him know what they find out, he pulled away smiling. Josh thanked him again before walking back to the waiting group.

He spoke to Art and Tom. 'Ben hasn't heard or seen anything. I've left word for the others to leave everything here and hurry to the complex. Let's get back.'

He remounted his horse and waved farewell to Ben before leading the way. They were now only an hour or so away.

They hadn't been travelling long, however, when they came across two bodies lying on the road. Nolan knelt down beside them, looking them over as the others watched. The story was much the same as at the relay station: killed yesterday after a seemingly quick fight. It was clear that the two dead who lay where they fell were unarmed farmers, not soldiers, so undoubtedly hadn't put up much of a fight. The raiders tracks were clearly noticeable.

Moving the bodies to the side of the road, laying them down in a more dignified position, it was agreed to leave them there for now. They swiftly moved on. Another few miles later, they passed an old barn with yet another body lying just outside. They didn't stop to look closely this time, merely slowing enough to take in the same picture as before. They hurried on up the road; they would soon be past the cornfields and approaching the grounds of the Bowles Mercantile complex of buildings and offices.

Finally, they began a long sweeping turn rightwards, away from the farming community, then into the buildings occupied by the employees, workers, engineers and rangers. Rounding a long stretch of drystone wall, a woman was walking towards them in the middle of the road, directly in their path. As they all halted, the woman ran towards them, reaching them in seconds.

'Oh, thank God someone else is okay!' she cried.

'What happened here?' Josh called out.

'Yesterday, it happened yesterday.' She spoke quickly, breathlessly. 'They came and ran straight through us – it all went so quickly. Before anyone knew what was happening, they killed the guards at the main house. Caused havoc. We didn't know what to do.'

'Who, who came?' Tom demanded.

'I ... I don't know, they just did, it all happened so quickly.' There was nothing useful to be gained from questioning her further.

Tom planted his feet into his horse, causing it to rush forwards. He headed up the road for the entrance to the complex that formed the inner sanctum of the company, including the home of the entire Bowles family. Josh and the rest of the riders quickly followed, hoping that everything would soon become clear.

THREE

Josh rode hard to catch Tom, dismounting as soon as he reached the large, imposing iron gates of the wall around the company's buildings. He saw blood spattered on the floor but could see no bodies accompanying it. While he looked through the gates for any movement, the rest of the group caught up.

Artur looked ahead at the offices and outbuildings and turned to Tom. 'I think whoever did this left as soon as they had finished but be on your guard.' He was already looking around for anything out of the ordinary. He radiated calm, a skilled fighter when needed, a leader of men. And a veteran of more battles and skirmishes than most others alive today.

'Let's just go see what we can do,' Josh said.

They headed towards the house in the centre of the complex, seeing people they knew. Josh felt massive relief at knowing there wasn't a total massacre at home as well. Everyone was hurrying about from one place to the next, the sunrise bringing light to the dark scene around them. Janner went off to see how his family had faired. Art took Nolan to the company barracks area, leaving Josh and Tom running to the left of the company buildings. Heading straight for the Bowles family home.

The home was a large, centuries-old manorial building, a mixture of concrete, wood and black-and-white plazt. The effect was one of efficient style mixed with an imposing air of wealth. There were hardly any buildings around constructed in this style and with these techniques anymore, which made it even more striking to those who visited. It was an ancient building which had been extended many times, built to last but also renovated well over the years, retaining the effect the original builders had intended.

Covering the short distance to the house took no time at all. Bodies lay in a neat row just outside the main door, each wrapped carefully in cloth. There were large patches of blood on them. Josh wondered if there were any more just like this around the place.

Tom threw open the large oak front doors. His wife, Amelia, came out of one of the side rooms. He ran to her and hugged her tightly. Josh could see tears in their eyes from across the hall. Taking a step back, he left them to their moment together, determined to find out what was going on.

His first thought was to head towards the kitchens, always the best place to find out any news, so he walked quickly across the black-and-white marble checkerboard entrance hall and headed into the heart of the home. As he went, he could hear muffled noises from throughout the house. Normally, it was such a vibrant and noisy place. Today, it just felt odd, removed from its previous familiarity.

Reaching the kitchen, he saw Anne Brixey standing in front of the window, her head and shoulders slumped down as she leant against the tiled work surface. Her normally neat long hair fell messily over her face.

Anne was Bowles Mercantile's second in command of security, Artur's deputy. While the others had gone on the trip visiting the Kernow Collective for trade talks, she had stayed behind, looking after the day-to-day running of the rangers and overall security. As she rested against the counter, she looked like she had been through the wringer over the last day.

Anne was a year younger than Josh, but right now she looked ten years older. Her wiry frame and taut muscles looked tense, her usual bright, piercing blue eyes now bloodshot and puffy. She normally dressed smartly with whatever she wore, but today her tunic was unbuttoned, her shirt hanging out. She looked far from her usual self.

'Josh!' Anne yelled, as she glanced up. 'Thank God you're all right. It's been a nightmare here.'

Josh moved to where Anne was standing, put his arms around her, and gave her a tight hug. 'Yeah, I've seen some of what happened, but I don't understand much more yet. I'm glad you're okay as well. What happened?'

'We're still piecing it together. We were attacked yesterday afternoon by about thirty men, and they were quick.' Anne's eyes told Josh she had seen some horrific sights over the last day. 'They didn't seem to be after anything, just rode in making a huge racket. Screaming and shouting to draw us out. As some of us ran out to see what was happening, they were swarming about, killing as many as they could before riding off again. We lost about twenty from the company and a similar number of locals before any of the rangers could arrive, but by then they had gone again. It was all over so quickly.'

'Did anyone recognise any of them?' Josh looked her up and down, so pleased she was unharmed.

'No, not one of them and they weren't wearing any type of uniform or anything. We killed seven of them by the end, but they had nothing on them to say who they were.'

'Do you know about the solar farm? We've just come from there – the relay station has been burnt down!' Josh briefly told Anne of what they had seen earlier.

'What! No, we haven't heard anything about anywhere else. We spent most of last night checking on everyone locally and trying to clean up. And the complex runs on its own solar supply, of course, so we wouldn't have noticed.' She stared at the ceiling. 'So, this is an attack on the company, then. It's co-ordinated.'

'It looks that way, but who's behind it? That's what we need to find out.'

'Has Art come back with you? I'll sit down with him and come up with a plan of what to do next.'

'Yeah, he's gone to the barracks. Where's Mr Bowles?'

'He was up in the northern areas yesterday, visiting one of the trade posts. He didn't take any of those new portable communications units as they're still not working properly, not until we fit the parts you were going to bring back with you. I sent a rider to brief him on what's gone on. I haven't heard anything back yet.'

Josh paused, thinking hard. 'Have you had any news from any of the other holdings or anywhere else yet?'

'A few of the rangers have come back from some of the more local outposts. The crop farms to the south are all fine and none of the honey-hive farms to the west have anything to report either. That's all that's come back so far. Hopefully, we'll know more later.' As Anne spoke her tone calmed.

'Good, well that's something then. How are you holding up?'

'Me? I'm fine. I hardly saw anything – I was down in the range when it all kicked off. The first I heard was when someone came to get me afterwards. When I got back to the house, there was just a trail of bodies scattered around, including the two comms operators. They'd been on a break outside at the time and it looked like they were caught off guard. So many bodies.' Anne fell silent for a moment. 'In all the confusion we asked Amelia to go and transmit to try to contact you lot. She just couldn't seem to get through. I'm not sure she knew what she was doing anyway. Whilst she was upstairs, the rest of us tried to help the wounded and dying. It was horrible.'

Josh wondered what the sight of the aftermath would have looked like, how it would have made him feel, understanding how affected Anne was by it all. He knew how words would hardly dull the pain, so he put his arms around her once again; this time giving her a much more affectionate consoling embrace. After a few tender moments, he pulled away.

Still gazing into Anne's eyes, he let his emotion show more than he normally felt comfortable doing. 'Well, I'm glad you're okay. It's a relief knowing you're here.' He had grown close to Anne over the last year; she had been the first person he had been able to let himself open up to in a long time.

'Don't worry about me.' Anne smiled, squeezing his arm before giving him a lingering kiss on his cheek.

'I'll try not to.' Josh blushed at the feel of her lips. 'Let's get everyone together to try and work out what to do next. Come on.'

Anne followed his lead.

By the time they reached the main hall, Tom and Amelia had moved to a window seat just to the side of the main doors. In the new day, the sunlight was streaming through into the hall, showing off its grandeur. They had been joined by their eldest daughter, Emily, and the three of them were sitting there, the relief that all were okay obvious on their faces. Tom saw Josh and Anne walking towards them; he stood as the two reached him.

'Amelia's been telling me what's gone on,' Tom told them. 'I just don't understand why, though.'

'I know,' Josh said. 'That's the question no one seems to know the answer to. I'm going to get everyone together to try and come up with some answers. Let's meet back here in a couple of hours – we could all do with a little food and some rest, though God knows I don't think I could sleep at all.' He turned to Anne. 'Anne, get Art and the senior staff and let them know what we are planning. I'm going into the town to see if anyone saw anything more than we already know. Tom, you stay here and have some time with your family. You're in charge until your father returns. I'll see you in a while.'

Josh and Anne walked towards the door, slowly heading out into the normally well-kept gardens of the Bowles estate. The lawns in front of the house showed the hoof marks of the attackers' horses. They hadn't attempted to get inside the building, just waited for people to come out, trying to defend themselves, then attacked ruthlessly.

They walked along in silence towards the main gates. Josh felt weary; with no sleep last night and an awful lot of adrenaline having flowed through his system, he was beginning to flag.

Josh stopped once they reached the gates. 'I'm going to get some breakfast at the Lodge and clean myself up a little.'

'I'll walk into town with you, before seeing what help I can give to Art. I could do with a break,' Anne replied.

They followed the path down to the buildings to the south of the main complex.

Around the Bowles Mercantile company buildings and offices, a thriving community had grown up over the last few decades. A large town dedicated to the needs of the leading enterprise of the area, which ultimately had grown into the capital of the new Bowles territory. As the company expanded and extended its influence, buying up and investing in local companies, people started to look to it for support and protection from the roaming groups of bandits hoping to plunder their lands.

'I can't remember the last time something as serious as this happened so close to our hometown.' Josh sighed as they walked along.

'It must be a long time.' Anne linked her arm into Josh's as they walked. 'The Bowles family has put a lot of time and money into the territory's security since before I was born. I can't believe anything like this would actually happen here – it's always been so safe.'

'I know. And the family is so well liked locally. This is something different.'

Anne glanced across. 'So, it's not people we know, then?'

'No. Bowles Mercantile control most of the businesses around here. That's what allows them to spend so much on security. I can't believe it's a local issue.'

They walked along in silence for the rest of the way.

As they arrived at the beginning of the town, Anne stopped, turning to face Josh. 'I'm glad you're back, you know. You go and eat. I'll catch up with you later.' She leant in and gave him another kiss on his cheek, before turning away and briskly walking off.

Josh smiled as he watched her.

The town that had grown up and surrounded the Bowles complex was one intimately known to Josh; he had lived here all his life and was friendly with many of the others living here. As he wandered down to the main square, he looked around, seeing the locals starting to go about their daily routine. For everyone he passed he smiled and said hello, but the replies were more subdued than normal. It was obvious how everyone had been deeply affected by what had happened yesterday. They were a close community.

Reaching the Lodge, Josh wearily climbed the few steps to the door. He opened one of the double doors and walked through; he headed for a table nearest to the window. Once sitting, he felt fatigue course through his body, making him slump into the chair.

'Hey, Josh, you all right?' The voice came from behind him; it was the owner of the Lodge. 'Glad to see you're okay.'

'Hey, Jesse, yeah all good. We've just got back to all this.' Josh relaxed as he saw her. 'I just can't believe it's happened.'

'I know. In all the years I've run this place I've never seen anything quite like it. It's absolutely horrifying.'

'Did you see any of it?'

'No, we didn't hear anything down this end of the town – by the time we did, it was all over.' She walked over to Josh, leaning down to give him a friendly hug, which Josh returned warmly.

'We're going to find out who did it and make them pay, you can count on that,' Josh told her as he pulled away, ready to sink into his chair once again.

'Well, I take it you need some food first. I'll bring you out some breakfast, you just wait there.' Jesse rushed away towards the back of the room. Ever the practical woman, he thought. Josh was glad that she knew him well enough not to want to talk any more.

He sat there, observing the town through the window, trying to process the events of the last few hours. He was exhausted but needed to be sharp – a good breakfast would help no end. The Lodge was quiet this time of the morning, but would presumably fill up shortly. He was glad of the peace around him for now.

The first order of business was to assess what damage had been caused to their facilities and to their people. Once done, they could start to repair that damage and move forwards. Then find out who was responsible. Josh hoped that Mr Bowles would be back soon; he always seemed to instinctively know how to deal with crises.

Jesse approached the table with a smile, laying out an assortment of foods for his breakfast. Fried mushrooms and oatmeal instantly caught his eye. He smiled his appreciation before she left him alone to eat.

Finished, he pushed the empty plate away, sitting back in his chair, sipping the remains of his drink. He was still dog tired but after some excellent food, and a short time to himself, he felt a much-needed burst of energy.

He headed to the counter, hearing Jesse in the kitchen. She turned and started to move towards him.

Josh gave her a weary smile. 'Thanks, Jesse, what do I owe you?'

'Oh, you're all right, on the house this morning,' she replied as she came out from the kitchen. 'Glad I can help in some way. I bet you've got your hands full now.'

'Yeah, you can say that again. Well, thanks again. The food was great. I'd better be getting on. I'll see you soon.'

'And you, Josh. Good luck.'

He walked out through the doors. Time to get back.

FOUR

Josh jogged down the steps, pausing at the bottom to look around. Most of the locals were going about their daily business, albeit under the cloud of the events from yesterday. He headed into town.

He noticed the local doctor's rooms were open. He approached the rickety-looking door and knocked twice. Hearing no immediate reply, and deciding that he didn't have too much time or patience this morning to spend on niceties, he pushed the door open with a loud creak before walking in.

The first thing Josh saw was the usual neatly stacked rows of medicines and herbs, each carefully labelled in different-sized jars. It would have looked like any other day in the doctor's rooms were it not for the large pile of bloody rags thrown into one of the corners. The doctor was scrubbing his hands at the sink. He turned his head as he heard the steps of someone entering, smiling as he saw who it was.

'Joshua, good to see you – how are you?'

'I'm good, thanks, Doc. We just got back an hour or so ago. I thought I'd try to understand what happened yesterday, see what the locals saw.' Josh leant against the wooden desk at the entrance to the rooms.

The doctor slumped against the sink. He had dark circles under his eyes. 'Good luck with that. As far as I know not many saw anything. I certainly didn't. The first I heard about it was when one of the groundsmen came to call me up to the main house. When I arrived it was utter mayhem, but everyone responsible for this appalling act had gone. I'm just resupplying at the moment before I head back out to revisit the wounded.'

'Is there anything at all you can tell me after seeing the bodies, the type of weapons or anything unusual you found?'

'I'm afraid not, my boy. Standard blades by the look of it – just a quick, sharp strike, I would say. I've thought about it over and over. I can't see anything which would give a clue as to who they were. I'm sorry I can't help you more.'

'Not your fault, Doc. I know you would have done as much as anyone. The first thing we need to do is work out who did this, then we might be able to work out why.' Josh was feeling tired again; it was surely coming across in his voice.

'If I do find anything out, you'll be the first to know, okay?'

'I know. Thanks, appreciate it. I'll see you soon.' Josh shook his hand before hurrying back out onto the street.

He walked along the row of old buildings in silence, watching the traders and craftsmen opening their workshops, day-to-day life resuming. They were a resilient lot, accustomed to adversity.

He made his way towards the town's centre. It had originally been built around a small, yet striking, concrete square, with an ancient carved-stone monument in the middle. It was in the form of an obelisk, three metres high and one metre wide. The lettering on it was all but illegible now after so long, commemorating someone or something that no one now remembered. It must have meant a lot to people in the past, so the locals maintained it as best they could.

Since the Bowles family had chosen the town as their headquarters, it had grown from its simple origins. There was now a hectic mixture of differing structures scattered around the old brick buildings, in a fairly haphazard fashion. From large wooden functional buildings, elegantly built like the Lodge, to single-storey reclaimed plazt ones, some built merely as a shelter over an open-fronted store where the owners could ply their craft. Others were larger, barn-type buildings used for the ancient trades which had made a comeback recently. One of these plazt and brick buildings contained the local blacksmith, another the glass workers. They all stood side by side with each other, giving the town a feel of someone having just thrown it all together, with no thought as to what the finished look would convey.

Josh moved from building to building offering his thanks or thoughts, whichever was needed. Yet each person he spoke to couldn't add to what Jesse or the doctor had already told him.

Tired, and a little disheartened by his time spent in the town, Josh decided to head back to the Bowles complex. As he walked, he saw the local pastor across the road, consoling a distraught woman currently in tears. Mose Tayl had been the pastor for a few years now. Josh wasn't a devoutly religious man. Maybe that was why he liked Mose so much – the pastor never forced his religious views on anyone but was more than willing to talk when asked about such matters.

Josh raised his hand, not wanting to wave at such a painful moment. Mose nodded slowly in reply.

Back at the iron gates, he saw a lot more people outside the house than before. It looked like Anne had gathered everyone they needed already. He walked briskly up the main drive towards Artur, who was standing to the side of the building, talking to a small group of staff.

'Hey, Art,' he called out as he approached. Just as he did, the group broke up, letting Artur turn to face him. 'What have you found out?'

Artur looked over with a weary face, his deep scar looking taut on his cheek. Josh realised the old man had known every one of the rangers well, to him they were like an extended family, and it was hitting him hard finding out who had died yesterday.

'It looks similar to what we found at the solar farm,' he said. 'They came in from the east, skirted round the main roads before approaching from the north of the buildings. Only this time they weren't after any buildings, just rode straight through, spending the time attacking whilst minimal defence was put up. Killed as many as they could before quickly riding off, similar as at the relay station.'

'Anyone get a look at them? Any ideas who they were?'

'A couple of the rangers did, yes. But they didn't recognise any of them.'

'So, we're still no nearer working out who did this, then, dammit.' Josh felt the rage rise through him.

'Not yet, no, but we will keep searching, if there is anything to be found we will find it. I've sent out a few of our best scouts to track where they went and see if there's anything else we can find out. We'll find them, don't you worry about that.'

As they were talking, Tom had been hurrying towards them. He took a deep breath before speaking.

'Dad's on his way home – a rider just came back and said that he will be here soon.' There was relief in Tom's eyes. He idolised his father.

Artur gave Tom his broadest smile at the news. 'Well, that's great news. I'll be glad to have him back here in charge.'

'When's he back?' asked Josh.

'An hour or so, they reckon. I'm going to gather everyone together in the main hall, so we are all ready for when he arrives. I'll see you in there in a bit.'

'I'm glad Mr Bowles is on his way back,' Josh told Artur, grinning at Tom's relief.

'We all are,' Artur agreed, clapping Josh on the shoulder as they began to walk to the house doors.

They were amongst a large group of people. The heads of all the departments had been urgently gathered; most had been in the area for an upcoming council meeting. They ran all of the companies of Bowles Mercantile and all looked deeply affected by the events of yesterday.

Josh saw Tom talking to everyone as they walked, letting them know what he had been told. As they began to hear the news that

Mr Bowles would be arriving soon, each face showed its own relief at the news. Eventually, once Tom had informed each person, everyone headed inside to the conference area of the house.

A thump right in the middle of his back made Josh jump. Leila Bowles grinned as he turned around.

He beamed as he caught his breath. 'Hey, Leila. You all right?'

Leila smirked back at Josh. 'I'm good, thanks, knackered but good. Glad to have everyone around right now, and it's good that Dad's on his way back soon.'

'Too right.' Josh gave her a large friendly hug, enveloping her small frame. 'I'm pleased you're okay too. When we heard Amelia on the communications, we didn't know what to think.'

'That I can believe. We just thought that any message going out was better than nothing. I'm just relieved you heard it. Tom told me you came back as soon as you could. Thank you.' She squeezed Josh tight before pulling away. She tied her long, curly hair into a ponytail, looking up at him.

'And I'm glad you're safe as well. Don't know what I'd do without my oldest friend, you know,' Josh told her.

Leila bowed politely, before hitting him gently once again.

Taking his arm, she walked with him towards the house where most of those waiting around had now entered.

As they walked, Leila spoke quietly. 'Tom told me about the solar farm relay station being destroyed and everyone there killed. It sounds terrible what happened.'

'All of them. It was horrendous.' Josh paused, picturing the people he had seen slain there, the scene crystal clear in his mind. 'And the attackers knew what they were doing, that's clear. A quick strike and it puts our lectric output down to incredibly low levels.'

Leila patted his arm. 'We'll get it back up as soon as we can – I'm going to take personal charge of it.'

Josh relaxed slightly hearing that; he knew that she would undertake the task better than anyone else could.

They walked through the large oak doors and followed the group to the left, through some even grander internal doors. Still arm in arm, the two of them were the last to go through.

All of the department heads, the security detail and various assistants were taking their places around an extremely long and highly polished plazt table, which could have held more if the occasion had needed it. The table was right in the middle of the Bowles forum, the main meeting place of the company.

The room was on the west of the house and was a later addition to the building. Originally it had been designed as a huge orangery, the tintglass keeping the room warm but never hot. But as the company grew, with more and more stakeholders involved, it was eventually converted into the grand forum where all the main assemblies took place.

A large ornate oak chair at the head of the table was where William Bowles ran his empire. On its left was where his closest advisor, his daughter Leila, sat. She was in charge of the company's investments – a genius when it came to figures or contracts – and running the business was made considerably easier for her father by having her in the middle of everything. She had dealt with all the Bowles Mercantile estate acquisitions and trading contracts since she was a precocious teenager.

Artur was already sitting in his chair on the right side with Anne behind him, ready to supply him with any information he didn't have at hand. The two were discussing some matter quietly as Josh looked over. Anne briefly looked up to give Josh a warm smile. Around the table, everyone was either taking their seats or just about to, the large number of quiet voices combining to make a kind of low rumbling sound in the room.

Leila let go of Josh's arm. 'Right, I'll catch up with you after.' She headed over to her seat, briefly chatting to Irving who was already sat down next to her.

As company quartermaster, Irving worked closely with Leila, supplying her with information about whatever she needed. The two of them knew everything that there was to know about the state of the territory.

Josh thought Irving looked tired; the overnight race home on top of the couple of weeks away on the trade mission weighed heavily on him. His unkempt wispy hair looked even more dishevelled than normal.

The older man had wanted to be on the trade mission himself, rather than send one of his juniors, to show how important the trip was to the company as a whole. He was fascinated by some of the technology revival techniques used by the Kernow, and he wanted to see for himself what they were doing. He was in his fifth decade now, having spent many of the past years reading as much about the old times before the Chaos as he could. He always told people how the technology that existed in those times fascinated him, as well as how they had lost it all.

In the large room the seating plan wasn't exactly a hierarchy radiating from the head of the table, although undoubtedly William's senior advisors sat next to him. It was clear that the nearer you were the closer you were to power.

Josh's seat was towards the other end of the table, but he didn't mind at all. It allowed him to steer clear of the politics he so hated, while still giving him a seat at the table, literally. His nominal role here was as the member in charge of maintaining the complex buildings and estate for William Bowles. There was a team of dedicated staff who looked after the estate, gardeners and woodworkers, whom he guided in the running of the complex.

However, that was not how Josh had been asked by William to serve him. Knowing that the young man was popular amongst the locals, William relied on him to be his eyes and ears on the ground. Josh helped the company by listening to what people really thought of how everything was run, ultimately reporting back directly to Leila and William himself. This bought the people's real concerns and problems straight to the leadership of the family, missing out all the normal lines of communications. All told, he liked to think of himself as a friendly trouble-shooter.

Josh had learnt to do this well during the last couple of years, and it soon became a popular move, which made everyone respect the family even more.

He took his seat next to the head of the algae farming division, an important part of the Bowles Mercantile company. The reintroduction of the protein-rich algae food bars and biscuits, combined with its large-scale manufacture, had brought about huge health benefits to the territory. Especially once combined with the honey produced by many farms in the area. This knowledge had all but disappeared since the fracturing of the workforce a century before, but now with a strong family controlling the local economy, more firm planning allowed the old industries to be brought back.

Josh shook her hand as he sat down. 'Everything going well?'

'Very well, thanks,' the woman replied. 'The new facility over at Shapwick is working out well. They've worked really hard setting up the flowpumps as the land there is quite silty. We're even going to put some of the new designs into use soon, hopefully.'

'Excellent, it's nice to hear some good news.'

As he was speaking a young girl rushed through the door, leant into Tom and gave him a short message before turning sharply and leaving.

Josh watched as Tom moved to behind his father's chair, his face beaming. The young Bowles dramatically raised both his arms, motioning for quiet. 'Colleagues, I've just been informed that my father has arrived and will be here once he has freshened up. He's been briefed on what's happened and he asked me to give all of you the same information, so we are all aware of the facts.'

Tom began to lay out the specifics of the two strikes. He updated the group about the solar farm station attack and the loss of life that followed. Anne then stood and briefed them on the assault on the main house, answering the few questions put to her as best she could.

The people around the table listened solemnly. Finally, Anne sat down allowing Tom to stand and thank her.

Suddenly, Tom fell silent. William Bowles appeared through a door in the corner. His tall, muscular body, topped by his thick, dark moustachioed face, gave off an appearance of command and strength. He wore polished black riding boots with a deep blue tunic and carried a brass-topped cane.

'Right then, everyone,' he said, his face stern and resolute. 'What the hell is going on?'

FIVE

The question hung in the air. Josh glanced around at those seated at the table, tentatively waiting for someone else to offer up any kind of explanation. Unfortunately, no one had any to give. William leant forwards, placing his cane and his large hands on the table in front of him, looking at his people. His eyes darted around, urging them to give him some news.

Artur was the first to break the silence, clearing his throat loudly. 'Well, we've all been briefed on what's happened,' he stated coolly. 'Now it's time we understood why and by who. I've sent out all our scouts and a number of the rangers, mainly concentrating on the north and eastern routes as that seems to be where they came from.'

'That's a start, but how on earth could this happen? Who feels that they can attack us like this?' William's voice boomed around the room, not quite shouting but almost.

Josh watched the blank faces in front of him all telling the same story: no one had any knowledge of who had committed such a monstrous act.

Anne ran her hands over her hair, smoothing down some loose strands before leaning forwards in her chair. 'We need to look at this logically. As Art said, the best information we have right now is that they appeared to come from the east and that's the way they've gone back. We've managed to track them that way already for a short while, hence sending the scouts after them. Some of the outlying locals we've talked to have confirmed this.'

Josh agreed with Anne. 'We can also say that they weren't your typical raiders – they weren't looting anything at all. Art, did you think they were after anything other than causing confusion? They didn't try to take anything in particular, did they?'

'Nothing. This was purely a strike on us and our lectrical power, I'm sure of it. They didn't touch any part of the pumping stations either and those are much easier to damage since they are mainly made up of scavenged parts.' Artur looked straight at William. 'It must have been premeditated. They came deep into our territory to attack the solar farm, then rode through the complex on their way back.'

Josh listened intently as Anne pushed on; he felt she was beginning to make progress. 'So, if they weren't raiders, they were organised with a purpose, which was to weaken us. And not just by taking lives – that seemed to be a secondary function of the attacks. The first target, the lectrics, was their main goal. The question is, who wants that enough to try something so bold?' She left the question hanging there.

William lowered his head, still standing. 'We all know that ever since the famine times, there's been gangs operating from the edges of the old capital, but it's never really been more than a minor worry. There's always reports of some crop stores going missing, machinery being stolen, minor problems really. We've put it down to the affected smallholdings' closeness to the wilderness of London.'

'Aren't those lands completely uninhabitable?' Josh asked. 'Without the land to grow crops on, the whole area is a polluted wasteland.'

'It is, but there've been some travellers telling stories of a larger collection of bandits than ever before. I must admit I didn't pay much notice to them. Maybe they were on to something.' William paused, looking around.

'And considering we have pretty good relations with our surrounding territories to the north and west,' Leila added, 'there could be a new player rising in the east.'

William pulled out his chair and sat down, turning his attention to his daughter. 'Have you heard anything more recently? Any approaches for trade or the like?'

'Nothing really, no. Just the same rumours you've heard, I guess. Trouble is, we don't have much information from those areas. There's been some rangers look around every now and then, but they never found anything of note.'

Artur spoke up, his anger showing. 'Whoever it is, we need to know if there is something more going on over there than we currently know. And if this was some form of power play by whoever is in charge, then we should cut it off at the knees.' He sat back, having said his piece.

One of William's assistants passed him a sheet of paper. William slowly read out the names of those who had died in the attacks. Once finished, he led the table in a moment's silent prayer for the dead.

At the end of the silence Artur struck the table hard with his fist. 'We should take a large number of rangers and go and make a show of our strength to whoever it was. Make sure they are thoroughly cleaned out.'

'How many could we get together quickly, Art?' William asked.

Artur thought for a moment, tallying the numbers. 'We can raise a hundred rangers fairly easily, over the next day or so. Most live in the immediate surrounding areas and we can draw the others from around the territory on the way. There's a few more to the west but they're too far away right now.'

Anne spoke up, with a hint of caution in her voice. 'We don't know what we're up against right now – that's a lot of lives to risk against an unknown enemy.' She looked at William.

William took a deep breath. 'I know, Anne. Believe me, I know. I care for all my people, especially the rangers who risk their lives for me. I wouldn't put them in harm's way, not if I can help it.'

Three seats away from Leila sat Henry Martgen, a small, shrill older man, wearing his small round eyeglasses. Henry sat on the board to represent the local farmers in the area.

Henry leant forwards to look at Anne, jabbing his finger hard at the table. 'May I remind you, that whoever they were, they came here and killed our friends and relatives. We need to strike back with utter conviction and not give them any chance of surviving. We are in charge of this territory and everyone needs to remember that.'

Anne responded. 'I'm not saying we don't, Henry, just that we don't know anything about them, whoever they were. We don't even know where they come from! We can't have such a casual attitude to sending people to their potential deaths!'

Henry stood, looking over his eyeglasses at the people watching him. 'If it's the same group I've heard of, then there's about thirty or forty of them – they seem to have grand ideas but are really just a motley crew of thugs.'

'When did you hear that?' Leila asked.

'A couple of weeks ago, if it's the same people we are talking about. One of the farmers out east needed some help in restocking his seed store after they took the lot, so I helped him with what he needed. It must be the same lot, mustn't it?'

Artur looked up from the notes he was taking. 'Stands a good chance – can't be too many groups like that operating in the same area. Thank you, Henry, that's good information.'

'It still doesn't mean that we know what we are dealing with, however,' Anne said, raising her voice. 'We don't know where they are either.'

'Then we go and look for them and we don't rest until they have been dealt with. I've represented farmers on this board for years now. We will be the first people affected if any more trouble comes our way.' Henry jabbed his finger down hard three times. His passionate response was clearly rousing some of the other members of the council, especially those who came from the east of the territory. As he spoke, a number of others were loudly agreeing with him.

William stepped in before the discussion descended into a shouting match. 'Thank you, Henry, I know how affected everyone has been here and I appreciate your candour. Please take your seat again.'

The noise in the room increased as everyone began a free-flowing conversation across the expansive table. Most agreed that they must act; they just all couldn't decide on exactly how.

William walked around the table, stopping to join in a few conversations as he did so. After a few such discussions he reached where Josh was sitting.

'So, Josh, what do you think?' he asked as he put one of his hands on Josh's shoulder, bending down to his eyeline.

Josh appreciated being asked; William had often told him how much he valued his thoughts. He respected the Bowles moral code and had grown up trying to live in a similar way.

Josh leant back, smiling at the man he was honoured to think of as a father figure. 'I'd like to think that going in there in numbers with a good force would sort it out, but what if it didn't, or what if it did and the next time it didn't? Wouldn't it be better to find out what's out there and try to come to some sort of accord?'

'Do you think it would be that simple?' the algae farmer sitting next to him asked.

'It's never that simple.' William gave a wry smile, shaking his head as he answered. 'Josh's answer is the right way – it's just not necessarily the best way, not after what they've done.'

'Whatever you decide, we will support you. You know that, William,' Josh told him.

Josh had grown up around the Bowles family; his parents had been senior members of the company. When Josh was orphaned, William Bowles ensured the young Josh was well looked after, organising his adoption by an older couple who ran the maintenance of the Bowles home. Throughout his childhood he had spent a lot of his time with the Bowles children, even taking some of their private lessons with them.

William muttered an acceptance to the support, but in a kindly manner, revealing to all he hadn't made his mind up. He walked over to the window, looking out to the fields beyond the complex.

Tom joined his father and they talked quietly. Eventually William grasped his eldest son by the shoulder; both of them stood in silence for a few moments before heading back to his seat. Tom, as heir to the Bowles company, stood behind his father rather than sitting. It was as William had done to his father, a tradition he was keen to continue.

As William approached the large leather seat, the general clamour around the room faded away to silence; everyone stopped their conversations and all the faces looked expectantly to their leader.

William took a deep breath, expanding his large frame. 'I must admit, it does look like there is a new group flexing its muscles in the east. We've all heard some stories over the last year, and what Henry has added today confirms this. These were no normal raids, by any means. They deliberately targeted our main solar farm, which will set back our algae basin and food production capacity. Whilst it isn't catastrophic, it is a major hindrance to us. It also shows us that they know where our strengths are – that means intelligence-gathering on their part. And the attack on the complex, well, that was designed to show off their strength to us, to get our attention. Well, they have it now.'

William waited, looking around at the council members. 'We must respond with a show of force. These people have killed those amongst us, with no mercy and for no reason. I agree with my head of security's advice to take a hundred rangers and crush whoever did this. I wish we didn't have to do this, but they have made this first move and we must finish it.'

For a few moments no one moved or spoke, then Henry Martgen rose to his feet. 'Thank you, William. This is the right thing to do. We must avenge those killed. You have our full support.'

One by one the others stood, all voicing their agreement. Some urged caution in how the task was approached, but in general the mood was one of sombre confirmation. It was part of the history of Bowles

Mercantile that major decisions like this always had the standing majority consent of the board members.

Finally, after everyone else had had their say, Josh stood and looked around. 'I'm not sure it's the right course of action, to be honest. I understand everyone's argument for it, but something doesn't feel right. Whoever did this surely knew that we would come for them – why would they push us like this?'

Henry rounded on Josh, spitting his words out. 'Irrelevant, it's been decided, a clear majority agree.'

'I was about to say,' Josh replied firmly to the older man, 'that whilst I have my reservations, I will, of course, agree with the majority decision.' He stared at Henry until the older man looked away.

William watched the confrontation with a wry smile on his face. Henry had always complained about Josh having a seat at the table, saying he represented no one and had no right to be involved in any decision-making. William had repeatedly shut down his argument.

'Then it is agreed. Artur, make the arrangements, please. Let me know when everything is ready.'

Tom spoke, still standing behind his father. 'We'll take a short break now to allow those involved to leave and start the preparations. When we return, I want to go through all the necessary actions we need to take to restore the solar farm back to full working order. We must ensure our food production isn't affected too much.'

William said a few quiet words to his son, then left the main room through his private door. Artur and Anne both left together, deep in conversation, planning the forthcoming mission.

Inside the reception hall of the house, there were streams of people rushing in every direction. Josh headed towards the main doors to get some air; he was still worried that there were too many unknowns in this situation, too much at risk. He needed to clear his head.

He made his way onto the lawn, standing on the dry grass, closing his eyes and breathing slowly. Although he had his doubts, he must prepare himself for what was to come.

Opening his eyes, he steeled himself, before walking down to the barracks where the preparations would be underway.

As Josh made his way down the side of the complex, heading towards the ranger garrison, he saw Artur and Anne had started with the preparations. They had gathered together seven messenger riders and were issuing orders to each of them.

Josh reached Artur, acknowledging him as he approached. 'Do you think we will be ready to leave in the morning?'

'Should be,' Artur answered. 'We've told some of them to tell the further away rangers to meet us along the way, so they don't have to come here first. I expect us to have everything more than ready by the time we leave.'

'What about you, Anne? You look worried?'

Anne nodded carefully. 'I am. I'm just not sure about this. But we're planning the route now. Hopefully some of the trackers we sent out earlier have found the way they went, so we can update it as we go.'

'I think it will be obvious the way they went,' Artur reassured them. 'You can't hide the tracks of that many riders.'

Josh admired the older man; he had listened to him tell of many skirmishes and battles he had been in, even a small tribal war when he was a young man in a different territory. Artur had seen all of the events in his life through the eyes of a soldier, one who was always seeking the best tactical advantage.

'Who's leading the teams, then?' Josh asked.

'William will be leading one and I'll head the other. We want to make sure that this goes seamlessly.' Artur's thin hair lifted in the slight breeze. 'The two groups will stay within a couple of miles of each other for safety.'

'Okay, I'd better go and get my things ready.' Josh watched Anne as he was speaking. Seeing the concern on her face, he smiled encouragingly at her. 'I'll see you before I go.'

'Don't worry, I'll take good care of him.' Artur laughed in Anne's direction, before carrying on with their planning.

Josh wandered down to the barracks to get the equipment he would need. Although he had a seat on the board and was a member of the Bowles inner circle, he still was a temporary ranger. As were so many workers from the territory. Over the last few years the numbers of full-time rangers had been decreasing steadily and part-timers rising. With the co-operation to the south-west and seemingly good, if not quiet, relationships with the other bordering territories, the regular fighting ability of the Bowles company had slowly declined.

Josh carried no rank, which allowed him to be a part of the troops and not above them, like so many officers were. Just like in his day job, it allowed him to understand how the people on the ground felt and thought.

The barracks was a hive of activity. Men and women rushing around, laughing and joking with each other. There was a palpable sense of nervousness amongst the rangers, which they were trying to relieve by lots of noise and joking around.

A few of them saw him passing, acknowledging him with a few words and lots of nods in his direction. Josh had spent many hours with many of them, both in training and in occasional real-life sorties. He walked a little slower as he was amongst them, saying hello to a few, but he didn't stop to chat.

He went up to the hatch built into the front of the structure. Leaning onto the windowsill below the only window in the side of the building, he peered in.

'Hey, Joshua, how're you doing?' asked the master of the rangers' stores. The master had been an old man when Josh was young, having worked for William's father, Jeremiah Bowles, as a young boy in the early days of Bowles Mercantile. He knew every one of the rangers and had a story for each of them whenever they wanted to hear one.

'Good, thanks, Master. Just here to get some things for the trip.'

'Of course.' He hurried away, gathering items from behind him in a rather random and haphazard way. 'I'll see what I can do.' And in a flurry of action, Josh saw water bottles, firestones, cooking cans and other assorted items being thrown into a bag with speed he wouldn't have thought possible from the old man.

Thanking him, Josh took the bag offered. He hurried back down the steps of the stores, partially to allow others to have their turn but mainly so he didn't get dragged into one of the master's old-time stories. He slung the bag over his shoulder, moved off to retrieve his sword and thought about tomorrow.

SIX

THE RANGERS WERE GATHERING ALL AROUND THE BARRACKS building, now overflowing due to the numbers having arrived from the local areas. The quarters were built to hold forty people inside, so tents and temporary shelters had been thrown up for the evening. No one minded, however. The nights were warm right now with the rangers focused heavily on their task. Josh spent a relaxing few hours chatting amongst the throng.

He spent some time looking at the men and women who were ready to ride blindly into this fight, wondering even deeper if this was the right decision. So many of the rangers here were part-time; in the last few years, a lot of the older ones had hung up their straps. Most of the new intake were young workers who joined for the enjoyment of weekends away from their families, not understanding the true need of the role.

Theirs was the first generation that no longer had anyone around alive who remembered life after the famine times, let alone any people who told of tales from before the Chaos.

As night fell, Josh made his excuses to the surrounding rangers, walking back up to the house.

He made his way through to Anne's small office towards the rear of the building. The door was slightly ajar, and he could see her flicking through a sheaf of papers. He stood in the doorway. God, she was beautiful. And not just that, she was fiercely intelligent. Driven too. She looked up and smiled.

'Come in.' She chuckled. 'Bit creepy just standing looking at me, isn't it?'

Josh felt a little sheepish at being caught watching her. 'I was just about to knock, actually.'

Anne stood and walked round the table to him. She took his hands in hers as she looked into his eyes, before putting her lips to his and kissing him quickly. Josh was caught off guard; by the time he knew what was happening, she had pulled away, smiling.

'Come back safe, please. I want to get to know you better.'

Josh stuttered slightly, attempting to regain his composure, suddenly very aware of his hands now gripping hers tightly. 'I'd like that very much too, you know.'

Anne threw her head back laughing, her neatly tied black hair whipping around her neck. 'Well, you better.'

'Umm, okay.' Josh leant forwards slightly, still flustered, to give her a tender hug for a moment.

They broke away from each other and Anne poured Josh a lukewarm mug of tea from the pot on a side table.

'I hear the trade mission went well,' Anne said, breaking the slightly awkward silence.

'It did. The Kernow really treated us well. We had a far more generous response than we'd expected – we came away with two more portable communications systems as well as spares and equipment for our current devices. They really are way ahead of us in that kind of thing.'

They both sat down as Josh continued, hurriedly trying to gather his thoughts after Anne's show of affection. 'As well as all that, they also agreed to increase the supply of moulding equipment for the making of relays for the solar panes. The ones we currently use were all made from cannibalising scavenged equipment, but now we can manufacture more ourselves.'

Anne nodded, a small smile forming on her lips. 'And in return for these vital supplies, the Kernow Collective will take more advantage of the Bowles expertise in algae farming and protein production. Sounds like a good deal to me. We're more than happy to let others use that knowledge.'

The algae processes had proved to be invaluable to their own territory, especially through the recent harsh winters of the last few years, and now the Kernow were interested in producing their own as well. It would hopefully cement the growing relationship, making the links between the two peoples deeper and more beneficial than ever.

They talked and talked. After a long time, Josh looked at the clock on the wall and realised how late it was. Where had the hours gone? Had they really been talking all this time?

Deep into the night, they embraced for one final time.

Anne looked into Josh's eyes. 'Be careful, okay?'

'I will. There's a lot of us going. I'm sure we'll be back pretty soon.'

They held each other tightly, Josh closing his eyes as he held the woman he had liked for so long.

Afterwards, he made his way back down to the sleeping rangers. He thought about Anne all the way there, grinning to himself as he did.

Reaching his pack under a large tree, Josh lay down. Before he could spend much longer thinking about his growing feelings for Anne, he drifted off into a fitful sleep.

When he woke, the morning had not yet started. Sunlight was just beginning to approach the horizon. Some of the older rangers were going through the sleeping others, rousing them, hurrying everyone to get some breakfast and get ready for the journey.

Josh ran the plan over in his mind: head due east at first light, then keep on that heading, following the trail left behind. Initial reports suggested the route just kept itself above the ever-expanding forest to their south.

William was walking around, chatting to his rangers, not discussing tactics but talking about their families and other jobs they had. The head of the Bowles family took great pride in knowing all his people, about their lives, about what made them tick. With each family, at least the elder members, still remembering their own grandparents' stories about the famine times, Bowles Mercantile was still a beacon of hope for the future.

By the time William had spoken to a good number of his people, they were ready to depart. Josh found his horse, already saddled, loaded his pack and stowed his weapon into it.

He was dressed in the plain dark green Bowles ranger uniform that all around him wore. Each senior member had their rank on the left sleeve of the tunic, with the Bowles insignia on the right sleeve.

William called out, raising his hand for silence. Once everyone was quiet, he called on Pastor Mose to speak.

Mose raised his head to the sky, placing both his palms up as he did. 'Lord, bless our people in their coming fight. Make them act with honour and justice against our adversaries. Bless William Bowles as he leads us into battle. Take these enemies into your grace and teach them your forgiveness.' He stopped talking, looking up into the sky, as everyone around him said their own silent prayers.

Thanking the pastor, William mounted his horse, quickly followed by the rest of his troops. Each ranger rode their own horse, owning one being the only requirement for applying to be a ranger. Dividing into the two groups as planned, they started out on their journey.

They made their way slowly through the surrounding town of Chilmark, the faces of the rangers thoughtful as each of them prepared themselves for what was to come. Passing the locals, who made way for them and clapped in appreciation of the task being undertaken, Josh saw faces of people he knew, hardening his resolve.

Eventually, they left behind the busy inhabited area so familiar to them, reaching the rolling plains of southern England. Quickening their pace, they urged their horses on.

Striding purposefully through the small makeshift camp, a well-built heavy-set man made his way to the tent of his superior. He was satisfied with how everything had progressed during the last few days, but these were delicate times and he couldn't afford to make any mistakes at all. He was weary but tried hard not to let it show; after all, he had a reputation to maintain. Dressed in a drab civilian coat, not his normal officer's tunic, he walked through the men around him, seeing their bodies stiffen as he approached. His thick, powerful arms strained through the coat as if it were made for someone much smaller than him. Bared teeth showed through his lips, either grimacing or smiling – he never indicated which one it was.

Approaching the tent, he nodded at one of the two men standing guard outside. The guard pulled the door flap back to let him enter.

Inside, at the end of the tent, was a large oak wooden table, covered in papers, neatly stacked. There were candles, drinking glasses and an assortment of writing instruments scattered around. To each side of the table were large chained oak chests. In front of both the table and chests were two large, rather shabby, red leather wingback chairs sitting on the flattened grass. One of these was already occupied by a weighty bearded man, who turned to watch the newcomer as he came in. While this was a temporary encampment, it was obvious that no expense had been spared bringing this amount of equipment with them.

Behind the oak desk sat their leader, thin and tall, clean shaven with slicked back hair and a high-collared coat covering his neck. If his neck had been uncovered the man in front of him would have seen two large deep scars which ran around his neck, almost from ear to ear. He had never told anyone where he got the scars from, adding to his reputation. This reputation was for total ruthlessness, not a man to be crossed.

'Captain, welcome, what have you got for me?' he asked in a cheery tone that belied his character.

'Everything's going to plan, sir.' Standing to attention in front of the desk, the man gave his report. 'We attacked their main solar production facility, rendered it totally out of action for months at least. We took the northern route as planned and had no problem at all. It's almost laughable how easy it was to travel through the territory without question.'

His superior behind the desk smiled, smoothing his hair back once more, before leaning forwards in his chair and waving his hand for the information to continue.

'We then ran through their hometown, made a good old mess of the locals and some of their troops and then headed out back here, leaving the biggest trail we could. We can't fail to be tracked.' He stopped, taking a breath finally, before waiting for the response.

'If they come, how far behind us are they?' asked the leader.

'If all goes as planned, they should be about a day behind. We've left a number of spies keeping a watch on them. They'll report back soon. We think they'll be here tomorrow or the day after at the latest.'

Behind the desk his leader gave a wry smile as he leant back into his chair. 'Good, good. Thank you, Captain. You've done well. Go and get some food and rest – we'll need you again soon enough.'

'Aye, sir.' The captain turned and left, leaving the two men alone.

‖‖

'Well, first part done, now for the fatal blow,' the portly man sat to the side said softly. 'Let's just hope it will be as easy.'

'You think it won't be?' The thinner man behind the table asked curiously, a slight frown growing above his eyes.

'I'm sure it will be, if they follow us and are as unprepared as we think they are.'

'They will, and they are.' Putting his feet on the table and closing his eyes, the man continued his wry smile.

‖‖

As the morning turned into afternoon, the Bowles troopers made good time following the tracks in front of them. The weather was set fair with firm ground beneath them. They stopped several times, as their advance trackers reached them to report on their findings. It appeared clear that the attackers had continued their way east and were obviously not a professional band as the covering of the tracks they had made was not enough to fool the rangers following them.

With the good news passed along the lines, the pursuit was rejoined. They would make camp at the end of the day.

They rode as the skies became clear of the wispy clouds from the morning, the sun beating down on them as they went. The riders themselves were quiet and the only noise which could be heard was the panting of the horses as they hurried across the landscape. Although they slowed a little as the day progressed, they still made good time.

After a brief stop for lunch, and to rest the horses a little, they rode on through the grasslands. Occasionally they slowed where the terrain made it necessary, but otherwise they relentlessly moved on.

They stopped as evening approached, to make camp for the night, the rangers and horses taking the opportunity for a well-needed rest. The second group of riders arrived shortly after the first and soon everyone was dismounted and taking the welcomed break. Within minutes, firestones had been cracked and campfires started.

The rangers were relaxing around the fires, eating their biscuit bars supplied by Bowles Mercantile the previous day. It made perfect food for ventures like this.

Supplementing their meal with some foraged food, the rangers soon were fed, watered and refreshed. They took the opportunity to relax a little, before they were ready for sleep. Setting up lookouts for the night, they felt safe for now.

In the morning, the rangers were keen to complete this leg of their journey. With some groans as they stood, stretching their weary backs, most were slightly less enthusiastic than when they headed out yesterday. But soon the troop had packed away their camp, remounted and were heading on their way.

Josh rode alongside Artur. 'Well, the weather's good at least. Keeps the spirit high.'

'Yeah, should make the day easier,' Artur replied. A little quietly, thought Josh.

'What's the plan then today?'

'It looks like we ride on until Herriard. We didn't ride too hard yesterday, so it shouldn't be too much.'

Josh sounded his agreement, put his head down and pushed on.

As expected, by mid-afternoon they had reached the small village of Herriard. There was only a scattering of houses and barns around a small ancient church, now utilised as a storehouse due to its insulating stone walls. The few who lived here were either inside working or out in the fields, so the rangers made their way through without much commotion.

Slowing to a walk, William led his troopers through the village to the outpost. The outpost was made to look like little more than a large barn on the outskirts of the village. But it belied its true purpose. This was where the Bowles influence over territory effectively ended, being the last place that was a sanctuary for any of the Bowles inhabitants.

There were thirty rangers waiting for them at the outpost, having arrived at stages throughout the day. As everyone dismounted and let the horses rest and drink, they all took this time to stretch themselves once more.

William Bowles gave his horse to one of his aides before heading to a partitioned area sat back at the end of the barn. He was quickly followed by Artur and Josh and then by two of his more senior lieutenants.

Inside the small room sat Alva Sinclair. She had overseen the outpost for the last year and had been waiting for everyone to arrive.

Seeing William approaching with his associates, Alva stood and smoothed her uniform before striding to the door to welcome her guests. She normally didn't bother with any type of recognised Bowles uniform, preferring her usual long utility dresses, but today she had dressed properly. Her usual long, wavy brown hair was gathered loosely back, showing her fresh oval face.

'Mr Bowles, sir, glad to have you here. Please come in, sir.' Overly gesturing with her hand, she motioned to them all to come in.

Josh could see she was nervous.

Alva was one of the younger outpost chiefs, having been sent here to the further reaches of the territory as her family came from the area. The Herriard outpost had been viewed as a quiet posting, mainly to watch over anything coming out of the old capital, which was normally not very much. As such, she was a junior officer with minimal experience, but she knew the area well and came across as competent and disciplined.

'Thank you, Alva.' William smiled kindly at her. 'You know Artur, don't you?'

'Yes, sir. Artur was very helpful to me before the posting. I spent a hectic few weeks training at the complex under his command.' Alva nodded to Artur who winked back at her.

'Ah, you've got a good career ahead of you, Alva. I'm proud to see someone I trained do so well,' Artur said.

Josh came forwards, shaking Alva's hand. 'Good to see you again, Alva. How's life been treating you?' He had worked with her on a few training exercises, always appreciating her determination in whatever she undertook.

'Good, thanks, Josh, good to see you too.' She began to relax. 'Please take a seat everyone and I will bring you up to speed.'

While everyone took their seats, Alva walked round to her chair behind the desk. She paused for a moment.

Alva stood tall and began. 'Now that you and your rangers have arrived, Mr Bowles, there's a total of one hundred and twelve of us here and ready to fight. We've received reports from four of the trackers over the last few hours and they all concur the group they've been following is headed in the direction of the pre-Chaos town of Aldershot. We've two more trackers still trailing them who hopefully will return soon with more information.'

Josh nodded as he took the information in. Alva had moved to the wall where a large map of the surrounding area was sited. She had already drawn the trail up to where they knew they were and then had put markers as to where she thought they might be heading.

Alva then went through the details of these areas, but a lot of it was based on old information – no one tended to go further east if it could be helped. After ten minutes she paused and looked around the room. 'That's what I can tell you right now. Any questions?'

'Do we know any more about them from what we've seen?' asked William, still examining the map in front of him.

'Only that where they have taken brief breaks, they haven't covered their tracks very well at all. They were in too much of a hurry, it looks like. The consensus is that they aren't very professional at all,' Alva answered. 'Apart from that, nothing else.'

Josh leant forwards in his chair. 'And are we sure that it's still the same number of riders that attacked us. No more have joined?'

'Yes, we've been looking to see if any have joined or left, but we don't think any have. As far as we can tell it's still the same grouping.'

'We all seem to be in the same position, then. No one knows much, really, do they?' Rising, William arched his back. 'Well, after we get some rest overnight, I propose we head out just before dawn and finally track them down and deal with them. Until then everyone should get some rest. Alva, would you go and sort out any supplies which are needed for us, please, and show some of the rangers the best place to set up as sentries while we're here, will you? You've done a grand job preparing for us.'

Alva stood, saluted and left the room. She looked more relieved than grateful.

As Josh was about to leave, William looked over to him. 'Thank you for coming, Josh, I appreciate it.'

'I wouldn't want to be anywhere else. It's an honour to ride with you.' He walked proudly as he left the room, so grateful was he for everything the Bowles family had done for him over the years.

Only William and Artur remained in the small meeting area. They sat in a comfortable silence for a few moments. They had been through so much together over the years and knew what each other was thinking without having to speak.

William was the first to break the silence. 'Well, without any more information it looks like we've just got to clear them out. I'll take the lead and you follow behind, Art. As soon as we find them, you flank round to attack the rear and take them unawares.'

'Assuming we find them,' Art muttered. Then spoke louder. 'It would be easier to plan if we knew more about them. I admit I'm struggling with this one. But I agree on the strategy. From what we've seen of them, they won't be expecting that.'

'Good, then let's go and give our old legs some food and rest before tomorrow.'

SEVEN

HIDDEN ON THE TOP OF A SMALL RIDGE TO THE NORTH OF THE village, nestling into a small cluster of trees, two men lay on the damp floor, looking down into the sleeping outpost. They were ready to leave immediately if they saw signs of the rangers preparing to head out for their final approach.

The two lay there feeling stiff and uncomfortable; they had been watching ever since the rangers had arrived last night. So far, everything Bowles and his team had done had been anticipated with some accuracy. The expectation was that in the morning, as soon as they saw things getting animated, they would hurry back to their own encampment and report.

As they lay there, they counted the number of rangers and horses, and made notes on everything they could think of. They had been sent to glean as much information as they could. Although they were too far away to see what type of weapons or equipment they had, they knew that their leadership had that information already from elsewhere.

Josh was awake just before dawn. He hadn't slept well at all. As he lay there, he watched Artur and his two senior lieutenants pacing amongst the rangers, checking on their troops. The three of them stopped nearby, standing by the large doors of the barn, silhouetted against the slowly brightening landscape.

'It's time.' Artur kept his voice low as he gazed outside. 'So let's get everyone up and ready to leave in an hour – that should give us a start just as the morning light allows. I sent some more trackers out earlier. Hopefully, they will be back with more information by the time we go. Let's hope we will be able to reach them before long and get this over with.'

The officers nodded curtly, a little tension in their faces, Josh thought.

Once the first few rangers had been awakened, the rest began to stir as a ripple effect spread throughout the troops. What started off as a low murmur of activity grew into a larger noise throughout as everyone rose from their temporary beds. Before long, people were taking in the orders being barked at them, before quickly and efficiently going about their morning routines of preparation for the coming day.

Josh rose, feeling the anticipation in his stomach. Although he was a ranger and had seen his fair share of scuffles and raiders, he was not a professional soldier. Nerves coursed through his body. Comforting himself that he was surely not alone in this feeling, he looked around, seeing the faces of the men and women nearby. They all wore similar expressions.

Mose walked amongst the rangers, checking on those he passed. Josh appreciated his strengths as a pastor, understanding people's needs. He remembered Mose telling him that he never tried to push his take on religion on them. He merely felt the need to show his compassion to everyone, and if that meant he got to tell them about his beliefs then so much the better.

Josh had occasionally discussed such matters with him, still learning about his own personal beliefs. He admired Mose's strong personal faith, which made him so comfortable in his own skin. Although Mose was an open man, he always hesitated about talking about his own history, preferring to talk about others' hopes and fears. The few times they had discussed where he came from made Josh think he had been running away from something or someone up in the north of the country.

Thankful for his presence, though, seeing the peace he brought to the ones he spoke to, Josh gave his own private prayer of thanks for the man.

Just outside of the barn, fresh water had been provided by Alva. Two large plazt troughs held enough water for drinking and breakfast preparation. Making his way to the queue he saw Nolan waiting in line. To some good-natured mocking by the surrounding rangers, he jumped into the line, missing out a good deal of waiting.

'Good sleep?' he asked his fellow ranger.

Nolan looked at him blearily. 'God no. I was next to the world's loudest snorer. I'm tired before the day's even started.'

'That's rich coming from you. I've heard you sleep before, you know.' Josh laughed at his friend as he rubbed his eyes.

'As opposed to your lordly sleep, I suppose.' Nolan gave a deep bow, grinning as he did.

Nolan was a similar age to Josh but his parents were a scavenging and trading couple from the Middle-lands. Whereas Josh had been raised inside the Bowles extended family, with their formal education and interactions with every scale of society, Nolan had grown up much more streetwise. He took every opportunity to remind Josh of his privileged upbringing.

Josh pushed the bowing man, a broad smile across his face as he watched Nolan stagger backwards slightly.

Reaching the water, they filled their canteens. They strolled over to the makeshift food station, taking a bowl of steaming porridge with a protein biscuit. Sitting down on an old overturned tub, the two ate their breakfast in silence.

Nolan had spent much of his childhood travelling into some of the abandoned outer cities with his family, finding enough scavenged goods to live on but never enough to settle down. By the time he was a young man, he understood the thrill and excitement of the outer cities. It was only when his parents died under the hands of some raiders that he had headed south, eventually coming across the Bowles territory.

Taking any job he could find, he found himself in work near the Bowles complex, eventually signing up as one of the few full-time rangers, making himself invaluable to his officers. He specialised in fieldcraft and observational techniques. As soon as he and Josh had met, they became firm friends, always looking out for each other whenever they could.

Finishing his meal, Nolan put his arm on Josh's shoulder. 'Don't try to do anything heroic when we find them, okay?'

'I know. I'll try to remember my training, don't worry. I've got no desire to do anything silly.'

'Good. We all need to do exactly what we've learnt.' Nolan looked around at the rangers. 'Especially some of the younger ones – they haven't even been tested properly yet.'

Josh knew that there were a large number of youngsters with them today but trusted the leadership and all the training they had received. 'I'll just copy what you do, then.' He beamed as he finished his drink.

Nolan laughed loudly as he stood, gently cuffing Josh on the back of his head as he did. Josh was sure he heard his friend still chuckling as he wandered off.

Finished eating, he wandered back to his pack, stowing his gear and cleaning the area around him, before hearing everyone being called together for a final briefing.

The rangers gathered outside the barn in full anticipation of their leader's commands. Josh gently pushed his way through the throng, till he was standing just a few feet away from where William had clambered onto a few stacked bales of hay.

William waved his hands down for quiet, a solemn but resolute look on his face. Once the noise had calmed down, he addressed his people.

'These criminals attacked our home without reason or provocation. It is our duty as upholders of the law to stop them ever doing this again. We're a peaceful territory, one which values the rules of order and peaceable negotiation. These people have no such moral leadership, so we need to ensure that they are dealt with as quickly as possible. For four generations, since the Chaos, we have fought against people like this, and we have always won. Today will be no different.' William hesitated, seeing the faces in front of him agreeing with him totally. 'But I remind you to be cautious today, as well as brave. Many of you have not faced a full-scale battle before. It will not be easy, but we will prevail. Our way of life will not be threatened, because you shall defend it.'

As he finished speaking, the crowd cheered for their leader. William clapped along with them for a few moments before quietening them down once more.

'Our trackers came back earlier. We know they stopped last night not much further along. By the time we arrive we can catch them unawares and deal with them quickly. Like yesterday, we shall split up into two parts. I will lead the way until we come close to them. Once there, Artur will take his group on a flanking attack. You all know your tasks well, my friends. God speed everyone.'

He beckoned Mose up to where he was standing, inviting him to lead the rangers in a final prayer. Everyone bowed their heads as he offered thanks for William's leadership, entreating victory on this day. Finally, he asked for a moment of silent prayer, urging everyone to make their own peace with what was to come.

Once Mose gave a single clap, signalling the end of the prayer, William jumped down from his position on the bales. He walked through the now raucous rangers as they cheered him, shouting his name. In the background the officers of the rangers were shouting orders above the noise.

Josh found his horse ready and waiting for him, saddled and bridled by the stable team. Leaving his camping equipment to the side of the barn, ready to be picked up once the attack was over, he slid his sword into its mount on the saddle. He mounted his horse, adjusting his stirrups quickly.

He still felt concerned by the actions his leaders were taking. He had thought again about mentioning to William his worry that they were following these raiders too easily. But he knew he had already raised his objections and didn't want to distract any further.

At the front of the mass of activity, William was already mounted, sitting proudly as he looked around, surveying the sight in front of him. He was soon joined by the rest of the leadership, before making their way to the road that led away from the outpost. The combined ranger force of Bowles Mercantile followed them. A quick check that all the leaders' chronos were synchronised meant they were ready.

Once they had left Herriard behind, the horses had a little more room to spread out, no longer having to move clumsily together. William pulled on his reins, making his horse turn his head slightly, so the leader could look at his rangers.

'Remember why we are doing this,' he called out. His voice was calm yet strong enough to carry across them all. 'We will make sure they cannot do this again. We stand for justice in this world – we will not go back to lawlessness, not again.'

The rangers looked at their leader; they nodded as he spoke and as he finished they all raised their right fist in the air. Seeing this, William sped his horse up and within seconds the first group was travelling hard along the route the trackers had set out.

Artur's team waited until William was out of sight to bring up the rear.

Josh was in the second assembly of rangers, positioned near the front. As he sat there, waiting to start, he could hear his heartbeat in his ears as the adrenaline flowed.

They moved out, slowly at first then fanning out amongst the trees and countryside, allowing them to travel along at a good pace. Without knowing exactly how far they had to go, it was a case of following William's pack in front, kept informed of what was happening by two messenger riders flitting between the two groups.

The sun was finally starting to rise, with the land taking on that dewy feel that came before the day was real. They were travelling at a good pace, covering decent ground when a horseman came hurtling towards them, stopping at Artur's horse. Immediately, Artur raised his hand high, telling everyone to come to a stop.

Josh was too far away to hear the conversation, but it was animated and there was a fair amount of gesturing and pointing by both participants. He presumed it was important. Once the rider had turned and hurried back the way he had come, Artur turned and faced them all.

'The trackers have found the camp a few miles up ahead. William has sent a team to assess it. In the meantime, we're to flank round half a mile and then position ourselves to their side. Once we hear the order we're to join in and take them before they know what's happening.'

Josh saw his fellow rangers sitting noticeably taller in their saddles; they were about to avenge their fallen friends and family. They would be making their lands ever safer. Following their leaders, they turned north to make their way to the position from where they would launch their attack.

It didn't take them long to circle around the bandits' camp. Making their final approach to their destination, they dismounted and tied up their horses just below the rise they needed to cross. Normally, they would have stayed mounted and charged with hooves and swords whirling, but the number of trees around the area was not the best for a mounted attack. They would do this on foot, only leaving a few messenger riders mounted for communication.

The bandits had set up camp in a wide circular hollow in the land. Around a quarter of a mile in diameter with young trees covering the ground all around, with only a few taller, more established trees spread loosely amongst them. Roughly in the middle of the area, a temporary camp had been erected, with one large tent surrounded by an assortment of sheeting for ground cover, presumably for sleeping. To either side were a few low and wide supply caches.

A few people could be made out walking around the camp, with a small number of horses tied up to one side.

There was a fire going in the middle of it all, with some people sat around it, the smoke lazily making its way skyward through the trees. The occasional laugh or shout could be heard.

The rangers slowed as they approached their holding position, crouching down as they travelled the final part.

As they reached the top of one side of the large hollow, Artur gathered his officers. 'Split the rangers into three teams. Spread out along the treeline with a small distance between each one. This should allow us a decent amount of manoeuvring when we attack.'

Josh was in the middle team of twenty or so. They moved as ordered to their positions, close enough to be able to reach the camp in less than a minute. Carefully, they all lay down on the damp grass underneath the trees, hiding as best they could behind the overgrowth. There was just enough to allow them a certain amount of cover.

Each ranger settled down, looking in the direction of the camp. The sun was now strongly out, with excellent visibility. Once all were ready and in position, Artur gave the signal to remain unseen but be prepared for the attack to start.

After sending a messenger to William, confirming they were ready, Artur moved along the line of rangers, making sure everyone was as calm as could be under the circumstances. Reaching the spot where Josh lay, he merely patted him on the back as he gave a quick wink to his friend. He moved on to the end of the line, where he took his place behind a large fallen tree and waited.

It wasn't long before the messenger returned. Artur called him over. He listened as the messenger relayed what William had said, before checking his chrono and turning back to his team. Everyone waited for the runner, who moved through the line issuing the order.

Ten minutes to attack.

Josh had taken his spot just to the side of a tall oak tree surrounded by a light amount of undergrowth. Just to his right was Abe Lomas, a slighter, older man than Josh and one he had known for a few years. Abe was the local brewer, along with his wife and daughter in the family business. He had a reputation for not backing down when it came to a fight.

'How you doing, Abe?' Josh whispered over.

Abe gave him a wry smile as he briefly looked at Josh, before returning his attention in front of him. 'I can think of better places I'd rather be, but yeah, all good, cheers.'

Josh chuckled at the comment, taking the relief that the moment brought to him. He was ready for what was to come, but he was still nervous about the whole affair. It all still seemed too easy.

The next few minutes seemed like an age to him. Time seemed to stop.

Suddenly, as they were all watching for any form of activity, several whistles rang out from the other side of the hollow. The noise carried well on the breeze. Although it was the prearranged signal that William's group was starting their attack, it took Josh a moment to understand what the noise was. Everyone on this side of the camp rose up.

Making their way over the undergrowth as fast as they could while holding their line, the rangers ran down the slope to the unaware opponents. They had planned for William's group to make one hell of a noise when they started, pulling in most of the resistance to that side. Josh's side were to stay as silent as possible on their advance, giving them the benefit of surprise to the rear.

As they ran, it seemed that everything was going to plan. William and his rangers could be seen on the other side of the area, already drawing the attention of the surprised bandits. Their group would reach the fight once William had already engaged, giving the bandits no place to go.

Almost at the camp, Josh saw the bandits rush to take on a defensive stance. It looked like they must have realised they were facing a considerably larger attack than they could deal with. Josh could see William in the middle of the charge, sword raised in the air. He was briefly transported back to his childhood, remembering an old picture book with a drawing of a knight charging into battle.

With only a few metres remaining until they would engage the enemy, the rangers slowed slightly and prepared themselves, swords raised.

EIGHT

ALMOST AS ONE THE BANDITS DROPPED TO THE GROUND AS A loud, sharp slapping noise rang out to the side of the advancing rangers. Immediately, Josh was aware of something sounding like a swarm of bees approaching them. By the time he had registered this, many of the rangers had been stopped in their tracks.

Looking left to right, not quite understanding what was happening, he saw foot-length metal-tipped darts sticking out of the legs and arms of many of the people around him. A lot of the rangers had been missed but a fair few were lying on the floor, clutching at various parts of their bodies. They would take no more part in the fight today. The bandits were using ranged weapons! As he looked around, he realised a good many more rangers were lying unmoving on the ground, dead.

Glancing to his right, Josh could just make out a wooden contraption to the side of the battlefield. A small wagon on two large wheels, built up at the front and hand cranks on either side, and he saw four men next to it cheering loudly. Not knowing what on earth he was looking at, he turned back to the kneeling bandits in front of him.

The bandits were climbing to their feet, revelling in the confusion and disorder spreading through the ranks of their foe. Many of the younger, more inexperienced rangers were showing their shock at the unexpected attack, not moving, just standing with wide-open mouths. The older members were calling out loudly, trying to rally them to restart the now paused attack. The more experienced rangers managed to bring everyone else under control, just as the bandits readied themselves for their attack.

The rangers advanced, less enthusiastically than before but determined nevertheless.

Putting both hands onto the hilt of his short sword before preparing to strike, Josh slowed as he reached the first bandit standing in front of them. As he started to swing towards the bandit, the man was starting a similar action. As they did so, their eyes locked onto each other in grim recognition of what was about to happen.

Being the aggressor, Josh had a certain amount of momentum propelling him forwards. He had the advantage, allowing the swing to come down a split second before the other man could complete his own attack. Josh's blade banged off the defender's, whose own sword lowered quickly against the force, before completing its deflected trajectory and slicing the man through the neck. He collapsed immediately, flopping to the floor without any more resistance.

Josh stared down at the crumpled man beneath him, dark red blood gushing out of the wound he had caused seconds before. Looking into the man's eyes once more, he saw a young, frightened man knowing he was about to die. He seemed far too young to be dying like this.

Josh dropped to his knees, all noise seeming to recede, watching death take this man he didn't know. He had felt like he was alone with his foe an instant ago, now the sounds of the newly raging battle assaulted his ears. He looked up, ready for the next fight.

Up and down the line, the rangers were fighting for all they were worth. A few more had fallen on the bandits' side, but Josh saw some had fallen on the side of the rangers as well. Pushing himself to his feet, he looked around for who to fight next.

Suddenly, unexpectedly, to both sides of the rangers' line, the leaves on the ground started to move. More men began to rise out of the very ground of the woods. At the same time, further bandits came out of the shelters.

Moving towards both sides of the action at some speed, these newcomers bolstered both front lines within seconds. Others headed to the sides of the lines, enabling the bandits to apply pressure to the flanks of the rangers. Josh felt a chill wash over him. They had walked straight into an ambush.

All Josh could do right now was focus on what was in front of him. As soon as he was on his feet, he saw an older, grim-looking man, snarling as he moved in his direction. Josh planted his right foot as firmly as he could in the ground, testing his weight as he did. He turned, raising his sword behind his shoulders and swung.

The oncoming man changed direction just as he watched the attack heading his way. Josh grunted as he lost control of the blade at the end of the swing, trying to regain his balance.

The bandit was now ready for his strike. He was carrying a hammer-like weapon, with spikes on the end, which looked extremely hazardous. Throwing his arm round in an arc, he bought the hammer down, aiming at Josh's head. Josh only just managed to duck, feeling the air brush his head as he got too close to the attack. But this time, he was ready. He thrust towards the old fighter in a clean direct lunge, piercing his stomach.

The bandit fell to the floor, growling as he did, his arms clutching himself. Josh kicked the hammer away from the stricken man as he looked around to find the next fight; this time, he didn't look down again.

|||||||||||||||||||||||||||||||||||||||||||||||||||||||||||||||||||||||||||||||||

The bandits' leader screamed the order to attack to his personal guard, admiring them as they leapt towards the fray. He had waited for the softening-up of the enemy to take place first, watching things play out with his teeth bared. As soon as they were in the right position, he shouted out the order for the second wave to join in.

Having become leader of these men through brutality and cunning, he was not a man to stand back and watch as others enjoyed such slaughter. His desire for power had driven him to the fore of everything his men did. Grinning, he raised his two short swords, one in each hand, before charging into the mass of rangers in front of him. Surrounding him were his finest fighters, making sure no harm came to their leader, although he had proven himself an elite swordsman time and time again.

They reached the right-hand flank of the rangers within seconds, seeing the shocked expressions turn to fear as the further numbers engaged. He was enjoying himself, slicing through the first man's neck with ease, showering himself in blood. As he did, he felt an electric thrill flow through his body; killing remorselessly made him feel alive. Wiping the warm blood from his eyes, he coolly observed his victim slump to the floor, before raising to strike at the next.

This enemy was much more adept at ducking his swing, however. His blade merely glancing the shoulder of the man. Blocking the retaliatory attack, he feinted left before whipping his wrist in an instant, slicing cleanly through his opponent's neck once again. It was his preferred strike of choice, a clean slice through the life-giving jugular of whoever he was fighting. He loved the way the blood jetted out, loved the essence leaking away from a dying body. Throwing his head back in ecstasy, he gave a guttural scream. He was eager to continue his butchery.

|||||||||||||||||||||||||||||||||||||||||||||||||||||||||||||||||||||||||||||||||

The two sides were now fully engaged, the area awash with the sounds of weapons clashing, intermingled with the shouts and screams of the fighters. It hadn't taken long for the bandits to be positioned as they had surely planned to be, attacking the front and rear of both groups of rangers.

Josh was fighting hard, side by side with Abe; at the moment, they both were holding their own in the general melee happening around them. But what had been expected to be an overwhelming attack had turned completely around. Now it was the rangers whose numbers were dwarfed, and positions compromised. Those in the rear were desperately trying to hold their own line rather than assist their brothers and sisters ahead of them. They were heavily outnumbered.

Artur was busy shouting orders at the top of his voice. Some of the older rangers understood instantly, ushering the younger members into their new, yet poorer, strategic position. They were trying to form a defensive double line as best they could, but some of the younger rangers were panicking and were more difficult to corral, especially as many were parrying the blows being thrust back and forth. Somehow, with great strength, they managed to form their double line: one line facing forwards towards the original attack with one now facing the rear.

Josh hadn't been able to turn, continuing to trade strikes with an angry snarling man a few feet in front of him. The man was strong, very strong, so each blow knocked Josh down slightly. Pausing, feigning tiredness without striking back, he made the attacker go for a quick double blow. Seeing him lift his weapon for the second time, Josh managed to thrust his own up into his opponent's chest. Pushing as hard as he could with both hands, he felt his sword break completely through the body before coming out the other side. The man fell to his knees, blood everywhere, before collapsing sideways. Josh was dragged down with him, struggling to remove his sword.

While on the floor, Josh drew a breath. He was already exhausted after fighting only three of the bandits – how he would carry on for much more he didn't know. His hands felt slippery with warm blood running over them; desperately, he tried to wipe as much away as he could, without having much success. He looked through the turmoil, trying to understand how the other team of rangers was faring.

It was a similar scene.

Through the trees and the bandits, Josh could see that William had recognised the danger from the new arrivals as well. He was shouting something to his own rangers, but what it was had been lost in the noise of the battle. At least William was still fighting fiercely, Josh thought, still able to assess how it was going.

Next to Josh, Abe's bloodied sword was flashing around like his had been a few seconds before. The older, fiercer man had already despatched four men by now, but each time he paused to catch his breath, more bandits filled the gaps where other colleagues had fallen. And just as their enemies were falling, so too were their friends and fellow rangers. Josh looked briefly behind him, trying to make sense of the horror around him. He gasped as he saw at least thirty rangers either dead or dying on the ground.

Standing unsteadily, Abe grabbed Josh's arm, pulling them both further into the fight, by now broken up into a number of smaller skirmishes. They quickly despatched two more of the younger bandits. As they did so, two other rangers reached them, all of them falling in behind a fighting trio from their own side. They were grateful to come to a small lull in the action. Drawing hard breaths before they had to re-enter the fray, Josh again tried to see what was happening with the bandits attacking the other rangers. He could see his own side valiantly fighting with ever mounting losses, but as his head turned to William's team, his heart sank.

One of the bandits had a long spear capped by a sharp metal tip. This younger man had been standing at the rear of the action for a few moments when Josh caught sight of him; he was wearing a long black coat, which for some reason Josh thought must have been very hot to fight in. He was probing the fighting rangers, standing behind the first wave of bandits, stabbing out with his makeshift lance. William was nearby, fighting ferociously with his lieutenants. Momentarily, Josh wondered if they had potential to turn the battle back their way.

But then the lance man whipped his right arm back, his spear dragging back as he did so. Without pausing once his arm was extended, he launched his arm forwards, releasing the spear just below head height. It flew silently through the air. As soon as the youngster had released the weapon, Josh understood who its intended target was.

Opening his mouth in a vain attempt to shout a warning to the man who had treated him as a son, he watched horrified as the spear carried on its path for a split second, before effortlessly gliding straight through William's upright body.

In what seemed like slow motion, Josh watched as his leader slumped stiffly forwards, like a huge tree toppled in the forest, a look of shock across his face. By the time William had disappeared from view, the scream that had been travelling to Josh's mouth finally realised itself.

The men immediately around William watched him fall; they faltered for a brief second, hesitant. The bandits saw this moment of weakness, screaming at the top of their voices before pushing forwards ferociously once again.

Josh sagged. William had fallen, the head of the company and rangers that he was a part of. The people he was fighting with had lost their commander. A dark haze descended over his thoughts.

Knowing he had to get this news back to home somehow, but too drained to run himself, Josh grabbed Abe by the scruff of his tunic, pulling his face to meet his own. 'William has been killed. We can't win this one.' He had to shout loudly over the noise around him. 'Get to one of the messengers, tell them to take the news back home – they must be told what's happening and especially that they were waiting for us. They knew we were coming! They knew everything!'

Abe nodded numbly. Josh pushed him towards a gap in the fighting near a small thicket of trees. He ran quickly, scrambling up a small bank, his legs pumping fast against the ground under his feet. One of the bandits saw him run and started to follow him. Josh intercepted the man, quickly despatching him from behind with one clean blow. Watching Abe disappear from sight, Josh said a quick prayer that he would make it out alive.

The two rangers around Josh sprang ready as more bandits attacked them from the side. Seeing the new adversaries approach, the three of them crouched with their swords ready at their sides. Josh looked down and grabbed a handful of dirt, which – as he raised his weapon to parry the first blow – he threw into the attacker's face.

Temporarily blinding the man, Josh took his opportunity and slashed at the man's leg. It was a fairly weak strike but had enough on it to make the target fall to the floor. Josh lifted his sword and thrust it down through the chest of the fallen man. The dying man had barely had the time to groan his last breath before another took his place.

Now battling side by side, the remainder of the rangers were fighting bravely against the now overwhelming odds. They were all together, the two groups having been herded towards each other during the battle.

The fight raged on, with more and more from both sides dropping to the ground with fatal injuries, but the bandits had more replacements ready to take the places of their fallen. The woodland floor beneath their feet was becoming harder to gain a footing on, with mud and blood mixing together, making the fighters slip around more and more. Both sides were understandably starting to tire, but unfortunately for the rangers their numbers were now too low to be able to put up any form of meaningful opposition.

Soon, they were down to fifteen rangers, with one dropping every few seconds.

Josh was defending himself against a huge ugly-looking bandit carrying a long, rough-hewn axe, dripping in dark red liquid. He threw the axe down straight at Josh's now moving head, which he only missed by a matter of inches. Pulling another smaller axe from his belt, he growled loudly ready for another strike.

He swung down again and again, against his sinking foe.

Josh was only just managing to keep his sword above his body, keeping himself alive by sheer willpower alone. On one heavy blow he turned his head sideways, lifting his sword towards the approaching axe, but was slow to react, with exhaustion totally taking him. He felt himself pushed down to the ground.

Peering upwards, the last thing he saw was the face of another man, laughing manically, swinging something large at him in what seemed like slow motion, hitting him square in the face. Josh's head slumped to the floor with darkness rapidly enveloping him. As he faded, he felt utterly bereft at what had happened.

‖‖

All throughout the battlefield, the voices of those injured and dying moaned, calling out to help that wasn't coming. There were some gruesome injuries to those on the ground. The ones still standing, still fighting, had their own share as they carried on with the contest.

Finally, with hope removed from the remaining Bowles rangers, the sheer weight of men against them told and they were all but gone.

Abruptly, a shrill whistle rang through the air making the bandits pull back from the fight. There were only five rangers left standing, still gathered together, drawing together to prepare for the final act.

As they stood there, ready to die, the leader of the bandits made his way through his men and strode towards them. Stopping a few metres away, he looked enormously pleased with himself. His face, neck and clothes were smeared with blood, just the whites of his eyes showing on his face. He still held his swords at his sides, dripping in the blood of the rangers. Calmly, he took a rag from one of his men to wipe his face first, then the swords, sheathing them while all the time watching his captives.

As he did he so he focused his attention on the defeated in front of him, removing his blood-soaked gloves before addressing them. He spoke in a calm but firm tone. 'Put your weapons down now and you will live. One chance, that's all you get.'

The exhausted rangers were taken aback by the manner of the man in front of them; at first, they looked at each other nervously. Then, one by one, they threw their weapons on the damp ground in front of them.

Initially amused at their obedience, the leader looked them up and down with a growing sneer. 'Good, get them tied up then go and look for any survivors out there and bring them here,' he commanded the man to his right. 'And tell the medics to tend for our wounded immediately.'

'Yes, sir,' responded the young man, rushing away.

NINE

Daniel Adams was only twelve but had been brought up in the saddle. His parents worked for the Bowles Mercantile blacksmith forges, serving all the horses throughout the company. Riding was a part of his upbringing ever since he could remember. For years he had sought to be a part of the local ranger force. As soon as he was old enough, he signed up to become a member of their messenger team. Although he desperately wanted a more grown-up role, he knew that at least for the time being he was a part of what he had always meant to be.

Right now, however, he was riding for his life. Terrified and alone, with the most important message he would ever carry.

Daniel had been waiting nervously with his colt, where all the horses were tied up. He had been looking after the tired animals, as the rangers headed towards where the attack was planned. At first, he wished he had been down there with them all, but he kept telling himself that he had an important role to fulfil.

Once the noise of the attack began, Daniel had grown more and more anxious. Having no experience of such things, he found it hard to imagine what was happening. He had heard the sounds from across the fields but couldn't see the battle. He told himself over and over he had confidence in the rangers.

As he watched for any clues, walking up and down the perimeter of the small field, he saw one of the rangers approaching him. Unrecognisable, splattered in dirty red mud, their head down as they ran towards him up the slight incline.

He watched the man approach, panting hard after his part in the battle.

'My name is Abe. I've just come from the battle. Now listen to me and repeat it back when I'm done,' the man blurted out as he reached the young boy and put one hand on his shoulder. Staring at him with wide fiery eyes, he made his words clear. 'It was a trap, they've been expecting us, they knew everything and were ready for us. William is dead, you hear me, dead. I don't think any of us will survive – they outnumber us and are well organised. We are lost.'

Daniel was aghast; he could hardly believe what was being told to him. He felt frozen with fear.

'Repeat the message. Do it!' barked Abe.

Daniel looked back, retelling the words he had been ordered to remember. Although stuttering slightly, he managed to repeat it to the older man's satisfaction.

Abe had nodded throughout as he listened to Daniel recite the message back, then grabbed the boy by both shoulders. 'Good lad, good. Now ride as fast as you can. Go to Herriard and let the outpost know. This news must get home – home to tell Tom Bowles what's happened.' He glared hard into the eyes of the frightened boy.

Daniel understood, seeing a small sense of relief in the man's face now he knew what to do. He quickly began untethering and making ready for his journey, adjusting the stirrups for hard riding. Only a few moments had passed before he jumped onto his strong chestnut colt, taking off as fast as he could. As he left, he looked round only once, seeing Abe running down the slope back to the fray, sword in the air, shouting as he ran.

Galloping through the local countryside, Daniel was trying to keep his mind on the task ahead. He would go as fast as he could manage to Herriard; he knew they would be able to help him there. Feeling more and more scared as each minute went by, his young mind was having trouble comprehending what the news he had been given would mean.

Looking down at his hands as he raced along, he saw that he was gripping the reins so hard his knuckles were turning white. He consciously tried to relax his muscles and calm his breathing – he couldn't afford to make a mistake here.

Without knowing how long he had been riding, Daniel came to a track he recognised as heading directly to the outpost. Turning onto it, he pushed on as hard as he could. He could feel the colt beneath him riding well, responding well to his erratic commands.

Heading at pace into the small village, he slowed slightly for the sharper turns. Hearing hooves skidding slightly on the dusty road, he slowed further, heading to where the rangers had stayed the previous night.

He had made it.

Shaking his head and breathing hard, the colt had clearly had enough of the journey home. Daniel jumped out of his saddle and ran towards the entrance, calling out at the top of his voice.

At the sound of his cries, Alva came out from one of the side doors, wiping her hands on a cloth she held in her hands. A young child ran around her until she shushed him and sent him back inside.

'What's the matter? What's happened?' Alva asked.

He tried to get everything out at once, but in his haste couldn't make himself understood, all the words just coming out garbled at once.

Alva bent down to his level, put both of her hands on his shoulders and looked him in the eye. 'Take a breath and calm down. You've got an important message, I can tell. Now slowly, what do you need to tell me?'

Daniel paused for a second before finally feeling able to tell his message. 'Mr Bowles is dead. They're all dead. They knew we were coming and waited for us. There's no one left.' He began to cry at the words he had just spoken. His task completed, the words now hit home.

Alva knelt there with her mouth half open, her eyes filling with tears. Slowly, she stood; her arms dropped to her sides. She turned, calling out loudly to the room she had emerged from. Answering her calls, a girl similar in age to Daniel came out, followed by the younger child.

'Anka, take Gerrit to your grandmother's. Tell her I will be over soon to explain – no time to get anything from the office. Go now, okay?' Her voice wavered as she spoke. Once the two children had gone, Alva turned again to Daniel, who hadn't moved at all.

'What's your name?' she asked him.

'Daniel Adams, but my dad calls me Dan,' he responded.

'Dan, did you see what happened?' Alva brushed the tears away from her face.

'No, one of the rangers, Abe his name was, told me to deliver this message to you,' he said quickly, barely taking a breath as the memory brought the panic back.

'Well then, Dan, we are going to make sure that we take this message back to the Bowles complex and give it to them, you understand?' She was ashen-faced as she spoke. 'I want you to now go west on this road for two miles and wait for me by the river crossing. I'm going to see what I can find out. Wait for me for one hour. If I don't come by then, head to the Bowles home. It's important this information gets back to them, understand?'

'Yes, of course.'

'Good, then get going. I won't be long.' Alva gave him a broad smile. 'You've done well so far, Dan. Let's honour William by getting the rest of this done.'

She led Dan over to his colt, helping him to mount up, patting his leg, before he took off, heading for their agreed rendezvous.

Alva watched Dan ride away until he was out of sight, giving her a moment to think. Once she couldn't see him anymore, she ran back to her office, her mind racing. With William and his rangers gone, she could hardly think of what would happen next, barely able to process everything she had heard.

She realised she was shaking as she ran. Slowing to a walk, she tried to catch her breath; she felt numb.

She reached her office and grabbed her tunic; she was buttoning it up when she called out to her older brother still working deeper in the building. He came out holding his three-year-old son, a questioning look on his face.

Alva looked across at her brother. Her face was flushing with anger. 'I've got to go and check out some disturbing news just in. I've had word that William and the rangers have got into a lot of trouble – it sounds like a real lot of trouble.' She paused, deciding how much she should tell him. 'In the meantime, make sure everyone gets to Mum's and tell them to wait there till I get back. I've already sent Anka and Gerrit over.'

She left her brother standing there, speechless at what he had heard. Hurrying to her horse, she threw the saddle on before fixing it tight. Within moments she climbed on, pulling at the reins, letting the horse know she was in a hurry. They were soon galloping towards where she knew William had led his rangers.

The tall man, clearly in charge of the proceedings, stood perfectly still as he proceeded to view the five defeated rangers in front of him. He watched as they had their wrists tied behind their backs before being pushed down to their knees.

The rangers were joined by three others from the battleground, all clearly worse for wear but not fatally wounded. The newcomers were tied and placed with their captured colleagues.

Josh was amongst those three. He had barely recovered from his knockout blow, having been found by one of the bandits as they searched through the wounded and dying. He knew he was suffering from a serious concussion after the blow, such was the headache he now had. His vision was blurred, and he couldn't make much out of the situation.

An aide approached the tall man, offering a large, clean, damp cloth, which he used to clean himself as best he could. Satisfied, he turned to give orders to a team of aides around him. One by one they went off to perform the tasks he had given them. As the final one left, the tall man was approached by a bloated man, who leant into his side, talking quietly so only he could hear. Both occasionally nodded or smirked as the conversation took place.

Finished, they both pulled away before turning once again to face the kneeling rangers. The leader pointed to two of the older rangers in the middle of the line. Immediately, bandits roughly grabbed them, lifting them to their feet before bringing them forwards.

'Take them to interrogation – they look senior men. See what they know.' He then examined the rest of his captives. He looked pleased with their downbeat appearance.

There were three women and three men kneeling in front of him. He sauntered up and down the line, clearly enjoying himself before he returned to his original spot in front of them all.

'I am General Noah Hill, commander of the New English Army,' he told the dejected rangers as they stared up at him, his arms opening wide. 'Our goal is to return this once-great country to civilisation, under a true leadership, a patriotic leadership. I will restore this nation to where it was before the Bannerman Declaration. We will again be as one. Gone are the days of splitting our land into petty tribes – we are here to overcome and lead England to its glorious future.'

The rest of General Hill's troops gave a short cheer as he finished speaking; he raised his hand while looking around, waving it up and down for quiet.

'Whilst it is regrettable that some of your own died today, it is necessary for us to subdue local warlords in order to progress. You will each be given a chance to contribute to our bold future. Each one of you will be put into service for a period of six months. After that, you will have a chance to join us and serve England – a new, reborn England.'

Josh peered up at him through his blurred vision, disbelievingly, not knowing what to think of this so-called general. It was not what he had been expecting at all. Events were happening too fast for him to process. William had died, along with many of his friends, and he was now a captive man, unsure of anything.

General Hill stood there serenely. He gave a small, brief, smile and then turned on his heels and walked away, quickly followed by a group of his lieutenants.

He made his way through the bodies, over to where William Bowles lay. Covered in mud, William was lying on his side on the ground, the spear still piercing his lifeless body. The general used his boot to roll his head towards him, so he could look into his eyes. Looking down with contempt all over his face, General Hill shook his head from side to side slowly.

'So, this is Bowles, is it? I'd heard better things about him. He didn't put up much of a fight, did he? String him up, so anyone who cares can see what happens to those who go against us.'

Two men standing nearby shouted for some rope; it was quickly brought over. After pulling the spear free before roughly tying William's feet together, one of the men slung the rope over a high, thick branch, quickly gathering it once it fell back. The two then pulled on the rope, until William was ten foot high in the air, swinging back and forth, upside down. They tied the rope to the trunk of the tree, before moving away.

The rangers watched them lift their leader up, with two vomiting at the sight. Josh briefly closed his stinging eyes, feeling tears falling.

General Hill remained motionless for a few more seconds, watching the body swing from side to side, before walking away to his tent without a second glance.

Once he had left, his place in front of the rangers was taken by a short, squat middle-aged man with a piercing stare. He wore some form of fur draped over his shoulders, which gave him an even-further-shortened look.

'I am Harris, and you will do everything I tell you to do,' he brusquely informed his captives. 'Do that and you will survive and thrive with us. Do anything else and you will die, simple as that.'

As Harris was talking, two men had started to tie the surviving rangers together as they stood up, with each having about a metre of slack between themselves and the next. Josh felt the heavy weight of the large rope pulling his arms down in front of him.

Josh's mind was swimming as he took in everything around him; he shook his head, trying to clear his vision. He realised he was being secured to the person next to him. It was Mary Howey. He breathed a small sigh of relief at finding her alive – he hadn't seen her since they left on the dash home. She was bloodied and dirty, a huge swelling on her forehead from what must have been a terrible blow. He put a hand on her shoulder to give what reassurance he could; she turned to acknowledge him through exhausted eyes.

With his sight growing less blurry by the minute, he looked around at the rest of the rangers tied up around him. He noticed Nolan at one end, his face bloodied and battered, but a look of defiance shone through.

Nolan nodded once at him while they looked at each other for a brief moment.

'Right, let's go,' Harris commanded, pointing to the man at one end of the line. 'You, follow me and keep up.'

Harris began to walk through the woodlands, accompanied by three others from this New English Army. The tied-up rangers walked along in file, following their captors, with occasional bumps and stumbles as they walked so closely together.

Josh took a close look at those guarding them. They were clearly men who wouldn't hesitate to kill one or all of them if the chance arose.

From behind him, Josh could hear one of the rangers quietly weeping and another one telling her to keep quiet and not to show any emotion. The weeping continued however, with Josh understanding completely how they felt.

|||||||||||||||||||||||||||||||||||||||||||||||||||||||||||||||||||||||||||

Riding quickly, Alva followed the tracks of the rangers from earlier in the day. From the discussions they had had, she knew to head towards some woodlands a few miles east of Herriard. Since she had set out, she had stopped every few minutes to listen carefully for any noises. Truth be told, she was utterly terrified.

She stopped quickly when she saw a group of horses in the distance, a few men moving amongst them. After tying up her own mare to the side of an old overgrown building, she moved closer to what she had seen, keeping cover as much as she could.

Getting nearer, she recognised the colours of the braiding on some of their reins. But when she saw the men, there was no one she recognised, and they weren't wearing any of the instantly recognisable tunics of the Bowles rangers. She gasped as she saw one of the horses being whipped harshly; this surely wasn't any ranger she would have been proud to work with.

Looking around, Alva carefully moved to the top side of the field near to the woodlands. Hearing noises just out of her eyeline, she knew she had to try to make her way nearer to find out the truth. She dropped to her knees and started to crawl.

It was likely only a few minutes, but it felt more like an hour to her. She reached a good vantage spot at the top of a small incline, where she looked down to a horrifying scene.

Through the trees, she could see bodies lying everywhere, ranger bodies. Friends and colleagues had been slaughtered mercilessly. She saw men laughing as they walked around the battleground, going through the fallen rangers' clothes, stripping them of anything of value.

Around the site, men kicked and spat on the corpses of her dead friends. At one point she thought she saw one man cut a finger off a dead ranger to steal a ring. Alva could see many more men than they had thought were there when they planned this last night.

Suddenly her eyes went wide; she was staring at a body hanging feet first from a tree. It took just a moment to realise who it was. Putting her hand to her mouth, worried she would scream out at what she had seen, she dropped to the damp ground. She quietly sobbed where she lay, not believing what she had witnessed.

Alva closed her eyes, trying to forget the image that was now seared into her mind. Taking a deep breath, still with her eyes closed, she said a silent prayer for the fallen. Through her horror, she knew she needed to calm herself so she could find out any information of use before she headed back.

Composing herself, she crawled forwards slowly, going as far as she could before the undergrowth she was hiding in thinned out. As she was surveying the gruesome picture in front of her, she made out the tragic figure of William Bowles suspended amongst the trees. She could see the rest of the rangers lying there in the mud. It was too much to look at for long. Her head slumped to the floor once again.

Abruptly, she felt something hard and forceful on her back. Looking around, she was horrified to see a bloodied man looking down at her with a callous smile on his face, his boot resting on her waist.

'What have we got here, eh?' the man asked. He laughed as he bent down to grab Alva's arms, forcing her to her feet. Alva struggled to get her hands free, but a hard fist to the back of her head stunned her, making her briefly submissive to the man.

Holding her arms with one hand and her neck with the other, the man pushed her and marched her through the battle site. They stepped over bloodied bodies while her feet slipped in the mud. Alva struggled to think but her dismayed mind was so groggy nothing came to her.

TEN

GENERAL HILL PUSHED THROUGH THE DOOR FLAP OF HIS TENT, chest puffed out, before taking his seat. He leant back contentedly, allowing time for the members of his senior team to take their place according to rank. He, just like the others filing in, was still covered in the bloody remains of the fight.

'Well then, gentlemen, I'd qualify that as an outstanding success. Rollins, what are the casualties like?' he asked one of the senior officers.

Colonel Rollins, in command of tactical decisions for the army over the last few months, was sitting to the left of the General and leant forwards as he began to speak. His muscular arms strained underneath his coat.

'We lost thirty-five men and another twenty won't make it through the next few hours,' he informed the gathered group. 'And that's against a force of over one hundred. As planned, they weren't expecting us to be a problem and our obvious superior fighting skills clearly showed. We've taken eight prisoners, two of which are to be interrogated as soon as possible. Three of the eight are women as well. Harris is taking them all back to base as we speak. We've also taken charge of all their horses – pretty good ones too, by the look of it.'

Hill's mouth turned up at one side at the memory of the victory. He gestured for Rollins to continue.

'And it looks like your contraption worked a treat, that Whacker or whatever it's called – it really softened them up before the fight. Took quite a few out with its perfect volley. I know we were concerned about its efficiency as a one-shot weapon, but it made a big difference.' Rollins finished his report, sitting back in his chair, looking extremely pleased with himself.

Everyone made their appreciation known to the General over his instruction to make the terrifying new weapon, whether they meant it or not. Although it had only worked a few times when they tested it over the last month, it had done its job when it was meant to, making an enormous difference. General Hill's gambit had paid off.

'Thank you, I'm glad it was made to work. Overall, not a bad day at all. Make sure we lose less men next time. We should perform much stronger against such rabble,' the General told them, with all firmly agreeing that they would do better next time. Leaning slightly to his left, Hill continued. 'And what do our spies say about the territory now, Iain? What kind of force is left?'

'It looks like we have just taken out most of their militia. There will be no more than twenty or thirty in the whole territory left now, if our information is correct. From what we've gathered over the last few months, they've ignored their military for some years now and so what you've just seen was most of it.' The voice came from the obese man with a wiry beard sat to the right of the General.

Iain Bates held no rank in the New English Army but was known to be the de facto number two, taking part in all its major decision-making. He had known Noah Hill for many years, being fiercely loyal to him, knowing him from before the Army had been created. He had gained a reputation for being utterly merciless over his time with General Hill, always ready to get involved in any venture which required cruel or heartless actions.

'And we're sure your information is correct?' ventured Rollins.

Bates glared back. 'Over the past year we've spent a lot of time and resources on spies along the southern coast and parts of the middle-lands of England. So yes, I'm sure my information is correct.' He sat back, allowing his expansive body to sag into the chair.

Hill was enjoying the friction between the two men, but he trusted Iain the most. Over the years they had built up a level of trust that hardly existed anywhere else in this new army they had created. 'Of that I'm sure, Iain. So, they're defenceless, then?'

'Not totally,' Bates replied quickly. 'Apart from these few remaining so-called rangers out there, there's the territory's people themselves. They appear to be fiercely loyal to the Bowles family, but that doesn't mean they will be able to put up much resistance, though, when we get there. More of an annoyance than anything.'

General Hill stood, placing his hands on the table in front of him. 'Then we continue as planned. We'll go back to headquarters today, let the men have a short rest, restock and then move onwards to finish them off. Dismissed.' He saluted, allowing the contingent of officers to quickly make their way out of the command tent. Only Bates remained behind.

Once they were alone together, the General looked over at his closest advisor. 'They were foolish, thinking they could take us on without understanding what we fight for.'

'They didn't know what to expect. We've been planning this for some time and we pulled it off perfectly. It won't happen another time – people will hear about us now and may be more prepared when we take them on.'

'And yet they won't be able to do anything about it. Nothing will be able to stop us now.' Hill leant back in his chair, relaxed and confident that his power was growing.

'Don't get complacent, though, Noah. We've had a great win today, but we don't know what tomorrow brings,' Iain cautioned him gently.

General Hill waved his hand airily, dismissing his caution. 'Enjoy today, enjoy it, there will be many more.'

Iain rose, saluted his superior, then turned and left the tent. Once outside, he saw the men gathering their belongings, ready to move back to the headquarters. He allowed himself a brief smile; this was indeed a most successful day.

Through the camp, Iain saw one of the younger soldiers struggling with a young woman – it appeared that he was bringing her towards him. He wondered why she hadn't been carted off with the rest of the women earlier. He watched with a tilted head and bemused smile as they finally reached the officers' area.

The young man came to a halt and pushed the woman to her knees; she looked up at the man with rage in her eyes.

Reaching down, Iain put his hand underneath her chin, lifting it so he could see her face completely. As he did so, he got a much better look at the thin, frightened girl in front of him.

He didn't look away as he asked the man who had captured her, 'And what's this, then?'

'I found her way over there, sir.' The soldier pointed to where they had come from. 'She was watching us and was trying to leave when I caught her.'

'Interesting. This might be useful. Full of possibilities,' Bates spoke quietly to himself.

'So, what are you?' he asked. 'Surely too young to be one of their rangers and you're too clean to have been fighting only an hour ago.' He let go of her chin and put his hands behind his back.

She spat at him. He merely looked at her, amused, before wiping the phlegm off his coat with his sleeve.

'Stay there,' he ordered, then called out to the men around the tent. 'Watch her, I don't want her harmed, understand?'

The men all saluted, as Iain turned and re-entered the leader's tent.

General Hill was still basking in his recent victory when his second in command returned.

'I think we've just had a stroke of luck,' Iain said. 'It looks like we've caught a scout. We could use her to send a message back to the Bowles territory. Give them the opportunity to surrender completely or face the consequences. Once they know that their leader and militia have been killed, they will have no other option.'

The General stood and walked round to the front of the desk. 'Yes, I see it now. Once they learn of our strength and purpose, they will have no option but to surrender and let us run their pitiful territory. A simple takeover will be a formality once they know of our power.' He hurried outside.

'So then, I understand you were watching us from afar, my dear.' General Hill spoke in a loud voice so the others around him could hear as well.

The woman glowered up at him yet remained silent.

General Hill swung his arm back before striking her violently across her left cheek with the back of his hand. She toppled over to her side; blood trickled from her mouth. Instantly, the soldier lifted her up to her knees, holding her until she was stable.

'You will answer me, girl. And if you will answer me truthfully, you will live. I want to send a message back to your masters about what's happened here, but I need to know they will get it. Otherwise, what's the point of you right now? So, are you a scout for Bowles or not?'

She nodded slightly, her eye and cheek swelling up from the trauma of the hit.

The General was satisfied at her response. 'Good. Listen well, girl. I want you to go back and take this message.' He paused, leaning down towards her. 'We are taking over. When we arrive at your territory, I expect to be welcomed with no further resistance. The New English Army will bring this country back to its ancient glory days. I am reuniting England after these lost decades of weakness and splintering. We will rise once more and take our place amongst our greatest warriors.' His voice came alive with fury and passion as he spoke the final part of these words.

Around them, the nearest men started to bang their hands on their chests in time. The effect was as impressive as it was intimidating.

Holding one hand up, General Hill turned to face the men, smiling at their reaction. He motioned for quiet before turning back to the woman in front of him.

'As I said, surrender and we will work to a brighter future. Resist and we will crush you as we have your rangers.' He knelt down on one knee, in front of his scared captive, stroking her cheek with the back of his hand and speaking softly to her. 'Tell your masters we'll be there soon.'

The woman stared back, eyes wide. Hill saw the fear written over her face, she understood the message well enough.

'Take her back to where you found her, then let her return to her leaders. She is not to be harmed, understood?' General Hill informed the men standing next to the woman before turning back to her. 'You're lucky – not many get warnings, you know.'

|||||||||||||||||||||||||||||||||||||||||||||||||||||||||||||||||||||||||||||

Alva was lifted to her feet, before being taken back to where she had been captured. Stumbling across the muddy battleground, she replayed the scenes between herself and the General through her foggy mind. He seemed sure of himself, that much was certain, as well he should having slain the ranger force. But she had also seen madness in his eyes; he was ruthless.

Having pointed out to her captors where she had come from, before they had taken her, she arrived at her horse, still tied up where she had left him. She was helped on roughly by one of the laughing guards, amused at his own manhandling of a young girl. Although her eye was beginning to swell badly so her sight was poor on her left-hand side, she held her head up, trying not to show any fear or weakness. Grabbing the reins, she rode off as fast as her head would allow, just wanting to get away from these people to somewhere she could think and process everything that had just happened.

Arriving at Herriard, she made her way into the village, heading straight for her office in the barn, untouched by the events of the last few hours.

Once in her workplace, Alva felt herself relax a little, but she felt cold both inside and out. She put on her overcoat and pulled it tight to try to warm herself, before hurrying outside.

Outside, Alva broke into a jog, pulling her horse behind her. She left the barn courtyard as quickly as she could, heading through the hamlet to her family home. Barging through the front door, she saw her mother kneeling in the living room playing with her grandchildren. Her mother rushed to her with pain in her eyes; Alva winced as her mum put her hand to her battered cheek.

She sent the kids into the kitchen and shut the door for some privacy. 'Mum, William and all the rangers are dead. It was a massacre – they've been planning this all along.'

Her mother's eyes went wide; her hands moved over her wide-open mouth as she listened to her daughter's news. 'Everyone?'

'It looks that way,' Alva said quickly. 'I've been to find out what's happened for myself – I got caught, but they let me go with a message for the Bowles family. I've got to get to Chilmark and let them know. You need to go, too. Take everyone and head south. I don't know how safe it will be around here now. Tell the others around to leave as well.'

'Are they coming this way, then?'

'Definitely. I don't know when exactly, but they will be, yes.'

Her mother nodded. 'I'm proud of you. I'll always worry, I'm your mother, but I'm so proud. Look after yourself – try and stay out of trouble, okay?'

Alva's eye started watering slightly. 'I will, Mum, I will.'

Her mother wiped a tear away from her daughter's face. 'I'll take the old carriage and head to our cousins. How much time have we got?'

'I don't know, but I want you to get going straight away. I'm leaving immediately for Chilmark. I'll try and send word to you as soon as I can.'

They moved in close and hugged each other tightly, not wanting to break away from each other. Delicately, her mother kissed Alva on the forehead before moving to the kitchen door. As it opened, the kids all streamed out around their aunt, and they held each other close. Then, after kissing and tightly holding each of the children, Alva hurriedly left the family home, heading back to her waiting horse.

Breathing heavily, she climbed up into the saddle and made her way onto the main track. Taking one last look around at the sleepy village they called home, she rode off to deliver her fateful message.

It wasn't easy to ride with one eye now completely closed, so to begin with she was cautious. She headed to where she had told Daniel to wait for her, hoping he would be there still. As she arrived at the ancient stone bridge, he was nowhere to be seen. Stopping in the middle of the bridge, she called out his name as loud as she could.

She saw the young boy step out from behind some trees, waving his arm, about fifty metres ahead. Alva kicked her horse on to reach him in seconds.

'Dan, you okay?' she asked.

The boy stared at her face; it must have looked horrific now the swelling had fully formed. 'Yes, yes, thank you. Are you all right?'

'No. But I will be. Come on – we need to get back as soon as we can.'

Daniel fetched his colt and jumped on.

Alva set off at an easy pace, initially to make sure the boy could keep up. She soon realised he was an excellent rider, which would make her job a lot easier.

Both of them rode rapidly across the fields and countryside Alva knew well. She hoped they would be able to continue like this for some time before they needed a rest. The journey would take them the rest of the day and a good part of tomorrow – it would be important to gauge their horses' fatigue as best they could, wanting to stop as few times as possible.

It calmed her slightly to know that the enemy, with that number of men, couldn't travel anywhere near as fast as her. When they came, she would be able to give some advance notice at least.

Racing along a dusty, worn track, she tried to stop worrying about things she could not control and to concentrate on her own ride.

ELEVEN

Josh had lost track of the time they had been trudging. His wrists were being rubbed raw from the rough rope tied tightly about them. So far, they had only stopped once for a brief pause, with Harris making them start going again before long. The rangers hadn't been allowed to talk to each other or to the guards. So they carried on, their heads down, looking just ahead of their feet.

Josh's headache had spread out across his whole head. At least his eyesight was getting slightly better, although his thoughts remained more than a little groggy.

Rounding a long, sweeping curve on the track they were on, Harris shouted for the group to halt. 'Our transport should be around here.' He growled as he spoke to both the soldiers before calling out to the surrounding area. 'Harris here – show yourselves.'

Two men called back in response as they appeared through the green canopy of the foliage all around, sauntering slowly down towards them. They shook hands with Harris.

Josh struggled to watch them pointing up the long slope while exchanging a few words with Harris. He looked distracted, even bored.

Harris ordered the prisoners to follow him to where the man had pointed. They started up again, bodies aching, making their way up to where a wagon was waiting.

Harris gave the order to climb aboard.

The wagon creaked and groaned as it started moving, but soon was travelling along at a fair pace. They carried on as night began to fall. Josh wondered where on earth they were heading to. Josh looked around at the faces of his fellow prisoners, seeing them still in shock at the events of the day.

Once the darkness came, the wagon moved slower through the countryside, but the driver seemed to know the area well. There was no talking allowed amongst any of the rangers aboard. Travelling mile after mile, Josh found they were heading in a north-easterly direction. Josh had never been this far east; as far as he knew this area was mostly uninhabited. Besides, anywhere further on was completely dead due to its closeness to the contaminated wastelands of London.

He found it odd that they were heading in that direction as he couldn't understand how anyone could live in or near to the ruins of the once-great city. He remembered his lessons as a child: there were no viable farmlands there and what soil there was had been poisoned from decades of oil and chemical use, leaving it barren and completely unproductive. He had heard tall tales from people, of life before the Chaos, about how tens of thousands of people had lived and worked there. But he could never quite imagine how that must have been.

One thing everyone understood, though, about that once-famous ancient city was that no one could live there now as it simply couldn't support any life.

Lulled by the constant moving of the wagon and the exhaustion from the stresses of the day, Josh felt his weariness inside growing. His eyes were drooping, and his body wanted to sleep. Taking in a few deep breaths to refresh himself, he was determined to stay awake; it was important to him to know where he was going, to understand as much about his enemies as he could. At least his head felt more like its normal self now, the haze in his mind had slowly lifted leaving just soreness behind.

Glancing over at the other rangers, he could see that most of them were asleep, but Nolan was staying alert like him. He looked over at his friend, seeing the same look in his eyes as he felt himself.

As the night and the journey wore on, they began travelling through old and decaying built-up areas. They passed line after line of tall buildings, with collapsed roofs and crumbling walls. Grasses and brambles spread everywhere, giving the scene something of a look of a rolling sea, with structures trying to rise from the depths. Everything was covered in a mossy green colour and the smell in the air was damp and musty; all here was decaying in front of their eyes.

Scattered everywhere were the rusting hulks of cars, mainly covered by creeping plants. These cars were the symbol of the old world, to the people of the new one. Where most people nowadays had a horse to travel around on, it appeared that everyone in the old times had one of these cars. To someone of Josh's age, it was an oddity, no more. They had learnt of times before the Chaos a little in their schooling, but more as stories and tales of caution than anything of usefulness.

But here there were so many cars, and it looked like they were everywhere. Josh was used to seeing small groups of the things, often hidden away in old fields where they slowly poisoned the soil as they decayed. But here they were so abundant it made him think once again of the stories he was taught as a child.

As they continued along, some of the structures they passed were surrounded by plazt fences, tall dark barriers walling off whatever was inside. But just as the decaying houses all around, these held no life in them either.

Trees grew everywhere, small saplings spreading out from their parents, the ground covered by the fallen leaves of the larger trees. But the place still had signs of its history poking out, just making itself heard.

Josh was uncomfortable at the sight of this ancient ruined city; it was not a place for the living anymore. He shifted on his seat, preparing for the long night ahead of him.

That night wore on, with the constant noise of the wheels the only sound. Occasionally, Harris would look round to survey his prisoners. His cruel smile taunting anyone who looked back at him. Josh knew he would enjoy any resistance – he was a killer and he enjoyed killing.

Quietly, they travelled on slowly through the darkness.

By the time the sun was just about to rise, they had covered a lot of ground. The wagon came to a steady stop just in front of a small wooden structure with a long gate closed at its side. Sat lazily around a fire were four men, who had watched the wagon approaching. As it pulled to a stop the men all stood and one of the younger members of the group stepped forwards to approach Harris.

Josh turned his head slightly to assess his surroundings, not looking directly at the approaching man. He wondered why they had stopped. He thought he could hear some noise off in the distance but wasn't sure if he was imagining it in his tired state. Ignoring it, he concentrated on Harris who had climbed down to talk to the younger man.

'I've got a shipment of prisoners I'm taking up to headquarters.' Harris' voice rang out in the quiet morning air.

'Yes, sir. Good to see you again, sir,' came the response.

'Let's sort out the entertainment first,' Harris growled as he turned to the wagon, ordering the rangers to climb down. One of the young men started tying and untying the rangers where necessary. Once the three women were separated, one of the soldiers started to lead them away from the main group. Clearly, they were going in a different direction to the men.

Chad, a young hot-headed ranger who was nearest to one of the New English Army soldiers, swung a free hand clenched in a fist at the nearest guard as he jumped to his feet. It glanced the guard's cheek as he slowly reacted to the attack. Unfortunately, Chad didn't put enough power behind it to make much of a punch. The guard was quick to respond, moving to make amends.

He grabbed the ranger with ease, putting his arm around his neck before throwing him to the ground. Seeing him winded, the soldier followed up by kicking him twice hard in the stomach. Chad covered himself in case of any further strikes coming in, as he coughed and moaned in pain.

Seeing their friend in trouble, Josh and Nolan both started to get to their feet but stopped immediately as the guard to the side of them stepped forwards, waving his sword in their faces. They slowly knelt back down.

Having watched the commotion with amusement, Harris sauntered over, a grin covering his face. He drew his sword as he reached them, standing over the man in pain on the ground before looking at the rest of the rangers. 'Any more trouble and the next one dies, got it?'

Chad was desperately trying to catch his breath, barely managing to nod his acceptance. Josh and Nolan stared, wide-eyed, but both grunted yesses in his direction.

Carrying on from before they were interrupted, the two guards took the three women away from the remaining men. Josh watched them walk through the trees, until they disappeared out of sight. The three remaining rangers were then loaded onto the wagon, two guards sitting behind them. Josh tried to make Chad as comfortable as possible; they weren't serious wounds but would hurt like hell for a while.

Harris motioned for the wagon to move on. He walked by the side of it as it rumbled up a track with a small gradient, between two lines of trees.

Josh watched the man striding along with his chest puffed out like a strutting peacock. If he hadn't been his prisoner, he would have laughed at the absurdity of the situation.

They soon reached the top of the track where the trees started to thin. Ahead of them was a large, imposing old brick and sandstone building, with a spire in the middle rising up, ending in a grey domed roof. It was surrounded by smaller structures, but none as grand as the central one.

From a distance he could see it was an ancient building, hundreds of years old, yet clearly built to stand the tests of time. As they moved nearer, Josh noticed the decay that had crept in. The grounds were covered in tall patchy grasses and clumps of tall nettles grew rampant around the base. The magnificent window frames were old and broken, patched up by wood or scavenged metal where the clear plazt had been broken years before. The roof was missing some of its tiles – attempts had been made to patch it up, but none looked like recent ones.

Smoke rose from the chimneys. In the calm of the morning the smoke clung to the roofs, shrouding the whole scene in a grey foggy mist.

Josh was impressed by the building, but not by its current state. Whatever was here, whatever this English Army was, they had either not been here very long or simply not looked after it at all.

They carried on past the central building, entering a large courtyard to its side. Several men were hard at work, with a steady flow of others heading in and out of the building. They all stopped to stare at the wagon and its contingent, as Harris gave the prisoners the order to climb down.

The three of them clumsily made their way off the transport, exhausted and stiff, until they all stood there in a line once more. They looked solemn. While Chad was looking at the ground by his feet, Josh and Nolan looked directly ahead at the soldiers.

Harris ordered one of the army men in the courtyard to untie the ropes, leading to much relief amongst the rangers as they rubbed their sore wrists. He walked slowly away from the group before turning around and addressing them.

'I know that you are thinking of trying to escape – don't bother. We will be taking the youngest to a separate facility.' Harris sneered. 'If you attempt to make an escape, he will die.'

Three of the men under his command walked over and removed the tormented young ranger. They hurried him off through a door sunk into the wall of the courtyard, his cries ringing out.

The remaining two looked on, aghast.

Harris spoke once more. 'You will be taken to your allocated jobs and assigned a co-worker to show you what to do. Do what they tell you. I'll tell you one thing. There are only two real punishments in the army: flogging or death. Try not to have either of them.' He finished with a laugh at this last comment.

Once Harris had stopped talking, Josh was approached by a balding, stocky man, who grabbed his arm gently before leading him round the side of the courtyard into the building. Nolan was taken in a similar way and each were led off in different directions.

'I'm Eddie,' the man said as he led Josh along. 'Listen to me and you'll be fine. I'll tell you what can and can't be done. If you want to stay out of trouble, follow the rules. The first one is don't be somewhere you're not meant to be.' He spoke quietly in an almost conspiratorial voice.

Josh went to speak but found he had nothing to say to the man.

'Try not to think too much. We've all been in the same boat, but after a while it gets better. There's plenty of food and they treat us well, as long as you do what you're told.' Eddie continued to talk as he led Josh through the maze-like corridors.

Josh tried to build up a mental map of the building, but it was so vast, with each passageway looking like any other. After a short time he gave up and focused all his attention onto this Eddie. 'What is this place?' he asked, without looking at the man leading him around.

'Not sure exactly. We've been here for about six months now. We found it when we moved on last time from our old base. It had a load of old military books and uniforms, so they think it may have been a museum or something.' Eddie spoke as if the situation they were both in was completely normal.

Josh stopped walking and stared at Eddie. 'And who exactly the hell are you? The men I was with have all been killed. I've been taken prisoner. What is going on here?' His voice had turned to a shout by the time he had finished talking.

Eddie sighed, looking down at the floor as he spoke. 'Keep your voice down. You've been taken by the New English Army, just as I was almost a year ago.' His voice cracked. 'There's no escape. I've known others who tried and have been killed. Besides, there's nothing left for me out there now.'

Eddie quickly turned and continued his way through the house, only this time without gripping Josh's arm. Josh had the presence of mind to follow him rather than be left wandering alone, especially if what Eddie had told him was true.

They walked down two more hallways until they came to a large oak door. Eddie opened it and walked through, Josh following the man cautiously. They were now outside again, in a much smaller courtyard than the one they had left earlier. It was cobbled with ancient smooth stones, and a small wall made of old crumbling stones surrounded them. Walking across it quickly they came to another door, which was open, and walked through.

It was a large room with a high ceiling above them. Josh immediately felt heat on his skin, the air heavy from a large fire raging in the middle of a fireplace to one side. Huge pots were placed on a metal structure in the middle of the room. Josh gagged as he took in a breath, the fetid air being taken into his lungs made him instantly nauseous. He coughed and struggled to breathe.

Eddie took his arm once more, leading him over to a window, which he opened, allowing Josh to take in some fresher air. He breathed heavily at the window before turning to look at the room again.

'Welcome to the tannery. Not everyone's choice, but it's warm and people tend to stay away from us.'

Josh was shocked to hear a hint of pride in his voice.

There were two other men working. Eddie called out their names, making them briefly look over at the newcomer. Josh noticed how nervous they were as they said hello to him.

But he had finally had enough of the smell and quickly bolted to the door, just managing to clear the threshold before he was violently sick. Wiping away the tears from his eyes, he took in a large breath before returning to the room.

Eddie stood there, smirking. 'It does that the first time you're in here, but it gets better. Right, I'd better show you what you'll be doing.'

Josh was shown around the various parts of the tannery. Each of the men spent a short amount of time explaining what they were expected to do, then let Josh watch them as they performed their tasks.

Hardly able to take any of it in, Josh felt his mind whirling with what had happened in the last several days. His head still hurt like hell from the blow he had taken. Suddenly trying to turn his attention to what he was being told was impossible.

After a full morning of watching the tannery's workforce while trying not to be sick again, Josh was physically and mentally exhausted. When they stopped for a brief meal of bread and apples in the afternoon, it was clear that neither of the two men who worked in the tannery with Eddie wanted to discuss their previous lives with Josh. No matter how much he kept probing them about where they were from. Eddie merely told him that once here it was easier to forget about what had gone before and concentrate on staying alive.

Josh remained determined to find out as much as he could about this New English Army and then escape back home. He wondered, however, how home would cope with the loss of William Bowles and his rangers.

TWELVE

Alva and Daniel made good time racing across the countryside, passing quickly through townships and settlements, only slowing when their horses tired. They kept away from the old places – they were too unsafe underfoot for fast travelling.

After one lengthy stint, Alva wanted to let the horses have some water and a short rest, stretch her own legs and possibly have a drink as well. She recalled that there was a brook a mile or so ahead of her. The day was warm, with few clouds in the sky; the sweat on both her and her horse dripped down their necks and bodies.

They reached the shallow river and dismounted, the horses breathing hard as they drank. Alva and Daniel stretched their tired backs out, before joining the horses at the water's edge.

The fresh water gave Alva a small boost – she was near her destination and could deliver her message. Deciding not to stay for longer than was absolutely necessary, they soon continued, but this time at a pace they could manage.

It wasn't long until the surroundings became more occupied, houses and buildings full of workers going about their lives. She was arriving at the outskirts of Chilmark, home to the Bowles family. Alva had last been here six months ago, but she remembered it well. Slowing down to a gentle walk, she prepared herself for what she had to say.

As they came around a small bend after a row of old, repaired houses, she saw the town square in front of her. They had arrived safely. Crossing through the town, she could see some of the people stop and stare at this badly injured rider and her younger companion.

They stopped at the complex's imposing main gates. There were two rangers on duty. One of them stood to approach her as she dismounted before them.

'I'm Alva Sinclair, in charge of the Herriard outpost.' She tried to sound authoritative, but she wasn't sure that was how it came out. 'I have urgent news for Tom Bowles and the council. I must see them now.'

The guard who had approached her now looked at her carefully. 'I haven't got a clue who you are. What do you want?' he asked gruffly.

Alva looked at him with as much strength as she could gather. 'I've ridden here with urgent information about William and his rangers – now show us in. Immediately.' Her tone must have convinced the guard. He told the other guard to look after the horses and motioned for Alva and Dan to follow him.

Tired but holding her head high, Alva strode forwards, with Daniel at her side, the guard having to hurry to keep up at times as they walked to the main house.

'Wait here,' the ranger told them as they entered the large lobby.

Pacing up and down, Alva tried to keep her breathing under control, wary of what she was about to say. Consumed by her own thoughts, she only partially took in the people working in the house as they walked by. She paused as she saw her disfigured reflection in one of the windows.

Just as she thought she'd been forgotten and was steeling herself to go and find somebody who could help, she felt a hand on her shoulder, making her turn quickly.

'Alva, I'm Anne Brixey, second in command here. I think we've met before, haven't we? My, your eye looks sore. We will have to have a look at it for you.'

Alva felt calmed by Anne's tone; she could feel her anxiety dropping. She had made it – she had brought the news home.

'Uh, yes we did, last time I was here, I think,' Alva responded, pulling away as Anne touched her sore cheek. 'And this is Dan. He came with me from Herriard.'

'Welcome, Dan. You look exhausted.' She called over her assistant, waiting to the side. 'If it's okay with you, Alva, I think Dan here could do with some food.'

Alva gave Daniel a tired hug. 'I think that's an excellent idea. I will see you soon, Dan, okay? I will call you if we need anything.'

The boy smiled with relief, before being led away to the kitchens by an assistant.

'Good. Now, can you come with me? Let's go somewhere more private.' Anne gently took Alva's arm, directing her to an ornately painted door the other side of the hall.

After closing the door behind her, Anne walked to her antique wooden desk and took a seat, signalling for Alva to sit in one of the chairs nearby. The room was a small office, with neatly stacked papers in piles around the desk, lending it an air of intimateness.

Anne opened a drawer and pulled out a small piece of cloth; after dipping it into a cup of water, she handed it to Alva.

'So, what news have you got for us?' Anne asked.

Alva patted around her eye with the cloth, gently wiping the dust and dirt away. She took in a deep breath, before telling Anne everything that had happened since William led the rangers to battle.

Anne sat there wide-mouthed as she heard the story unfold. Alva knew it was hard to take in. She couldn't believe it herself still. After Alva had finished, they both sat in silence for a minute.

Anne leant back in her chair, her eyes wide open. She ran her fingers through her hair, stopping when they supported her neck. 'And you saw no survivors at all?' Her voice wavered as she spoke.

Alva lowered her head; a tear rolled down one of her cheeks. 'No, none. All the rangers I saw were dead. If there were any alive, then I didn't see them.'

'My God. William gone! And all the rangers, everyone. This is horrifying – how could this happen?' Anne put her hand over her mouth. 'Josh!' she whispered. 'We need to get everyone together and let them know what's happened. Alva, will you come with me?'

They both headed out of the office room back into the main hallway. Anne headed to a set of dark double doors; knocking hard, she opened the door and entered immediately. Alva followed behind.

The chamber was the personal office of William Bowles, where Bowles Mercantile was run from. It had first been used by Jeremiah Bowles, William's father, many years ago. It was the first part of the house to be refurbished and utilised when he had acquired the main building.

Alva looked around as she walked in. It was hard to take in her surroundings. She saw fine small tables and bookshelves. Pictures hung on the walls: animals and landscapes, some of people from long ago times. In the centre of the room was a large oval table, its sheen partially removed from years of wear by the family, covered in a myriad of papers and paperweights. Behind this central table were two desks, each more organised. Sat at these were Tom and Leila Bowles, running the operation while their father was away.

The Bowles siblings looked up at the same time. Seeing the tired and dirty Alva behind Anne, both faces took on a worried look.

Anne started speaking as soon as the doors were shut, looking at both of William's children in turn, her voice breaking as she did. 'Alva's returned from where William and the rangers engaged the bandits they were following. I'm sorry, Tom, Leila.' She paused, obviously trying to find the right words. 'William and the rangers, they've been killed, all of them.'

Alva felt tears start again; she wondered if they would ever stop. She was trying to stay strong, but it was so hard.

Leila was the first to stand and walk over to them. Tom stayed sitting there, his eyes glassy, staring ahead.

'Are you sure? What happened?' Leila's words came out stilted, monotone.

Alva took a step forwards to come level with Anne. 'I'm sorry, it's true, I saw it myself. I received a message from the battle from one of the messengers, telling me the news. I went to look for myself. Then I saw them all.' She paused, remembering the horrific sight of the battlefield, before continuing. 'I saw them all dead, and William was one of them. They caught me and took me to someone called General Hill, who told me to tell you they would be coming for you all and taking over the territory. He called it the New English Army. He said it's dedicated to restoring England back to how it was once.'

Leila leant back, steadying herself on the oval table before looking at Alva.

'Thank you for bringing us this news. We must gather the council together.' Leila spoke like she was on autopilot. She turned to face Tom, who was now looking out of the large window behind his desk.

'I will inform the council members and get everyone together,' Anne told the both of them. 'I'll let you know when they're all ready.'

As Alva left, she saw Tom and Leila embrace each other with their heads buried into each other's shoulders.

Anne called one of the house workers over. 'Take Alva to the doctor in town. Tell him to look at her injuries.' She turned to Alva. 'Get that eye looked at, then come back when you're ready.'

Alva acquiesced. 'Okay, I'll be back soon.' She headed off, following the house worker.

The rest of the afternoon at the Bowles residence was spent in a flurry of activity. Most of the members of the council were nearby since the previous assembly was only a few days before. Only two were far enough away now to merit not being included. Messengers were sent instead to update them on the terrible news.

Leila and Tom spent the time inside their family's office alone. Occasionally they were interrupted by Anne, giving them brief updates on how everything was progressing. For much of the time they alternated between grief and shock. Their mother had died many years ago when they were young, and since then their father had played both roles for them. He had been the focus of their lives for so many years.

After the initial shockwave of the news, they struggled to focus on what needed doing. Leila was having more success than Tom at facing the situation; he withdrew into himself in front of her, allowing her to do most of the talking.

Finally, late in the day, Anne knocked on the door and entered, announcing that the council was ready for them. Tom stood, looking nervous. As the eldest child of William, it was time for him to take the reins of the company and all its associated decisions.

Leila understood what her brother was feeling; looking at his darkened eyes she whispered, 'You'll be okay. You knew this might happen one day. I'll be there to support you.'

Tom didn't answer. He kissed his sister on her cheek before leading the way to the council chamber.

The council members stood as Tom and Leila entered. All offered their condolences.

Leila went to her seat, leaving Tom looking at his father's chair. She watched him standing behind it as he motioned for the others to sit. He wasn't ready to take the position just yet. She smiled at her brother as he looked around the large table.

'Thank you for coming. You all know the news. We are here to work out what to do next.' His voice held firm as he spoke.

As Tom was speaking, Leila noticed Irving sitting nearby, ashen-faced, in shock.

The first to speak was Gabriel Wells, an older, greying man. Gabriel had been the representative for some of the larger merchants and traders in the area for many years. He was one of the wealthier members of the council, having helped William out many times with loans or assistance of manpower.

'Tom, Leila, I offer my condolences at the news of your father. He was a great man who led this territory well. I owe William many debts, not all of which are about money. Whatever I can do for the both of you, I will.'

Brother and sister thanked their old friend. Leila felt reassured to have him around at this time.

Gabriel continued, looking at Tom still standing behind his father's chair. 'Tom. I know this is hard for you, but your family is still the majority shareholder in this company. You are his eldest child, you have been trained to take over from William. The company needs its figurehead. I call for a vote to make you the new directeur of Bowles Mercantile.'

Leila quickly raised her hand. 'I second that.'

One by one, everyone around the table agreed. Tom was now officially in charge of the company. He pulled out the chair before slowly taking his place at the head of the table.

'Thank you, Gabriel. Thank you to all of you. I promise I will try to do my best running the company.'

Leila reached across, patting his arm gently. She would support her brother in any way she could.

Gabriel spoke again. 'May I suggest that we also confirm Anne Brixey as the new head of security. I know that Art looked on her as a fine deputy and she will honour him as she takes over.'

Leila agreed. 'I think that's an excellent proposal. Anne, will you accept?'

Anne looked around the room, then finally at Tom, who managed a small smile. 'Of course, thank you, I will do my best for you.'

Leila thanked Gabriel for the advice; she understood it was meant as a way to get the meeting started and was grateful for the assistance. She intended to take control of the gathering, recognising her brother was overwhelmed by it all. Starting by outlining the situation. 'As everyone knows, we are now effectively defenceless. Whoever this person is has wiped out the majority of our ranger force, having more troops than we had, by far.' She paused, trying to lower the anger in her voice, but decided to let it out. 'It also seems to have been a trap. They knew we would come after them in retaliation for what they did. The question is, what will they do now? From what Alva tells us, it appears they are definitely coming for us, and soon.'

Gabriel cleared his throat and leant forwards. 'I would agree – of course they will come and take what they have now made helpless. If they intended on taking out our defence, that's the only obvious next step. Otherwise, why bother?'

To the right of Gabriel sat Shad Thoms, a younger man, with long dark hair pulled back and a full black beard flowing down from a friendly heavy-set face. Shad was one of the two elected members of the council; he was a scavenger, a promising lectrical worker and popular amongst the locals.

'Can we get any help from Kernow? We get on well with them, don't we? And we've just had a very good trade mission with them,' Shad asked plaintively of the faces looking at him.

'They are the closest territory, of course, but whether they would I'm not so sure,' Leila answered. 'They're well known for not wanting to be involved in others' affairs.'

'You have family there, don't you? Surely that would count for something.' Shad was almost pleading now.

Tom spoke up, pale-faced. 'My mother was from there, yes. But we don't really know much of that side of the family, I'm afraid. Anyway, it would be the Collective who would decide. But it is something to consider, I agree.' He looked across at Leila who signalled her agreement with him.

As Shad sat back in his chair, Henry Martgen looked at Tom through his eyeglasses, staring hard at the younger man, and then looked down.

'Maybe we can try and find a peaceful solution with them, then.' Henry spoke each word carefully to the table.

Gabriel glowered at Henry and his suggestion. 'Are you mad? They have just killed our rangers and William himself. Do you honestly expect them to come here and negotiate a "peaceful solution"?' Gabriel spoke the last two words in a higher pitched voice, imitating Henry.

Henry stood and looked like he was about to shout insults at Gabriel, but Tom banged the table and ushered him to sit.

'I know that you two are not the best of friends, but I will not allow it to spill over into this meeting. We are here to find solutions, not carry on old arguments.' Tom paused, looking shocked. He sounded like his father.

Henry sat back, flustered and still visibly seething.

'If I may, I'd like to ask Alva to speak,' Anne volunteered to the group. 'She saw what they did. Maybe she can give you some insight.'

Without waiting, she turned and gestured to Alva for her to talk to the council.

The young woman took a few moments before she spoke. 'You all know what happened. I'd like to tell you what else I saw. These men, all men, seemed wild, feral even. Absolutely vicious in their attack.' Alva paused again. 'They aren't the type of people to negotiate anything, let alone peacefully. The things I saw them do to the dead … they are not honourable people. And this general, he had a madness in his eyes. He wants to be all-powerful and won't stop until he is.'

'Then there's only one thing to do: take everything we own and leave,' Gabriel said, with little emotion in his voice.

Leila was shocked at the notion. 'But what about the working families around here? Everything they have is tied to the land – we can't expect them to leave suddenly like this.'

Gabriel glanced at Leila. 'It's either that or face whatever is coming, and with no defence how will that turn out?'

Everyone around the table went quiet.

'Before all hope is lost, I must say Henry may have a point,' Tom said. 'I think someone should go and try to negotiate with them. At least we can find out, one way or the other, if it is possible to find a peace. If I understand this general correctly, he will enjoy having us go to him. It's dangerous but our only play right now. We have no defence left.'

Now that Tom had backed this approach, more and more of the council started to agree with the prospect of meeting them. He looked squarely at Leila. 'I should go, I should represent us as head of the family.'

'No, that's a bad idea. We've just lost one head of the family and I think it's too much of a gamble for another one to go. We can't risk you so soon after – the family needs its head.' Leila had made her mind up on this matter. 'I'll go.'

Tom had the beginnings of a scowl on his face.

Henry spoke up immediately. 'I think Tom should be the one to represent us. He is the head of the company after all now.'

Leila raised her hand. 'No, I will. There will be no further discussion on this matter.'

Henry sat back in his chair and crossed his arms. The rest of the council showed their reluctant agreement. Irving nodded his ascent, still hardly able to speak.

Gabriel stood up, looking at each member in turn. 'Thank you, Leila, we appreciate it. But however well-meaning it may be, I think it's a fool's errand. We need to think of the worst before it's too late. Tom, will you speak to Kernow and see what they can offer us if the worst comes to pass?'

Tom answered quietly. 'Of course, I'll contact them as soon as we finish here. Anne, I want you to get any rangers that are left in the whole territory back here. Also, get as many of the workers from the surrounding area as you can here – see if any will fight with us if needed, but let them know what is happening.'

'Of course,' Anne replied. 'I'll send out as many riders as I can. I'll let people know what's coming our way.'

'Good. I suggest you all help out where you can. I shall go and try to contact the Kernow and see what help they can offer. Thank you, Leila. I suggest we all meet back here in two hours.'

Leila stood and kissed Tom tenderly on the cheek, before turning and leaving the room, shoulders sagging.

THIRTEEN

Josh felt terrible during his first night with the New English Army, barely able to relax, let alone sleep, on a musty bed in a draughty room. Twelve other men were in the same room as him and at times during the night he heard at least three of them quietly sobbing. Hour after hour he lay on the thin wooden cot, one thin blanket to keep him warm, staring up at the ceiling in the dim moonlight, determined to leave this place as soon as he could.

After ending his work detail yesterday, Josh had been taken to see the Army's supply officer; yet another severe man who seemed to take pleasure in the new captives' discomfort. All the new workers were issued with a dyed-black shirt they were told to put on immediately. The man then proceeded to bark commands at them for half an hour, which basically all boiled down to the same thing. Obey the guards, don't make trouble, and anyone attempting to escape will ensure the death of another as well as possibly themselves.

There were two other newcomers there with Josh and Nolan; both were young and looked absolutely terrified. Josh had wondered where they had come from, worried how long they would last here. Once the pointless introduction to army life was over, they had been sent to their sleeping quarters.

As dawn broke, the first light made its way into the room. Josh took in his surroundings. He hadn't paid much attention last night as he was shown to the room. The walls were covered in peeling paint, the antique plasterwork flaking off all over the walls. Everything looked and smelt damp. They were on the third floor and right below the roof, which looked like it wouldn't keep much water out when it rained.

As he acclimatised to this dingy place, he heard the sounds of the building coming alive. Suddenly, a loud whistle was sounded from somewhere and within moments everyone was sitting up, stretching their tired limbs.

'Breakfast! Make sure you're not last – there's never enough food,' Eddie shouted at Josh from across the room, near one of the broken glass windows. As Josh looked over at the man, he saw him dressing as quickly as possible.

Taking that as his cue to get ready, Josh pulled on his trousers after shaking them free from some of the dirt of the previous day. They were still covered in dark stains, which he tried not to focus on. He then put on his Army-issue black shirt, one he was resolute not to wear for long. By the time he had laced up his boots and was putting his first arm into his tunic, he was the last out of the room. Following the sound of the rest of the hurrying men, he made his way downstairs.

He ended up outside the rear of the building towards the end of a large queue. Josh looked carefully at some of the others around him. Most were younger men, with unkempt hair and grubby skin. All were wearing similar black shirts above a variety of different coloured trousers. There was plenty of pushing and shoving amongst them as they moved closer to the food being served.

Walking up and down the queue were much neater, better-dressed men. Their guards, albeit not looking too carefully at the people they were watching. All were armed and looked well fed, definitely able to quash any trouble that got out of hand.

Waiting patiently, Josh felt himself jostled a few times, but otherwise the queue for breakfast was a relatively quiet one. Arriving at the food, he picked up a bowl and moved to the long table with large steaming pots on. A miserable skinny man in his later years scooped a ladle of the hot stew into his bowl and grunted for him to move on. Josh did so, faintly bewildered by the whole situation, grabbing a good-sized strip of bread as he went.

Moving away from the servers, Josh looked for a place to sit. He saw Nolan a short distance away. He walked over and sat down, not too near to draw attention but near enough to be able to hear anything they might say to each other. As he sat, he saw Nolan give him a quick wink.

'You okay?' Nolan asked, carrying on with his breakfast.

'Yeah, not too bad, you?' Josh took a bite of the bread and started chewing while looking around the area.

'All good, trying to work out what all this is about.'

'Same here. They seem organised, even if it is in a pretty chaotic way. Everyone I was put with is extremely scared but seems content to go along with them.' Josh noticed everyone was eating quickly, with their heads down.

'Yeah, I've seen the same.' Nolan took a spoonful of his stew and grimaced. 'God knows what's in this.'

Josh tried the food in his bowl. It tasted stale and greasy, but he knew he had to keep his strength up so he forced it down.

Abruptly, another whistle sounded, with everyone going quiet and looking up towards the man making the sound near the door to the building. A guard led a long line of men out towards the feeding station, each was tied loosely to the one next in line. It was noticeable that they were either the very young or the very old. About halfway down both Nolan and Josh saw Chad, the ranger that had been taken separately after being with them in the battle.

'So that's where they keep the ones to force us into working with them,' Josh whispered, watching the nasty scene. A lot of the men around them seemed to be looking at someone they knew and who bound them to this Army. 'Clever way of enforcing discipline.'

Nolan grunted his agreement as he watched the trail of captives take their food back into the house.

'What about the women? I wonder where they are?' Josh asked.

'Not a clue. We need to keep an eye out to see if we can find where they are.' Nolan finished his food and placed his bowl on the ground. 'So, what have you been told to do? I've been assigned to scavenging.'

'Tannery. God, it's rank in there.' Josh squirmed at the thought of another day in the insufferable place. 'Let's try to find out as much information as we can and compare notes next time we meet.'

Another whistle rang out, making everyone stand and return their bowls, ready for another day serving this self-styled General Hill in the New English Army. Josh quickly finished his stew before making his way to his work detail.

In the tannery, Josh was assigned to assist Jaan, a shy fellow in his late twenties who spoke quietly and seemed withdrawn into himself most of the time. Josh tried a few times to strike up a conversation but made no headway at all beyond a few words. By the time a short lunchbreak was called, he had gleaned only a few small details about the man.

Jaan had told him he was originally from a small coastal town to the north of Canterbury in the far southeast of England. He had joined the New English Army a couple of years ago, but whether it was voluntary or forced he wouldn't say.

Jaan had mentioned that the Army hadn't been around for that long before he had joined. Josh tried to probe further but Jaan clammed up, not wanting to talk about it anymore. Josh left it for now, hoping to return to the subject another time.

As the two of them finished talking, Eddie walked over with a concerned look on his face. Gently taking Josh's arm, he led him to one side.

'Some advice, lad,' Eddie said in a low, hushed tone. 'Don't go asking too many questions. You never know who will find out.'

'Why? Why should they care?'

'Doesn't matter why. Just try and keep your head down, that's all.'

Josh had finally had enough of everyone around him meekly accepting their fates and keeping their heads down, as Eddie said.

'For God's sake, you're all acting like slaves here, like there's no hope left.' He blazed at the room. 'How can you accept being treated like this and letting them tell you what to do?' The anger he felt leached out of him.

Oddly, apart from Eddie, the others in the room just carried on with their work – everyone carried on with what they were doing. Josh looked around for some form of emotion, but none came from those with their heads down.

Eddie grabbed Josh's arm harshly, pulling him outside the main door to the tannery. The wind had whipped up a little as the two men moved to a corner of the yard.

'Lad, you need to appreciate a few things about the men in here.' Eddie kept his voice quiet. 'Before you act like you're better than us, why don't you try understanding things first?'

Josh had calmed down a bit by now and looked uncertainly into Eddie's eyes. 'I didn't mean for it to come across like that. I'm just amazed by how accepting everyone seems to be of all this.' He waved his hand around at the buildings.

'Many haven't accepted it easily, especially the older ones. Take Jaan in there – he lost his family to the Army before he was taken. They raided his village, killing many and taking whatever they wanted. He was helpless for months after that, but he's functioning now, at least.'

'But he's with the men that killed his family. How can he serve with them?' Josh asked. 'I just don't understand.'

'Because they broke him. He has no fight left in him now and so he serves them. He has the occasional freak-out but mainly he just gets on with things. There's three ways people get by here. Choosing to join, being broken, or pretending to be a part of it.'

'So, which one are you?' Josh's eyes narrowed as he asked the question.

Eddie sighed. 'Me, probably a bit of all three, but I tell myself I'm acting the part of a man trying to preserve his own life. I had no family worth speaking of and no friends I was taken with, being a bit of a lone traveller and all that. At first, I thought I would leave somehow one day, but I let myself get comfortable, I guess. Telling myself that at least with them I'm fed and safe.'

Josh shook his head at what Eddie was saying. 'But they attack and kill innocent families, take what they want with no thought of others.'

'I know.' Eddie hung his head, looking at the floor. 'I'm not proud of myself. I just try not to think about it.'

'Then by your actions you condone what they do, helping them in what you do. You're just as bad as they are.' Although Josh knew the situation was more complex than he was making out, he felt disgusted at the way these men were acting. He stormed back into the tannery's hot and stinking room, feeling nothing but revulsion for this Army and its men.

General Hill was gazing out of the window, as Iain and the rest of the senior ranking officers filed into his office. He continued gazing out as they stood there waiting for him; he loved to project an air of authority, even to his most trusted advisors.

After a suitable amount of time, he turned and walked over to his antique bureau, situated at one end of the long, elegant room. Around him were paintings of battles and acts of warfare through the ages; he felt at home amongst such images.

He sat down into the high-backed, ancient leather chair, and leant forwards on the table.

'I trust the men are rested and recovered?' he said to the watching collection of officers.

'Yes, General, we've also restocked the wagons and are preparing to be ready to leave whenever you give the order,' a young wiry man with greased-back hair responded. 'We have also redistributed the weapons we took from the battleground amongst the men.'

'I take it the men enjoyed the female company they had last night?' Hill smirked wickedly at the question.

Colonel Rollins spoke with a crooked smile and a gruff tone in his voice. 'Very acceptable, General. They appreciated the new intake.'

'Good, good. Got to keep morale up. Well then, gentlemen, I think it's time we made our way to our new home.' General Hill relished the thought of what was to come. 'Let's leave this unproductive land behind us and take what we need to really rebuild this fallen country.'

The cadre of officers in the New English Army spent the next hour discussing the route they would take to the Bowles residence at Chilmark, often letting the conversation move off on many tangents. Each officer told of what they were looking forward to taking the most from the current occupants.

All the anticipations, however, centred around the one thing they all desired the most: power. Every member of the Army's inner circle had got were they were by being ruthless and brutal, and they expected to carry on that way once the grand plan had been carried out.

Iain Bates, however, didn't join in with the occasional gossip around the table. He knew that General Hill would kill any of these men if they ever got too powerful, as he had done to the occasional officer before. He understood that any form of challenge to the General's authority would never be accepted and so always deferred in everything which could be construed as a challenge to this man he had followed for such a long time. Acting like this kept him safe and able to guide the Army much more than these others.

Once the meeting came to its end, the officers left the room with their orders. They would be leaving soon for the final assault on the prize. General Hill walked to the window, looking out at the green countryside to the west. He mulled to himself that after so many false starts, this would be the break he had been waiting for.

Josh spent the rest of the day keeping his head down, listening and observing, as he completed the tasks he had been given by Eddie. Inside, he was still seething about the apathy of these people, their tacit acceptance of what was being done. Surely more of them felt like he did. Somehow, he would free himself from this dangerous so-called army.

As he worked, he noticed that Eddie would occasionally glance over at him, as if about to say something but stopping himself every time. The others in the room meekly continued as if his outburst had never happened. The one thing he knew was that he needed to find some stronger allies in here than these people. He was eager to get together with Nolan again; together they surely could come up with a strategy.

Once the end of the day came, the sound of the food whistle rang through the buildings. As in the morning, everyone quickly made their way to where the food was served.

Standing in a quieter line than in the morning, Josh looked round to find Nolan but couldn't see him anywhere. He hoped he wasn't late and hadn't missed what little food they were given.

With his food, Josh sat where he had eaten breakfast that morning, hoping that Nolan would join him soon. As he ate, Eddie wandered over, sitting down next to Josh.

'You okay?' Eddie asked.

'Yeah, just looking for someone I came in with,' Josh replied, not really wanting to engage with the man too much.

'What detail was he given?'

'Scavenging, I think he said.' Josh continued to eat while still looking around.

'Ah, sometimes they go out for a day or more.' Eddie obviously wanted to talk more than Josh. 'He might not be back till later or tomorrow.'

'Right, thanks.'

Eddie twisted his body a little to face Josh more. 'Look, I know you think that by not resisting them, I condone what they do. Maybe you're right, maybe I should have fought them, but I'd be dead if I did. There's nothing I can do to change all this.'

Josh looked at Eddie thoughtfully. He didn't want to berate him again – maybe Eddie could be useful to him after all.

'But what if there was something you could do?' he asked the older man.

Eddie looked around, taking in the positions of the nearest men to them. He lowered his voice before answering Josh.

'You could get yourself killed talking like that to the wrong man.'

'Are you the wrong man?' Josh narrowed his eyes. 'Or do you want to do the right thing?'

Eddie sat back, taking a moment before he replied. 'I won't let on what you're thinking of, no. But I'm no fighter – any one of those guards would kill me before I'd put a step out of place.'

'You don't always have to be the best fighter to win a fight,' Josh said. 'I've got no intention of staying here. I just need to work out how to leave. I think you probably want to as well. You just don't know how to.'

The two men sat in silence as they finished their meals. Josh wanted to believe that he could trust Eddie and hopefully gain an ally in this place.

Another whistle, telling the men mealtime was over. The two rose and replaced their bowls before making their way to their room. The evening was spent with the rest of their roommates. Some telling stories of their past lives, others staying quiet and not getting involved at all. Josh took little part in the events before night came, lying on his bed thinking of the family and friends he had left behind. Anne was foremost in his thoughts; he stifled a tear thinking of what she must be going through at home.

Unsurprisingly, Josh had another restless night's sleep. It was lightly raining outside, making the air through the whole house smell even damper than yesterday. Water slowly dripped through the roof, falling onto the floor. At the sound of the now inescapable meal whistle, everyone hurried down to eat their breakfast.

Standing in line, Josh noticed Nolan just being served. He breathed a small sigh of relief that he was okay. Noting where Nolan went to sit with his food, Josh continued to wait for his before joining him.

'Missed you last night.' Josh sat down on the damp grass near one of the walls.

'Yeah, out with the scavs. Although it wasn't the most organised thing I've ever done.' Nolan took a large mouthful of stew before continuing. 'Not even sure what the whole point of it was. I can't even see the point in half the stuff we were collecting. It's not what I'd call useful. Everyone just wants to be seen to bring the most stuff back rather than work out what they actually need. I mean, who needs old jewellery or trinkets here?'

'Glad you're back, though. I wanted to talk through a few things with you that I thought yesterday.' Josh looked around to make sure no one could overhear them. 'I'm sure that there are guys in here who would want to come with us if we tried to get away.'

Nolan thought for a minute. 'I'm sure there are but are there any we could really trust to help us? I wouldn't want to risk my life to most of this lot.'

'True, but I'm sure there's some in here who would be good. I think we're going to need some help at some stage.'

'Got anyone in mind?'

'There's a guy I work with, Eddie. I'm pretty sure he would help us.'

'Okay, I'll take a good look at some of the lads I'm working with, see if there's anyone in that lot who can help us.'

The two of them finished their food in silence, the cool drizzle on their faces as they sat there. When the shrill noise of the whistle arrived signalling the end of mealtime, they exchanged glances as they stood then went off to their separate work details.

FOURTEEN

Leila had been in a heated meeting with Irving, Alva and Anne for over an hour now. Tom had spent the time up in the communications room for yet another exchange with the Kernow Collective.

Outside, the security detail, which would be guarding Leila on her proposed trip, was busy preparing for their journey, planning out potential routes. Leila had decided to take two of the company's bodyguards for the trip, Ty and Simon, who were two of the strongest and most imposing rangers left. They had both only just returned from the south of the territory that day, having been horrified to hear of what had happened to the rest of their force. They would be an imposing sight to anyone thinking of trying to ambush the team along the way, but all of them been fully briefed on what to expect from the enemy.

Irving had been listening again to Alva's details about her encounter with this so-called army, asking her question after question till she was exhausted.

Leila poured some water from a large glass jug for the others around her as Tom stepped into the room.

He walked over to where the three were sitting and sat down on a nearby chair. He still looked shell-shocked from the news of his father's death, his eyes dark. The others looked expectantly at him, waiting patiently for him to speak.

'Well, I managed to get through to Matthew Taylor, finally. We've been speaking for the last half hour,' Tom told them.

'He's the head of the Kernow Collective, has been for seven years,' Leila informed Alva. 'How much do you know about them?'

'Not much really. I know their reputation, though,' she replied.

Leila gave a small laugh. 'Ever since the Chaos times there's always been a tension with them, for good reasons some may say. But the two territories have had good relations for some years – look at the good trade between us now. And that's where our mother was from. She was a distant cousin of Matthew. Dad met her when he was down there one year.'

'I know their bad reputation in our territory,' Tom interrupted. 'But we can trust Matthew when it comes to the family's survival.' He turned to Leila. 'He passes on his thoughts and prayers to us, Leila. He was appalled at what happened to Dad and has offered as much help as he can.'

Leila looked out of the window at the mention of her father, speaking with tears forming in her eyes. 'And what help can he offer us? They can't defend us, can they?'

'Not like that, no,' Tom answered. 'But they are willing to help in other ways. They extend an offer of sanctuary to anyone who wishes to take it. He will personally take our family into his house, should we so desire.'

'And that's it? We run away? We can't do that!' Leila exclaimed.

'No, we came up with something else as well: he offered to move their border temporarily eastwards about forty miles to take the solar farms and algae protein production centre at Somerton under their protection.'

'They want to take it over?' Irving barked.

'No, we can move there and run it as our own, but they will make it clear to anyone who is interested that they will protect us. They will send some of their militia for a show of force. It is our jewel in our family's assets and if we can keep hold of it, we may just have a future after all.' Tom leant back, looking at the others taking in what he had just said.

'It means leaving our home.' Leila had a tear in her eye. 'And everything we've built.'

Alva leant forwards. 'May I offer my thoughts?'

Leila motioned her to talk. 'Of course. You don't have to ask.'

'I don't believe this general will accept anything other than full surrender and if that happens you won't be able to stay here anyway. They want to take everything you own, and they won't hesitate to kill everyone to get it, so you lose this place either way.'

Anne had been quiet for a while, sitting there listening. She joined in, offering her take on the situation. 'We should plan to take everything of value to Somerton. If we can hold there then at least we've got a backup plan if the worst happens.'

'I agree. It will take us a day or so to prepare. We should start immediately if we want to make sure we leave nothing of value behind.' Irving looked a shadow of his former self.

'And what about the people who can't move, whose livelihood is in the lands they work? What about them?' questioned Leila.

Tom put his hand on his sister's shoulder. 'They're after us and our production means, not the locals. All we can hope is that they aren't bothered about hurting the land workers, at least until we can come back stronger somehow.'

'So, we give them our home, our lands, and leave, just like that.' Leila felt more tears welling up inside her.

'I assure you, Lei, we may leave here temporarily, but we will be back soon. We live to fight another day,' Tom told his sister.

Leila stood, only just holding her rage at bay. 'I can't believe we are thinking of doing this, though. Plan all you like, but there must be another way. It's time I left to go and try to talk to this insane general. Let the council know what is happening and prepare to go to Somerton as a last resort. I hope I return with better news.'

'I'd like to come with you,' Alva volunteered. 'I don't want to stay here without helping more. And besides, I know what he is, and I'm not afraid of him.'

Leila thought for a moment then gratefully accepted her offer, wishing they had more people like the young woman in front of her.

Tom made his way to stand behind his father's chair, now his own. He gripped the high back tightly, giving him some comfort in what he was about to say. To a silent room he told of the help the Kernow Collective was offering, both in sanctuary and protection if they decided to retreat to Somerton. Tom didn't dwell on it long, merely giving them the facts before allowing the council to speak.

Gabriel was the first to offer his thoughts. 'It's the only way. We must take the offer. At least this way we keep our lives and freedom.'

'And what about the people who can't just up and leave, eh?' Henry Martgen rose to his feet and leant on the table, his eyes full of anger. 'I for one have farms and fields – without those I have nothing.'

'And what will those be worth under the rule of this New English Army?' Gabriel countered.

Henry glared at Gabriel, the hatred for the man blazing in his eyes. 'It may be the same as now. They will need supplies and maybe we can arrange to supply them. You go, take your things and leave, like the coward you are.'

'Are you mad?' Gabriel showed his amazement at the suggestion. 'These people will only take what they want – they won't become bloody customers, for God's sake.'

Tom stepped in to stop this argument before it went any further. 'Enough. We're going to prepare to take everything we can down to

Somerton but wait until Leila returns from meeting with this general before we finally decide. It gives us a little time to get ready. It saddens me deeply that we're in this situation, but we are where we are, and we need to deal with it. We're all free people here. No one will be told what to do and no one will be left behind if they want to come with us.'

The council broke into a number of smaller, heated discussions; it was important that everyone said what was needed to be said.

Eventually, Leila entered the room, looking around at the council. 'I'm leaving now to see what can be done. I hope I return with better news.' She walked over and gave her brother a Bowles salute before turning away.

The members banged the table in front of them, slowly at first then building louder and louder as Leila left the room followed by Anne and Alva. One by one the others left, each with their own decisions to make.

Tom, Irving and Gabriel remained.

Gabriel had always been a pragmatic businessman, willing to go wherever the profit was. But he also had worked with William for many years, making a successful living being so close to the family.

'Whatever you need, Tom, I will help out. Your father was good to me and always fair in our dealings. I can't see how I can stay here, not now. But I will not just cut and run from you.'

Irving smiled at the words. 'Thanks, Gabriel. It's transport we're going to need more than anything if we do leave, that should be our priority. Our purpose now is to save William's family and holdings as best we can.'

With Tom agreeing, the three of them started to discuss how to treat the coming days.

|||||||||||||||||||||||||||||||||||||||||||||||||||||||||||||||||||||||||||||

By the time Leila had changed into her riding gear and gathered her travelling party together, it was nearing evening. The horses had been chosen and readied for a fast journey; time was of the essence. She was joined at the stables by Alva and the two rangers, Ty and Simon. They were all eager to get going, even knowing the dangers they faced once they did. They knew where they were heading and were just waiting for Leila to give the order to start. She looked at each one and then bowed her head, giving a short prayer to her lost father. Grabbing the reins and gently nudging her mount she moved away, followed by the others.

The journey was expected to take a day and a half. They didn't plan on stopping much, just enough to rest the horses where necessary. Travelling through the first night, good time was made, with everyone making small talk to pass the time.

Ty told how he and Simon had been away for the last few weeks, having been stationed down at the Bowles salt production facility on the coast near Overcombe. They had been having some minor issues over the recent months with thefts and sabotage of machinery.

They had planned on staying for a further couple of days, once the problem had been sorted out. But after hearing the news, they hurried back to the Bowles complex.

They both agreed that at least now they were helping the cause, even after what had happened.

By the time first light was showing it was clear the horses could do with a rest and some water. They slowly trotted along for a few miles before finding the ideal resting spot next to a low riverbank. Pulling up and letting the horses drink a while, they all took their own opportunity for a rest as well; the journey would take them the rest of the day if they travelled hard.

Henry Martgen was up early as always, having spent the previous evening sat outside on the porch of his large single-storey ranch at Chitterne. He had started building the structure himself twenty-five years ago, adding to it every few years as time and resources would allow. Henry saw himself as a shrewd man, a realist and someone who would do whatever needed to be done to ensure his family's survival.

He had come from a farming background; his father had toiled for many years to provide his family with enough food to eat. Sometimes they had only just made it through some harsh winters. But it had taught his family a lesson in self-reliance and adversity – and also one of never having to rely on other people.

Henry lost his older brother when he was a young man; he had gone to protect a neighbouring farm from raiders and had been killed during a brutal fight. Afterwards, his brother was honoured by all the locals at a thanksgiving feast. But during the service the younger Henry resented the kind words being said, promising himself that when he had his own family he would never put anyone ahead of them.

By the time his father passed away, Henry was a widower with three children, two sons and a daughter, his wife dying in childbirth. The farm he inherited was operating profitably and was producing plenty of surplus produce to sell, enabling him to afford a standard of living his father had hardly ever dreamed of.

His first accomplishment on taking over the farm was to raze it to the ground and rebuild a much larger wooden building, in the style of an old-fashioned ranch. He had the goal to become an important man in the area, one who would be treated with deference and respect.

Henry focused on building up his connections through the surrounding area over the next few years, being generous where necessary with his time and resources. But always he did this to help his own position, never with true selflessness. As such, he had climbed to a position where he was respected but never liked. People could never find anything bad to say about him but also never really took him to their hearts.

One of Henry's sons, Godfrey, was just like his father. Raised to be someone who learnt how to use people for his own needs. Henry had always planned for him to take over the farm when he eventually passed. Godfrey, however, was a restless young man who, at the age of nineteen, wanted adventure before settling down to a life of farming and family. So, one day, two summers ago, the son had come to his father and told him of his plans.

His vague plan was to travel north to the Middle-lands, passing through the ancient schools along the way to see if the stories were true. He wanted to experience the world outside of his own sphere but also to bring back news of the outside world. At first his father was reluctant to let him go, but after a few weeks of Godfrey making his case repeatedly, he relented and bade him well in his travels.

Life continued in the Martgen household as normal, with Henry often wondering what life Godfrey had built for himself. There had been no word from him since the day he left, until one morning, six months ago, he rode up the lane to the ranch.

Godfrey was welcomed back warmly, with a large meal held that night in celebration of his return. The evening was a happy reunion for the whole family. Godfrey told of his travels and what he had seen but seemed reticent to talk of his most recent days.

By the end of the night, Henry and Godfrey were strolling around one of the fields they owned and farmed. Pausing under a large old oak tree near to a small stream, Henry looked at his returned son with a piercing gaze.

'What's on your mind, son?'

Godfrey looked right into his father's eyes. 'I'm here because change is coming, Dad. There's a group in the east that's heading this way and I don't think we can resist it. But there's an opportunity for us to work with them.' He paused for a few moments before putting his hand on his father's shoulder. 'It's either that or lose everything you've worked for.'

Henry was shocked by his son's statement, but he knew his son and knew he wasn't prone to exaggerating things. 'Tell me everything you know, then, and we will deal with whatever it is.'

'There's this man, Noah Hill, but he calls himself the General. He's built a small army over the last couple of years and he's now set his sights on the territories in the west. He preaches a message of power, of returning England to its previous glories before the Chaos.' Godfrey sat down, followed by his listening father.

'Apparently, it all started out with him rising to take control of a small band of raiders on the east coast somewhere. Through sheer ruthlessness and ambition, he marauded his way along the coastline, picking up some of the most dangerous men around as they went. He then started to style himself as the general of an army, one he calls the New English Army.'

'My God, how many does he have with him?'

'A few hundred in all. Most are fighters and the rest are there to support their needs. He hasn't lost a fight yet with anyone and he feels that he can go wherever he wants to next.' Godfrey leant back, looking at the sky as he took a breath.

'And how do you know all this?' Henry asked.

'Because I'm part of it, Dad. I joined a few months ago, and I've been with them ever since. Now, don't get me wrong, I don't really believe in all he preaches, but he is the strongest authority in that area, and it was the best way for me to get on in life, I felt.'

'I can't blame you for that. Just be careful and make sure you're always on the winning side. If you do that, you'll be all right.' Henry patted his son's back twice. 'So, you've come to warn us, then?'

'More than that, Dad. When I heard about rumours of the General's plans, I went to him and explained I was from this area and you had influence around these parts and would be...' Godfrey hesitated. 'Err, amenable to helping him out rather than being on the other side. I know you haven't always seen eye to eye with the Bowles family.'

Henry gave a smile to his son, turning into a grimace as he thought of past slights. 'They've never treated our family with respect, thinking themselves better than the rest of us. I'm sure William's father wasn't a saint. How else would he have built the complex and earned his fortune? I'd be happy to talk to this general and see how we both could benefit from working together.'

'I think it's the right choice, Dad. We want to be on his side in what's coming. We can leave in the morning. It's good to be back with you again.'

FIFTEEN

Josh felt stronger than the previous day, finally managing to get some sleep after a laborious day of working in the stinking tannery. He had spent the day gently probing the others about their pasts, wary of not pushing anyone too far. Slowly some of the men started to open up to him, allowing him to listen to the stories being told, quietly taking in everything that they said.

He had only been in their company for a couple of days, but the others had started to accept him as one of their own and were becoming much more talkative than on that first day.

As was regular now, once awake everyone hurried to the food station. But this time there was something different to a normal morning; it was clear that something unusual was happening. Although the food was prepared and ready to be dished out, everyone was being ushered towards the end of the eating area, with some of the senior army figures waiting near the other end. The workers milled around, grumbling about the change in schedule. Once everyone had arrived, General Hill and his lieutenants strode out into the middle. Hill's second in command – Bates, someone had called him – stood next to the leader, glowering at the men around him.

The General wore a broad smile across his face as he looked around at the men in front of him, clearly savouring the moment. His coat had, as ever, the collar raised high. Everyone immediately went quiet, ready for the General to speak.

'As you all know,' he started, his voice resonating across the area. 'We have won a great battle against the weak forces of the Bowles territory. It is now time to take what we have won: their land and their production. We'll make it work for us and it will make us stronger in return.' Many of the men close to him cheered immediately at the declaration, soon followed by the rest of the workers.

Hill motioned for quiet, continuing his speech. 'I have given the order for us to begin packing up. We will move directly to the Bowles headquarters. We have worked hard for this day, men. Finally, we have a place where we can begin the process of restoring England to its rightful place, where we will be its new creators.'

Again, the surrounding troops cheered noisily for their leader. Again, followed less enthusiastically by the others further away. General Hill took some time to speak briefly to a number of the men closest to him, all smiles and backslapping, before re-entering the building, followed by his senior staff.

As soon as he had left the kitchen, staff banged on the pots in front of them, indicating that breakfast was to be resumed for everyone.

After the now-tedious morning stew, once more without Nolan who appeared to be off on some scavenging outing again, the tannery was alive with sounds of working and talking.

Josh was again paired with Jaan. They had worked well yesterday, and Josh was sure to act as friendly as he could around the man. Asking small questions to get him to open up had worked so far; today he would push harder to find out more.

As they were preparing the barrels, Josh wondered how to move the conversation to the Army. His co-worker seemed to be in a good mood today and it looked hopeful he would talk more when asked. After they had finished making the pungent mixtures, with both taking a few minutes' air, Josh casually struck up a conversation.

'How are we going to move all this stuff? Some of it must weigh a ton.'

'Ahh, they've done it before, they'll manage it again,' Jaan replied slowly.

'Really? When did they move last time, then?'

'In the spring, when we moved here, and they've moved a few times in the last couple of years. It's hard work, but it can be done.'

They moved back inside to their benches, ready to start more of their tasks.

Josh took a while before speaking again, not wanting to appear too keen in front of Jaan, who was talking more now than he ever had before.

'Wonder why they keep moving?' he finally said.

Jaan didn't respond instantly. He stopped what he was doing and leant onto the table in front of him. His breathing grew quicker, his hands were clenched into fists. 'Because they're like locusts, taking somewhere and then stripping it to its bones. Soon there's nothing left to take and so they move on to the next place.' Jaan had turned his face to the ground now, clearly getting angrier as he spoke.

Josh was shocked at the words coming out of Jaan's mouth, unsure how to treat this outburst. It was the first time that he had seen any form of emotion from the man since he had been here. Normally, for Josh, it would have been natural to try to comfort Jaan, but he wanted to see what else he could learn before he dried up.

'All this talk of a new England, it's pathetic. They say all these things – stability and progressing towards the future.' He stared at Josh, eye to eye. 'Lies, all lies. They just take and take then move on to take some more. They kill and steal, until what? Until there's nothing left, that's what.' Jaan was almost shouting the words at this point.

The rest of the workers in the tannery stopped their work and looked aghast at the scene occurring in front of them, as if by association they would be drawn into what was happening.

Jaan rose to his feet, his cheeks reddening, his fists shaking. He stood there for a moment, his upper body and arms trembling. Suddenly he walked towards the door and threw it open, stormed out and marched across the small courtyard.

Josh looked over at Eddie, who had been watching since Jaan's outburst had begun. Josh shook his head, before following Jaan out of the door.

Following quickly through the courtyard and into the main house, Josh wasn't sure which way he was meant to go. Seconds later, he heard shouting coming from one of the corridors; it could only be Jaan, so he rushed towards the direction of the noise. When he turned the corner, he saw Jaan a few inches away from one of the soldiers, screaming at him. The poor man was so worked up he was barely making himself understood.

A small shudder flowed through Josh as he watched Jaan move towards the guard and push him hard in the chest with both hands. Seeing the shove, another soldier ran towards the scuffle with his sword drawn, hanging down beside his body. Everything seemed to happen in slow motion as the second man reached Jaan, slashing him across his back.

Jaan immediately arched backwards, his hand reaching round by instinct to where he had been hit. Showing no pain on his face, he started to turn around to see his assailant, anger the only thing showing now. Before he fully twisted his body, he was stopped by the sword sliding into his stomach, gripped by the powerful hand of the soldier who slowly pulled it out, causing blood to stream out of the wound.

Jaan's hands went to his stomach.

Slumping to his knees, he looked down at his hands, covered in his own blood. He was facing Josh by now. With a look of relief and a small smile on his lips, he fell forwards onto the stone floor, dead.

For a moment, everything was still, with the three men staring down at the lifeless body. Then the soldier who had killed Jaan saw Josh standing there and marched over to him.

'Come with me,' he ordered as he grabbed Josh's arm and pulled him down the corridor. He barked at the other soldier, 'And get someone to clean that up now!'

They stepped round Jaan, the blood smoothly spreading out all over the floor, getting it onto the soles of their shoes. Looking back, Josh noticed the soldier was leaving bloody footprints as they walked to a small room.

Shutting the door behind him, the gruff soldier pushed Josh to the wall, staring at him intently.

'What's your work detail?'

'We're from the tannery,' Josh answered, trying to control his breathing.

'What were the two of you doing in the house, then?'

'I was trying to stop Jaan. He just lost it and ran out of work. I didn't want him to get hurt, so I followed. I don't know what got into him and made him act like that.'

The soldier let Josh go and took a step back, still looking at him suspiciously. 'Well, you've seen what happens when someone tries to cause trouble: they're put down. Am I going to have any trouble with you?'

Josh bristled at the man's words but understood the game to play here. 'No, sir. I just want an easy life, that's all.'

The two of them stood there, looking at each other. Abruptly, the soldier gave a lopsided grin and walked to the door and opened it. 'Good, now get back to work. But I'll be keeping an eye out for you now, you understand?'

Josh showed he understood as he walked submissively past the man and out of the door, making himself look very troubled as he left to return to work.

He retraced the bloody steps leading back to where the fight had occurred. Jaan's body had been moved, but the floor had a black stain where his body had been. Cautiously walking around, making sure not to tread on any of the blood, he reached the outdoors.

Outside, Josh knelt on one knee. Taking in some deep breaths to calm himself, he tried not to retch at the memory of what had just occurred. He could still see Jaan's eyes looking at him the moment before he died. What a waste of a life, he thought, what a waste.

Standing and walking a few times around the small courtyard with his hands on his head, Josh tried to understand what had happened to Jaan. Had he pushed him too far, reminded him too much of losing his family? Josh felt guilty at being the one to push him to breaking point, but it was the soldier who had killed him – he was the one ultimately responsible.

But it showed that many of the men inside this Army could still be strong enough to fight back if given the chance. They just needed the right leadership and motivation. How he could help them with that he wasn't sure yet, but it was something at least.

He just hoped that others would be more of a success than Jaan.

Once back inside Josh approached Eddie to let him know what had happened to Jaan. Keeping his voice low, he explained the events of the last few minutes. Eddie sat back onto a rickety stool, running his hands through his hair.

'Dammit, he was a good lad. He's had a few outbursts before, but never anything this bad.' Eddie thumped his fist onto the table; the rest of the workers in the room looked at him. He turned to the enquiring faces, frowning. 'Jaan's dead, he went off on one in front of one of the soldiers, they killed him.'

Everyone looked shocked by the news, but soon turned away, carrying on with their work details. The room was quiet.

Eddie came over to help with Josh's work, replacing Jaan at the bench. They spent the next hours mainly in silence, working throughout the day until their evening meal.

A good distance away from the crowd, Josh was eating thoughtfully when Nolan approached, sitting down next to him. Nolan looked tired and drained of his usual energy; his clothes were dirty and covered in dust.

'When did you get back?' asked Josh.

"Bout half an hour ago. We were out scavenging, pretty useless things again, when we were called back by a messenger rider. God knows why. No one told us anything.'

Josh told Nolan about moving to the Bowles territory, following up with what Jaan had told him and then the events that led to his death. Nolan said he felt bad for the man he never met, another victim to this madman, Hill.

They fell silent for a while. Josh processed the day's events.

If the Army was planning on moving to the Bowles territory, they must either be sure that there wouldn't be any more resistance or didn't care. Probably the latter. A perfectly understandable gambit considering the loss of William and the rangers.

'This doesn't sound good,' Nolan muttered carefully, staring at his bowl. 'Although there's no rangers left, I'm sure Tom and the locals will try to rally round to stop any assault from them, no matter how pointless it may be.'

'I was thinking the same thing. And they won't stand a chance at all against Hill.'

'What can we do from here? We're pretty limited in our options.'

Josh closed his eyes, thinking hard. 'I don't know, but I know we just can't do nothing, can we?'

'If this whole place is moving on, then it's a perfect opportunity for us to escape and get home,' Nolan suggested, finishing the food in front of him.

'What about Chad and Mary and the others?' Josh asked. 'We can't just leave them to be abused or killed – you know what happens if escape attempts are made.'

'I don't know, yet. But we can't stay here, and this is an opening that might not come up again. There's going to be a lot of confusion, moving this many people and goods. We need to take it.'

Josh knew that Nolan was right but was concerned for the other rangers held captive here. 'I know, but let's see what we can do for them at least.'

'I think Chad and the other hostages are assigned servants' duties to the leadership. There're so many guards around them, there's not much trouble they could get up to. I saw the man that brought us here that first day with some of them yesterday, and they sleep separately as well.'

Josh thought for a moment. 'What about the women? I haven't seen or heard anything about them since we've been here.'

'No, me neither,' Nolan replied.

'I don't want to imagine what they're going through.'

Both went quiet for a time. He could imagine; that was the problem.

Josh finally broke the silence. 'We need more information, and some help if we can find it.'

'Agreed. What about that Eddie you've been talking about? Do you think he would be up for helping us?'

'Possibly. I'll talk to him later and sound him out.'

Just as they had finished talking, a group of soldiers strode noisily into the middle of where everyone was eating. The clamour quietened expectantly.

The lead soldier looked around and spoke loudly, so everyone could hear. 'As you all know, we are on the move once we've packed up. I'm looking for volunteers to help us tonight to prepare the wagons for the journey.' He looked around at the uneager men.

Only a handful of men stood and raised their arms, until suddenly Josh nudged Nolan's shoulder and stood himself. Nolan was up a second later and they both raised their arms.

The soldiers walked amongst the crowd, accepting most of the standing men. When one reached Josh and Nolan he looked them up and down before grunting. 'You'll do.' He beckoned the two of them to follow him to the other volunteers. They joined a group of twelve, where they were led away to where the wagons were kept.

Marching along in a poor impression of eager helpers, they reached a large, rickety old barn. The ancient doors were shut and chained. The twelve men were told to sit and wait until the quartermaster arrived shortly. They all happily took the opportunity to relax in the evening air.

'What was that for? I'm already knackered,' Nolan complained under his breath to Josh.

'Might get us a bit of leeway tomorrow if we can make ourselves central to operating these wagons. Tell them we used to make and service them, that sort of thing.'

'You might get away with it. I don't know a damn thing about wagons, though.' Nolan sighed as he lay back against a dusty pile of hay.

'Worth a try at least,' replied Josh. Nolan returned a smile.

The quartermaster was not what they were expecting. He was a small, officious-looking man wearing what could best be described as an old-fashioned tunic and tie, who walked with a slight limp in his right leg. He looked like an ancient office clerk at best, not someone in charge of stores and equipment in an army.

He split the volunteers into four teams; each team was then assigned to two guards. After he opened the barn and gestured for the others to follow, everyone walked to their evening assignment.

Most of the wagons were in fairly good order, not needing too much attention to ensure they would be good for the coming journey. There were three wagons at the rear of the barn, however, which could easily be described as being in total disrepair.

Seeing these were next to his work detail, Josh walked around the nearest one and then looked at the other two. The quartermaster saw Josh in the corner of the barn.

'They've had it, not much we can do there, I think,' the smaller man told Josh.

'I think we could get one working one out of the three, if you wanted me to look at it for you,' Josh answered, trying to show the right level of eagerness in his voice.

'You know much about wagons?'

'A little. Our village had one which kept breaking and so I kind of learnt how to mend them.'

The quartermaster looked at the wagons and pile of bits in the corner. 'If you can, that would be a great help, go a good way to assisting the effort and all that. I'd appreciate it, too. I'm Miles, by the way.'

Josh introduced himself before going to work on the dilapidated wagon in front of him, all the while making sure he was giving the impression of being eager to help. He worked through the remaining hours of the day, watched carefully by the soldiers and the quartermaster.

By the time the moon was high in the sky, most of the others had left the barn. But, finished, Josh took a step back and admired his handiwork. The wagon, while being fragile, was perfectly useable. The evening had also given him time to relax mentally and concentrate on something other than recent events; for that he was grateful, in a way.

As Josh was reflecting on his work, the quartermaster came over, looking at the now-useful wagon. 'Good work, that will make a difference.'

'Thank you, sir,' replied Josh.

'When we are on the move, I'd like you to work with my team, just in case of any breakdowns or problems. Where is your normal work assignment?'

'At the tannery, sir.' He hoped he wasn't laying the enthusiasm on too thick.

Miles looked like he appreciated it, though. 'No problem, then. Report to me when we are ready to set off.'

Josh thanked him before being left alone at the end of the barn. Sauntering to the large wooden doors, he met the last remaining guard.

The guard took him back to the main building. Josh moved along the corridors, pleased with himself. Happy to finally get to his own bed, he collapsed onto the low cot and fell asleep immediately.

SIXTEEN

THE TRAVELLING HAD BEEN HARD. THEY RODE INTO THE surroundings of Herriard still alert, on the lookout for any signs of the army. Slowing to a walk at the outskirts of the hamlet, to allow the horses a small rest, they ventured cautiously through the now deserted streets.

Leila saw Alva trying not to look at the buildings, concentrating on moving forwards. When they finally reached the other side of Herriard she stopped her horse before turning to talk to the others. 'Alva, where now?'

'The battle was ahead east a couple of miles or so. We could skirt round the battleground, rather than see everything there.'

Leila realised Alva was concerned that her father was still there, where he had died. She desperately wanted to see for herself what this madman had done to him and the rest of the rangers, but inside she knew that she only had a limited amount of emotional strength left. Her father had always tried to teach her not to be overly sentimental; this was the ultimate test.

'Let's try and find their base first. We can come back to this after to pay our respects.' Leila glanced over to Ty and Simon; both nodded in solemn agreement.

'And keep an eye out for anyone,' Alva told the three of them. 'There might be some scouts around.'

Taking the wider track at the crossroads, they moved at a cautious pace, on alert heading into enemy territory. They soon came near the battleground. Leila looked up and saw a large number of birds flying overhead. Getting nearer, she could smell the rancid stench of the results of the battle. It had been warm recently and it told. Trying not to retch, Leila looked away.

Suddenly, Simon told them to wait where they were and rode off. He was gone for only a few minutes, but when he returned his face looked drained. Leila asked him where he had been, but he just muttered quietly about checking something out.

Leila felt angry at not being answered; she wasn't in the best of moods near this place. She was about to question again when Alva leant across, shaking her head.

'He was laying your father down,' she whispered, not making eye contact.

He had been trying to spare her seeing her father swinging from the trees. She turned to face him, lowering her head out of respect and thanks. Simon did the same.

She moved them on. Covering her face with her neck scarf as she passed, Leila tried hard not to look at the mass of bodies lying there. Fortunately for her, everything was so dark and covered in mud that she couldn't make much out from this distance.

As they had hoped, the sheer volume of numbers of the moving army made tracking easy. Occasionally, Ty would dismount and take a closer look, but there wasn't much need for their tracking skills here; they could merely follow the trail easily from the saddle.

Subdued, the group followed the trail through fields and woodlands, which eventually gave way to ancient buildings and forgotten constructions. They were skirting the area near to London. Leila felt more and more nervous with each passing minute. They had all grown up with tales of this place; she had no desire to see if they were true.

They moved on in silence, the rusting skeletons of a huge number of cars scattered along their journey. Although she wasn't particularly superstitious, this land felt cursed, somewhere people weren't meant to be. They hurried on, keeping their heads down and their eyes focused forwards.

Ty was in front when he raised his hand as a signal to stop. He pointed in front and to the left of him. A slight curl of smoke could be seen rising behind a thicket of trees.

Leila gathered them together, so they could begin to discuss their strategy for what was to come.

'We come here as representatives of the Bowles territory, answering his message,' Leila started. 'We request talks – what else can we do?'

'It will be obvious we're not here to fight. There's only the four of us. I agree.' Alva looked at Ty.

Ty breathed in heavily, before giving a long sigh. 'I get that, but I don't think we should all go in. There's a chance we won't come out again, and if we don't the council need to know that at least.'

Simon agreed. 'I think that's right. Alva, you should wait here. We will go in as Leila's guards. It's what they will be expecting.'

Alva held firm. 'No, I've seen what they do. I want to show him we will not be cowed by him, that we will always bounce back.' Her voice had grown louder as she'd spoken. Leila could see how much it meant to her.

'Simon, I want Alva to come with us. She's done so much already for us, we owe her this. I want you to go back to Herriard and wait for us. If we aren't back in a few hours, go back to the complex and let the council know.'

Simon looked at Leila for a moment. 'If you're sure, Leila. Then good luck,' he told the three of them as he turned back. 'I'll see you soon.'

Making their way towards the smoke they had seen, they reached a small hut, next to the road. Leila approached it and called out firmly to the occupants inside.

A young man emerged from the hut. He rushed out and instantly stopped, seeing the horses and riders in front of him. He looked extremely flustered and unsure as to what to do.

Leila spoke as commandingly as she could, hiding the fear inside her. 'I am Leila Bowles, daughter of William Bowles, and I'm here to see General Hill.'

The young soldier stared at the riders. He was joined outside the hut by a second youth of about the same age, but this one looked calmer and appeared to understand the situation better.

'I can take you to him. Leave your horses here,' he instructed. 'And your weapons.'

Leila nodded to Ty and Alva. The three of them dismounted before handing over the swords they carried on the horses' saddles. Once they were disarmed, the soldier visibly relaxed, telling them to follow him.

Walking in silence up the road, then over a large grassy area, Leila looked around trying to get a feel of the place they were being led to. The great stone building they were heading to seemed decrepit, yet still ominous to her as she would soon meet her father's murderer. She was determined not to allow her emotions to take control. She would make her father proud.

They arrived at the main entrance and were told to wait. The soldier spoke quietly to a guard next to the door then rushed inside.

Ty put his large hand on Alva's shoulder; her nerves were showing. 'You'll be fine, lass. I won't let anything happen to you here.'

Alva smiled. 'Thanks, Ty, appreciate it.'

The three stood there awkwardly. Leila wondered if the General would make them wait for long as a childish gesture of power. She could see Alva taking deep, rhythmic breaths, and could only guess at how hard it must be for her to have come back after what she experienced last time.

Quicker than she thought would happen, the large double doors opened. A grim, solid-looking man approached them eating a large chicken leg.

'The General is out in the stables. Come with me.' The man strode off at pace to the left side of the building, quickly followed by two armed guards. Looking at each other with some bemusement, Leila and the others followed.

The stables were not what they were expecting. It was an impressive brick building with bales of hay dotted around it. The doors were open with a few soldiers scattered around, presumably standing guard.

Stopping and holding his hand out, the man threw away what was left of the food he was carrying and told them to wait. He disappeared into the dark inside, leaving everyone standing there, waiting.

Moments later, several other men walked out, standing to attention by the doors. Followed by a looming figure that could only be General Noah Hill.

The General walked to a few feet away from the Bowles representatives, taking off his gloves and giving them to one of his men to his left.

'Welcome, Leila Bowles. Apologies for not meeting you in person. I was giving my stallion a thorough brushing down – so important to keep a good appearance up, don't you think?' He gave a short bow before turning to Alva. 'And thank you for delivering my message, girl.'

Leila wanted to pounce on this general and grind his face into the dirt but kept herself calm, her face impassive in front of this monster. She looked him directly in the eyes. 'We are here as representatives of the Bowles territory. I trust we will not be harmed because of this meeting?'

'You have my word, my dear. The fighting is done, is it not?' General Hill put out his arms and showed both his palms to Leila as a gesture of peace before looking around at his men; all were smirking as he spoke.

'Good.' Leila's voice had a bite to it as she spoke. 'Then we come to negotiate with you. To find a settlement we can all be happy with.'

Looking comically confused at the statement, the General tilted his head to one side. 'Negotiate? But, my dear, you misunderstand. We are taking over. There is nothing to negotiate.'

'But what about our people, those who live and work with us?' Alva spat at the man in front of her.

'And they will become my people, our people. They will work for me and for the New English Army. It's merely you and your family that we will replace. We will become the new owners of all of the Bowles holdings.' Narrowing his eyes and lowering his voice he leant forwards slightly. 'Girl, your father is dead, all your rangers are dead, you are defenceless. We are readying for the journey as we speak. Tomorrow we march to take over from you. We are strong, and you are weak. That is how England will rise again – the powerful will rule once more.'

Leila stood there unable to speak, mouth slightly open. What could she say to this man who stood in front of her so antagonistically? Stuttering slightly, she tried again. 'But these are free men and women, they are peaceful and forward-looking. That is how the territories will be successful, through hard work and co-operation with likeminded people.'

Hill chuckled at the words. 'How small your vision is. You talk of territories, I talk of England once again. Your hope is based on letting people gently crawl out of this mess our world has got into. I will lead them out of it strongly and swiftly. It has taken us far too long already.' His cheeks were reddening as he spoke.

'What? By killing and taking innocents? By forcing yourselves on others?'

He took a small step forwards, his eyes glowering with emotion. 'People like you will never understand what we are doing, will never see the potential of what can be done. Done by someone willing to sacrifice for the future.'

'Oh, I understand all right. You are willing to let others sacrifice, but what have you ever sacrificed? I don't see you struggling to live or hungry. No, you're a taker. Nothing more, nothing less.'

Looking at the grinning man in front of her, Leila could control herself no more. She swung her hand at this evil standing there, slapping him hard across the cheek. He grabbed her arm after it struck his face and his fierce grip pulled her close to him.

Behind them, the soldiers had drawn their swords and were ready to strike at the General's command. Ty changed his stance, ready for action at any time. Alva stood there, mouth wide open at what was happening.

General Hill put his free hand into the air. 'Hold,' he commanded. 'We're not going to have any more trouble here.' Leila's face was so close to his she could feel his breath. His eyes wide open in front of hers. He grasped her by the throat, then pulled her ear to his mouth. 'Any more of that and I will feed your girl here to my troops, understand?'

Leila whispered back, her constricted throat allowing nothing more. 'Yes.'

Letting her go, he pushed her a few feet away. Rubbing his cheek, where a red welt was appearing, General Hill spoke calmly. 'That's the only time you ever lay a hand on me or my men. We'll call it even for the death of your father. Now, you have my answer, there will be no further discussion. When we arrive, we take control of your family holdings, and kill anyone who gets in our way. Now run along before I change my mind and give you to my dogs.'

Leila hated the way he was clearly enjoying this show of generosity, making a show of it for his troops.

The General marched back towards the doors to the stable, pausing before he went inside. 'And if I were you, I'd be long gone when we arrive.'

The guards were smirking as they were left alone with Leila and her two companions. Sheathing their swords, the guards ushered them firmly away from the house and grounds, walking them briskly towards their horses.

|||||||||||||||||||||||||||||||||||||||||||||||||||||||||||||||||||||||||||

Josh had been rushing back and forth between the wagons and the buildings for supplies for most of the day, as part of his temporary assignment to the travelling detail. The transports were now almost ready for the journey, with only some small repairs left. On one of his final trips, he was carrying a bulky amount of rope. Coming to the barn, he dumped the load on the floor, stretching his back before gathering his thoughts about the impending journey.

Out of the corner of his eye, he saw a small group walking up to the main stables area. They were some distance away, but oddly he could see two women amongst them. Looking around and seeing that there were no guards nearby, he moved towards a wall nearer to the direction they were travelling.

Reaching the wall's end, he leant against it, casually looking like he was catching his breath after his exertions. Lifting his head slowly, he now had a good view of the entrance. Seeing who was there made his eyes widen; he stopped breathing for a moment with the shock.

Leila was there, with Alva and a ranger. Running the possibilities through his mind, he could only think that she had come to negotiate with the General, considering what had happened to the rest of the rangers. Something which he didn't think would be possible, but he understood their need to try.

Josh watched the scene play out, wincing when Leila slapped the General's cheek. He only relaxed when he saw his friends were allowed to walk away, realising he had hardly breathed while he stood there. Desperately wanting to shout out to them to let them know he was alive, he clenched his teeth together, knowing it was the wrong thing to do right now.

He dreadfully wanted to rush to Leila, to show her some comfort at the loss of her father, the father she was so very close to. Josh felt the loss deeply as well, of course, but couldn't imagine how she must be dealing with everything right now. He only just stopped himself from heading over to tell her how much he cared.

After seeing them walk away, Josh hung his head, closing his eyes as he felt tears falling down his cheeks.

He could easily imagine how the meeting had gone.

Feeling sad for Leila's last futile throw of the dice, he hurried back to the barn to continue with his preparation for the journey.

||||||||||||||||||||||||||||||||||||||||||||||||||||||||||||||||||||||||||||||||||

After their meeting with Hill, they were marched back to the small hut where they found their horses as they had left them. With no talking from either side, Leila, Alva and Ty checked the horses tack and mounted up. They quickly left the Army behind them.

They rode in silence for a while; Ty was the first to break it. 'Nice slap, Leila. Although I did wonder if he would run you through there and then.'

Leila managed a wry smile. 'I couldn't help myself. What a self-righteous pompous prick. He deserves more than a slap.'

Ty chuckled. 'That he does. Unfortunately he's got an army behind him. And that makes him very dangerous indeed.'

'I agree, and I don't think there's anything we can do to stop him right now. We need to retreat and live to fight another day.' Leila was sad but determined. 'Are you okay, Alva?'

The younger girl nodded. 'I'm fine. I just wanted to show him I wasn't scared of him.'

'Well, you did that very well indeed.'

They rode on in silence, no more words seemed needed amongst the three of them. After a short ride they found themselves coming up to the battleground, once again smelling it before they could see it. Stopping at a nearby field, Alva and Ty sat on their mounts waiting for Leila to speak.

Leila rode on slowly. She desperately wanted to search amongst the fallen, to bury her father, to honour his body with a decent funeral. But how could she bury just one man amongst all the other fallen. She now knew that this New English Army would be coming tomorrow; any time wasted might cost more lives and she couldn't tolerate any more death.

Remembering how her father always tried to teach her to be caring but not sentimental, she spoke while still looking at the scene of death in front of her. 'These are not our friends or family, just their bodies. My father lives through his words and actions during his life, not after his death. We cannot honour all these men in time. We need to get home and let everyone know what is really coming. One day we will return.'

Holding back her tears, she moved on. Once passed, they paused briefly to look back. In the far distance they saw dark clouds slowly rolling towards them.

Pulling hard on her reins, Leila started off. She pushed the horse to a canter in order to reach Simon at Herriard as quickly as they could, then to hurry back on to home. The news they carried was not good. Leila could see no other option but to leave the home she had grown up in.

SEVENTEEN

THE RAIN ARRIVED WITH A VENGEANCE IN THE EARLY HOURS
of the day. By the time Josh and the rest of the Army were up and ready
for breakfast the downpour was sheeting heavily, leaving large puddles
littering the grounds of the base.

After a hastily prepared breakfast, all the men went hurrying to
their duties. Finishing loading the remaining goods of the Army onto
the wagons was the first order of the day, with everyone involved in
the organised mayhem. The rain carried on relentlessly throughout the
morning, never looking like stopping at all.

Josh spent the first few hours working on the last wagon to leave the
barn. Minor repairs were needed, if he was honest, but it was warm and
dry inside, so he felt no need to hurry the job. He did, however, want
to speak to Nolan – today, new recruits were not allowed to wander
around the base on their own. The guards were out in force everywhere.

After finishing his work, he stood in the door to the barn. Two
figures were walking towards him, a couple of guards he didn't recognise.

One of them called over. 'The boss wants everyone together right
now. Head to the food area. He doesn't want anyone to be late.'

Josh nodded to the guard and jogged round the barn, where he saw others heading to the main building. Seeing Nolan walking amongst them, he headed over and slowed to match his pace on joining him. The rain soaked through his clothes as he did.

'Hey, you okay?' Josh asked quietly.

'Yeah, I'm glad you're here. I wanted to speak to you before we go,' Nolan replied, looking straight ahead as he spoke, brushing water off his face.

'Yeah, me too. I think it's going to be the best chance to get away during this move. I wanted to hear your thoughts.'

They stopped talking as they joined the throng heading to the food yard, moving to an emptier area at the rear. Leaning against the wall, which provided a small amount of relief from the rain, Nolan carried on their hushed conversation.

'I've heard some news about the women. Apparently, they are being taken separately from the Army. I overheard one of the guards saying that they didn't want any distractions along the way.'

'Damn.' Josh wiped water away from his hair. 'If that's the case then I don't know what we can do for them right now.'

Nolan shook his head. 'Nothing, I'm afraid. We'll have to wait for now, until we can get some help back at home.'

'And what about Chad?' Josh asked.

'If that was me being held hostage, I would rather you escape to get help and damn the consequences to myself. It's a harsh choice, but one I'd want you to make.'

Josh took a deep breath, letting it fully out before answering. 'I know. It doesn't make it any easier to do, though. We haven't spoken to Chad about it, given him the option.'

'And we might not be able to speak to him before we leave, so we have to make the decision now.' Nolan frowned. 'So, do we try or not?'

'We try.'

Hearing a small commotion coming from the other side of the crowd, they both looked over at the door, seeing the leaders of the

Army walking through. Last of all, General Hill strode through, a waterproof cloak covering his clothes. He looked amused at something as he surveyed his people.

Josh made the appearance of listening to what he was saying, but was deep in thought and paid no attention to whatever it was. As the General finished his rant, Josh and Nolan looked at him with renewed hatred.

'We are now ready to leave, men,' General Hill roared to the expectant crowd. 'When we arrive and take charge, we will take our first step to controlling the south of England. And soon after that, we shall take our first steps to taking the whole of the country.'

Cheers rippled out through the gathered crowd. Beaming as he took his applause, the General walked amongst his army. Stopping often to acknowledge those he recognised, he spent a good amount of time chatting and sharing jokes with his soldiers. It was noticeable that he was very closely guarded as he walked amongst them. Once he had done his rounds he waved to the crowd before strutting back into the house.

'Right, then,' a deep voice boomed. 'We leave in one hour. Everyone make sure they are ready and at the correct detail. Come on, then. Let's go get ready.'

Josh didn't react immediately, merely watching all around him waiting to leave the yard and head to wherever they were needed. As the numbers thinned, he and Nolan started walking to the door. Wishing each other luck, they went their separate ways.

Josh hurried to the tannery, where Eddie and the others were moving the last of the room's supplies. Eddie came over and gave his arm a firm slap.

'Good to see you. How are the wagons going?' Eddie asked.

'All ready. Should be fine as long as the ground isn't too soft with all this rain.' Josh took Eddie's arm and led him outside where he could speak in private. Eddie dragged a large blanket over himself he had taken from the tannery, to protect himself as best he could against the weather; throwing Josh one to do the same.

He glanced around at the empty courtyard. Seeing they were alone, Josh made his pitch to Eddie.

'This is it. We can make a break for it during the move. Are you in? Do you want to come with us?' Josh's voice was hushed. 'I think it's now or never. It's the perfect opportunity.'

Eddie looked at Josh, indecision etched on his face. 'How am I going to do it? You're young and fit – I don't think I'd stand a chance of running away.'

Josh pulled the blanket over himself a little more. 'If we can get away without them knowing, then they won't know where to look when they find out. There will be massive confusion over the journey and that's our chance. It's not a matter of fitness, it's one of opportunity. I'm not sure yet how it will happen, but we will find a way.'

'Oh, what the hell. I'm in. I don't want to stay with this lot any longer. If I can help then count on me. Thank you, thank you for making me realise.' With a small grin, Eddie turned and re-entered the tannery.

Hoping that he could count on Eddie, Josh made his way back to where the wagons were now almost fully loaded. The rain had eased to a light drizzle, but the skies looked like they had much more to give over the course of the coming day.

He walked over to the quartermaster, waiting patiently to one side with another man who would also be helping with the wagons as they travelled.

One by one, the wagons were lined up, with some of the soldiers and support staff milling about. Everything the New English Army owned was here, ready to move to the Bowles territory. Horses lined up against the wagon train, being prepared for the journey. Some ready to pull the wagons, the others the soldiers' rides. These soldiers would keep everyone in line during the expedition – these would be the ones Josh had to find a way to slip past.

Miles gathered the maintenance team together. 'All right, we are going to be responsible for making sure no time is lost with breakdowns or failures. Mind you, looking at this weather, I'm sure that most of our time will be used getting the wheels out of the mud.' He gave a small chuckle at the comment, then frowned as no one else joined in.

His second piped up at the comment. 'I've made sure each team has plenty of rugs and straw to help traction in this weather, sir.'

'Good. We will each be looking after a number of carriages. I will be moving up and down the line at all times, making sure nothing too serious happens. For God's sake, if it does, make sure you call for help. I do not want to get on the wrong side of the General by holding up this transport, you hear?'

The assembled crew all quickly agreed.

'Go to your stations, then. We're moving out imminently.' He dismissed the team, who hurried off in different directions.

Arriving more and more quickly now, the members of the New English Army were jostling and shoving to try to get some of the limited seating places for the journey. Each time someone thought they had a space some higher-ranking member arrived, throwing that person off, till eventually the wagons were filled with stores and people. The support workers were to walk in the middle of the convoy, lines of lower-ranked soldiers amongst all the workers for security.

Most had arrived and were in position when everyone looked to their left, back towards the buildings they were leaving behind. The last arrivals were ushered to the rear of the line. They were the hostages, tied together in three lines. Paraded in front of everyone, driving home the reason for their existence. The noise died down as they walked past.

Rage built inside him and Josh stiffened at the sight, his hands clenched.

Suddenly he felt a hand on his shoulder from behind. One of the older guards stood there, his sword tapping against his leg. The guard shook his head; Josh glared at the guard, trying to control his breathing.

'Easy, lad,' the man told him sternly. 'No point dying today.'

Josh pulled his shoulder away, before realising he was in a futile position. He raised his hands in supplication, and his shoulders sagged as he swore to himself he would make these people pay.

The last to arrive were the General and his leadership team, heading to the front of the line. Their private transport was second from the front, covered for the weather, of course.

With a long blast of a whistle, the journey began.

It took longer than expected to get the caravan moving along, all the wagons carrying heavy loads. Many of the men who had climbed aboard were soon told to get off and walk, much to their displeasure. In the wet conditions around them, it would not be a pleasant walk.

Josh strode along, next to one of his allocated carts, making a show of checking the wheels every now and then. Aware of the mounted soldiers around him, he wanted to look as keen and committed as he could to the cause.

They moved along at a good pace with no major problems through the rest of the morning, continuing well into the afternoon. The ground, while wet, was still firm. After a long hot summer, most of the recent rain here hadn't had much effect on the roads they were travelling on.

For many hours they stuck to a solid path with long sweeping curves. Spongy and soft on top, but hard and solid underneath a few inches of soil. Josh was sure it was one of the old-time highways, although how they made such a thing he wasn't sure. They were part of stories told to children, but he had never really understood how or why they would be needed.

With no problems with any of the transports so far, Josh had little to do but walk alongside. Hearing noises behind, he saw that the kitchen staff were moving up and down, ready to deliver a lunchtime meal. They delivered first to the General. Josh caught a glimpse of a basket of roasted chickens being lifted up to greedy hands. For the others, the now unvarying stew and hard bread was being served.

Eating while walking along wasn't the easiest way to eat but at least it was filling. Quickly taking a drink from one of the water carriers, Josh at least felt ready for the coming escape.

Throughout the day they forged onwards, the rain keeping everything damp with its constant falling. They left the ancient road in the afternoon, moving onto a smaller one. Heading through the countryside.

Twice they had to repair a damaged wagon, whose wheel was wobbling badly on its axle due to its poor fitting. But apart from that, the repair team had little to do and the Army rolled on relentlessly.

As the sun slowly headed down, the light dimmed in front of them and the dark clouds that had been following them during the day began to move nearer. The poor weather they had felt all day turned from small drops of rain to larger, heavier ones. From behind them cracks of thunder could be heard, still many miles away but heading quickly in their direction.

The harder rain made the already soggy ground worse, threatening to become hard work to travel on if it continued at this pace. The men who had overcoats or homemade ponchos pulled them tighter. The others pulled anything they could find closer over their tunics, tying the material up as best they could.

The transports at the front came to a halt. Josh watched as several men climbed out of one of the leading wagons, approached a clearing, and stood there talking. With all the agitated pointing going on, it was clear they were discussing the best route to take. It didn't take them long, though, as they clambered aboard once more and soon started off again.

Turning at a large crossroads, Josh soon understood what those men had been talking about. It seemed they had left a good route and turned onto a rougher, muddier one. He could only assume this way was considerably quicker. The wagons started to slip and slide as they moved along with the rain continuing to lash down.

Gradually, they made their way along the chosen route. Although it was slower than before, they still rumbled along, mile after mile, towards their destination. Josh had little to do – the wagons were holding up well in the deteriorating conditions – so busied himself clearing the mud from the wheels every now and then.

The guards on the horses were hunched over their steeds, makeshift ponchos over their heads, trying to stay as dry as possible. They had stopped observing everything around them, now looking bored and tired.

Finally, it was clear they could go no further. The transports stopped and everyone was ordered to pitch their shelters to take refuge from the rain. Soon there was a haphazard tented village around the wagons.

Josh was billeted with the other maintenance men. They huddled together, trying to keep themselves dry as best they could next to a small fire. They had only been resting for a short while when the quartermaster stuck his head under their canopy, water dripping off his head as he looked in on them.

'There's a splitting axle on one of the middle wagons. I'm worried it will fail. I need someone to sort it out.' As he spoke, the damp men all tried not to catch his eye, most looking down at the ground.

Josh sighed heavily, trying not to look too keen. 'All right, I'll come and have a look.'

The others grinned as Josh stood up to leave. Once outside, Miles slapped him on his shoulder. 'Good lad. Right, it's this way.'

They trudged through the mud, stopping occasionally to knock the worst of the mud away from their shoes. Josh felt himself getting cold and wet through all over again. After making their way through the tents, they reached the wagon with the problem. Josh knelt to look underneath; it was clear that the axle wouldn't last much longer in its present condition.

He stood up again, hands on his hips. 'Yeah, it doesn't look good. But I think it can be sorted. I'll need some tools and rope and can get straight on to it.'

'Good. I'll take you down to where the tools are and let you get on with it.' The quartermaster walked down the line with Josh. They reached one of the heavily laden wagons and Miles passed Josh the tools needed for the job. They took down a length of rope and walked back to the breaking cart.

After dropping the rope on the ground, the quartermaster drew his coat closer to himself. 'I'll let you get on with it, lad. Let me know if you need anything else.'

'Yes, sir.' Josh stood there as he was left to carry out the work. There was a tired and uninterested guard watching occasionally about five metres away. He was now in a hopeful position.

Not too far away Nolan was awake, sitting at the side of one the tents. He had watched as Josh had marched down the transports. He stood up, making as if to go to relieve himself near the treeline.

Josh saw him stand and yelled out loudly to make himself heard against the rain. 'You there, come and give me a hand with this.'

Nolan looked uninterested at first, then annoyed at the request. The nearby guard shouted right at him. 'Go and help him! He's on official business.'

He ambled over to Josh, who showed him the repair he was doing and how he needed help. Making a show of assisting, Nolan helped Josh lever the wheel up ready.

They worked slowly, lowering the wheel on the one side before they went around to the other side to do the same.

With no one now watching they could talk, finally.

'We'll get this done and tell the guard there's a couple of other ones that need doing and I'm taking you with me to help. I did promise Eddie he could come with us, but I don't know where he is,' Josh whispered.

'There's not much chance of looking around for him either with the guards watching. I feel bad but what else can we do?'

Josh wiped the mud away from his hands. 'Hang on. I've got an idea. You stay here, and I'll be back.'

He crossed to the other side and approached the guard. 'Do you know where the tannery people are? I could do with some leather strips for the repair.'

The guard wasn't sure but told Josh to ask one of the guards further towards the middle of the convoy. He did so, soon finding the tent where some of the tannery workers were.

Eddie was resting near one of the wheels of the tannery cart. With Josh nudging him, he looked up through drowsy eyes.

'I need some leather for a repair I'm making,' Josh said, winking so only Eddie could see.

'In this weather! I'll get some for you, then,' he mumbled as he stood.

Getting some strips from the top of a hessian sack on the wagon, Eddie looked at Josh questioningly.

'Follow me,' Josh told him and walked away. He wanted to say more but knew he couldn't yet.

They reached Nolan and carried out the last of the repair. It would hold temporarily, but not for long. Josh wanted it to fail after a short while of use, to slow the transport up if they did make a break for it.

Shouting out to the guard, the rain still falling hard, Josh thanked him. 'Cheers for that. We're off to mend the other one now.'

The guard nodded half-heartedly, returning to his miserable watch.

Josh crossed to the other side of the convoy; there were no tents on this side because of the thick brambles covering the side of the highway. They moved down part of the way before crouching together.

Eddie spoke first, shivering. 'Are we really doing this? I'm worried I might hold you back.'

'Nah, you'll be okay,' Nolan answered. 'I reckon we've got a good few hours before they start again at first light. And they won't be coming looking for a few escapees, I think. That's if they even know we've gone.'

Josh looked at the two of them. 'I hope you're right, but we need to get a good distance away just in case. Let's do this, let's go.'

The three of them crawled through the brambles. The thorns pricking their faces and hands, making them bleed into the water running over them. It took them twenty minutes just to reach a clearing. When they stood, they brushed themselves down and hurried along to a nearby treeline.

Josh looked back, a free man once more. 'Well, we know where they are heading. We need to head away from them to begin with. To give us some distance. Then we can decide what to do once we are clear.'

Nolan pointed. 'Let's head north as far as we can, find somewhere warm to hide out, maybe dry off, too.'

'I'm all for that.' Eddie was already breathing hard.

'North it is, then.' Josh felt exhilarated at no longer being in servitude to the General.

They slithered down a small bank behind the trees, starting to jog once they reached the bottom. Keeping a good pace would be hard in this light and weather, but they started to leave the New English Army behind.

EIGHTEEN

As soon as Leila arrived home, she had a long, sobering discussion with Tom. Exhausted, she left to find some food and take the opportunity for a quick change of clothes, while messengers were sent to each of the council members.

After changing into fresh outfits, Leila and Alva were relaxing, slumped on the two comfy couches in Leila's office. Eating fruit and protein biscuits, they both sat in silence.

'I can't imagine how everyone is going to react to the news.' Alva looked over at Leila, her face absent of hope.

Leila gave a small wry laugh. 'I can. Each one has already made their mind up – this has just confirmed it, that's all.'

She looked around at the pictures and ornaments, reminding herself of her family's influence here. She wondered if she would ever return once they left.

Tom walked in with Irving, both with stern looks on their faces.

'I've given the order. We're starting the move,' Irving informed Leila. 'Our priority must be to not let anything of use fall into this Army's hands.'

Tom continued with the bad news. 'All of the lectrics we've gained from Kernow over the last few years will be first to go. We only have a small amount of communications, but I don't want them having it. Everything to do with the lectric supply to the solar panes as well. We might not be able to take it all with us, but we will make it unusable to them.'

Leila interrupted, thinking of the people not just the materials. 'Have we heard of any messages back from the council? What have we told the locals about what's going on?'

'Nothing yet from any of them.' Irving wrung his hands together, hard. 'And there's many rumours going around, of course, but the people around here are pretty much in the dark, I guess.'

Leila lifted herself up slowly, her body sore from the long ride. 'Then I'll go and tell them what's happening. We owe it to them.'

'I think we should plan to leave tomorrow morning.' Tom looked at the floor. 'I don't want to cut it any closer.'

'Agreed. Let's concentrate on taking everything that is valuable to restarting our home and business. Anything else doesn't matter.'

Tom managed a smile at his sister's words. 'Ever the pragmatist, eh? Just like Dad.'

They headed outside. There was much to do.

The complex was a hive of activity, everyone rushing around. Leila admired every one of them. She knew them all so well and was desperately worried for their futures. Tom and Irving went off to organise the move, leaving Alva following her awkwardly.

They walked briskly through the gates and headed into the surrounding town, finally reaching the square at its centre. By the time they arrived, news of them coming had ensured a large crowd had gathered. Standing on a large crate in the middle, she raised her arms, gesturing for silence.

'People. Friends.' Considering keenly all the questioning faces, she began. 'As most of you know by now, my father and the rangers went to confront the bandits to the east. They did not return. We've all lost people we love.'

The crowd had gone deathly quiet. So many had been affected by the slaughter. Some of those gathered were holding back tears, others looked angry or scared.

'When I heard what happened, I went to negotiate with these people myself.' She saw relatives of those who had died looking plaintively at her. 'I'm sorry to be the one to tell you but there is nothing we can do to stop them coming here. They intend to take over our holdings and production. They told me that any resistance would be met with brutal force.'

The crowd was clearly stunned at the news. The noise level started to rise as they finally understood. Couples put their arms around each other. Some started to cry, others shouted out.

The loudest was coming from a furious man who was making his way to the front of the mass of people. He reached the front, pointing his finger at Leila, his face reddening by the second.

'They can't do that. Our families have worked hard here to make a life for ourselves. We are not going to just give that away!'

Leila took a step forwards with her arms open, trying to calm him. 'I know how you feel. The only thing I can say is that they promised to work with those who stayed and offered no confrontation.'

'And you believe that?' the man asked.

Leila paused before answering; she didn't want to lie to anyone. 'I don't know. Maybe, maybe not, but I don't think they are trustworthy at all. What I can offer is that the remainder of my family are moving to our holdings at Somerton. We have been offered support by the Kernow Collective. They will send their militia to make sure we can hold out. Our border will, at least temporarily, be moved back to there.'

The crowd had listened to her speak, but more questions were coming. A tall, frustrated woman shouted at her. 'And how will we move everything there? Our lives are tied to the land. We have equipment that's heavy.'

Another voice cried out. 'So, the Kernow are taking over to the west and we give this other crew our lands to the east. It's fine for you – you'll be all right with everything you own. All I have is my home and fields.'

Angry men and women were now shouting all through the crowd, some arguing to fight the coming army. Others were angry at Leila herself for not offering more protection.

Leila tried to speak over the questions coming at her thick and fast but was struggling to make herself heard. All she wanted to do was try to answer some of the questions thrown at her but she was getting nowhere. She felt tired to her bones.

Suddenly, from behind her, a loud sound of metal on metal pierced through the noise. Everyone stopped shouting as they looked to see what it was.

Alva had grabbed a long metal pole and was beating it against an old iron railing which surrounded the monument in the square. Looking up at the people in front of her, she stopped when the shouting had died down. Striding over to stand firmly next to Leila, she threw the pole down before speaking.

'We are here to give you the facts of what we know. Do you forget that Leila lost her father? Does she feel any different to any of you?' She paused to look around at some now distinctly sheepish faces in front of her. 'They have killed most of our rangers. We cannot defend ourselves anymore. Now, we have gratefully accepted the offer of help from our friends at Kernow. No one believes this is fair or just or reasonable, but we are where we are and we either deal with it right now or God help us when they get here.'

Leila put a hand on Alva's shoulder, quietly thanking her for her help. She then braced herself and faced the crowd once more. 'We believe they will arrive in a day or two. We think that if you are going to leave, you should leave in the morning, with us. We will offer as much assistance as we can to anyone who needs our help.'

One man raised his arm before asking his question. 'What about those who aren't here? The farmsteads miles away from here?'

Leila looked down at him. 'We have sent all of our messengers out to all parts of the territory. We are letting as many people know as we can. I hope everyone hears what we are doing, but I know that some won't. I will live with that for the rest of my life.'

One older woman Leila knew called out. 'We know you will help us as much as you can, Leila. The Bowles family has always looked after its workers and territory well. We know you're hurting too.' The woman turned to face the crowd. 'Our grandparents and great-grandparents suffered much. We've all heard the old stories about the famine times their parents endured after the Chaos. And how they scratched a living in the dirt for years after that. Yet here we all are now, living not surviving. This is nothing to what they had to go through. Now we must move again, leaving possessions behind, yes, but not our lives. It is a small sacrifice compared to what they went through.'

Leila bowed to the woman, grateful for her words. 'Once we are there, I promise that everyone will have somewhere to live, somewhere to work. We will rebuild and never let this oncoming army sleep soundly. And one day soon, we hopefully will be able to return to our lands.'

The mob had now settled. After Leila's last words, cheers and clapping rang through the crowd. Leila waved them calm again. 'Go and pack if you want to come with us. We hope to leave in the morning. If you need any help then let us know.'

The crowd started to thin, small groups discussing what they had heard, walking away from the square.

Leila hugged Alva. 'Thank you. I think a lot will come with us, at least I hope they will.'

'They know they are better off with your family. I just hope the ones who stay behind are treated well by the General and his troops.'

Leila sighed at the unlikely thought.

The complex and its staff were in a highly disordered state throughout the day. Boxes and sacks were brought in and quickly filled. Once packed, everything was brought out to the front of the house, ready to be loaded onto transports for the journey west.

Once each wagon was full it was sent off on its way; there was no need for everything to travel together as there was still a small amount of time before the New English Army was expected to arrive. In the distance to the east, dark ominous clouds looked like they were heading towards them, but for the moment the weather held fair.

Many of the people from the town were also arriving, bringing their scant belongings with them. Many of the traders from the town had helped those without transport to carry as much as they could. As each wagon left for Somerton, those unable or too weak to walk were placed on top, their families walking alongside. Within hours, a long train of transports and people carrying their worldly possessions stretched away from the Bowles complex towards their new home.

By the time early evening had arrived, all items that had been prioritised for travel from the complex had already left; much of the livestock was now being moved as well. A great assembly of sheep, goats and llamas headed west.

Pausing briefly for a hot mint tea, Leila and Alva had wandered outside, resting against one of the small walls that surrounded a kitchen garden.

Leila gazed wistfully into the distance. 'I think we're going to make it out of here, at least before they arrive.'

Alva frowned into her tea. 'Yeah, that's something at least. But I can't help thinking about those who are choosing not to come.'

'I know but we can't make them. We've given them the information we have – what they do with it is up to them.'

Alva sipped her warm drink. 'What will that general do to them?'

'I don't know, Alva. I just don't know.' Leila sighed.

As they were taking their break, Tom came out looking for his sister.

'We're pretty much done in the house. It's a shame that we can't take any furniture with us, but everything else has been loaded and is ready to go. I can't believe everything we have can be taken so quickly. What would Dad say? My first act as head of the house and directeur of the company is to retreat away from our land.'

Leila stood to hug her brother. 'That stuff doesn't matter, we can make more possessions. We're doing the right thing. We can leave and regroup. One day we'll come back to our home.'

Tom stood a little taller at his younger sister's words. 'Thank you. Sometimes I think you should have been the eldest – you're better at this type of thing than me.'

Leila laughed properly, the first time in days. 'God no. You're welcome to it.'

'Right, more to do, then. Let's get this done.'

They headed back to the house to continue the evacuation. Reaching the main doors, they saw a group of riders approaching them. Seeing it was Gabriel with his family and entourage, they waved as the horses stopped nearby.

Gabriel dismounted and walked over. He shook the hand of Tom firmly and hugged Leila paternally.

'We're off now but I wanted to stop by and see you before we go. We're heading to our Warmwell community near the coast.' Gabriel smiled, sadness on his face. 'I wanted to remind you that your father and myself worked together for many years. And your mother and my wife were great friends, as you know. Anything I can do for you, you just need to ask. I want to return to my home before long, just as bad as you do. And you are the family to do it. I know I am seen as someone who only looks out for myself, but I swear to you I will support you as much as I can. Whatever you need, ask me and if I can help, I will.'

'Thank you, Gabriel. You don't know how much we appreciate that.' Tom shook his hand again in appreciation.

Leila had a tear in her eye as she thanked Gabriel. 'Hopefully, we will be asking for your help sooner rather than later. Thank you.'

'Your father would be proud of both of you. I've also brought a few more wagons for you. I hope they help.'

Leila saw a number of larger transports pulling up at the gates. 'Thank you again. My father chose his friends wisely indeed.'

They all embraced once more, knowing time was short.

'We will return,' called Leila as Gabriel mounted his horse.

'We will return!' Gabriel shouted loudly as he turned and glanced back. With his arm raised and his fist in the air, he led his party away from the house, westwards bound.

Buoyed by Gabriel's gesture of solidarity, they hurried back to finish the loading of the complex's property onto the wagons and transports. About half had already left. They would be done soon.

'Alva, thank you for all your efforts. It's appreciated,' Tom said. 'I'd like you to ride with us to Somerton. I want you to have a position with us when we get there – we would be lucky to have someone like you working with us.'

Alva's eyes went wide at the offer. 'Oh, thank you, sir. It would be an honour.'

'Good, good.' Tom almost had a smile on his face, almost. 'Right, first job for you. Go and find Anne and Irving. Let them know we want one last meal in the house tonight. We will meet you all here as soon as possible.'

Alva grinned as she strode off towards the barracks.

The final evening at their family home was a solemn occasion. They ate what food had been left out, inviting all the workers who hadn't left to join them. Some of the locals had already left, heading west; some had come to the house and had been invited to stay for the evening.

By the time night had fallen, everyone settled down for an uncomfortable night's sleep.

Not being able to sleep at all, Leila and Tom both stayed in their father's study. They hoped to take in as many memories as they could before they left.

They stayed up till the early hours, reminiscing about their childhood and other happy memories. Leila talked a lot about their mother – how they wished she could have been around to see them grow up. She had made a kind of peace with her mother's untimely demise many years ago but knew that Tom still felt mightily pained by not having her with him.

Eventually, with the fire having burnt down to glowing embers, they both fell asleep in their chairs for a few precious hours of rest.

At first light, Irving woke the two of them up. Once they were both awake, he gave them a brief update. 'All the wagons have left. We got an early start. It looks like the weather is going to get pretty poor.'

Leila looked distractedly out of the window. The clear sunny day yesterday had given way to dark and moody clouds. Standing up and stretching her aching limbs, she saw her brother doing the same.

Irving continued with his update. 'Everyone from the area who wants to come with us has started off as well. It's all going to plan so far.'

'Thanks, Irv. And I know how much leaving this place hurts you as well.'

Outside was totally quiet, the last of the long train of people were a few minutes' walk in front of them. Coming up from the stable were Anne and Alva, leading five horses behind them. A slight drizzle had started in the air, promising much more to come soon.

Leila stood there, holding back her feelings. Glancing to her side, she saw a tear slide down Tom's cheek. 'I thought I'd be the emotional one, not you.'

Tom wiped it away casually, not bothering to hide it. 'Thought I'd do it for the both of us.' He smiled tenderly at his sister, before giving her a long hug.

Irving helped them all on the horses before climbing onto his own. 'Should we say a few words?'

Leila looked at the house and then looked to the countryside. 'No, no words could do justice to how we feel. We'll be back one day. Save them till then.'

With that, they urged their mounts onwards, through the gates and off to their new home.

NINETEEN

THE THREE RUNAWAYS HAD HURRIED, TRUDGED AND SLOGGED their way across miles of muddy fields, using rivers or streams to disguise their route when possible. By the time first light started to arrive they were all utterly spent. The rain had slowed to a light smattering halfway through the night, finally stopping an hour before dawn. Eventually, they came to a halt near an old rickety hay barn, breathing heavily and covered from head to toe in dirt.

Collapsing clumsily on the ground, they lay there for a moment, catching their breath.

Nolan broke the silence. 'For an older and fatter man, you kept up well, Eddie.' The whites of his eyes smiled through his muddy face.

Eddie laughed, causing a coughing fit. 'Why thanks. I don't think I could do it again though, if it's all the same to you.'

'Nor do I,' Nolan agreed, laying his head back on the floor.

Josh sat up. They had made it away from the Army, but he wondered if they had been followed. He mentioned his worry to Nolan.

Nolan stared up at the sky. 'Doubt it,' he said firmly. 'It would be impossible to follow us the way we came, especially with all the precautions we took. Even if they could track us, they need to move off early with the delay last night. I think we're clear. My best guess is that they don't even know we've gone – don't even care, to be honest.'

Josh glanced over at his friend, then towards the way they had come. He wanted to believe that they would not be followed, but he wanted to make sure. 'I hope so. We should find somewhere to safely rest and hide away in.'

'Well, this crappy barn won't be any good. Let's head over to that higher ground over there and see what we can see.'

Eddie groaned at the mention of more walking.

They headed uphill for a while. At the top, they had a perfect panoramic view of the nearby countryside. Josh searched the landscape, desperately trying to find some sign of any Army members looking for them. There was nothing.

He could, however, see a small hamlet a mile or so to the north. He was too far away to tell if anyone was living there, but it was somewhere to aim for at least.

He clapped his hands together. 'Come on, then. Let's get there as quick as we can. At least the weather's a bit better now.'

Eddie's shoulders slumped again, before they filed off towards the distant settlement.

|||||||||||||||||||||||||||||||||||||||||||||||||||||||||||||||||||||||||||||

The tired-looking guard was making his early morning rounds, making sure everyone was readying themselves to travel as soon as the order was given. The quartermaster approached him as he was checking around one of the wagons. Standing to attention, the guard waited for him to pass. Instead, he came right up to him.

'Have you been on watch all night?' Miles asked. 'I'm trying to find one of my repairmen.'

'Most of the night, yeah. When did you last see him?'

'Midnight or so. He was working on the wagons.'

'Probably catching some sleep, then, if he was up late.'

'Indeed. I'll keep looking.' The quartermaster turned to continue looking through the waking men.

He had walked the length of the column of wagons and men three times now, making it look like he was inspecting the transports. He didn't want to look again; that would draw more attention. He knew he should report a missing man, but he also knew how that might affect him. There was no way he was being held responsible for someone else escaping. Deciding to protect his own neck, he walked back to his wagon and gave it no further thought.

||||||||||||||||||||||||||||||||||||||||||||||||||||||||||||||||||||||||||||||||

Reaching the small collection of houses, Josh looked around for signs of life. At this time of day the locals should have been up and working, but there was no one about. Knocking at a few of the doors made it clear that all the buildings were empty.

The three of them stood there exhausted, confused and hungry. It was not a difficult decision to make to enter one of the houses. Choosing one at the end of the row, they opened the front door and made their way into the kitchen.

It was a small, ancient thatched cottage with low ceilings and a welcoming homely feel. The kitchen was warm and dry. Josh made a fire in the hearth to boil some water. Within minutes they were drinking a warming tea and eating some of the fruit from the bowl near the window.

'So, where is everyone?' asked Eddie.

Nolan slumped down into a chair. 'Not sure. Could all be out working somewhere, I suppose.'

Josh looked around the kitchen and walked into the main room of the house. 'No, it looks like they've shipped out, and quickly. There's things out of place and marks where stuff has been moved.' He went into one of the bedrooms, coming out after a brief look. 'Most of the clothes are gone as well. Whoever lived here has left.'

'Do you think they knew what had happened and what was coming, then?' Nolan wondered.

'Maybe. How, I don't know, but maybe,' responded Josh.

Eddie drained his drink. 'Well, if that's the case I'm going to see if there's anything to change into. I'm soaked through, covered in grime, and need a change of clothes.'

As soon as Eddie headed to the bedrooms, Josh and Nolan looked at each other and rushed after him. They weren't going to let Eddie have the best pick of whatever clothes were left behind. Racing each other, they spent a hectic few minutes stripping off and grabbing the nearest and best clothes they could find. It was a welcome relief from the stresses of the last few days.

Once all were changed into ill-fitting but clean new clothes, Eddie went out to the back garden of the cottage. He brought in a large bucket of water and they relaxed a bit more, washing their faces and heads as best they could.

Nolan was the first to share his thoughts. 'We need to head back to Chilmark – let them know what's coming. See if we can help.'

Josh finished washing his face. 'Agreed. I saw Leila at the Army base. It was clear she was trying to negotiate. And it was even clearer that the General was in no mood to give any ground. We need to get back.'

'And what exactly can we do, faced with Hill and his soldiers?' Eddie asked. Josh noticed the fear in his eyes.

'We fight them, again and again,' Nolan told him firmly.

Eddie shook his head. 'Hard to do when you're dead.'

Josh stepped in. 'Eddie, this is our family, we have to offer whatever help we can. You have no obligation to stay with us. You're welcome to come, but we won't think any less of you if you don't.'

Eddie shrugged his shoulders. 'All right, I'm in. You're not getting rid of me that easily. But I'm no hero, so don't expect me to act as one.'

Nolan leant over and clouted his back. 'Thanks, maybe we can't help much but let's be better than that bunch of murderers.'

Josh smiled at the two of them. 'Let's see what we can cook up, get some food inside us and work out how we're going to get home.'

They rummaged through the kitchen cupboards; Eddie went outside to search for anything he could find growing in the garden. It wasn't long before they were preparing a salty vegetable and mushroom stew from everything they had found. They spent a peaceful hour cooking and eating the best meal they had had in days.

Josh knew Eddie wanted to rest further, especially after having such a hard night slogging through the mud, but Josh insisted they continue. 'We need to find out where we are exactly,' Josh told them. 'Let's get on the road for a while and see where it takes us. We'll still head away from the Army before we turn westwards. We then can find somewhere to have a few hours' sleep.'

Eddie and Nolan agreed, and soon they were walking along a single-track road with their spirits high. Thankfully, the weather had taken a turn for the better. The storm they had been caught in yesterday had moved on, and although the sky was still partly cloudy, they were dry at least. They walked through the countryside till the sun was high in the sky, with a pleasant cool breeze blowing across their faces.

They came to a fork in the road. One way continued north and the other turned west. Deciding that they were far enough away from the Army's convoy, they headed west towards their destination.

The road ran straight for miles, the three of them making good progress. Inevitably, however, the pace they were making was slowing considerably. And it wasn't just due to Eddie. They had all been awake and travelling for too long; rest was needed, if only for a short time.

Keeping an eye out for a suitable place to rest, they walked another mile before seeing a cowshed in one of the fields. Making their way cautiously to it, they saw that it had been unused for a long time. It had an ancient corrugated roof which looked mostly weatherproof; it made them fairly optimistic about keeping dry if the rains were to return.

Insisting he took the first watch, Josh let Eddie and Nolan settle down to get some rest. Eddie was asleep within seconds, not long followed by Nolan. Josh took a seat and leant back against the doorframe to the cowshed, making himself comfortable and ensuring a good view. As he forced himself to stay awake, his thoughts drifted while he listened to the snoring of his companions.

General Hill stepped down from his carriage and stretched his back. They had made good progress so far on the journey and would soon be at his destination. He again pictured his prize as he stood there. The resource-rich land of the Bowles territory. He would move in, build up his army with all the wealth that came with the land. Then he could branch out to take over the remainder of the south of England. Especially the Kernow vagrants and fishermen in the far west – how they had gained such a reputation for talent with old-time lectrics was utterly mysterious to him. Probably untrue, he thought. Once the south was his, he could then think of moving into the Middle-lands. Maybe one day soon he would reunite the whole of England, with him as the sovereign of the land.

He walked over to Iain Bates, who was in the process of gathering the leadership team around him. They all saluted as the General approached. He saluted them back.

'Iain, what's the update from our scouts?' he asked his second in command.

'It looks like they've left the main residence and surrounding buildings, just like you told them to. We can't find any damage or anything. I think we can just walk in and pick up where they left off.'

The General gave a deep rumbling laugh. 'I knew they would turn tail and run, the cowards. They saw what we did to their pathetic rangers and couldn't face us again.'

Iain agreed. 'I think we should send a small retinue of soldiers in first, just to make sure there's no one setting up an ambush or the like.'

General Hill nodded slowly. 'Very well. I want to get going again soon. I'm eager to see our new home. Where's the quartermaster? Find him and let him know we must be ready to leave very soon.'

Iain turned to one of his junior officers, motioning for the man to do as the General commanded. The man left quickly.

They spent a short amount of time discussing the next steps they would take on the final leg of the journey. It was agreed that they would allow the Army a final rest now, making sure all transportation was ready for the rest of the journey. The command was given to cook up some more of the food for the soldiers, with a group of hunters being sent out to see what game could be caught for the meal.

Once the orders had been issued, the leaders of the Army gathered once again in the largest carriage. The most ruthless and cruel people in the fledgling army, all after power and wealth.

'After we acquire the Bowles hometown, I want all remaining opposition ruthlessly crushed,' Hill told his team. 'You have your list of the places which we think will offer the most resistance.'

'Of course, General. I hope the information is good, Iain,' Rollins said pointedly.

Iain Bates bristled a little at the comment. 'My spies in the surrounding area are first class and the information will be extremely accurate, all mapped out and ready to be dealt with. Jarek has overseen it himself.'

Bates was referring to his deputy, Captain Jarek Nowak, one of the cruellest men Iain had ever met. He had no morals, was highly intelligent and had no limits to his depravity, a one-man killing machine. He had risen quickly in the Army over the last year. Normally, once captured, men took a month or two to become part of the Army. Jarek was accepted by all within a week, killing his handler in front of everyone for some perceived slight. Bates didn't trust him one bit but was prepared to use the sharpest tool he had when he needed it.

'I am giving him the task of suppressing any opposition immediately,' Hill said, watching the faces of the men around him.

'Keep a tight leash on him, sir,' Iain said politely. 'He can go too far sometimes.'

Hill brushed his suggestion away with a wave of his hand.

The food soon arrived, allowing them to take a short break as they ate. Other officers came and went from the carriage, delivering information or taking orders away.

As they were finishing eating, they heard a commotion outside. Heated voices and barked orders cutting through the air. They stepped out to see what was happening.

In front of them were two men, kneeling in front of a couple of soldiers. The men on the floor were dishevelled, looking worriedly around.

'What have we here?' asked General Hill.

The soldier nearest came to attention and answered immediately. 'We found them trying to escape, sir. I was at the end of the column and got them before they could get away.'

'Good work, good work.' Hill sneered. He walked up to the potential escapees, eyeing them up and down.

One of the men looked up. 'We were just looking for some food, that's all – we weren't trying to escape.' The other man nodded furiously, joining his comrade in the obvious lie.

'We will not accept deserters,' Hill firmly told the pair, his voice rising so the rest of the men around could hear. 'An army is only as strong as its weakest link. This New English Army needs ruthless yet dedicated men, ones that you could be if you take the chance.' He took a step back and threw his dagger down on the ground in front of the two men. Seeing this, his personal guards took a step nearer to their leader; he raised a hand to calm them. The two deserters looked at each other.

'One of you will take this knife and kill the other one. They will then be allowed to continue to be part of our movement. That is the type of man I want in my Army. If you don't, you both will die.'

The two men looked up at the General, then at each other. It seemed an age before either of them moved. The man to the left sprang at the knife, grabbing it before the other had time to register what was happening. The newly armed man lunged at the other, knife glistening as he moved. In one slick movement, he slid it straight into the side of the neck of the horrified victim, who was only now bringing his hands up to protect himself.

Keeping the pressure on the knife as the blood streamed out of the pierced neck, the aggressor forced the other to the ground as he slowly died. Blood was pouring out over both of them. Trying to speak but only managing a wet, gurgling noise, the dying man looked accusingly at his murderer. As soon as there was no movement from his victim, the man stood up, gently throwing the dagger to the feet of one of the soldiers. He grimly looked into Hill's eyes, fear covering his face.

The General was enormously pleased with the scene in front of him. Looking at the silent mass around him, he dared anyone to challenge his authority. All stood quiet in front of him, no one able to look away.

'Go and rejoin your unit. But we will be watching you. Do not step out of line again. Am I clear?'

The blood-soaked man came to attention at once. 'Yes, sir.' He saluted as best he could, before pivoting on the spot and hurrying away.

One of the General's personal guard stepped forwards. 'I know his commanding officer, sir. I will personally speak to him to tell him one more step out of line and he dies.'

Hill nodded at his guard. 'Yes, you do that.' Suddenly, he slapped his thigh and walked back to his carriage, everyone else still watching him.

Before he climbed back up, he paused and looked back. 'We leave in thirty minutes. Ready the horses and wagons. I want to be there as soon as I can.'

TWENTY

Just outside the ancient village of Somerton sat Bowles Mercantile's main source of wealth: the solar and algae farms. It was surrounded by many associated small manufacturing businesses, grown up around the area due to the abundance of lectrical power. Receiving a levy of one third of everything sold by these companies, in return for free lectrics, Bowles Mercantile had made its fortune.

As they reached the town, Leila and Tom were being briefed by one of the mechanics.

'We've been working day and night to build a functioning relay station to distribute the lectric. So far there's lectric restored to one of the algae farms, as well as a small section of the immediate surrounding area,' the worker told them. 'It's going to take a lot more work to have the power back to the levels before the attack, but we can get there in time. Luckily, the panes supplying the energy are virtually untouched.'

Good news, finally, thought Leila. 'So once lectric is restored, we can restart the businesses so important to the local economy.'

'That's the aim, yes.'

'Well, keep up the good work. We'll come and visit as soon as we're settled.'

The mechanic thanked them and headed back to work.

'Our people will be here soon,' Irving told them. 'It's going to be a massive operation, looking after them. Food will be the priority for now.'

'I know. We'll have our work cut out,' Tom responded.

They had raced ahead of the straggling convoy of people and animals to make sure they could organise the disorder that would ensue when so many arrived at their temporary home. Somerton itself was not a large place – Leila could travel through it on horse in only a few minutes. But it was surrounded by field upon field of wheat crops. They had already been harvested for the year and so there was plenty of space for an improvised camp in the short term.

They finally reached their father's summer residence in the centre of the village, now their only home.

Somerton Manor was a gothic building, centuries old, a home away from home for the two siblings. They had spent many an enjoyable summer here in their youth. While they knew that they couldn't house everyone in comfort nearby, it would act as an excellent waystation while they worked out the finer details.

Waiting for them as they arrived were the staff of the small manor house. They had been kept informed of all the latest events and were aware of what was coming.

The first person to greet Tom and Leila was a kindly, grey-haired, elderly man, shuffling rather than walking because of his age. Claude had been the housekeeper at the manor for the Bowles family since Jeremiah Bowles first acquired the property decades ago. He, along with an extended family, had run the house ever since. His wife had passed away many years ago, so he and his two children had made lives for themselves running the manor with a passion. He was now assisted by his grandchildren, who had taken the baton on with pride.

Tom went to shake his hand, then grabbed the old man and hugged him tenderly. The two looked at each other as Claude offered his condolences. 'I'm so sorry to hear about your father, Thomas. I cannot express my sorrow to you.'

Tom brushed yet another tear away from his eye. 'Thank you, Claude. I know you two were close. Now I must ask you to help the third Bowles generation to run this place, if you're willing?'

Claude smiled affectionately at the boy he had known since he was a child. 'Of course, Thomas. It would be an honour.'

Leila approached and followed Tom with hugs and kisses for her old friend. Claude's family had also now joined him outside and soon the subdued welcome was complete.

Leila was speaking to Sanaa, Claude's eldest granddaughter who did most of the organising around the house with one of her younger brothers. 'There's going to be a lot of people arriving soon, tired and hungry. We must make them comfortable until we know what we are doing with everyone.'

Sanaa understood what was needed and headed off to start the preparations.

Tom continued discussing events with Claude, updating him on the past few days. His eldest grandson arrived, welcoming them with a huge hug, sorrow in his eyes for their loss.

When Claude had heard of the plan to move as many people to Somerton, enlisting the help of the Kernow Collective, his family had set about organising and readying themselves for the task. He quickly moved on to updating Tom and Leila with his news. 'We've been communicating with the Kernow engineers for the last few days. They say they can get a larger temporary relay station up and running in a day or two when they start work. They will only be able to use a quarter or so of the solar capacity, but it will mean we can get the protein production up and running pretty quickly. We just won't have much extra lectric to share around for a week or so, but we will have enough food to go round.'

Leila felt relief wash over her. 'Thank God for that. There's going to be a lot of people around here soon – at least we will be able to feed them all.'

'Not to mention the Kernow militia that's going to be hanging around,' Claude grumbled to both of them.

Tom smiled at the old man. 'They are here to help, Claude. I know you're not their greatest fan, but in this they are our friends.'

Claude didn't look like he believed a word Tom was saying but held his tongue for now. 'As you say, Thomas. Shall we go in and discuss what to do?'

Tom put his arm around his old friend. 'Yes, good idea. We are expecting one more guest soon. I've invited Matthew Taylor to come and plan our way forward.'

Claude's eyes opened wide. 'The Kernow leader? What the hell is he coming here for?'

'As I said, they are coming here to help. These are strange new times and we need all the friends we can get.'

They walked into the ancient stone building. Many of the travellers were still some way away, allowing a few moments' respite.

They spent the next couple of hours catching up and reminiscing about old times. The time was a refreshing one, both physically and mentally.

During one particularly long tale from Claude, a knock on the door interrupted them. Leila was grateful for the break in the story as they welcomed one of the house workers into the room.

'There's some visitors on horses asking for you, Mister Bowles,' the girl informed them, before holding the door open, waiting.

Tom stood, motioning for Claude to stay where he was. 'Thank you. I'll come right away. It's okay, Claude, you stay here. Thank you for cheering me up.'

'You go on,' Leila told him. 'I'll be out in a moment.'

|||||||||||||||||||||||||||||||||||||||||||||||||||||||||||||||||||||||||||||||

Outside, dismounted and soothing their horses, were seven riders. They were dusty from a long journey but didn't look weary at all. They were tall, well built, with thick beards on the men and long braided hair on the women. When Tom appeared, the leader of the group confidently strode over. He had a full black beard and long messy hair down to his broad shoulders.

He smiled, shaking Tom's hand with both of his own. 'Thank you for inviting us, Tom. I'm sorry we had to meet each other again so soon, under such terrible circumstances.' His voice was deep and powerful, more than matching his large frame. 'I want to assure you that we come as friends and I bring the Collective's sincere condolences for the death of your father.'

'Please pass my thanks on to them, then, Matthew. We're grateful for the help you have offered us as well.'

'You're welcome. Your father was a good friend to Kernow, and to me personally. We want to work together to rid ourselves of this upstart army I've been told about.' The large man turned and introduced his second in command. 'This is Cador, my nephew. If you're ever in a tight spot, he's your man.'

Cador smiled awkwardly at the introduction. Although a powerful young man, he looked nervous. His head was shaved, bar a week's growth, with his beard mainly falling from his chin rather than his cheeks. His build made him look like someone you wouldn't want to fight with, yet he was quiet and polite.

Matthew introduced the others in the party. After, Tom called over the waiting stable boys to help the Kernow with their horses. Following a brief chat with Matthew to confirm his orders, some of the travellers went off to see how they could assist the incoming people.

Tom led Matthew and Cador towards the house. 'You must be thirsty after your trip.'

'Parched. I could do with a drink,' Matthew replied happily.

'Right,' said Tom. 'Let's go inside. We can discuss our plans.'

Leila came out from the house to greet their new guests. She had never met Matthew but had heard a good deal about him from their father in her time. Introducing herself, she shook his hand reservedly, feeling slightly unnerved as she saw him taking a long look at her.

'It is a pleasure to meet you,' Matthew said to her, dwarfing her hand between his much larger two. 'I must say how much I can see your mother in you. You are the image of her, just as I remember.'

Leila instantly dropped her guard and smiled. She had been young when her mother had died and although her father had always been there for her, she had few memories of her mother.

Tom broke the moment. 'We were just going inside. Let's get our guests comfortable.'

Having this man standing there, who had actually known her mother, was an enormous pleasure. Hearing Matthew talk about her likeness made her take his arm and lead him towards the house.

'You must tell me more about Mum. Dad told us plenty but I'm sure he didn't tell us everything.'

Matthew looked down at her. 'I'm sure there's a few stories I can dredge up. I'm sorry about William, Leila. I was horrified to hear what happened.'

Leila patted his arm. 'Thank you, that means a lot. I know you and Dad were great friends.' She led him through the main door to the manor, followed by Tom and Cador talking about the journey.

They moved into a large room on the right-hand side of the old manor. With its low ceiling and stone floor, it showed the age of the house with its hundreds of years of history. They sat either side of a large unlit fireplace, black soot lines above it from centuries of use. Pale wooden beams crossed the ceiling, with twisted wood panelling finishing off the effect.

Sitting back into the comfy sofas, Matthew and Cador drank fresh apple water poured from a large glass pitcher served by a youngster from the manor. Tom and Leila sat back, allowing their guests to quench their thirst.

The jug was almost empty before the conversation turned to the current situation. Matthew was keen to stress that Kernow was now just as concerned about the Army as they were.

'We need to make sure that they do not settle and build a stronghold for themselves. Men like this, once successful in one venture, will not stop trying to grow further,' Cador stated, looking at each of them in turn. 'We need to find a way to rid ourselves of them as soon as we can.'

Leila brushed her hair away from her face. 'Of course, but after they slaughtered our rangers, we barely have anyone left able to fight compared to them. We can probably muster up thirty or so. And unless you're going to send five hundred militia here, I don't see how we can.'

'I don't think we can bring that many, but we can bring about two hundred. When we heard what had happened, the Collective's council all came together and agreed to show our full support to you. It was unanimous, all seven regions. As it stands, that's all the men and women we can gather right now – I wish it could be more. We need to think what we can do with them. But at least for now it's enough to make them know that they won't be able to take any more territory off you.'

'Then what do we do? Thank you for being able to bring such a number, but I doubt that they alone would take on the whole Army,' Leila said.

Matthew stood up, walking over to the window. 'That's what we need to work out. We probably can't take them front on, so we have to come up with a different plan of attack.' He turned back. 'We'll think of something, I promise. I suggest we get a war cabinet together, my staff and yours. Together we can come up with a plan to defeat this madman.'

Tom walked over to the Kernow leader. 'Matthew, I don't want you to think me ungrateful for all the help you are giving us, as we truly are. But why are you taking on such a risk? I get that Hill is a truly horrific neighbour to have, but this seems above and beyond that.'

For a few seconds, Matthew gazed at the view from the window without answering. He released a deep breath. 'It is something we at the Kernow discussed before I left to come here and, to be honest, we've been talking about integrating with the outer world for some time. This army arriving has just given voice to many on our council.' He stopped, looking intently at Tom. 'Many of us know the stories of what our grandparents' parents did after the Chaos. How they cut themselves off from the rest of the country, kept as many people out as they could, condemning people to die without any help they could have offered. We know what people think of us. This is the time to make amends.'

Leila cut in. 'It's hard to understand how bad those times were.'

'I'm not saying that I would have done anything differently than they did back in those days. They really were the worst of times, calling for tough measures. But no one is left who lived then, nor knew anyone who was alive at the time either. It's time we atoned in some way for those times. This seems like exactly the type of help that will make the Kernow respected again, if it works.'

As he finished, he turned to face the room.

Leila was unsure of how to respond to such honesty about his past. 'All I can say is thank you, then. My father often spoke of how honourable the Kernow were, and not just because Mum came from there, either. Hopefully, others will see just how right he was.'

'We thank the council for your decision, Matthew,' Tom said. 'Once we get everyone settled, we can meet and plan our next move. Our people should be starting to arrive anytime now. It should take a day or so to arrange things for them. Will your militia be here soon, Matthew?'

'Indeed, sometime tomorrow.'

'Good. At least we can start to feel safe again, for now. I should think the General will want to settle in anyway, before he then finds out where we have all gone. It's time to start getting everything ready for the arrivals.' Leila called one of the house staff, telling them to take Matthew and Cador to their room to rest. The girl led them away, dwarfed by the two huge men.

'Well, that went better than we could have hoped for. Don't you think?' Tom asked his sister.

'For now, yes. I'm just concerned that some of our people won't like being told what to do by the Collective. They aren't the most popular of people around these parts, remember.'

'They will just have to lump it, then,' Tom protested. 'Without them, we don't have a chance.'

Leila walked over to her brother and held his hand affectionately. 'I know, I know. Just be aware of it, okay? I want to save our energies for fighting the General, not each other.'

She put her arms around her brother, hugging him tightly. He depended on her so much now; she had to guide him through these terrible times.

Over the course of the night, and all through the next day, refugees arrived from the Bowles territory. Whether some from the more eastern territory would come at all was not yet known. Many were temporarily settled around the buildings dotted about the manor house farm. Houses and barns became full of exiles. Others carried on further west, hoping greater distance would make them safer. Once all the buildings were full, the field started to become a sprawling mass of tents and canopies.

Leila, now joined by Anne, supported Irving in the settling and organising of the people. It appeared to help take his mind off the loss he felt for William. Claude lent the assistance of his local support staff, too. Messengers were sent further afield with requests for help or places to house the incoming.

At around midday, the Kernow militia arrived. Two hundred fighters, about a quarter of whom were on horseback, marched to the surroundings of the small town. They set up a camp in a large field to the west of Somerton. A small stream ran to one side, which was used for cooking and washing.

The encampment consisted of rows and rows of pale-coloured tents, neatly placed in lines, making a square with a larger tent in the middle. This would be the officers' planning area. Kernow flags fluttered on each corner of the structure.

The building of the camp was something that most of the locals looked on with horror. To have a different territory's militia building such a thing right in their backyard was something that brought fear to the older men and women. The stories that had been passed down by their great-grandparents of the warlords and feuds from the famine times were still held in the back of their minds. For the younger ones, they tried hard to believe that they were allies here to help.

By the end of the day, the stream of arrivals had slowed to a trickle. Most had been found somewhere to stay, even if temporarily for now. The manor house itself was bursting at the seams, but everyone was much more relaxed than they had been for some time.

In the pleasant evening air, Leila was taking a trip to see the progress at the solar farm. She was accompanied by Anne, Alva and Cador, Matthew having left to discuss plans with his militia. The solar facility was only a mile or so from the manor house, so they had chosen to walk rather than ride. The talk was light-hearted for the journey, Cador telling stories of his home life while being asked a huge number of questions along the way.

He was a part of Matthew's large family of copper miners, one of the resurgent occupations over the recent decades. It was playing a vital part in the reintroduction of solar technology and had made his extended family quite rich over recent years. It was obvious that he was passionate about his work, but he also talked of a passion for reading. Alva was entranced, hearing of some of the old books he had read, and he delightedly told her he would show her them. The brawny man seemed impressed by such a keenness to read.

Arriving at the solar farm, they saw that two large transports had arrived from Kernow, stocked with the replacement lectrics and other vital elements for the new relay station. The Kernow engineers were already busy at work, watched by Bowles mechanics. The lectric lights around the station were glowing bright; it felt like a small island of calm in the darkness.

Leila talked to some of her men who seemed upset that the Kernow people had taken over and weren't giving them much to do. Leila tried as best she could to smooth away their gripes, explaining how it was speed needed here more than anything. She tried to explain that they had much more expertise and could do everything a great deal quicker, but she understood their complaints. She made a mental note to discuss this with Matthew when she next saw him.

TWENTY-ONE

GENERAL HILL LED HIS NEW ENGLISH ARMY INTO CHILMARK. He rode at the front of the convoy, closely followed by his officers, feeling like a conquering hero taking his spoils. He had seen hardly anyone on the ride into the area; the people would be cowed and scared of showing themselves.

Holding the reins to his horse in one hand, the other resting on his hip, he knew this was his greatest triumph yet. With such a territory under his control there could now be no one able to resist him. This area would be more fertile than the east part of England with its small offerings. This huge swath of land was ideal. The only authority, albeit small, left now in the south were the fishermen pirates to the east. In good time he would subjugate them as well.

One of the advance scouts arrived from the complex. Hill carried on without stopping as the rider turned his horse. Waiting to be spoken to, the young scout followed a few feet behind.

Making a show for his troops, Hill spoke loudly so his voice carried. 'Report, then, scout. Have they left their home for us? Or are there any remaining behind ready to die?'

The scout stiffened. 'All empty, sir. We've searched the surrounding areas, up to a mile around. As far as we can see, they've all gone.'

'Excellent news, just as I expected,' Hill announced, slapping his whip against his thigh. 'I knew they would run away with their tails between their legs. No one can stand against us, no one.'

He dismissed the scout. Turning to Iain, who was riding just slightly behind to his left, he let himself smile broadly at his old friend. 'No words of caution, Iain? No comments about watching our backs?'

Bates glanced across, his eyebrows slightly raised at the not-so-subtle dig, but he kept his emotions in check. 'Not this time. I'll give it to you. It is indeed a superb victory, taking this territory over. All credit to you, General.'

Hill fully agreed with his second in command. He faced towards the town and pushed his horse on a little faster. He was impatient to arrive. He could see for the first time the buildings he would take over.

The town was eerily quiet; there was no movement at all as they made their way through. He could hear his men getting louder as they saw places to stay in or eat in. He didn't mind the slight lapse in discipline – they deserved what they were about to take.

They finally came to the large, open iron gates of the complex. Hill raised his hand for the following train to stop. He dismounted, breathing in the air before walking to one of the scouts at the gates. The scout saluted then turned towards the house, shouting loudly to inform others of the General's arrival.

Hill glanced back at his troops; they were waiting expectantly. Motioning for his officers to join him, he once again turned to view his plunder. His closest men gathered around to wait for his orders.

Still staring at the building in front of him, he barked his commands. 'Scouts say it's clear, but don't trust that to be the case. I don't think they will leave anyone behind, but there may be booby traps or the like. Send some of the new people in first to check them out. Then get the men stationed where you can and start to unload the wagons. I want everything set up as soon as it can be.'

Two of the officers saluted before heading to the gates to start the task of settling into their new home. Hill, followed by Bates and the remaining leaders, walked across the neatly kept lawn towards the main door of the building.

Standing there waiting for them was the scout captain; he had spent the last hour personally ensuring the main building was safe to enter. Saluting as his leader arrived at the doors, he opened them wide, informing the General that it was all clear.

'Let me show you to the largest office, sir,' the captain pompously said. 'It has the best views and I think you will find it more than suitable.'

Hill grinned his acceptance, following behind as they moved through the large entrance hall to the office selected.

The captain opened the door to William Bowles' old office, allowing the small group to walk through.

'Excellent,' breathed the General, looking around, admiring the splendour of the room. 'This will suit me perfectly.' He walked to the chair behind the desk, feeling extremely satisfied. Glancing around the room, he could see there was a fair amount of paper strewn around the place.

Sitting down slowly, he gestured for his officers to take seats in the various chairs in the room.

'Feels good, doesn't it?' He laughed.

The four sitting in front of the desk agreed, still looking around the room.

'We can get settled in immediately, then we need to start their production up again,' Bates informed the gathering. 'I can't see it being too hard – it's just under new management, that's all.'

'When's that spy of yours going to be here to fill us in on the nuts and bolts of this place?' Rollins, sitting back comfortably, asked Bates.

Bates answered slowly, barely concealing his dislike for Rollins. 'I've sent a rider to bring him here. Hopefully, he'll be here before the end of the day. I've lent him some of our spies over the last few weeks, so we should be fully up to speed once we're done.'

'Good. In the meantime, send out some hunting parties,' General Hill said. 'Let's get some good food inside us all. Then we can start planning how we are going to organise everything, gather tributes and men. I want to make our army even stronger. We have our destiny to reach.'

They continued talking for a while more. A junior assistant brought in some wine from the General's personal stock, which was enjoyed as they took their time deliberating on the events of the last few days.

As evening drew in, the kitchens were fully up and running. The hunters had caught a good amount of meat, which was being cooked up, and throughout the complex spirits were high. The barracks had been taken over, although there wasn't enough room for all the soldiers and the supporting workers. A number of tents had been pitched for the moment, with promises made to take over some of the buildings in the town the next day.

After hungrily eating a well-cooked meal, Hill and Bates were exploring the complex, investigating the structures and surrounding buildings. As they walked, they spoke to some of the men settling in. The soldiers showed their appreciation to the General for such a victory, standing to attention with salutes and cheers everywhere he went.

It was safe to say that both Hill and Bates were somewhat overawed by the size and standard of the facilities. The Bowles family had created something special here. What puzzled both of them was just how easy it had been to take it all away from them. As they strolled, a junior officer approached, informing them of the arrival of Henry Martgen.

Henry, with his son Godfrey, had been taken into one of the smaller side rooms in the main house. The General arrived to meet them, Bates following closely behind.

'Henry, thank you for coming.' Hill waved his hand as a gesture for them all to take a seat. He called out for an assistant to bring some wine for himself and his guests.

'Of course.' Henry sat on an old sofa, relaxing slightly at the tone of the General. 'How may I be of assistance?'

Bates spoke first. 'You've been extremely helpful so far – the details of Bowles troop numbers and weapons skill you gave us really aided our plans. We appreciate what you've done for us. What we need now is to know where the best farms are, the most livestock, that sort of thing for supply. But first, we want to know everything we can about the state of the territory. What have you seen and heard since the Bowles clan fled?'

Henry took a deep breath. 'Well, Tom Bowles and that sister of his left the day after she arrived back from meeting with you. They went with the remaining rangers and all of the complex staff. That young man you lent me saw them load a hell of a lot of boxes onto their wagons before they left.'

'Only to be expected,' Hill commented.

'It appears that they've headed to the town of Somerton,' Henry continued. 'It's where their largest protein facility is, just by the lectric farm your men took out. They've a small manor house there. I'm guessing that's where they plan to hole up and regroup.'

'I thought they would have fled further than that,' Hill remarked, absentmindedly rubbing one of the scars on his neck. 'No matter. It makes it easier to finish them off at our leisure, I suppose.'

As he was speaking the door opened; a young boy brought in a silver tray with a flagon of wine and expensive glasses. They waited in silence while he served them all drinks before closing the door on his way out.

Henry took a sip of the excellent wine before carrying on with his report, looking slightly more relaxed now. 'They also issued a statement before they left, offering homes and jobs to anyone else who wanted to join them. I am afraid to say quite a few took them up on the offer.'

Bates leant forwards at the news, a worried expression growing on his face. 'How many left with them? More importantly, how many essential workers stayed? Farmers might not be too much trouble to replace but what about the power workers, the ones who know how to run their lectrics?'

Henry was hesitant. 'I'm not exactly sure at the moment. I've sent the men you supplied to investigate these specific areas.'

'I'm sure it will only be a temporary blip,' Godfrey butted in. 'Once we know where we are, we can start to plan out what resources need allocating where.'

Bates stared hard at the father and son in front of him.

Henry recovered his composure slightly before continuing. 'I've already taken steps to take over some of the abandoned farms local to here. My workers and I will have them back to normal levels of production within a couple of days. There won't be any issue with these, at least.'

Hill nodded sagely as he took in the information; it was all as he was expecting. 'Good. I will send some of my men to oversee everything soon. You have been a great help, Henry, a true friend of England.'

Henry drained the remaining wine from his glass. After a short discussion about some mundane parts of the local area, Henry thanked everyone and left with his son.

||||||||||||||||||||||||||||||||||||||||||||||||||||||||||||||||||||||||||||||||

Bates stood after Henry and Godfrey had left the room. Excusing himself to the General, he followed them outside.

Catching up, he called Henry's name out loudly.

Henry stopped dead and turned back to see Bates walking towards them; his shoulders sagged slightly.

'I thought you might want to tell me what you didn't want to tell the General.' Iain squared up in front of the older man.

Henry's mouth opened a good few seconds before any noise came out. 'It's not that I withheld information from him, I just wanted to confirm it before I can guarantee it.'

'What information?'

'About how many have left the territory.'

Iain took a small step nearer, only inches away now, looming over the older man. 'And how many do you think have left?'

Henry took a deep breath. 'I think most of the highly skilled labour has gone, all of the traders have moved out, a hell of a lot of livestock was taken with them, too. A good percentage of the farmers stayed. They didn't want to leave their land, you see.'

Godfrey continued with more bad news. 'From what I've heard, they took most of the lectrics, just leaving the panes which are useless on their own. I think some of the Kernow are helping them – that's where they got all the lectrics from in the first place anyway.'

Bates took a small step back, disturbed by what he had heard. 'We expected to have some loss of people and assets, but this sounds like a level we hadn't anticipated. We need that lectric power. It gives us the taxes, not farms. Damn. Lectric will drive the General's next stage, allowing our allies to access it, not our rivals.'

Henry stuttered. 'I'm sorry.'

'No wonder you didn't want to tell him, God knows what he will say when he finds out. And it's damn well not going to be from me. This is your mess.' Snorting at the two of them, he stormed back to the house without another word. Stamping back through the doors, he was muttering under his breath. 'And I'm not going to tell him either, not until I can blame somebody else. I'm not going to lose any favour because of this.'

Seeing Rollins and Jarek talking in the entrance hall, he called for them to follow him. He knocked and they entered Hill's office.

Iain exuded calm. 'I'm not sure how much use that Martgen will be. Didn't seem to know much about what was going on. He's had five of my best spies for long enough now.'

Hill looked at his second for a while. 'Well, go and find them and talk to them yourself. That man is a means to an end, that's all. For the moment he's useful. When he stops being useful, kill him.'

'Just don't want him misleading you, that's all.'

The General stood behind the desk, his fists balled up, and leant on it. 'Since when have you given a damn about what someone does? Just sort it out, yes?' His temper was starting to rise.

'Of course. Apologies.'

Hill seemed to take the acquiescence of his deputy as a sign of his loyalty. He waved it away benevolently with a flick of his wrist before sitting back down in his chair, his anger subdued. 'No harm done. Now what other news have we got?'

'I think we should start with sending some of the troops to the town and neighbourhood,' Jarek proposed. 'Let's make some examples of the locals straight away, make sure everyone knows who's in charge. We need food for the next few days anyway. Why don't we impose taxes immediately? We start to take a proportion of the food from farms, say a third or so. Anyone who resists is quickly dealt with, with extreme prejudice. That should send them all a message.'

'I'm not sure that's the best way to go initially,' Iain said. 'Maybe we should start a little less forcefully. We don't want to see any more people leave to follow the Bowles family.'

'What do you think, Rollins?' asked the General, ignoring Iain and annoying him no end.

'We need to start as we mean to continue. We do need food initially, so we do need to start collecting it as tax.' The tactician answered slowly and carefully, as was his way. 'And anyone who disagrees with us needs to know that won't be accepted.'

'Of course, I agree with that. I just think we need to be a little more circumspect to begin with, that's all. We don't want to lose any more people.'

Hill leant back. 'You're both right, as it goes. We need food and provisions, so let's start organising how to bring those in from our new territory. And we will be sending a strong message to those who resist us. But we won't be taking it out on the farmers or workers themselves.'

The three looked quizzically at Hill.

'We need to send a message without harming our workforce. So, leave them be, but if you meet resistance, there are other things we need.' Hill had a contemptuous look in his eyes as he spoke. 'We need daughters to entertain the troops. Sons to join the Army. I will leave it to your discretion, then, Iain, but get it done.'

Bates nodded, accepting the order. 'Very good, sir. Jarek, let's send out some teams. Each one to have a wagon and driver, a couple of mounted soldiers and some foot soldiers. Get each one to take some workers to carry and load the wagons. That should do it.'

'Yes, sir. I'll have the supplies flowing in by the morning.'

The three saluted and left the room.

TWENTY-TWO

Josh, Nolan and Eddie had struggled hard through the muddy conditions. They had somehow managed to keep up a reasonable pace over the landscape for most of the previous day, always keeping away from any populated areas to avoid any unnecessary dangers. They still didn't know exactly how far towards the centre of the territory the Army had penetrated.

Eddie had held the two others back a little; he was nowhere near as able as the two of them. But Josh didn't begrudge him being with them. He often reassured him when he apologised for his lack of fitness, which he constantly did.

Once Josh started to recognise parts of the local area, it lifted his spirits no end; he felt that being so near now he could start to make a difference in whatever defence of Chilmark was needed. They felt a renewed purpose but took more care as they got nearer the town.

Nolan had suggested that they didn't approach from the east. It would be more sensible to approach from the north – that way was less populated and less developed with more areas of cover if needed. It would add a few miles onto their trip, but they felt it was worthwhile.

Finally reaching where they had planned to be, not far from the complex, Josh told the others to take a break to rest. They found a secluded area beside a small stream covered by dense trees, ideal for their purpose.

Josh sat down, taking his shoes off, resting his feet in the cool running water. 'We're only a couple of miles away now and we still haven't seen any sign of the Army yet. Are we ahead of them or behind them?'

'Have to be behind them. We've travelled a longer route on foot. They must be on the outskirts of Chilmark by now,' Nolan replied, doing the same as Josh with his feet.

'Do you think that they are preparing to take the complex immediately, then?'

Eddie, who looked exhausted, was lying back against a thick tree trunk. 'I don't think they'll wait – it's not their style. They'll have a plan already and will just attack straight away. They're not ones for subtlety.'

Josh was thinking hard about all the different possibilities. 'You're probably right, so we need to find out for ourselves. We need to get close to see what's happening.'

Eddie gave a small sigh, but Josh had already decided to give the older man a rest.

'Eddie, me and Nolan are going to take a look at the complex. I want you to stay here. No offence, but we will be quicker without you, and we both know the area really well.'

'God, none taken. It makes complete sense. I don't think I've got much more in me right now. Shall I stay here and wait?'

'It's as good a place as any,' Nolan told him, looking around their position. 'When we go, move over towards those overhanging branches and settle in. And don't come out until you hear us again, okay?'

'Got it. Once I'm there I won't want to move, believe me.'

The three of them relaxed for a few more minutes, eating some of the foraged food they had collected during the day and drinking fresh water from the stream beside them.

Feeling as rested as he could be, Josh dried his feet and stretched out his tired muscles. Wanting to be careful, he would allow a good couple of hours or so to reach Chilmark; whether they would be able to reach the complex was another matter. Would they run into the Army at some point?

Eddie crawled into his resting spot and pulled some branches over himself. Bidding him farewell, they headed on their way.

They ran low and hard across the landscape, stopping and starting between various types of cover, the two of them in silence. Josh thought about what they would find on their arrival at their hometown. Keeping a close watch on their surroundings, they still didn't see much activity for the moment.

Josh was eager to find out the state of the complex. He wondered how much resistance the remaining people would give to the Army when they came. Would the General give any quarter? He didn't believe so but couldn't bring himself to think of the consequences. Occasionally he glanced across to Nolan, who was running alongside him with a grim look on his face.

Halfway there, they headed down a thin, overgrown trail. It was covered by small saplings on either side, thickened out with dense brambles growing everywhere. Slowing to a stop, Josh looked at Nolan questioningly. They could hear a woman shouting in the distance, with real venom in her voice, followed quickly by a deathly silence.

They made their way up the path, moving through the hedgerow when there was a small break in the thorny brambles. It took them a few clumsy moments to get through to the other side but when they emerged, they had an excellent view. They crouched, looking down a long clear slope at a farmstead at the bottom.

In front of an old, small brick building they watched as a woman cowered on the ground, a hand to her face, looking up at a man standing above her. His fists were clenched; it was clear that he had hit her to the floor and was more than ready to strike her again. There were a few others standing around them, watching silently as it played out.

They couldn't hear what was being said but the man was giving the woman orders, with the result being the woman started once more to protest loudly. She sat up, remonstrating with her attacker, who leant forwards and punched her viciously once more. It was a clean punch to her temple and she instantly fell unconscious to the ground.

Nolan looked across at Josh. Josh shook his head; not only were they outnumbered but he wanted to know more about what was going on. Nolan settled down, grumbling, his face reddening.

They could tell it was the New English Army. Or at least a few of them. The black shirts of their uniforms were instantly recognisable. As Josh and Nolan watched, men started bringing sacks of grain and bundles of vegetables, loading them onto a wagon. This went on until the wagon was half loaded. The lead soldier had a brief word with one of the men waiting around and signalled to one standing in front of the door of the house.

He opened the door; two young boys and an older girl ran to the woman, still lying on the floor, not moving. The daughter held her mother's head, stroking her hair as she started to come back to consciousness. Slowly sitting up, still dazed, she looked at their home where two men were bringing out her husband, arms tied behind his back.

They brought him to the soldier in charge, pushing him to his knees. Josh winced inside, thinking the man was about to be murdered in front of his young family. But the soldier appeared to merely spend a few minutes telling him something, before turning and signalling for his troops to move out. The captive man looked at the ground for the whole speech.

Josh breathed a sigh of relief that the family had been spared. But before he could relax fully, he watched as the soldiers walked over to the daughter. They both leant down towards her as she was comforting her mother, grabbing her by the arms and dragging her away towards the slowly moving wagon. She was lifted up and thrown into the back of the cart. The two soldiers then walked behind it, glancing round furtively to make sure they weren't followed.

The two boys watched with their eyes wide open, crying as they saw their sister manhandled. But the mother pulled them both into her, stopping them from chasing after her. The father, still kneeling, watched submissively as his daughter was taken away.

The soldiers moved out, leaving the family on the ground together.

'Should we go and help?' Nolan asked.

'We could, but there's nothing we can do for them right now. Let's follow the soldiers to find out where they're camped. We can do more good that way.' Josh looked at the family one more time. 'This is probably happening in other places as well.'

They crawled along the hedgerow, to follow the wagon and troops.

Keeping a good distance away, the two of them watched the wagon as it rolled along a wide-open road. They didn't appear to be in any rush to get to where they were heading.

They followed them for about a mile, always keeping their guard in case they ran into any more of the Army. As the wagon headed over a small rise, Josh took hold of Nolan's arm, gesturing for him to follow. They moved to an overgrown briar patch, kneeling down to talk.

'This doesn't seem right,' Josh said. 'The complex is just over that hill – where is their encampment? I would have thought they would have set up a couple of miles away.'

Nolan looked as confused at Josh; they both came to the same realisation at the same time. The Army must have already taken the complex.

Josh stood up, still careful to keep himself covered by the foliage. 'We need to see the complex. If they're already there, then what's happened to everyone?'

'I don't know. But they might be all over the area, so we need to be as careful as we can getting in close.'

'Agreed. If we can get around to the west of the complex, we can approach through the cornfields. Those haven't been cut down yet so might allow us a bit of cover. There's a good view that way with no roads or buildings. We can get pretty close if we're careful.'

Knowing the area as well as they did, it was easy to make their way through the more overgrown areas of the countryside. They had already managed to travel for quite a way before seeing any more signs of life.

Hiding behind an old collapsed barn just to the side of a large mill pond, they watched another wagon and soldiers steadily making their way in the direction of the complex. The cart was heavily loaded as it rolled noisily along the dusty road.

Josh could feel his anger rising. It was clear that the General had already started to loot the territory. Taking some deep breaths before setting off again, he was determined to channel his anger against the Army somehow.

By the time they had reached the cornfields, evening was approaching. Clouds were moving slowly in the sky; the shadows formed made Josh feel slightly less vulnerable.

Ahead of them, they could see the roof of the main building, with its supporting outbuildings in the background, but at this distance nothing more. Keeping low and moving as quietly as they could, they made their way closer. The corn only reached to their necks, so it wasn't a comfortable way of walking.

What normally would have been an easy stroll took them almost half an hour. Their legs were cramping as they were having to keep so low, making them stop repeatedly for small rests. Finally, they reached one of the small drainage ditches running through the fields, allowing them to stand almost upright with a clear view of the house and its surroundings. What they saw left Josh speechless.

All around the house were New English Army soldiers. Some were resting, some were issuing orders to the support workers. Wagons were clumsily scattered around the grounds, with their cargo of sacks and boxes strewn everywhere. Workers were carrying loads towards the house and buildings they were now claiming as their own.

Sitting down in the damp ditch, Josh put his head in his hands. Nolan slumped backwards against the small bank. Neither had words to say.

Needing to look again, Josh stood. He was determined to dispassionately view the scene in front of him. The buildings and grounds looked the same as when he had left them. There didn't appear to be any damage to the area at all, not even smashed windows. More importantly, he couldn't see any bodies lying around. It made him wonder how much resistance there had been when the Army had rolled in and taken it.

Josh recognised a large man as he walked into view. He was issuing orders to a younger soldier. He wandered slowly around, the junior taking notes furiously. With a wave of his hand he dismissed the assistant, then stood there without moving as he stared out over the fields.

Josh lowered himself slightly out of instinct. He was sure he couldn't be seen but he didn't want to take the risk. For a minute, he observed the man he had seen after the disastrous battle. It appeared that they were looking directly at each other. The man turned away, strolling back in the direction he had come from. Josh quietly breathed out, realising he had been holding his breath for what seemed like ages, before sitting back down to speak to Nolan.

'I … I can't believe it; they've taken it already.' Josh was distraught.

Nolan shook his head at the words, covering his face with his hands as he lay there.

'I can't see any signs of fighting either. It all looks clean. Untouched even.' Josh was quiet. 'What happened here? I can't believe they didn't try to make a final stand at least.'

'Maybe they left when Leila returned?'

'Maybe. I just don't think that's likely. Surely they wouldn't have given up their home that easily?'

Josh sat back, his mind wandering to all his friends who lived, had lived, here. He pictured Anne in his mind, someone he wished he had had time to get to know more. What had happened to her? How would he be able to find out if she was still alive? He didn't know how he would answer those questions.

Nolan stood, taking a longer look at the complex, trying to glean anything further from what they were looking at. They moved across the field to get a different view, but there were no other signs they could find to change their initial thoughts.

They made their way back through the fields, night fast approaching. No words passed between them for some time as they made their way back to Eddie.

Eddie was fast asleep when they arrived; Josh gently shook his shoulder to wake him. He sat up quickly, taking a moment to realise where he was.

'So, did you find them?' he asked, rubbing his eyes.

'Yeah, we damn well found them all right,' Nolan exploded. 'They've already taken the complex – they're settling in as we speak.'

Eddie gave a long, deep groan. 'I'm so sorry to hear that.' He was quiet as he extracted himself from his temporary sleeping area, standing and stretching his back once he was out. The three of them stood in the moonlight, waiting for someone else to speak.

'So, what now? Where do we head from here?' Eddie asked his two companions.

Josh looked over. 'There's nothing we can do here right now. We need to find somewhere to rest, try to find some allies. I hope they've come as far west as they're going to for now, so let's keep heading in that direction. There's a farming community that way I know; hopefully, they won't have been touched yet.'

'Okay, it's a plan. Lead the way, guys. I won't hold you back any more now I'm rested.' He put on his tunic, buttoning it right up to his neck to keep the chill of the night away.

Nolan took the lead, the three of them gently jogging along in single file through the countryside, with Eddie keeping up with the pace. Josh was further behind, still close enough to hear any directions from the two ahead, but wanting to have his own space around him.

Over the next few hours they ran and walked silently, trekking across the countryside, occasionally pausing to get their bearings.

Deep into the night, Nolan called a halt to their journey. He motioned to Josh to approach. He needed his friend to take over and lead the way now, not knowing the place they were going to.

Josh took the lead, guiding them through the night. He knew he wasn't any help to anyone when he was moping at the rear, so he tried hard to force himself to focus on the task at hand. They were tired, hungry and feeling very downbeat right now, but they had to keep going.

They stopped as they came through a treeline. In the moonlight, they could make out a farm over the other side of the slope. There were no lights on and from where they were nothing looked too much out of place. Deciding the risk was minimal, they made their way through the orchards.

Having reached the front of the farm, Josh bounded onto the wooden porch and firmly knocked on the door. After hearing nothing immediately, he banged again a little louder.

'Ben, Ben, are you in?'

A low light came on towards the rear of the house through one of the windows; they heard a voice calling out from inside, telling them to wait just a moment.

The door opened slightly. Josh took a step back to make himself clearly seen in the moonlight. On seeing him, Ben Sanderson quickly threw open the door before hugging him tightly.

'Josh, what are you doing here? Come in, come in.' The old man waved his hands as he spoke.

'I'm here with two friends if that's okay, Ben?'

Ben looked at the two others a few feet away. 'Of course, now quickly inside, all of you.' He hurried them in, before checking no one else was outside. He locked the door before leading them to the kitchen at the rear of the building.

TWENTY-THREE

Leila sank back into a large comfy chair in the corner of Tom's now cluttered office. Stacks of files were piled high against one of the walls, material she wondered whether they would ever need again. Tired, she closed her eyes as she released a long drawn-out sigh. They had all been working non-stop for the last two days. Organising the arrivals from the old territory, while trying to keep track of everyone and everything, had been a huge undertaking. At least now most of the arrivals had been sent to local farms and surrounding villages, with a stream of messengers riding between the various places of sanctuary.

She had sent her brother to bed a few hours ago, to get a little sleep. They were planning to hold a meeting with the Kernow representatives later that morning and she felt it important he was as fresh as possible.

Security was their priority, that much was clear. With the arrival of the Kernow militia the day before, there was at least a feeling that they were temporarily secure from the Army. How long that would last was up for debate.

In the back of her mind Leila was concerned how temporary all this was. With such a large proportion of the territory gone, and the remainder now solely dependent on the Kernow Collective, what was to become of the Bowles family and their holdings? With such a small number of rangers to call on, how could they defend themselves in the long run?

She rubbed her eyes, then face, trying to rid herself of the weariness she felt deep down. She knew that she needed to just focus on each day as it came right now, let the future take care of itself.

Feeling a hand gently shaking her shoulder, she was suddenly startled. It was Claude, standing above her with a cup of hot steaming tea. Leila felt slightly confused, before realising she had fallen asleep.

'I only let you have a couple of hours, Leila,' Claude told her in his soft voice. 'I think you needed it.'

Leila was extremely grateful. 'Thank you, I think I did.' She took the cup with both hands and sipped.

'Can I get you some food? You must be hungry by now.'

'I'll come with you to the kitchen, Claude. I don't want to be a bother,' she said, as she placed the cup on a nearby table.

Claude smiled, helping her up from her chair. 'Nonsense. It's always a pleasure.'

They made their way through the house. A few people were still working, speaking in hushed tones. Reaching the kitchen, she said hello to Sanaa, who was working over one of the huge counters.

William had always managed to make his workers feel like part of his extended family, and with the staff of this house it was no different. Leila was a few years older than Sanaa, but the time Leila had spent here, growing up, made her feel extremely close to Sanaa.

Sanaa waved, smiling broadly in their direction. Her happy demeanour was the perfect antidote to the events of the last few days. With her long brown hair tied up in a messy bun and an apron covered in more flour than appeared to be on the table, she motioned for them to come in.

'Just knocking up some bread for those in the house,' she told them, returning to pounding the dough in front of her. 'The temporary kitchen we've set up in the main barn is hopefully making enough for everyone who stayed around here last night.'

Her grandfather walked over to her and kissed the top of her head tenderly. He then walked to a small wooden door in the corner, opening it to reveal the neat pantry.

He gestured to the opening. 'What can I get you, Leila?'

Leila thanked them both, looking at the shelves in front of her. She was grateful for the food, greedily eating an apple followed by several slices of bread with a rich raspberry jam slathered over them. While eating she wondered how long they would be able to feed all of the people they had brought with them. The harvest had been good this year, but unless they managed to immediately restart production of the protein foods, would that be enough?

The worries of our age, she thought. Food and security. Would they be able to answer both of those questions before someone took them away?

As Leila was eating, Claude helped Sanaa with the bread, loading the baking trays before sliding them noisily into the hot oven in the chimney place. Watching and listening to the gentle laughter between them both, Leila felt a pang of jealousy as she remembered her father doing the same.

Leila thanked them again as they continued baking. The sun was rising through the windows and she wanted to prepare herself for the day. She wandered through the halls of the manor, every step reminding her of much happier times from her youth. Outside, she could see how beautiful the morning was: a warm orange glow rising over the treetops with thin wispy clouds slowly drifting overhead. It looked like it would be a lovely day.

She sauntered across the front lawn, enjoying the cool wind blowing across her face as she heard a sound to her right. It was Cador walking alongside Anne, with Irving hanging back slightly, heading in her direction. Smiling warmly at them, she waited till they reached her before saying good morning.

Cador and Anne stopped, returning her welcome, but Irving was not so forthcoming. With a grunt aimed loosely in her direction, he continued past them all to the house. They watched as he traipsed out of sight.

'What's up with him?' asked Leila.

Anne shook her head slightly. 'He's been like it for a while now. He wanted to know more about the Kernow militia, but they weren't exactly keen to tell him much at all, I'm afraid.'

'Our garrison commander felt he was asking intrusive questions,' Cador said sheepishly. 'I think it's all a little blown out of proportion, if I'm honest. I tried to reassure him, but I might've made it worse.'

Anne chuckled. 'You did come across a little patronising. I don't think Irv is used to being spoken to like that.'

'I'll apologise when I next see him, then. And I'm sure Matthew will want to speak to our commander about it as well.'

'Nonsense. Irv's just used to having all the information available.' Leila took Cador's arm, guiding him towards the house. 'There's bound to be some initial tension between our two groups. It's up to us to smooth that out. I'll speak to him and tell him to let it go.'

Cador looked appreciatively at Leila. 'Thank you. Please make sure he knows I meant him no disrespect.'

Assuring him that she would, she led them towards the house. The activity around was now gathering pace as everyone started out on their duties for the day. The large makeshift camp in the big field to the south was also waking up. Fires had been started and water carriers were beginning to move between the river and the people.

Leila was quiet as they walked alongside each other. The most important meeting of her life was due to take place soon and she hoped they could forge a way through together.

Three Kernow men were wandering through a small secluded wood, looking for any local game they could find. They had travelled hard for the last few days, and though they had been provided with dinner and breakfast at their camp, it was always good to have a bit of extra food. Even though they were all experienced trappers and hunters, they weren't being particularly stealthy.

After a few unsuccessful attempts at catching a particularly tasty-looking rabbit, they gave up and walked on the bank of a stream running alongside them. It wasn't long before they heard a noise not far ahead. Dropping to their knees, they made their way to a point nearby where they could find out what was making the sound.

There were two youngsters fishing on the side of the bank, chatting to each other as they cast their lines into the slow-moving water. From the look of it, it was a good place to catch fish, as they had already caught and laid out two decent-sized fish on the bank. The three of them looked at each other, deciding that they wouldn't mind a part of the action as well.

The men stood up and walked towards the youngsters. Just as they were within talking range, one of the Kernow slipped down the bank, calling out as he fell. The one next to him rushed to his aid, telling him to hold on.

Hearing the sound, the two children spun round. They stood there for a moment, mouths open. At the sound of the second man urging the first to get a move on, they dropped their fishing lines before running fast in the opposite direction.

Having regained his balance out of the slippery mud, the man climbed back up the bank and joined his friends.

'What's wrong with them?' he asked the other two, laughing at what had just happened.

'God knows,' the nearest one replied, a big grin across his face.

'Well, they've left the fish and I'm still hungry.' He leant down, gathering the fish into a cloth pulled from his jacket pocket. Tying a knot in it to make a perfect carrying pouch, he walked back up the bank. 'Let's head back but stop on the way to cook these up.'

The three of them strolled slowly back the way they had come, looking forward to a nice meal along the way.

Anne was waiting quietly outside the manor for Matthew, thinking that they would be soon sitting down with a view to coming up with a plan. Unexpectedly, she saw a group of people hurrying towards the house. As they approached, it was clear that they were unhappy. She stood up, sighing at whatever this latest drama was.

They were next to her in no time at all, with most of the people speaking at the same time. Anne looked at the small throng of people in front of her, raising her palm to gain some sense of order. She recognised a few of them and hoped that they would know she would help if she could.

'One at a time, please,' she yelled at the crowd. They quickly quietened down, with one of the men stepping forwards.

'A couple of our lads were attacked earlier on. It was those Kernow folk, we know it was. Everyone knows it was, and we're outraged! What are you going to do about it?'

'Tommy, isn't it?' Anne asked the man. He confirmed it was before she continued. 'Now, tell me what happened, but calmly, please.'

He told how a band of burly Kernow militia had snuck up on some of their boys while they were out doing a spot of morning fishing. How the lads were terrified as the men charged towards them, screaming and shouting, and the boys had run away in fear.

Anne listened thoughtfully to the story. When he had finished, she took a moment before responding.

'Are either of the boys here now?'

Tommy turned and gestured to a boy to approach. He stood in front of Anne, head down and quiet.

Anne went to one knee. 'What's your name?'

'Alfie,' the boy answered.

'So, Alfie. Is this all true?'

The boy nodded quickly.

'And why do you think it was the Kernow people?' Anne asked him in her even tone.

217

'They were dressed just like the others we saw yesterday. And they had the same swords as well. My uncle is a blacksmith and he teached me about the different types.'

Anne thought for a moment, looking into the boy's eyes. 'Well, I will get this sorted out, I promise you. Okay?'

He nodded again, just managing a quiet thank you at the end.

Standing, Anne eyed the still-angry crowd. 'Tommy, you and Alfie are welcome to come into the house whilst I sort this out. The rest of you can return to your camps. You have my word this will not go unchallenged.'

The crowd slowly dispersed, mumbling as they went. Everyone was riled from this affront by the Kernow people. Leading Alfie and Tommy into the house, she again assured them everything would be worked out. She took them to one of the side rooms, telling them to wait there while she dealt with it and promising to send them food and drink.

Walking through the hallway, she saw that Matthew had arrived with his team. Tom and Leila were just greeting him, with introductions taking place. Joining them, she too welcomed them all before taking Tom and Leila to one side.

Anne recounted the story from the boy. Tom was visibly worried at the thought of having to confront Matthew with it; he didn't want to risk their support at this crucial time. Leila, on the other hand, seemed more than willing to stand up for what she felt was true.

'It's about what's right. If they really have done this, then they aren't the people we want to ally with.' She put her hand on her brother's shoulder. 'And Matthew will want to know one way or the other anyway.'

'Okay, but please be tactful,' Tom pleaded with his sister.

Leila went to Matthew, where she gently took his arm and asked him to have a moment in private with her.

Tom watched as they headed into her private study, the door slowly closing behind them. He turned to Anne. 'This won't mess this all up, will it?' he asked her delicately.

'I'm sure it won't. Well, I hope it won't,' was all she could manage.

After five minutes the door to the study opened. Matthew strode out, marching directly to Cador who was waiting with the other Kernow members. A short, animated discussion then took place, which ended with Cador rushing out of the house.

Anne peered through the window. She watched as he climbed onto his horse at speed, before racing away from the manor.

Matthew approached Tom, now rejoined by Leila. His face was definitely redder than it was before the news had been delivered to him.

'I've sent Cador to the camp to investigate,' he told the three of them. 'If we are responsible for this, I promise you the men who did it will be punished.'

Tom was obviously embarrassed as he spoke. 'I'm sorry we had to bring this news to you, Matthew. I hope we can sort it out.'

'Indeed. So do I. But if this is just a baseless accusation, I myself will not be happy either. Especially, as you know, as we came here to help. I suggest we postpone the planned meeting until Cador returns from our camp.' He bowed slightly before heading outside, followed by his staff.

Tom stood and watched them walk outside. He turned to Leila and Anne, looking worried.

Leila tried to reassure him. 'We'll sort it out, don't worry. Matthew seems a reasonable man. Leave it with him for now,' she said. 'We've got plenty to be getting on with. Let's wait till Cador comes back. Okay?'

Anne spent the next hour pretending to do some work; she suspected everyone else was the same, their minds so focused on what might happen that no one could concentrate on anything else. At the sound of horses approaching, they all rushed to gather just outside the main door. Leila stood next to Matthew, both looking calm with a nervous edge. Having been summoned to the front of the house, the young boy Alfie waited patiently just to one side. His father put a protective arm around him.

A small group of people from the camp had been waiting near the manor, just around the side, where they presumably thought they couldn't be seen. They made their way to near the front of the building as five horse riders approached.

Cador dismounted, telling the others to do the same and wait where they were. His tone was not a content one and he marched towards Matthew and Leila grimly.

'Sir, Leila. I know what happened, and I think we can sort this out,' he stated firmly. He waited for Matthew to give his consent before continuing. Walking back to the horses, he brusquely ordered three of the riders to follow him. 'You three, come here.'

The three followed Cador sheepishly to a few metres in front of the boy and his father, the fourth walking separately over to Matthew. They leant their heads slightly forwards, allowing their long hair to partially cover their faces. Cador walked directly to Alfie, kneeling down when he reached him.

'We owe you an apology, young master,' Cador began. 'But if you will come with me you will also hear an explanation.' He put out his large hand to take the young boy's. Alfie's father nodded, patting him on the back to encourage him.

The mismatched couple walked to the three guilty-looking men. Cador approached the first one, telling him to explain. He, too, now knelt down to Alfie's eye level.

'My name is Elfrick. I owe you and your friend an apology. We meant no harm at all. My colleague here merely stumbled down the bank as you were looking over, and I fear we scared you. I understand how we must have looked to you, but I assure you we meant you no harm. We took your fish as we thought it all quite funny and we were hungry; for that I am truly sorry.'

Anne breathed an audible sigh of relief, seeing Matthew give a wry smile at the same time.

Cador turned to Alfie, speaking so the crowd could hear as well. 'However innocent it may have been, and I assure you it was, it does not excuse their actions, especially as they have admitted taking the fish that Alfie left behind. We have a strict moral code amongst the Kernow and these three have stepped outside that today.'

The crowd muttered in agreement.

Cador now addressed the crowd themselves. 'For the next two days, these three shall work tirelessly in your camp. Cutting wood, making fires – they shall be your workers. We want to show our apologies to you. Hopefully, this will make some amends. And of course, we will give the boy more than enough fish to replace that which was taken from him.' He emphasised the last point. 'We have also brought our pastor with us. She would be most grateful to offer any assistance that she can, spiritual or otherwise.'

The Kernow pastor, a middle-aged kindly-looking woman, stepped forwards. She gave a small bow to the assembled people watching her.

Leila called over one of the farmhands, instructing him to take the three bashful men, who were taking this in good spirits, to the camp to set them up with some work. The Kernow men walked in the direction of the crowd, who appeared to be amused by the whole event now rather than their initial anger. The pastor followed, soon chatting to some of the onlookers as they walked.

Matthew approached Cador, grasping him firmly on both of his arms. 'Thank you, Cador. Well done. I was worried for a minute there, but you handled it beautifully.'

Leila gave him her thanks as well, promising him a fine wine with his meal tonight. She took his arm and walked him to the manor house. They were finally ready to plan the next stage.

TWENTY-FOUR

'WHEN ARE THESE DAMN LIGHTS GOING TO BE WORKING?' General Hill thundered from his bedroom on the first floor, waving his hand over the light plate for the tenth time. Slamming the door behind him, he stormed downstairs.

Hearing the shouts coming from above, and the noise coming down the old wooden stairs, many of the officers on the ground floor quickly left to perform their duties elsewhere.

Unfortunately for Iain he could not follow their lead. Standing to attention as Hill burst into his office, he prepared to have the discussion he was hoping to save till later. 'General, good morning.'

'Is it? I expected to take over this territory and have it running as normal immediately.' Hill's voice had cooled down somewhat from the noise upstairs, but it still had an edge to it. 'I was promised lectric power as soon as we arrived. Where are the lights in the house, Iain? Why don't they work? And what about the communications equipment we've heard so much about?'

Iain had spent the previous night meeting with his spies, listening to their reports. He had listened to the same story over and over again.

His fears about the state of the immediate surrounding area of the territory appeared to be confirmed.

He gathered his strength before laying out the situation for the General. 'It appears that the Bowles family took most of the parts and linking equipment, which run their lectric grid. We're looking into it, but without specialised equipment we can't access the power yet. I'm afraid our guys aren't used to these more, ahhh, sophisticated systems.'

'Then find the ones in charge and get them to make some more,' Hill told him tersely.

Iain sat at the desk, picking up one of the large stacks of papers on the side and making a show of riffling through them. He was trying to buy himself some time before he spoke. Finally, he looked up. 'We're trying to find some way as we speak. But yes, we'll have to make some if we can't find any immediate way to get to the power. It looks like their local system is working okay, as we know that they continued to have power after we took down their relay station. It's just a matter of connecting it all up now. I've got our best men on it as we speak, but they are having to learn a lot as they go. I've also sent out some men to look for the right people who either know more about the system or who can make some parts for us.'

Hill fell into one of the chairs. 'I have spent all my energy making plans and strategies to restore this mighty country, but I need men to back me up. It is my destiny to bring order and how can I do that if I'm being let down? I need that lectric on immediately. If we get these lights going, it shows our men we have completed the next stage of our grand plan. We can then restart the businesses around here, and the tax that, of course, comes with them.'

Iain leant forwards; it was time to lay everything on the table. With both his hands flat on the smooth wooden surface in front of him, he began. 'I don't know how long that will be. Up until now we haven't found anyone who knows about this sort of thing, sir. It appears that everyone local who did know anything went with the Bowles family.'

This was as good a time as any to get everything out in the open. He continued. 'In fact, it appears that a large majority of the locals have left as well. Most of the traders and tradesmen are gone – it only appears that the majority of farmers have stayed.'

He remained in the same position, without moving, as he carefully watched his old friend absorbing everything he had just heard. They had known each other for many years now, but lately Iain had noticed a growing mania in him. This belief in himself as the saviour of England, which had once been merely a way of styling himself, had taken him over completely in recent months. It had grown now into an unshakable confidence in his destiny. Unfortunately, that was making him unpredictable as well.

Hill stood, his eyes seething with anger. Without a word he opened the door, walking through to the large hallway beyond. Iain followed him, as his duty commanded. The others working in the house made way for them, keeping their heads down and making no eye contact. People were all too aware of the General's moods.

Outside, Hill stopped abruptly on the lawn. He looked straight ahead while standing bolt upright. His hands were shaking. Iain remained a few feet behind, waiting patiently. Slowly, Hill brought himself under control, breathing slower with his hands now calm. He turned to look at Iain.

'They will pay for this. I have made a mistake in overestimating the people of this territory. I believed people were hungry for stability and peace, everyone working towards a goal of reuniting this magnificent country of ours.' Although Hill was looking directly at him, Iain could tell the General was really talking to himself. 'I allowed them to make their own choice. I shouldn't have done that. I will take that choice out of their hands from now on.'

He approached Iain, putting his hand firmly on his shoulder. 'Where did they all go to, Iain? I want them all back. I want them all working as they should, for the benefit of our movement.'

'I've sent out scouts and riders to find them already. We will soon know.'

Hill removed his hand, walking round his motionless friend. His eyes seemed distant. 'Good, very good.' He slowly made his way back to the house, pressing his hands together hard.

Iain Bates silently breathed out, realising he had been holding his breath. Watching his old friend walk away, he knew that there would be plenty more bloodshed to come because of this. After a moment gathering his thoughts, he went directly to the barracks.

He knew he had to have some good news soon; it would be down to him to provide some of the answers that were needed. He also knew that he needed some others he could lay some blame on as well, just in case things didn't go as planned.

At the barracks, he saw his deputy lounging under a tree just outside the first wooden building. Smiling to himself, Iain made his way to where he was sitting.

Jarek watched as his boss confidently strode towards him. Most men would have stood and saluted but he merely grinned, giving him a half-hearted salute as he stayed put.

'Got a job for you and some of your boys, Jarek,' Iain told him. 'I need to find out where everyone went when they left here. Ideally anyone who has experience with these damn lectrics.'

Jarek casually stood, brushing the dirt off his tunic and trousers. 'When do you need to know?' he airily asked.

Iain had always allowed Jarek plenty of leeway when it came to the line of command. He recognised his unique talent and made allowances for it, sometimes too much it now seemed. Right now, he was in no mood for his brand of impertinence.

'Immediately,' he barked at the younger man. 'And remember who you are damn well talking to.'

Jarek promptly stood to attention. 'Of course. I'll send out some men straight away, as well as going myself. They most likely went further west, possibly south. They have good relations with the Kernow, don't they?'

Iain confirmed that they did.

'Then west is most likely. I'll head that way myself but send out enough men to cover the whole surroundings.' He waited to be dismissed before rushing into the barracks.

Iain took a seat outside the barracks' main entrance. He sat there with a scowl on his face, observing everyone's movements as they rushed around. Jarek wouldn't need to look over at his boss to know his every move was being watched. Less than half an hour later, scouts had been sent out to all areas, to search out where the Bowles people had headed.

Last to leave was Jarek. He had gathered his gear before leading his horse to where Iain was still sitting. 'Sir, hopefully we should have news within a day or so. With all our scouts out, there's no way we can't find them.'

Iain nodded once, a hint less threatening. 'Good. The General knows that many of the people with needed skills have left the area with that Bowles family, and believe me he is not happy about it. He wants them back.'

Understanding spread across Jarek's face. 'Leave it with me, I'll find them.'

Wanting to spend the next few hours keeping well out of the General's way, Iain decided to tour the local town to gain a better understanding of their new surroundings. Information was what he needed, more so than ever now. Especially if he wanted to know who to lay blame onto. He would start at some of the production buildings scattered around the immediate area; it would give him some time to think.

Calling for a couple of guards who were on a break outside of the barracks to follow him, he headed out of the complex's gates and into the old town of Chilmark. It wasn't that he expected any trouble – there were too many soldiers now occupying everything for that to happen – but this place still had a foreign feeling about it, and he wanted to be completely sure of his own safety.

Walking into town, he was aware that the only people around were the Army's own men and its workers. None of the locals had stayed.

He could understand that to a certain extent; they had expected a large number of those closest to the Bowles family to leave with them. But absolutely no one had stayed who lived nearby. It appeared that Henry had been telling him the truth.

Most of the old skills could be replaced easily. They had many men who were proficient in metalwork, leather tanning, and the like. And, of course, the majority of farmers had stayed behind. No, it was the technology people they lacked; they needed men trained in lectrics – how to get it from the panes and windmills scattered all over the countryside. He had been made aware of a couple of men who had some sort of rudimentary skills, but nothing near what they needed. They also needed to find someone with communications skills, replicating the ability of the Kernow to talk over long distances. What a boon that would be to have.

Iain assessed the goings-on all around him. The local inn had already been taken over by the cooking staff, supplied with some of the stores taken from the local farms already. He could hear the sounds of his men relaxing coming from within; he could also hear a few subdued cries from some of the women who had been brought in to entertain them.

He stopped to speak to one of the senior officers, currently organising the takeover of the local buildings and stores, asking how everything was coming along. The officer, a man Iain had trained himself, updated him on its progress. They were aiming to have the majority of places allocated by nightfall, with billets for everyone who needed one.

Well, at least something was going to plan, he thought to himself, before wandering over to one of the workshops. Opening the door to look around, he saw it seemed to be part scavenged materials on one side of the room and a sorting place on the other. One thing of interest to him were the piles upon piles of covered wires scattered over one side of the floor. Behind that were varying sizes of metal and plazt scraps, organised into crates piled high. Maybe this was where they could start repairing the sabotaged lectrics around the complex.

Iain went back over to the organising officer he had left a moment before.

'Something else I can help with, sir?' he asked.

'Why haven't you assigned anyone to that building over there yet?'

The officer looked down at his notes. 'It just looked like a load of scavenged stuff, sir. We've been assigning more important tasks up to now.'

Iain frowned at him. 'Well, I'm making it a priority now. The General wants the power on immediately – that place could be important to us.'

At the mention of the General, the officer stiffened visibly. 'Yes, sir. I'll get it sorted straight away.'

'Who's in charge of trying to get the lectrics back on at the moment?' Bates enquired of the man.

'That's Rees, sir. He's around here somewhere trying to work it all out. I'll send for him at once.'

The officer saluted and approached one of his aides in the square. Iain watched as the message was sent to fetch this Rees. He could see the exact moment the General's name was mentioned, such was the fear he instilled in his men.

Iain looked around the square, inspecting the activity taking place around the town. There were enough guards around to keep the workers on their toes as they occupied the buildings. They would be settled in very soon, then they could plan for the next phase.

He was aware that they needed many more men if their aim of becoming the dominant force in the south of England was to be realised. It would be a priority to ramp up the conscription straight away, but he knew they needed the power on to offer new blood something special. These young men would be seduced by the advances the Army could deliver. Lectric for all – well, at least those loyal to the General. Of course, easy access to women wouldn't hurt, either.

Hearing a sound behind him, he turned to see a scrawny man with his grimy hair tied back running towards him. The guards instantly took a step forwards, raising their weapons at the oncoming male. Iain waited till he stopped in front of them, panting a little after his run over.

'I'm Rees, sir.'

'Put them away.' He waved at the swords. 'This here is one of the most important men around today.' He walked over to Rees, putting a friendly arm around his back and ushering him towards the store with the wires. The guards dropped into step behind them.

Rees struggled to catch his breath as he was swept along. Opening the door before leading him in, Bates turned to face the young man.

'So, I hear you are our lectrical expert, Rees?' He gestured with his hand around the store.

Rees hesitated. 'Um, well I know a bit, sir. My dad was a scavenger and often we messed around with lectrics. We sometimes used to set them up when we found some panes before selling them. I'm quite good at making batteries as well.'

Iain walked over to the pile of wires lying on the floor. He picked up a handful of them before beckoning the young man over and giving them to him. 'And you can use all of this for it?'

'Not all, sir, no. Most of the wires will work with lectrics, but a lot don't. The ones with metal in work fine, but a lot of them don't even seem to have metal running through them. My dad never understood what these clear ones were for, but it's easy to sort out those from the useful ones.' Rees seemed to relax as he spoke.

'Good. So you know what to do, then. The General is keen to restore power to the complex and then further afield. It appears you are the man to do that for us.' Iain spoke while looking around the store, not wanting to look at the man before his response came.

Rees was quiet. They both knew what he was being asked to do. Success would mean a position of importance in the Army. Failure, however, would mean his death.

'I will try my best, sir. It's not going to be easy, though. I haven't got that much experience with larger systems.'

Iain turned to look into his eyes. 'It needs to be done, Rees. I don't need to tell you how important it is to the General.' He watched as the younger man showed he truly understood what was being said. After pausing to allow it to sink in, he smiled benevolently to reassure him. 'You will report directly to me. If you need more resources, you will have them. Pick some men to help you. I will assign you your own guard as well to make sure you have complete freedom to come up with the solution.'

Rees saluted. 'Thank you, sir. I will do my best.'

Iain headed to the door. 'Then let's hope that's good enough,' he said menacingly, without looking back.

Once outside, he told the guard what had been decided; the guard headed inside to speak to Rees.

He could tell the General some positive news now at least; whether or not it worked was a different matter. He now had someone else to blame. Feeling much better about the whole situation, he wandered back to the complex.

TWENTY-FIVE

Josh waited just outside the large farmstead, drinking down a large mug of tea. Closing his eyes for a second, he felt the cool morning air on his face bringing a welcome moment of calm after the events of the last few days. Although he had slept well since his arrival, albeit for a short time, he felt the fatigue deep inside him still.

Although arriving at the Sanderson Farm late in the night, they were welcomed immediately by Ben. Seeing how hungry and tired they all were, Ben had brought out some bread and jam for them to quickly eat before ordering them to get a few hours' sleep. They had gratefully agreed to wake early to discuss everything they knew; there was simply no point doing it late at night with the state they all were in.

Josh could hear the others arriving in the kitchen. He drained his drink and headed back inside. Ben's wife, Kay, stood near the table sorting through the clothes they had been wearing when they arrived last night. Before they slept, they had dumped them in a pile on the floor of the kitchen. Seeing the state of the clothes when they arrived, she had found some of their son's old things for them to wear instead.

She smiled at Josh as he re-entered the kitchen. 'I'm going to give these a wash and see if I can save them at all, but it doesn't look good.'

'Thank you, Kay. Although we might be gone before you've had a chance.'

'No problem. I can always keep them for you.'

Nolan walked in with Ben, gossiping away like old friends. Ben had made it clear that any friend of Josh's was welcome in his home.

Kay hurried round, cutting some of yesterday's bread ready to toast for breakfast. The three men sat down at the table, pouring themselves drinks as they relaxed.

'Should I get Eddie?' asked Nolan.

Josh grinned broadly. 'No, let him sleep. If we need him, we can wake him up in a bit.'

Finishing a large sip of tea, Ben leant forwards on the table, looking serious. 'I'm glad you're here, Josh. Yesterday was so frightening. A group from this so-called army came and took a load of our crop from the harvest.'

'So, you too? We saw them do it to another farm yesterday, only they took away their daughter, as well as the harvest.' Nolan had a pained expression as he recalled the scene.

Kay was horrified. 'Oh my, thank God there's only the two of us here at the moment. So, we got off lightly, then, just losing some crops.'

'Where's the rest of the family?' Josh asked.

'They're down visiting family on the coast. They should be fine down there, thank God. At least for the moment. They were taking a few days away after the first harvest was brought in.'

Josh was relieved at the news. 'I'm sure they will be, and I'm just glad you're both okay.'

Kay leant over Josh's shoulder, placing a plate with some warmed bread and marmalade in front of him. 'What are you doing here, Josh? Why have you come back from Somerton? And in such a state as well.'

Josh was utterly confused. 'Somerton? I haven't been to Somerton for ages, Kay.'

Ben was in the middle of moving a piece of bread to his mouth but paused at Josh's comment. 'Isn't that where everyone went?'

'Where who went?' asked Nolan.

The four of them looked at each other curiously in turn, before Kay broke the silence.

'Well. Before this damn Army arrived, messengers were going around telling everyone who wanted to go, to go to Somerton. Tom and Leila made it clear that they would retreat to there for now and help anyone who wanted to leave before this Hill guy took over the complex.'

Josh and Nolan stared at each other for a moment, before they both sat back in their chairs with huge grins spreading across their faces. Hearing a slight bumping noise from further inside the house, everyone turned to see a still-sleepy Eddie walking into the kitchen, rubbing his eyes.

'That's the best night's sleep I've had for months.' He looked at the two men he had come so far with, smiling broadly at him. 'What's up with you two?'

'We were just wondering the same thing,' remarked Ben.

Josh stood up and walked over to Eddie so he could give him a large pat on the shoulder. He then gave Kay a long, affectionate hug.

'Oh, thank God. It looks like we got it wrong,' Josh told them. 'We thought Tom, Leila and everyone had tried to hold the complex against the Army. But they left before they got there. They've moved to Somerton to regroup for now, by the sound of it.'

Kay smiled in understanding. 'I thought you had gone with them. I didn't realise you didn't know.'

Josh laughed. 'Nope, we've been away for a while. But now we're back and it all doesn't look as bad as it did yesterday.'

Eddie was still standing in the doorway. 'That's fantastic news. Oh, guys, I'm really happy for you, really happy.' He turned to Kay. 'Umm, is there any more tea or toast there?'

Kay laughed and ushered Eddie to the table, preparing him some fresh breakfast with a fresh pot of tea. Josh then proceeded to tell of what they had been up to, since the news came which made William Bowles and the rangers leave the complex to take on this New English Army and General Hill.

Ben sat there listening intently, occasionally interrupting to clarify a point or ask a question. Tears formed in his eyes more than once. Kay continued to fuss around everyone, keeping herself busy during the terrible tale. More than once she stopped what she was doing, covering her open mouth with her hand when she heard some of the more horrific aspects of what had happened.

When they listened to the story of the battle, one Josh had more than a little trouble telling, about how William had died and the slaughter that followed of the rangers, Nolan got up and walked to the window, gazing out silently.

Once Josh had told all they knew, Eddie told his story about the Army. What he had seen and heard over the last year was horrendous, but everyone insisted on him telling them as much as he could. He broke into tears more a few times. As he told of the women the Army took for the soldiers, his voice was no more than a whisper. At the end he couldn't help but apologise for having been a part of the Army, even if it was as a partial captive. Kay gave him a large hug, assuring him that he wasn't to blame for any of it. He didn't look like he believed her.

Finally, Ben brought them up to speed with the events of the last few days in the territory. Filling in the gaps that Josh had been wondering about all morning.

After sitting in silence, Kay was the first to stand, the remains of the breakfast needing to be cleared away. Trying to lift everyone's spirits, she now began talking of preparing sandwiches for lunch. Having spoken for so long, and about such difficult subjects, the men left the kitchen to take a walk outside.

They strolled through the upper orchard.

'They must have had help, someone giving them information about us. They knew how to draw us in after the initial attack. It was far too easy – this was a trap well sprung. They knew when we were coming and how many of us would be facing them.'

'Who would do that, though? And how would anyone gain by doing that?' Nolan asked as they walked across the field.

'That's the question, isn't it? Who would benefit from doing it? I can't quite believe anyone in the territory would benefit from such a change for the worse. Not if they truly knew what this General Hill was like.' Josh stopped at the end of the field, turning back towards the house.

'One thing the General always let everyone know was that he knew things, about people and places around us,' Eddie said ruefully. 'And we knew he had spies amongst us in the workers, people who would get certain benefits from dropping their fellows in it. He must have had spies here as well – it's how he operates. Sorry I don't know any more than that.'

'Not your fault. And that says that he must have had someone on the inside. Thank you.' Josh reassured his new friend.

'Does it matter anyway?' Nolan asked. 'It would be good to know, but it won't change anything now, will it?'

'Maybe not, but someone like that living amongst us is dangerous. We need to find out who it is.'

Over the next few hours, they relaxed as much as they could inside, before eating the lunch set out in front of them. They were finally beginning to feel good again after such comfort and care given to them by Kay.

After lunch they said their farewells to the Sandersons, promising to keep them updated with any news and insisting that if they needed anything at all then they should just let them know. Kay hugged each one of them in turn. When Josh said his goodbyes, she kissed his cheek, urging him to be careful; he had a tear in his eye as he agreed he would.

Ben led them to the outbuildings at the back of the farmstead, where he opened one of the small barns to show them the trap he used to travel around the local area. It wasn't much but it would get them to

Somerton a little quicker than walking, with a little more comfort than they had experienced since escaping the Army.

Josh was reticent to take his main form of transport away from him. However, once Ben had pointed out that there would be a lot less travel around the place for the foreseeable future, he accepted the gift gracefully. They harnessed up the youngest of Ben's three horses and led it up the farm drive before the three of them jumped into the trap and headed west for Somerton.

Their spirits were high, their stomachs were full, and the sun was shining. It was the complete opposite to only a day ago.

Although the ride wasn't comfortable in the least, with some bone-jarring bumps in the road, it felt like a grand way to travel. By late afternoon they had made good time and weren't far away from Somerton.

Passing a couple of hamlets almost at the end of their journey confirmed everything Ben had told them. They saw people all over the area, obviously refugees from the territory who had made their way to safety. There were fields of tents and shelters, different colours of sheeting making a patchwork covering the ground. Though he felt sad at the sight, Josh was pleased at how many had come this far. He became determined to make sure it was only a temporary solution.

After clearing the fields with the people in, they pulled into the narrow drive leading up to Somerton Manor. They rode halfway up before parking the trap to the side of the drive, then made the short walk to the main house. There were a lot of people working, with a few stopping to watch as they walked up the drive.

From around one of the corners Sanaa was leading some of the kitchen assistants towards one of the side doors. She paused for a moment, seeing the three men approaching. Realisation spread across her face and she ran as fast as she could towards Josh, almost leaping at him when she reached him. She threw her arms around him.

'Josh, Josh, oh thank God. They said you had been killed with all the rangers. Oh my God.' Tears started to stream down her cheeks as she held on tight.

'It's good to see you, too, San.' Josh laughed as he felt the bear grip getting stronger. 'We were there, but we're okay.' He managed to push her away, still holding her arms while smiling broadly.

Sanaa abruptly rushed off, shouting she had to let the others know. Nolan and Eddie grinned to each other at the sight. After the events of the last few days, it felt good to be amongst friendly faces.

Within seconds, Leila and Tom were hurtling through the front door.

'Josh!' cried Leila, rushing to him, another tight hug following once they reached him. 'Nolan, you too,' she said as she saw him standing next to them. 'I can't believe you're here, that you're safe.'

Tom was shaking Nolan's hand vigorously, grinning at Josh as he did.

'We got taken after the battle but managed to get away, eventually.' He pulled away from Leila before bringing Tom near and looking sympathetically at the both of them.

'I saw your father fall. He led us so bravely, fighting till the end.' He brushed away a tear. 'We were ambushed by a larger force than we expected. But he led by example till the end – he couldn't have been a better leader. There was nothing I could do, I'm sorry.'

Tom shook his head. 'We know, Josh. He was a great man and a great example to us all. Don't even think about blaming yourself. I know you would have done everything you could.'

Leila, not managing to hold back her own tears, agreed. 'Josh, it would have meant a lot to him for you to be there at the end and even more to be here now. That's what you need to hold on to.'

Josh breathed a small sigh of relief, thankful they were able to welcome him back with such grace. He had wondered how they would feel about him returning alive, not having been able to stop the awful fate that had befallen their father. He heard an exclamation from behind him; turning quickly, he saw Anne rushing towards them.

Reaching him, she stopped a few inches in front of his face, looking him up and down with wide eyes. Before Josh could say anything, she kissed him as she wrapped her arms around him.

Josh looked into her eyes. He went to speak but realised he didn't have anything to say. He pulled her in again, for a softer, gentler kiss. Before long they heard some coughing from the side of them. Looking that way, they saw everyone grinning while watching them. With sheepish grins on their faces, they turned to face the others, firmly holding each other's hands.

After Eddie was introduced, Tom ushered them all into the house, through to his office.

It took them a good couple of hours for both groups to fully understand what the other had been through. Questions had been flying from side to side as they all listened intently to the stories. The quietest moment was when Josh told the story of seeing William Bowles fall in the midst of the battle. They all sat in silence for a long time after he had finished.

Towards the end of the discussion, Alva joined them. She was thrilled that Josh and Nolan had returned to them, listening to their tale with tears in her eyes.

'And that's when we found out from Ben Sanderson about the move to Somerton. I can't say how relieved I was to hear that you had made it here safe and sound.' Josh relaxed back in the chair, taking a large drink as he did.

Leila looked over at Josh. She had stopped crying, but her face was still red and puffy. 'We are due to meet with the Kernow again shortly. We've had a number of meetings with them so far, but we haven't really come up with a plan yet. We've mainly spent the time organising the arrival of the Kernow militia and our own evacuees. I'm sure that the extra information you can supply will be vital to the plans we must come up with.'

'Of course. I'm pretty sure they have someone on our side feeding them information. I can't believe they didn't, not after knowing so much about us.'

Tom stood, running his fingers through his hair. 'We need to work out how to find out, Josh. Worst case the person might still be around us now, still aiding them. If we do come up with a plan, we can't allow it to fall into their hands again.'

Leila agreed. 'Absolutely. But first let's have a break before we meet with the Kernow.' She turned to Nolan and Eddie. 'Let's go and find you some fresh clothes and you can clean yourselves up a bit.'

Eddie looked delighted, having not experienced such kindness for a long time. Everyone filed out of the room, off to tend to their own matters. Josh and Anne decided to go for a walk around the manor's gardens.

They walked in silence to begin with, arm in arm. When they reached an old wooden bench just next to the stream, they sat down to talk.

'When I heard that you weren't coming back, I couldn't believe it,' Anne said as she looked into Josh's eyes. 'It was then that I realised how much I felt for you and how, somehow, I always knew we would get together, but always thought we had all the time in the world.'

Josh nodded. 'I know. It's time to get on with our lives, isn't it, instead of waiting for things to happen to us. After what's happened, who knows how long anyone has.'

Leaning towards each other, they kissed again. The sun was spilling through the trees, with the stream in the background.

As they sat there, together, Anne leant her head onto his shoulder. He wrapped his arm around her as she pulled him in tight. They made the most of a few perfect minutes together. Now they had found each other again, they were determined to ensure a future for themselves.

'What are we going to do?' Anne asked as they headed back.

'I don't know yet. But whatever we do, we'll make sure we win.'

TWENTY-SIX

Buoyed by their total victory over the Bowles family, the New English Army settled into their new hometown. Morale throughout the ranks was high, even amongst the support workers, not normally known for their unwavering allegiance.

The Army had occupied the barracks, pleased that the sleeping quarters were no worse than their last ones and in many cases much better. Although the previous occupants had taken much of the bedding and stores with them, those could be easily replaced in the coming weeks. The settled-in soldiers soon found that with secure roofs, clean running water and a working boiler system, they would be living the finest they had for a long time. One of the worries before the move had been about the standard of their new accommodation; that had now been completely forgotten.

With the news that supplies were already coming in as well, many of the younger soldiers felt that this Army might not be too bad after all. The senior officers had also spread the news that a large influx of young women was expected over the coming weeks. The soldiers knew exactly what this meant.

The workers were spread out a little further. Some – those trusted to be close to the General – were stationed in the complex itself, with the remainder in the surrounding town. The town afforded each worker a decent place to settle, much more than had ever been allowed for them before. But a large number of soldiers were stationed around them, patrolling the area, making it clear that the lowly workers were still property of the Army.

General Hill and his senior officers had taken over the first-floor bedrooms of the main house for themselves. Downstairs was being modified for the Army's needs.

One of the first changes to the building Hill undertook was the creation of a war room, out of the council chamber used by William Bowles before him. Having had the long wall cleared of all its useless paintings, he was creating a large-scale map of the south of England. He was adamant on it being accurate, as it was to be used as the main planning area for his plot to dominate the surrounding territories.

Luckily, their previous headquarters had held many charts and atlases. He had often spent hours poring through these old records when he had free time; now he wanted to be able to see his future kingdom in greater detail. Two young men had been tasked to draw the plan on the wall. They had started to measure out the distances, beginning with the coastline to the south.

Hill wandered in to check on the start of his pet project, casting his eye over the initial markings on the walls. Congratulating himself, and urging the illustrators to accuracy, he was pleased with what he saw.

Iain Bates soon followed, looking at the wall with somewhat less enthusiasm than his boss. 'We've had a good number of scouts back today.' He spoke softly near the men. 'We should sit down with the senior officers to take stock of our position. That will allow us to plan the next stage.'

Hill, still looking at the wall, nodded sagely. 'Indeed, although I already have the next stage all set in my mind, Iain. But I suppose it will be useful for all the officers to have total understanding of my goals.'

'Shall I get everyone in here, or leave these two to their job for now?'

'Get everyone in here. I want our war room to start living up to its name, don't you think?' He hadn't looked away from the embryonic map while he had been speaking.

'Of course. I'll round everyone up and get them to gather here, then.' He left the room, leaving Hill with his thoughts.

Pleased with himself, he spoke informally to the workers. 'You two. Take a break for an hour or so. You are doing fine work.' The two placed their tools to one side carefully, thanking the General before making their way outside.

After admiring the developing drawing, he made his way to the head of the long oval table, running his fingertips along it as he moved. 'This was the seat of the Bowles family, from where they ran all their holdings. It's all ours now and we will run it with an iron fist for the glory of England.'

Iain Bates was talking with Jarek as they walked into the room, the gross bearded man almost the complete opposite of the lithe younger one, the lack of morals the glue that bound them so closely together. Rollins also was discussing matters with his second in command.

The next one in was Bryant, in charge of the support workers and a vicious, unfeeling man. The General himself had handpicked him to oversee the workers and prisoners, recognising that this was someone who would not tolerate any form of dissent from those he oversaw. He had transferred away from the Army to the worker side last winter, quickly excelling at his new task.

The other senior officers soon followed, saluting to the General at the end of the table before taking their seats.

Finally, the quartermaster, Miles, arrived with a case full of papers. He speedily found a seat, spreading many of the papers out around him before cleaning his eyeglasses as he squinted around the room at the others.

When all the officers had sat down, only one half of the huge table was filled.

'Welcome,' the General began, 'to our first war room meeting. We are the heart and soul of the New English Army. The decisions we make here will have consequences for the whole of England in time.'

The officers all banged their fists on the table furiously, joined by Miles attempting to follow their lead. A couple of the nearby officers smirked at the sight of the small man copying them.

'Thank you. Thank you. And I assure you that all of your names will live forever, once we forge ahead with our destiny.' He paused, watching the growing pride on his men's faces. 'But we must first get down to business. I want to hear all of your reports of our position as it stands. I think it would be good to hear from our quartermaster to begin with.' He gestured over to Miles, who was hurriedly arranging his papers in front of him.

'Thank you, General. Well, the move went very well indeed. We have unloaded all of the supplies we brought with us. Indeed, we have already restarted most of the processes which were underway at the old headquarters. Most of the buildings in the town have been assessed and are now occupied by the necessary workers. The guards already have everyone at work and under control.'

Miles hesitated, looking at the General, before continuing. 'The Army is settled into the barracks. It will, of course, need updating from the rangers' needs but we are already planning the necessary changes. I have already discussed these matters with Colonel Rollins in depth. We have plenty of supplies and food at the moment, especially with the tax starting to come in from the territory. I've started to evaluate some of the buildings for a secure local storage facility. It needs to be fairly large, and it will need extra guards once the tax really starts flowing in. It seems that the Bowles family had no suitable storage places here. Apart from a few other minor issues, which I won't bother you with now, I'd say we are in an excellent position for the foreseeable future.' He sat back, wiping a drip of sweat away from his forehead.

The General showed his appreciation to the quartermaster. 'Thank you, Miles. Just as we expected. Keep up the good work.' He turned to Rollins. 'And the Army?'

'Mainly in good health and barracked well. The injured from the fight against Bowles are all recovering well – the facilities here will definitely help on that score. I've issued some promotions to those who showed exceptional leadership during the battle. They are detailed here for your final sign off.' He passed the list to the General.

Hill cast his eye briefly down the names of men recommended for promotion. 'Of course, they fought well. Confirmed.'

Thanking him, Rollins continued. 'We are, however, below our previous strength due to the losses we incurred. We now have less than three hundred trained soldiers or guards. Now, although we have wiped out any resistance from the immediate area, I think it is imperative that our first task should be to increase those numbers. I would like to see a large recruitment drive as soon as possible, conscript anyone who is deemed suitable for us. We need time to train them, of course, but we will need more soldiers for the future.' Rollins sat back to allow others to comment.

The group spent the next half hour discussing the best way to increase their numbers so heavily. A couple of the officers urged caution, advising how difficult it would be to integrate so many so quickly.

After much disagreement from the two sides of the argument, the General raised his hand. 'I agree that we must not dilute the passion and drive our Army has. But it is clear that we need to increase our numbers. Strength is one of our greatest assets, and we must grow stronger and stronger.' He turned to Bates. 'Can we do this quickly, Iain?'

'With care, yes. Once we demonstrate how much their lives will improve, we can. We must give our soldiers the best in everything, something to fight for. There are some ready to be promoted from the support workers already, I believe.'

Bryant offered his agreement on that point. 'There are some worthy younger men, yes. And I think it will do them good to see they can be promoted up to the Army. Something to work hard for will give the rest of them more of a purpose.'

Hill liked the answer. 'Good, then we shall start immediately. Send out your troops, Rollins, bring new blood into our Army. And take a look at those who we think are now ready to make the move internally as well.'

Rollins made some notes on his pad in front of him, thanking Bryant for the suggestion. As he did so, two of the kitchen staff brought in some welcome drinks and food. As soon as the spread had been laid out on one of the side tables, they took a short break before they continued their planning.

Once finished, Hill placed a palm firmly down on the table, looking at the others. 'One of the most important things we need to get sorted out are the lectrics. This is vital to our progress over the coming months. Offering lectrics to our elite will ensure their loyalty. Iain, where are we on this?'

Iain stood and walked to the door leading out into the main hallway. Standing to one side, he theatrically waved his hand over the clear light plate on the wall, flooding the room with light as the lectric flowed. Allowing a moment for those in the room to appreciate the sight, he waved his hand once more to turn off the light. The men sat around the table burst into applause, with Hill sitting back, satisfied, in his seat.

Iain proudly walked back to his chair. 'We've restored the lectric to this house and its surrounding buildings. Our team worked throughout the night with great success. We're currently working to extend this to the town around us, allowing some of the larger production services to be restarted.' He sat down in his chair, looking extremely pleased with himself.

The General leant over to his second in command, grasping his shoulder with a smile. 'Excellent. I knew it would only be a matter of time. Your team has done well, Iain. When do you think we can start sending it further afield?'

'We're not sure yet. The system around here was just about manageable – we don't know what we're dealing with elsewhere yet.'

Hill frowned slightly.

'But my men are on it,' Bates said, 'and we should have some news very soon.'

'Make sure you update me regularly. I want the lectrics working.'

'Of course.'

They moved on to other less important topics over the course of the afternoon, the General's enthusiasm driving them on. Finally, as evening started to fall, the meeting came to an end, allowing the tired officers to set about their duties.

Rees had informed Bates as soon as the lectrics were fixed. He'd finally worked out the linkages to the panes in the early hours, although it took him till the morning to make the necessary repairs.

Iain Bates arrived just as Rees was finishing his stew. Rees looked exhausted.

'Well done on the house lectrics,' Bates told him. 'What else have you found? Can we restart the rest as well?'

'Well, the main building and surrounding structures inside the walls, all these can just about be fed by the panes inside,' Rees explained. 'There's also an ancient mechanical generator as well, run on some form of alcohol by the looks of it, for times when more is needed. But the town appears to have no way of supplying itself. It has to come from somewhere else.'

Bates found himself angry at the news. 'Are you sure?'

'I'm afraid so, yes. There's just not enough supply around here.'

'Right. So, the rest of the lectric must come from that solar farm, west from here. I wasn't expecting that, I must admit. I thought the town would have a secure supply of its own. Dammit.' He turned away to look around the town. 'Can we restore lectrics here without that supply?'

'I'm afraid not, sir. The need's too great and there's just no way to supply that much given what we have here.'

Iain's mood dropped. They had been so sure that the town would have its own lectrics. The plan had been to move in and restart the productions within days; now it looked like only what they had brought with them would be up and running immediately. Without some of the more advanced processes, it would hamper the General's plans no end.

'Is there a way to route some of the lectric from where it is working to the town?'

Rees shook his head. 'I've looked at that. For a start, they're both on completely different systems. Even if it was possible, there wouldn't be enough to run what we want. What we have is fine for the lighting, heating and cooking, but not much help down here.'

'I was afraid of that.' Iain walked away, calling out as he did, 'Come with me, we're going to see the General.'

Rees's eyes went wide. He hurried along with Iain through the town and up to see the General.

Iain left him standing nervously outside as he entered to brief the General. Eventually the door opened, and Rees was summoned inside.

General Hill was standing in the middle of the room, one of his hands rubbing his neck, looking annoyed. Rees approached apprehensively. Bates had taken a step back and watched the young man breathing hard.

When Hill spoke, his voice took on a careful staccato style. 'I hear you can't get the lectric working in the town.'

'No, sir. What we've already restored seems to be about it for now without more supply.' Rees spoke quickly.

Hill glanced over to Iain, growing angrier and angrier. 'You told me the town would have its own supply, did you not?'

Bates now stood at full attention. 'It appears we, I, predicted wrongly, sir. I apologise.'

Hill turned away from both of them, moving to gaze out of the window. He stood there, fists clenched. No one moved.

Still looking out the window, he finally spoke. 'So, what you're saying is that we need that damn solar farm we attacked.'

Bates stiffened even further, expecting the worst. 'It appears that way, yes.'

Hill faced them once more, looking at Rees. 'You may leave.' Rees left the room as quickly as he politely could.

'Dammit, Iain. I thought you were sure they were self-sufficient here.' He appeared to be calming slightly, much to Iain's relief.

'It's what we had been told, and to be frank that's the correct way of doing things. I can't believe they didn't plan it to be.'

Hill turned, thumping the table with his fist. 'So, we need that damn place, then. Well, we shall just go and get it.' He faced his second once more. 'I want plans to get it, Iain. You know how important it is to us. We must have lectric to give away. It will allow us to control the population.'

'Yes, sir.' Iain saluted, then briskly headed out to prepare for their next move, relieved that he had a chance to make amends for his mistake.

TWENTY-SEVEN

ALTHOUGH THEY COULD HAVE HOSTED EVERYONE IN THE LARGE dining room in the manor, Leila had opted to take the meeting outside. It was a beautiful autumnal day, thin wispy clouds occasionally passing overhead. A number of chairs were arranged in a semi-circle by a brook that ran to the side of the house, with small tables holding drinks dotted around.

Josh and Anne arrived first. They both sat to one side of the semi-circle, happy to be together.

He greeted Alva as she arrived with Cador. Josh had noticed how smitten she was with the him. He stood and shook both their hands.

'It's pretty impressive how they've set up their camp so quick, don't you think?' Alva asked Josh.

'They've done well, absolutely.'

Cador agreed proudly. 'Ah, just good organisation, that's all. They're a good bunch – they listen well.'

'I'd love to meet more of them. You must tell me when you're next going there,' Alva blurted out a little too quickly. Josh smiled at the young woman's keenness.

'Well, I'm impressed by your eagerness to learn, my lady,' Cador said with a teasing tone.

Alva blushed a little at the comment.

They were followed by three of the Kernow militia leaders, representing the Kernow Council along with Matthew.

Last of all, Tom led Matthew and Leila out from the house down to the waiting others. Pulling a couple of chairs out of the line, the three of them sat facing everyone. Everyone went quiet, waiting for their leaders to open the proceedings.

Tom was the first to speak up. 'Thank you all for coming. It's a historic meeting, as authorities for both territories are here in one place for the first time in a long time. Whatever we can decide here will have great repercussions on both our lands.'

The Kernow leader smiled kindly at the words. 'Indeed. And as a gesture of goodwill, we have started installing at the manor one of the newer communications systems we brought with us, to work with some of our own more portable ones. It should be up and running pretty quickly. Hopefully we can put it to good use.'

Leila stood, walking around the listening people. 'Thank you, Matthew. Now, we all know what's happened and we all know where we are now. I would like to invite Josh to tell you what he knows about this New English Army. We all know what he has just gone through.'

Leila sat again, inviting Josh to tell his tale. He briefly told of the journey to the battle site, explaining how they had been tricked into a false sense of superiority. It was a sombre tale of how this General Hill knew when and where they would be coming, along with numbers of rangers. Everyone listened intently.

Although he could tell them all he knew about the Army, he wished he knew more about the tactics they used. Unfortunately, all he recalled was his own personal fights against the individual soldiers he had killed. He particularly described how he heard, then saw, a large number of projectiles flying at them before the fighting began but he couldn't explain where they came from. This, in particular, brought sounds of anger from the Kernow.

'So, they were using ranged weapons then? Damn cowards.' Cador grunted.

'Only once at the beginning, but it was a colossal assault against us.' Josh tried not to think back to the moment as best he could. 'We never recovered.'

One of the Kernow leaders showed his anger. 'It's disgusting. Ranged weapons are fine for hunting or target practice but spineless to use in battle. Personal honour requires hand-to-hand fighting. It's the honourable thing to do.'

'They aren't honourable,' Alva told them. 'Not in any way.'

'We've followed this rule for many decades now. It's been that way since after the Chaos,' Matthew offered. 'Ever since those ancient leaders risked others' lives rather than their own by ordering such attacks. But now we know they don't hold such values.'

Josh continued recounting the story. He faltered slightly telling of the loss of William and their ultimately futile attempts to keep fighting. When he told of his capture he once again asked for forgiveness from Leila and Tom, both of whom waved such a request away once more.

Regaining his composure, he began discussing the Army's previous headquarters where he had been taken afterwards. The Kernow people asked many questions about numbers of soldiers and support staff, about their level of technology. It quickly became clear that they had no real knowledge of lectrics, something the Kernow were extremely relieved about.

Josh went into as much detail as he could about the General and his senior officers, how they acted and what he thought they would do in unknown circumstances. He was convinced that while they called themselves an army, it was more a case of everyone looking out for themselves.

What was useful was the description of the convoy the Army used to travel to the complex. It allowed them to fully understand its size and strength. Upon him describing how they held separate the group of hostages to ensure the others' compliance, a few of those listening began to get obviously riled once more.

He mentioned the escape only briefly, spending more time on what he had seen on their way home. They were particularly interested in how he had observed the farm being ransacked for supplies, undoubtedly the way the General would be going about running the territory if he had his way.

Surprise and shock rippled through those listening as he explained about the young girl being taken from the farm, turning to disgust as he explained how women were being taken to be used as playthings by the higher ranks of the Army.

Leila realised that three of the female rangers had been captured along with Josh. 'Josh, our women, were they taken for such a role?'

Josh could only nod his reply, lengthily pausing before continuing.

At the end of his tale, he sat back and let out a long breath, spent from the account. It was a good few minutes before anyone spoke again.

Matthew stood, making his way over to Josh. 'Thank you for that, Josh. The information will be invaluable to us. What you went through was horrific. I can only thank God that you made it home.' He continued as he walked around. 'I think the one thing it shows us is that although it calls itself an army, it is no such thing. The morale and discipline in a real army is not earnt by fear, by hostages, by terror – it is earnt by respect. No, if we can break them apart, they will fold easily. They won't rally around their officers like a genuine army would. They have no underpinning of honour nor respect. Take out their leaders and they are nothing. I'm sure that many would gladly leave if they could.'

'You're right there,' Josh agreed. 'But the General uses the Army as a shield around himself. He won't let himself be apart from it at all. And even with your militia, they still have the numbers, even after the battle.'

'Then we need to find a way to split his shield.' Cador leant forwards, his voice firm. 'Make them use their soldiers in different areas.'

Anne smiled in understanding. 'Yes, draw out a large number of them. If we can split them up, we can take them on.'

'But is there any way we can achieve our goal without much more loss of life?' Tom looked nervous. 'We've already lost so many. Can we really ask our remaining people or even the Kernow to do this? Matthew, you've been more than helpful so far, but our numbers are so low, this would be your decision to make.'

Matthew looked at Cador. 'If we let them be for now, we will be next. Of that I'm sure. Right now, we are the same.'

'Then, thank you. But how do we do it?' Tom asked.

Josh felt a thought forming. 'I've got an idea there.' He paused for a moment. 'We can launch attacks on some of the more noticeable parts of the territory, ones which they'll have to deal with. If we plan the timing right, we can get part of the Army out dealing with them. Ideally, we can pick some targets where we don't have to damage too much either. A few large-scale farms for instance, threaten their supplies.'

'I believe they used to call it guerrilla warfare. From the old records it appeared to be a useful way of attacking a larger force,' Cador told them.

'What about the relay station? Could we lure some of them there? They must have realised by now that most of the lectric comes from there, surely?' Anne asked.

Leila leant forwards in her seat. 'What about this traitor you believe they have in our midst, Josh? If we knew who he was we could feed them some false information.'

'I know, but how do we find out who it is?'

They discussed in depth the landowners, producers and traders. By the end they had narrowed it down to only a few, but still were having trouble believing it could be any of them. It was decided that whoever it was would have remained behind, making the most of their betrayal.

Josh suddenly had an idea. After saying he would be back quickly, he rushed off towards the house.

It wasn't long before he returned, walking alongside a slightly confused Eddie.

Josh presented Eddie to those he hadn't met. 'I'd like to introduce you to Eddie. He helped us escape from the Army. They held him captive for a year. You can trust him, as we did with our lives.' Eddie gave a small, embarrassed bow.

'Eddie,' Josh said. 'Did you know of any spies the Army had in our territory?'

'Not the names, no. It was widely known that the General had an excellent spy network. It was one of his many boasts around the headquarters. But I didn't know any of them by name. Sorry.'

Leila approached. 'Did you ever hear of anyone called Tromas at all?' He was the most likely, they had decided, having been a rival of William for years.

Eddie shook his head. 'No, never.'

'What about Amerston, or Hessat?' Leila started reeling off a list of names out of frustration.

'Wait! That one!' Eddie shouted.

'Which one?'

Eddie paused before looking at her. He frowned while whispering the name again and again. 'Martgen, I've heard the name, I'm sure.' He hesitated. 'Yes, there was a junior officer with that name. Bit of a creep, if you ask me ... Godfrey! That's him. Godfrey Martgen. Tall man he was.'

'Henry had a son called Godfrey,' Leila exclaimed. She described him to Eddie. He was nodding furiously as she talked, agreeing with everything she said.

Tom looked aghast at the revelation. 'Henry Martgen! I know he was a bit of a thorn in Dad's side, but would he really betray the territory? Can we be sure he even knew his son was in the Army?'

'Sounds damn likely, doesn't it?' called Cador. 'It's too much of a coincidence not to be.'

Josh stood, placing his hand on Anne's shoulder. 'There's only one way to find out. I'll go to his farm to see what I can find out, feed him all the false information we want. A traitor will always use any good material he has. If it is him, and it works, then we know who led to the downfall of your father. The more I think of it the more it makes sense, but we need to know one way or the other.'

Leila held her brother's arm. 'I can't understand why Henry would do it. But I can't understand why anyone else would do it either. It just seems odd that it sounds like it was his son that Eddie met in the General's service.'

Tom looked over at Josh, pain etched on his face. 'Okay. Find out, Josh. I hope he wasn't involved, but find out for us.'

Josh was determined to dig up the truth. He didn't need any more reason to find out, having more than enough questions in his own mind already. 'I will. Then we need a plan to split up their soldiers. What false information can we pass along? What will make the General divide his troops?'

The group fell silent as they pondered the next step.

'We need to make the General think that the Kernow are making a play to capture a large part of the Bowles territory. Maybe with a view to pushing further east as soon as they can. We can play on the fears that exist, of the Kernow leadership and militia.' Anne looked apologetically at Matthew. 'Sorry, Matthew. We know it's not true.'

Matthew looked unconcerned. 'No, I agree. It will sound believable, I get that.'

'I could tell him that a small group of us have been ordered to search the territory for any friendly help we could get. Maybe even hoping some of the rangers are holed up in places, not knowing what to do,' Josh added.

'Make it known I'm holed up in Somerton with my few remaining loyal rangers,' Tom said. 'That I'd tried to create an alliance with the Kernow but failed. Tell him how we're looking to regain as much of the territory as we can. But make it look hopeless.'

Anne carried the idea further. 'We should say there's about seventy Kernow soldiers here. After talks broke down, Tom was left helpless in his father's summer residence, while the Kernow concentrated their efforts on taking over the solar farm and protein facilities. That's enough to make him bring half of his troops or so, surely.'

'And we are bringing more of our people in a week or so to complete the annexation of the rest of the Bowles territory,' Cador offered. 'If this all gets back to General Hill, surely he would send a large force to beat the Kernow threat to the prize. Allowing us to take back your home as he does.'

Josh listened and agreed. He hoped the General would be keen not to allow them to threaten his new powerbase. It was the best option of splitting the troops, allowing an easier strike on the Bowles complex.

It was agreed that Somerton was fairly safe for the time being. If the plan worked, it would allow their militia and rangers to sweep south-east, ready to attack the complex. They would also maintain a small but visible team at the solar farm to make it look occupied but with orders to withdraw immediately if the scouts saw the Army approaching; they reasoned that if no one was there then presumably no damage would be caused to it.

They would also launch a number of raids on some of the larger farms nearby, drawing out some more of the soldiers, leaving the homes intact but burning a number of the crop stores, making the Army nervous about their own stomachs for once.

By the end of the meeting everyone agreed with the plan, but Leila had a final question. 'What happens if Henry Martgen isn't the traitor and he relays none of this information?'

Josh thought for a moment. 'Once I've told him everything, I'll stay close by and see what happens. If he is indeed a traitor, then as soon as I leave he will send word. We can also send a scout or two to watch the complex to see if he arrives. If he does then we know. I'll ask Nolan to go. He'll know where to watch from – we've already been there once and got quite close in safety. He can use the same approach.'

'And if he isn't the traitor?' Leila repeated.

'Then I will tell the General myself.'

Everyone gasped, looking at Josh worriedly.

'What on earth do you mean?' Tom asked.

'I've got out already, I'm sure I can get back in again.' He squeezed Anne's hand slightly. 'But let's hope it won't come to that.'

Leila walked over to Josh, looking at both him and Anne. 'Are you sure?'

Josh nodded. 'It's the best shot we've got. I'll be on my own, so I can travel fast. Yes, I'm sure. I think I should get going as soon as possible. The longer we wait, the worse it is for the whole territory.'

Leila gave him a firm hug, kissing his cheek as she pulled away. 'Right, let's get some proper planning done, then, before Josh leaves.'

They all headed into the manor, to Tom and Leila's office. Eddie said his goodbyes to Josh before leaving the group to head back to his tent. Josh and Anne stood close together throughout.

It didn't take too long for a more detailed strategy to come together. Trying to keep it simple was their main goal, with uncomplicated tactics. While Josh would be on his mission to Henry Martgen, they would launch a series of rapid, small attacks to targets around the complex. Not too near, but not too far either, just enough to get some of the soldiers away from the main body of the army. Every little would help when it came to their ultimate confrontation.

Nolan had arrived and was brought up to speed with the plan. Knowing exactly where to go to keep an eye on the complex, he assured Josh he would get his part of the plan completed. They agreed that he should take someone with him, just in case anything was to happen on the way.

Alva instantly put her name forward. 'If you'd allow me to go, I would be honoured.'

'Shouldn't it be someone more, umm, experienced?' Tom asked.

Cador stood, walking over to the young woman. 'She's more than capable, I strongly believe that.'

Alva blushed slightly at the kind words, looking around at the watching faces.

'I agree,' Anne added. 'She's proven her worth already. Nolan, are you okay with Alva coming with you?'

'Don't have a problem with it at all, all good with me. Ready, Alva?'

Grinning broadly, she stood to attention. 'Yes, sir.'

Tom was outgunned with all the support for her; a little abashed he looked at Alva. 'Okay then, good luck.'

'Then let's go and plan,' Nolan told Alva. 'Josh, when do you want us there?'

'I reckon about midday tomorrow. I'll travel tonight and hopefully speak to him in the morning. If all goes well, he should want to go there straight away.'

'Good, then we'll get there for the morning and be ready. Good luck.'

Cador looked down at Alva, leant to her ear. 'You be careful out there, you hear me. I don't want anything to happen to you, okay?'

Alva's cheeks reddened a little. She looked up at him before she spoke. 'I will be. I just want to do my part, that's all.'

Cador put his hand on her shoulder. 'Good, now be safe.'

Alva and Nolan left to prepare for the trip, promising to be extremely careful as they travelled.

After checking that everyone was satisfied with all they had planned, Josh said his farewells. He headed out of the room, then building, on his way to the stables with Anne.

Anne was the first to speak. 'Be careful. I couldn't bear losing you now.'

'I will be, I promise. I'll be back before you know it.'

They looked into each other's eyes for a long while, smiling as they did. Eventually, Anne placed her arms on Josh's shoulders, wrapping herself around him, giving him a long, lingering kiss. He held her firmly as he kissed her in return.

After one final hug, Josh mounted his horse and headed down the lane. Anne watched him leave before she headed back to the others to begin the task of sending out their attack units.

TWENTY-EIGHT

JOSH HEADED SOUTH FOR A WHILE, AIMING TO SWEEP FAR around the occupied complex at Chilmark. He needed to avoid its immediate surroundings, where the Army looked to be in control. For large swathes of his journey, it was possible to race as fast as his horse would allow, the open landscape affording him such a bonus. Although the rains had brought an abundance of water recently, the ground was still fairly firm underfoot.

A few times he saw squads of soldiers ahead of him, never more than a few men on horseback accompanied by a wagon. It was the same scene they had come across the other day, being played out across the local areas of the territory. This needed to be stopped before it affected too many people. Managing to stay well away from them each time, he made good progress towards his destination.

As he rode, he wondered how long the Army would stay around the complex and its town. They had only just settled in and so surely wouldn't be thinking of occupying the further away areas yet. If they took their time, it might just buy them the time they needed.

He continued to ride right until the darkness began to envelop him so much that it was unsafe to travel any further on horseback. The clouds above had covered what little moonlight there was and the Martgen ranch was not more than a few miles away. He found a small paddock to leave his horse in. He took off its bridle and saddle, and secreted them under a patch of long grass covering the end of the field. Then he secured the old wooden gate and headed off on foot.

It took him well into the early hours to reach the outskirts of the Martgen land. He saw no one as he made his way through the trees, but visibility was so poor he had to be careful not to trip. Tired, he reached a good position where he could view Henry's home. He settled down for some food and to grab some sleep; he wanted to be sharp when he had the conversation.

Relaxing as best he could at the base of a large oak tree, he closed his eyes for a moment.

He opened them what felt like only a second later, but the sunrise was already throwing its first rays over the land. He had been asleep for a while, although his body certainly didn't feel like it.

Stretching, he rose from the damp floor, prepared to meet Henry. Keeping an eye out as he approached the door, Josh couldn't see anything out of the ordinary. He wasn't sure what he was expecting to see – the Army troops hanging around? Probably not, but he knew that if Henry was indeed the traitor then he had to be aware of everything.

He leapt up the few steps to the wooden porch surrounding the ranch and knocked rapidly on the front door. He wanted to look like he was trying to get inside quickly, stealing hurried glances over his shoulder as he waited.

After knocking a few more times, he finally heard steps inside. Hearing the bolts slide, he took a step back. It swung open outwardly revealing Henry Martgen standing there, still wearing his nightclothes. Josh watched as initial astonishment flickered briefly across the older man's face, before quickly being replaced by an expression of seeming concern. Looking over Josh's shoulder at his grounds, Henry hurried him in.

'Josh, my lad, thank goodness you're okay,' he managed to stammer out, trying to regain his composure. 'Welcome, welcome. I thought you had suffered the same as all the other rangers. But I'm glad you're alive, welcome.'

Henry closed the front door, relocking it fully behind him. Then he led Josh through to the kitchen, offering him a seat at the table. Henry cleared up the remains of the previous night's entertaining left at the table before he sat down opposite Josh, ready to talk.

Josh leant back, showing how relaxed he was now, being with a friendly face. He recounted his tale of recent events, describing the battle without many details. When it came to after the battle, he left out the fact he had been taken by the Army; he didn't want to imply any knowledge of it whatsoever. He explained how he had been knocked out early on in the fighting, only coming around much later, after everyone had either died or left.

Henry listened politely to how he then made his way back to the complex, before heading off to Somerton with the rest of them. But when Josh started talking of when the Kernow arrived, Henry appeared to show much more intense interest.

'And I don't think there's any way forward with them now. They've made it clear they want the solar facility, and they're going to take it whether we like it or not. They know that Tom isn't in any position to deny them anything.'

Henry listened intently. 'We all knew they were never to be trusted – people with a history like that do not change their ways. And what is Tom going to do about their ultimatum?'

'Honestly, there's not a lot he can do now. Me and a few others volunteered to go and speak to our friends, to find out what support we have left in the territory.' Josh looked hopefully across the table.

Henry gave a dry smile. 'Well, I support Tom, of course I do. But we have no men to speak of other than farmhands. And I haven't heard of any of our rangers since the battle. But whatever I can give, I will give freely.'

'Your support will mean a lot to Tom, I'm sure. We're nowhere near being able to fight either the Army or the Kernow. At the moment, everyone is still reeling from the death of William. All we can hope right now is to defend Somerton Manor. I'll keep looking for any support we can find. The best hope is that although the Kernow take the west, we can somehow rally to defeat this general in the future and take back the rest of our lands. I'll tell Tom that we can count on you then.'

'Of course. Where will you go next?' Henry asked.

'South. I'm going to try and reach the algae farms. There's a few of us left. We just need to work out how to rally together after everything that's happened.' Josh emphasised the fatigue in his voice as he spoke.

Henry moved over to the stove, pouring a warm drink. 'I wish you well. If I have any news that will help, I will be sure to send it to Tom.'

Josh gratefully accepted the drink placed in front of him. 'Thank you, Henry.' He watched closely as Henry carried on clearing up near the sink.

'So, how many of the damn Kernow are at the solar farm?' Henry asked.

Was Josh reading too much into it or had Henry asked that trying to be a little too casual? Now was the time to play along and see if their fears were justified.

'At the moment? About seventy or so.' He pretended to be crestfallen, running his hands through his hair. 'Nothing to us normally, but with our rangers so few, more than enough to keep us at bay.'

'And what do you know of what's coming?' Henry asked quickly.

Josh was now becoming more and more convinced of Henry's involvement with the Army. His inquisitive demeanour combined with the way he had steered the conversation around to here pointed to it. 'We pretty much know exactly. Tom had a kind of showdown with their leadership. It all devolved into a huge slanging match, where they said they were expecting about another hundred to arrive in a week's time. When they arrive, they will solidify their grip on the area completely.'

Henry paused against the countertop, before looking round once more. 'So that's their goal? To take over the facility and the lands around, then?'

Josh's shoulders slumped. 'It looks like it, yeah. Leaving Tom and Leila with the farmlands of the manor and some of the moors to the south of them.'

'I wish I could do more, Josh, I really do. But we're trying to keep our heads down as a family at the moment, to see what this Army does next.'

'Of course. I wouldn't expect anything else yet. Have they been here at all?'

Henry looked around the room. 'No, no, not yet, no. Haven't seen or heard anything yet.'

'Thank God for that. Henry, thank you for your hospitality. I'll pass your kind words on to Tom and Leila.' He rose and the two shook hands.

They walked to the door, Henry wishing him all the best. Josh headed out, turning back to wave his thanks as he reached the lane. He hurried quickly down the track until it curved away and could no longer be seen from the ranch. Doubling back on himself through the surrounding woodlands, he made his way to where he had an excellent view of anyone who would be leaving or arriving.

He needed to see what would happen now. If Henry was involved somehow with the Army, he would get the information to the General as soon as possible. If he didn't, then while he may still be the traitor, it would remain unproven for now.

Josh didn't have to wait for long. It couldn't have been half an hour before he watched Henry walk out the door, heading to the stables across the yard. He reappeared from the stables and proceeded to ride off west at a pace, towards the Army.

It seemed their fears were well founded. There was no other explanation for what was happening; Henry had done everything a guilty man would do. In no doubt whatsoever, Josh began to head back to his horse. By now Nolan would be making his way to the complex, to see if Henry was off to see the General.

Having done his part, he looked forward to heading back to Somerton, particularly to see Anne.

||||||||||||||||||||||||||||||||||||||||||||||||||||||||||||||||||||||||||||

As Henry rode along, he ran through what he had just heard. The information Josh had given him was surely invaluable to General Hill. He knew, from his previous meetings with Iain Bates, one of the main aims of the takeover of the territory was the lectric power the Bowles family had harnessed. If the Kernow did indeed take over the main source of that power, it would not bode well for their ambitions.

With this new information, he could potentially be able to expand his own holdings. But he must play this cleverly. Hill himself was not someone he could overtly push for any favours. It was Iain Bates with whom he must negotiate; the man understood the need for deals and arrangements. They had already agreed to leave his lands alone when they arrived – now it was time to extract some more concrete promises. There were a couple of local fertile farms he had always coveted. Now was the time to offer this information in exchange for those farms.

Exceptionally pleased with himself, he rode westwards as the morning sun warmed his back.

||||||||||||||||||||||||||||||||||||||||||||||||||||||||||||||||||||||||||||

Nolan and Alva had left Somerton at midnight, aiming to use the darkness to their advantage. The ride was uneventful; they reached the outskirts of Chilmark while it was still dark. Having secured the horses, they made their way slowly to the edge of the field where they could keep a watch for Henry in the morning. Nolan stayed awake while Alva caught a couple of hours' sleep.

Once morning came, they were ready to make their way through the field to get a clear view of the complex's entrance. Nolan had already explained where he had watched from previously, so they wouldn't need to talk once underway. He described Henry Martgen for Alva: a short, balding man with thick round eyeglasses which made him quite easy to spot. It would be made easier for them as they had brought one of the Bowles family's opticals, kindly leant to them by Tom for the mission.

As they started to make their way to their vantage point, they suddenly heard a sound coming from the track around the field. Unsure of where exactly it was coming from, they both dived into the undergrowth of a thicket next to them. It wasn't the best cover, but it was the best option available. As they did, they hid a knife each inside their tunics.

From around the curve of the track, they saw two soldiers approaching their position. It was going to be close as they passed nearby. Nolan drew Alva closer to him.

The two men were almost on top of their position, when one of them abruptly stopped. He drew his blade with one hand as he put his other one out to get his companion's attention.

Standing only a few feet away, he called out, 'Hey, what are you doing there?'

Nolan slowly got to his feet, looking sheepish. 'Umm, sorry we were just taking a rest.' He winked at the soldier, smiling as Alva joined them while smoothing down her clothes.

The soldier looked at the two strangers in front of him. 'I don't care what you were doing. How did you get here? This is meant to be a restricted area.'

Nolan put his palms face out in deference. 'Sorry, we didn't know. The name's John. We were just out last night and ended up here.'

The other soldier, blade also out now, cautiously made his way towards Alva. 'What's your name, girl?'

'Maggie, sir,' Alva replied shyly.

'And what were you doing here, then, Maggie?'

'Like John said, we'd been out walking last night and came across this spot.'

As they talked, the first soldier had been looking intently at Nolan. He stood there tilting his head slightly. 'I know you, don't I?'

Nolan held his passive stance. 'Umm, no, I don't think so.'

Suddenly the first soldier shouted at the two of them. 'Get on your knees.' He raised his blade as he issued the command. 'You're one of the scavengers in Clak's outfit!'

Nolan started to kneel, taking his time as he did so. Alva was quickly down, watched uncertainly by her own guard.

'Are you sure?' the man towering over Alva asked.

'Yeah, I haven't seen him since we left, but I'm sure.' He looked down at Nolan, who was on one knee. 'What are you doing here? Tell me.'

Nolan launched himself upwards. With one easy movement he pulled out his knife, and thrust it deep into the soldier's neck. As the blood gushed out all over his arms, he quickly withdrew the knife and turned to where Alva was kneeling.

The second soldier was trying to process what his eyes were seeing. He had a puzzled look, but that quickly changed to determination as he saw his comrade fall to the ground. He grabbed Alva's hair, placing his sword by her collar. Making his stance firm, he looked over at Nolan, now standing covered in blood.

'Drop the knife or I'll kill her right now,' he shouted.

Nolan froze.

'Drop it now!' The soldier was becoming frantic.

Nolan looked at Alva. She nodded as best she could with her hair being held.

Dropping the knife and raising his bloodied hands level to his shoulder, Nolan sighed deeply. The soldier looked satisfied with the result of his command, then pushed Alva heavily to the floor. Alva gave a cry as she collapsed, staying where she fell. She wanted the soldier to think she was a useless girl lying on the floor; with one glance up at him, she realised it was working.

As the soldier advanced slowly towards Nolan, Alva rose and rushed at him from behind. Before the soldier could turn, she had stabbed deeply into his side with her knife. He gave a cry of pain before lashing out with his arm, catching Alva across the face and knocking her backwards.

Taking his opportunity, Nolan picked up his own knife and ran at him. Unfortunately, Alva's knife had only wounded the soldier. Nolan raised his knife ready to strike the fatal blow. It was when he was only a couple of feet away that the wounded man thrust his blade forwards, straight into the oncoming Nolan.

The metal pierced right through his abdomen. Sliding out his back, blood leaking out as it did. Nolan looked down at his death, horror creeping across his face. His last act was to swing his knife arm and plunge it deep into his killer's neck. The two of them stood for a few seconds, before collapsing clumsily together.

Alva scrabbled across the dirt on her hands and knees, rolling the soldier's body away from her friend. She cradled his head in her hands, looking for any signs of life. Running her fingers over his lips, she tried to feel his breath. She shook him gently, pointlessly. As she realised he was gone, her shoulders sagged and her head dropped.

She stayed there for a minute, feeling tears roll down her cheeks. Looking around at the gruesome scene in front of her, she felt alone and helpless. But she had a job to do, an important job. One which Nolan would want her to finish before she got home safely. She braced herself, determined to carry out the role, vowing to honour Nolan by completing it.

Alva worked as quickly as she could, dragging the two soldiers deep into the field. There was a drainage ditch a little way in, which would hide the bodies perfectly. She hauled them by their legs, unbothered by any clumsiness on her part. But when she took Nolan, she took her time, trying to be as respectful as possible. Gathering some of the foliage from the field, she covered them as best she could.

Turning her attention to the track, she looked at the ground covered in patches of blood. She broke a branch off the nearest tree and swept the area, clearing away any signs that remained. In a kind of trance, she made it look as best she could.

When she finished, Alva knelt in front of the temporary grave she had made for her friend. She had been raised a God-fearing girl, so felt it only right that she should say a prayer for the dead. Deciding to say two prayers, a longer and more thoughtful one for Nolan and a curt one for the soldiers, she closed her eyes.

Done, she made her way down through the cornfield to where Nolan had described. Removing the optical from its case, Alva removed the lens cap and powered it up; it was still fully charged. Alva had seen Nolan check it before they left and remembered how he had gone about using it. After a while of fiddling with the zooming controls, she felt she understood it enough. Satisfied, she settled down to wait. Trying hard to concentrate on the task ahead was going to be an almost impossible ask, but she would give it her best shot.

She made herself comfortable, still in shock, as tears flowed down her face.

TWENTY-NINE

SINCE THEIR ARRIVAL, THE NEW ENGLISH ARMY SOLDIERS HAD been enjoying life in their new plush headquarters. The senior officers had held meeting after meeting, hunkered down in the offices downstairs in the main house, splitting their time between celebrating their success and planning their next move.

General Hill had walked amongst his men, praising and thanking them, while irritably urging his leadership team to come up with a plan to get the lectric supply up and running as soon as possible.

Throughout, there was a feeling that the General was on to something; maybe he really was able to subdue all those who resisted him. His latest victory was cementing his reputation, especially with the newer, younger members.

The reports from the scouts about the solar farm contained the news they feared: a large number of people were working in the area, closely watched by what looked like militias on horseback. None of the scouts had been able to get close enough for a full count on the numbers involved, wary of the mounted guards patrolling the area. But it was clear that there was a lot of work being undertaken at the facility, the next place they needed to subdue.

With this information, the discussions between the senior officers centred on whether to strike head on or attempt to draw the armed fighters away and fight them on their ground. Hill favoured the second option; after all, had it not worked with the Bowles rangers so successfully, and indeed at times before that? He liked the opportunity to set up an ambush, drawing his enemy in where his ruthless tactics could be pursued.

The issue that could not easily be resolved was how to draw the enemy out. Subsequently, during the planning sessions, support for the full-on attack was gaining momentum amongst his officers. Hill wasn't pleased by the move away from his preferred method of slaughter and so, not for the first time, called a halt to the proceedings to give himself some time to think.

Allowing himself some space, he opted to take a stroll around the grand gardens of the old Bowles home, admiring the amount of time it must have taken to look after the grounds. He made a mental note to continue keeping the gardens looking so pristine, a break from the stresses of leadership. One of the hardest struggles he suffered from was finding men to achieve his goals, as few were as driven as him to ensure a united England. He increasingly was finding that many did not live up to his needs.

As he walked through the grounds, he rubbed the skin around the scars running down his neck. Although he was used to the constant tightness around them, lately they had felt more tender than normal. He painfully recalled the events when he had been given them, a young boy learning a harsh lesson in life. With a quick shake of his head, he focused on current events; there was no need to spend time worrying about the past.

Stopping at the top of the rear gardens, he saw Jarek approaching him, three soldiers following closely behind. Stopping and standing to attention, they waited for their leader to speak first.

Hill was annoyed at having his relaxing stroll interrupted. 'Jarek, what do you want?'

'We've reports that a number of farms have been attacked and set on fire, General.' The younger man showed no emotion as he talked. 'Three to the north and two to the east.'

Hill breathed in slowly, trying to slow his rising anger. 'Bloody savages. Burning their own people's farms now in response. I can't say I'm not surprised – if they can't have it then damn those who have. That's the mindset of the people I'm dealing with.'

The soldiers in front of him remained impassive.

'We need to send out some armed patrols. It's something we should have done earlier as well as the tax collecting.' He turned away to look at the rolling landscape. 'Jarek, organise some teams to go out there and show ourselves. I don't want to give anyone the impression we are not in charge.'

'Yes, sir. I take it we are to enforce our rule with a suitable show of strength?'

Hill glanced over his shoulder at the young killer and caught his smirk. 'Indeed, I think it's time to put the hammer down a little. Keep these damn people in order for me.'

His peace shattered, Hill started to walk back to the house, only to see Iain hurrying towards him from the gates. With an internal sigh, he recognised that fool Henry Martgen walking alongside him. Straightening himself, he waited calmly until they had reached him.

'General, I think you need to hear what Henry has to say. It's particularly relevant to what we have been discussing over the last day.'

His interest piqued, Hill signalled for Henry to talk. 'I've information about the Kernow militia, and their plans over the next week. I came here as soon as I heard.'

'Go on.' Hill looked curiously at Henry.

'I've had a visit from one of the Bowles family's closest people – Josh, his name is. Apparently, he and a few others are touring the territory trying to find out who's still on their side,' Henry told him earnestly. 'But he also said the Kernow intend to use this opportunity to take over the western lands, now that the Bowles hold on them has gone. He said these Kernow don't seem to know much about your army or think it will be too much of a problem to them. They'll push to the solar farm and stay there, letting you have the rest of the Bowles territory.'

'Did he give you any detail on that?' Hill replied rudely. 'I could have guessed that's what they would plan to do myself.'

'He did. They currently have about sixty or seventy of their militia guarding the solar farm; apparently, that's where they're planning to make their base. Their next move will be to bring another hundred militia within a week or so. That's everything I was told.' Henry sagged slightly as he finished.

'This man, do you believe what he says?' Iain asked sharply.

Henry nodded quickly. 'I do. He was on the Bowles council, one who William looked on as family. Fairly pointless in my estimation, but he is close to the family.'

The three of them stood in silence while the General processed what he had heard. If the Kernow took over that solar facility, with its major source of lectric for the territory, it would throw everything he had worked for into the unknown. They must take it before any more of these brutes could arrive.

Hill smiled graciously as he placed one hand on Henry's shoulder. 'Well done, Henry. Once more you have proved yourself to our vision for England. I will ensure that you are handsomely rewarded for your loyalty.'

Henry gave a small bow of his head. 'Thank you, General. I'm just glad I could be of some use. I do have one small favour I would ask of you?'

'Go on.'

'There are a few farmsteads around my own holdings that would be run better under my control. And of course, you will receive more supplies and taxes from them with increased productivity. With your permission, and support, I could ensure that was the case.' Henry paused hesitantly.

The General gave a small chuckle. 'I think we can manage that. The farms are yours, Henry. Any trouble with the current occupants, let me know. In fact, you can take a few men with you on your return, just to let these farms know I have agreed this.'

'Thank you, General, and of course if I hear anything else, I'll let you know.' Martgen gave a small bow before leaving.

'Iain, we must take that facility immediately,' Hill snapped loudly as he started to head back to his office. 'Maybe that idiot traitor Martgen will be of use to us after all.'

'I think you're right, Noah. Everything he said would fit with what our scouts have seen there. And it would make sense for these Kernow folk to grasp the opportunity of a larger territory for themselves – it's a perfect time with the demise of the Bowles family.'

'We can easily beat their current number, but I don't want to have to attack when they have more men if I can help it. And when we take it, when their reinforcements arrive, we can send them right back again straight away.'

Before entering the building, Hill called over one of the younger soldiers. He gave the order to gather his senior officers. They had to finalise their plans.

Alva let out a long sigh. She had watched the meeting between General Hill, his second in command and the other man through her optical, focused in closely on her target. The balding man fitted Nolan's description perfectly, right down to the small round eyeglasses. Content she had seen what she needed, she sat down to pack everything away ready for the journey home.

Her mind filled with hatred for the man she had just watched talk to General Hill. She came to the conclusion he was worse than anyone in the Army, a traitor to his own people who had actually made a choice to betray his own. She could not understand how someone could do that; he had blood on his hands for everyone who had died because of his actions.

Carefully, she made her way back through the field, pausing as she came to where Nolan's body lay. Promising to come back as soon as she could to give him a proper burial, she continued on her way. The track was clear this time, giving her a clear run back to the horses.

Alva readied her own horse but was unsure of what to do with the other. She needed to ride fast, especially if she saw any patrols along the way. There was no way she could get the other horse to follow her at any speed, so she removed all his tack and opened the old gate to the field. The horse looked unsure as to what was happening, deciding to stay in the small enclosure. Alva was at least satisfied that he could leave if he wanted to.

She set off, retracing the journey they had made earlier. Although she was still suffering from the events of the last few hours, she was determined to get the message back to Somerton. And even more determined that she would make this Henry Martgen pay for his crimes.

|||||||||||||||||||||||||||||||||||||||||||||||||||||||||||||||||||||||||||||||||

Heading to the war room, the General felt energised by this new turn of events. As he walked into the room, he paused to view his masterpiece on the wall.

The first phase of the war room's territorial map had been finished this morning. The illustrators had completed the whole of the south of England, with major towns and places of interest included. The surrounding seas were painted a cool light blue, with an acknowledgement of the French coast right at the bottom. Internally the lands had a light green background, with darker greens for the ever-expanding forests dotted around the landscape. There were some markings for where the old cities would be drawn on, lifeless places no longer inhabited.

There were no identifying marks for any of the territory borders, nor names attached to these areas. The General had given the order for it not to include any such distinguishing marks, such things being temporary in his eyes. What was included were the strategic places relevant to any conflict. Strongholds or militias they had known or heard about, places of extreme importance to the rebuilding of the country. The solar facility at Somerton was one such place.

He was lost in thought, standing there as the others filed in, taking their seats around the table. After a moment, Hill made his own way to his seat at the top. As he did, the room fell silent. He looked around his team, making eye contact with each officer.

'I have it on good authority,' he began theatrically, 'that the Kernow want the lectric supply over at Somerton. They will not have it. There are seventy of them there now and more will be coming to complete their takeover soon. We need it ourselves as part of our grander takeover. I want a plan to take it for ourselves. Immediately.'

Rollins leant forwards, his hands together. 'When will these extra men be coming, sir?'

'Within the week, and maybe a hundred more will arrive. Separately, neither should be a problem. Together it might cause even us a few headaches. We would still win, of course, but why wait? Your thoughts?' Hill sat back in his chair, indicating to the others to talk.

They all agreed quickly about the need to strike as soon as possible. It seemed they had been dealt an excellent piece of information, one which would make their goal easier. The discussion didn't take long – all agreed that it would take around half of the soldiers for the task. They would aim to leave the next day.

Iain, however, expressed his concern about leaving the base they had only just captured with less than half of the troops.

'And who will they have to defend against?' Rollins asked with a hint of amusement in his voice.

'I don't think anyone will come against our headquarters itself. I'm just pointing out that with these new patrols heading out into the territory, it will leave a smaller force than we normally have to defend ourselves.'

The General was unworried. 'As you say, there's no one left to defend against. And there's also the workers — they can always be called upon if needed.'

Iain acquiesced to his leader. 'Of course. Just pointing it out, that's all.'

'Does anyone else have any issues with the plan?' Hill asked the rest of them pointedly.

A few of the others around the table looked uncomfortable. Shaking heads signalled that no one wanted to say anything.

'Excellent. What is our current fighting strength?'

Rollins reeled off the figures. 'There's two hundred and eighty fit men ready to fight, another twenty still recovering from the previous battle against the rangers. Around thirty have been promoted to junior ranks from the workforce in the last couple of days and have already been given some basic training. We've sent forty out patrolling the territory, dealing with the areas where fires had been started.'

'And we've paused the tax-gathering parties for now,' Iain butted in. 'There's more than enough food for the immediate future.'

'Good. Rollins draw up some plans for the attack. I want to know by this evening how we will be doing this. I will be leading the attack, of course. Once we have succeeded, I will return here to continue our important work, leaving a defensive contingent to defend our new lectric supply.' He stood, leaving the room to his lieutenants.

|||||||||||||||||||||||||||||||||||||||||||||||||||||||||||||||||||||||||||||||

Hill was lounging in one of the interior rooms, reading one of his old hardbacked books, its edges bent and the colour faded. He was relaxing underneath a tall standing lectric lamp, which covered the immediate surroundings in bright light. Seeing his second enter, he closed the book before gesturing for him to sit down.

Iain ran through the plan the officers had arrived at, explaining a few of the points in depth. It had been decided they would take one hundred and seventy soldiers, arranged in two battle groups, to take and hold the solar farm. That would leave seventy to defend the new headquarters. They needed to take some prisoners, although ideally not the Kernow men with their savage ways. It would help them continue to restock the support workers.

When he had finished, Hill put the book to one side and sat forwards.

'Sounds good, clean and simple. Let the others know I approve the strategy.'

'Very good, sir.' Iain rose to leave, but Hill stopped him.

'I've been thinking,' Hill added. 'About when we have dealt with this Kernow threat and sent them back to their own territory with their tail between their legs. We could head down to where the rump of the rangers is in hiding with Tom Bowles. There would be plenty of workers with him we could take. It's not far, is it?'

'Not at all, no. It would finish them off once and for all, I agree. And once they're dealt with, there's no reason for everyone to stay there. They will return to where they came from and bring their trades back to their homeland. Good idea, General.'

Hill waved his compliment away; he knew it was an excellent idea already.

THIRTY

W HILE J OSH WAS VISITING H ENRY, THE MANOR AT S OMERTON was a hectic place. Preparations were rapidly being made for the coming attack on the Bowles family home.

Anne had been with Leila and Cador outside, organising scouts and supplies. Taking a moment for a small break, Leila took Anne to a bench for a chat. 'We'll know one way or another soon. Josh can look after himself – he's already proved that.'

Anne shook her head. 'But returning to the Army … I can't even bear to think about what they'll do to him. We know what they're like.'

'Have faith, Anne. Faith that he'll come through for us.'

'I'm trying. It's just too hard right now.'

Leila wrapped her arms around her friend. 'I know.' Her voice betrayed her own anxiety.

Cador wandered over. 'That Josh is one brave man. You should be proud of him.'

'We are, incredibly,' Anne replied, brushing herself down.

'Then let's get ready for his return, yes.' Clapping his hands quietly, he smiled at them.

Leila considered the hulk of a man standing in front of them; he constantly surprised her with his positive approach to life.

She stood, pulling Anne by her hand. 'Absolutely.'

With Cador and Leila walking on either side of Anne, they went back to their work; there was plenty to do.

A few long hours later, Josh came riding up the drive to the manor. Anne ran to where he dismounted. Throwing her arms around him, she gripped him tightly to her.

Josh held Anne, finally allowing himself to relax after his race back. He smirked. 'Glad I'm back, then?'

'Oh, I guess. Hardly noticed you'd gone, to be honest.' She laughed, giving him a quick peck on his lips, before calling a stable hand over to look after the tired horse.

Josh walked with Anne to meet Leila and Cador. 'I fear Henry is involved after all. During the journey back, I replayed our conversation over and over. I'm convinced by his demeanour and the questions he asked that he is the traitor. He left pretty soon afterwards as well, just as we thought he might. We just need to have it confirmed by Nolan.'

They all headed indoors, calling Tom so Josh could explain his reasoning. Tom listened intently as he heard Josh recount the meeting. All they could do now was to wait for Nolan and Alva to either confirm or refute his conclusion.

Tom left to update Matthew. Josh knew he was taking the news of Henry's suspected betrayal badly. It was one thing to be attacked by an outside group, but to have a member of the council shown to be complicit in his father's death was utterly horrifying.

With Anne leaving to continue the preparations, Leila and Josh wandered through to the kitchens. Josh needed some food after his travels. As he ate, they talked of old times together, managing to laugh at some of their exploits from when they were children. Leila told him she welcomed the break from more serious matters. She, too, was distressed by what had happened, even though she hadn't shown it as much as her brother.

As they were tidying up the kitchen, Sanaa and her assistants arrived to start preparing meals for the rest of the residents. Wanting to give her all the room they could, they left and headed back into the manor. Taking a rest in some chairs in the foyer, they were joined by Cador, who looked restless. They settled down to wait.

They didn't have to wait for long.

Hearing a noise, Josh jumped to his feet to look out of the window. He could see Alva arriving. They all rushed outside.

Cador reached Alva first, and stopped as soon as he saw her arms covered in dried blood. He took her hands and began to check her over for any signs of injuries.

Alva pulled her hands away slowly. 'It's not mine. It's Nolan's. A patrol found us as we were about to watch the complex. Nolan killed them both.' She looked down at her blood-stained hands. 'But one, he got Nolan at the same time. Nolan died saving me.'

Cador put his arms around her, allowing Alva to rest her head on his shoulder. 'They will pay for it, I promise you that.'

Josh grabbed one of the young workers who were watching the scene unfold and ordered them to go get Tom and Matthew. He felt utterly bereft at the news. Another friend dead, a good man gone. If he needed any further motivation to rid the land of these murderers, this was it.

Alva had regained her composure a little as Tom and Matthew hurried towards them. Standing a little straighter, she ran her stained red fingers through her hair and brushed away the remaining tears.

Leila made a gesture to the approaching men, making it clear not to be too inquisitive of her right now. She looked into Alva's eyes before asking her to tell them the results of the assignment.

Alva confirmed Henry Martgen's role in the whole affair. As soon as she described him in detail, no one doubted any longer that he was, and had been, feeding the Army all the details they could desire. When she started to retell her story of Nolan, Leila stopped her. She led her away to get her cleaned up.

Tom and Matthew were dismayed to hear of Nolan's death. Yet another body to add to the General's crimes.

Tom, Matthew and Josh went to Tom's office. Now they knew the truth they could act accordingly. Leila and Anne joined them as they sat down; Leila had left Alva in Cador's care.

Tom was the first to speak, angrily. 'That settles it. Henry has indeed been informing to the Army. We must accept that he told them all the details of the ranger's attack on them. They knew everything. All those deaths ... my father's death is on him.'

Leila showed her anger, matching the emotion in her brother's voice. 'There's no way the General can ignore the possibility of losing the solar facility. Without the lectrics it supplies, they can't possibly start the surrounding industries up.'

'Let's pull our militia from the facility, carefully as they may be watching them. We can leave the engineers there for now, letting them know if there's anyone coming – we have communications up and running with them now,' Matthew told them all. 'Let's prepare to launch the assault to regain your home.'

Leila approved. 'We think that's the best way forward, too. What happens if they don't take the bait, though? We can't make a move with the whole Army there, can we?'

'No, I'm sorry. I wish we could, but this does depend on them doing what we think they will.'

'I believe they will go for it, though,' said Josh. 'I don't think the General's pride could take him losing out to anyone. This is too good a chance for him to win again. That's what he lives for.'

'That's all this man thinks about: winning battles. He doesn't care about the people or the future. This must end now.' Tom thumped the table as he spoke, disturbing the glasses scattered on it.

Leila put her hand on his shoulder. 'It will, Tom, it will.'

Anne looked at Tom. 'I will send out as many scouts and trackers as we can muster. As soon as the Army heads out, we will hear about it – then we can make our move.'

Matthew agreed. 'And I will start to bring everyone together. We need to travel quickly once we get the word. As soon as they turn up at the solar facility and it's empty, they're going to realise they've been tricked and head back straight away. But I'm sure we can travel much faster than them. I've already stationed guards around our camp. They are keeping an eye out for any inquisitive scouts the Army has out there. I will send them out further. They'll make sure our route is clear before we go.'

'Let's get going, then. I think this will happen quickly.' Cador had just entered the room, looking ready for a fight. 'This General is a reacting soldier, not a cautious one. We should be ready to go as soon as we can.'

The meeting broke up. This was indeed their best chance of dealing with the New English Army, but more of the people they knew and lived side by side with would die taking that chance.

Josh tagged along with Anne, ostensibly to give her any help he could. But it was also good to spend some more time with her, especially with such a dangerous task approaching. He helped organise the scouts, explaining where to go and what to look out for. By late afternoon fifteen had been sent out, ready to keep a watch on the Army's movements.

Stopping work briefly to grab some food, the two of them ate down by the stream. It was a beautiful, crisp evening.

'Do you think this will work?' asked Anne, as they finished their meal.

'Honestly, I don't know. It stands a good chance if all goes well, if we are reading the General as well as we think we are. If it doesn't, I just can't see how we get a better one.'

Anne looked down at the stream, watching the sinking sun's reflection on the water. 'It will work, it has to.'

Josh put his arm around her, kissing her quickly on her cheek as he did. 'I'm glad we found each other. There's no way I'm going to let this madman take it away.'

After not long enough, one of Anne's deputies came running across the lawns to them. Duty called again, it seemed. Anne kissed Josh goodbye before heading back to the lower field, leaving him to return to the house to see if he could offer any assistance.

When he walked in it was apparent that although everyone was hyped up and ready for action, there was nothing more to do. Messages had been sent and troops were getting ready for action.

Leila stopped as she was passing. 'Hey, you. How's Anne?' she asked with a big grin on her face.

'She's good, thanks.' Josh wondered why his face felt a little hot.

Leila linked her arm through his and led him to her and Tom's office. 'You make a good pair, you know.'

'I hope so. I still can't believe we're an item.'

'It's been obvious for ages how much she likes you. How did you not know?'

Josh was puzzled by the comment. 'Really? Oh.' He shook his head at the thought.

'You're an idiot, that's why.' Leila laughed. 'Always have been.'

Before Josh could respond, they arrived into the room with Tom and Matthew. They waited until everyone was seated before detailing the plan. Josh saw Alva sitting to the side; she had washed off any remains of her earlier combat and was watching events with a blank expression.

Matthew was the first to speak. 'We've pulled back most of our militia from the solar farm. I've scattered scouts around to keep us updated on whatever now happens there. Our engineers have set up the field comms unit a couple of miles to the north of it, so we have instant updates sent here if anything happens we need to know about. Some of the older technicians there have withdrawn already – they're not fighters so wouldn't be of any use in the upcoming attack. The ones remaining will hurry out of there when we tell them, so shouldn't be in any danger.'

'Thank you, Matthew,' Leila said. 'Anne, where are we on our scouts?'

'All sent out,' Anne answered. 'I've arranged them between here and Chilmark as agreed, all round the complex. And also along the Army's expected route just in case any turn back for whatever reason.'

'How many rangers have we got ready?' Tom asked Anne.

'Thirty or so. But half of those aren't exactly the most experienced we've ever had.'

'Matthew,' Tom said, 'when we launch our attack, it should be me leading it. I need to be seen to be the one taking back the complex, our family home.'

Cador started to voice an objection, but Matthew stopped him. The Kernow leader paused before answering. 'I understand where you're coming from, Tom. I know how it would look if it appeared that we'd just given it to you after we took the place. But our men and women only take orders from our own leadership.'

Josh leant forwards, elbows on his knees. 'Why don't you make it clear that you both are together in the lead? After all, it's clear this is a joint effort. That way Tom leads as well as you. If all goes well it's going to be clear how much you helped us, and how close we are going to become as territories anyway.'

Matthew smiled at the suggestion. 'Good with me. Tom?'

'Yes, a joint campaign. But I must retain the final command.'

'It depends on what that command is, though,' Cador interrupted. 'I won't send our people to do anything foolish.'

Tom rose to his feet. 'And what's that meant to mean?' He glared at Cador, waiting for an answer.

After rising slowly, Cador walked nearer to Tom. 'Just that I don't know how you will lead. I worry that you'll be too emotional to be able to focus on the bigger picture. So, to give you complete command would be a reckless act.'

'Too emotional? Damn right I'm emotional,' Tom bellowed. 'They killed my father and took my lands – who wouldn't be emotional?'

Cador lifted his open palms to his chest. 'I rest my case.'

Leila and Matthew now both stood next to their counterparts. Neither of the men wanted to give any ground. The four of them started to talk over each other; voices were raised with no one managing to make themselves heard above the din.

There was a loud crash. Everyone stopped talking, looking towards the corner of the room. Alva was standing amongst the remains of a glass vase, now shattered into a thousand pieces on the floor.

Her voice wavered yet was loud and forceful. 'I've just finished washing off the blood of a man who gave his life to save my own. He's now lying in a ditch covered in grass. Hundreds of men and women have already died, having no funeral or prayers said for them to help them move to the next life. I don't even know if my own family are still alive or dead. So why am I standing here, listening to who wants to be able to say they are in charge? How much more blood will we have to wash off before this ends? Does saying you're in charge matter that much?'

She finished with tears streaming down her face, unable to speak any more. Glaring at the four leaders, now quiet and abashed, Alva opened the door and stormed out.

Anne hurried after her. Everyone was completely silent.

Josh stood, half amused, half exasperated. 'Well, the youngest one here has just told you lot, hasn't she? Tom, Matthew, a joint command should mean just that. A joint command. Once we have set the plan in motion, there shouldn't be that many battlefield changes. And you'll both have different responsibilities once everything's underway. Cador, remember why we're all here, please. So, let's sit down and plan this. Remember we are not the Army. That's what we're fighting against. Okay?'

Tom was the first to hold his hand out to Cador, who gladly accepted the gesture. The four of them still looked sheepish from the true words harshly spoken.

Cador offered his apologies to everyone in turn, as Matthew did also to Leila and Tom.

'Good,' remarked Josh. 'I'm going to check on Alva. Behave, people.' Satisfied they wouldn't return to arguing, he left the room.

|||||||||||||||||||||||||||||||||||||||||||||||||||||||||||||||||||||||

Once Josh had closed the door, any remaining tension dissipated. Alva's words had had a profound effect. Subdued, they returned to discussing the plan to attack the complex if Hill took their bait.

They planned to approach from two directions. One squad was to head for the town of Chilmark itself, making itself very noticeable as they cleared through the streets, having split into four smaller sections. The second squad was to wait just outside the main complex entrance. Hopefully, once the first had been sighted and reported on, the soldiers from the barracks would be tasked with heading into the town to defend it. As soon as the soldiers had left the complex, the second squad would then attack them at their rear, thus hitting the Army on both flanks.

It was agreed that Matthew would lead the initial town attack, and Tom would lead the complex attack group. This would allow him to be first to retake his home if all went well. Cador came up with the idea to include both territories' people in each part of the attack, which was agreed by all. This allowed a true mixture of Kernow and Bowles, which would send a clear message to everyone involved that they were truly on each other's side.

Within the hour, an overall strategy was agreed upon.

|||||||||||||||||||||||||||||||||||||||||||||||||||||||||||||||||||||||

Everyone gathered together. Josh chatted to a calmer Alva. Cador had been the first to apologise to her after her outburst, assuring her he would make it up to her in some way after the forthcoming action.

After explaining the plan to the satisfaction of everyone assembled, Tom stood to say a small prayer for the men and woman taking part. Everyone stayed standing in silence for a short time after, before breaking away to head to their stations.

They now had to wait for news about the Army. Would they take the bait? Or had they wasted their time? Would they have to come up with a different plan? It would be a long night until those questions were answered.

THIRTY-ONE

Hill gazed out of his bedroom window at first light, after a restful night's sleep, watching a light mist floating across the surrounding fields. As he stood there, he felt once again his destiny driving him forwards; his passion for a strong England would make his name famous down the ages. He had taken the first step; the next one would be just as critical.

He could hear his Army preparing for the day's sortie to the prize: the lectrics. The final piece of the puzzle to allow him to drag this miserable country back to civilisation. He had risen and dressed early today, keen to get on with things. Slapping his leather crop against his leg, he headed off to lead his Army.

Outside, Iain and Rollins waited for their general. As they saw him coming, they stiffened their stance. Hill walked towards them, motioning for them to follow him down to the road, to the waiting horses.

'All ready?' he asked as they headed through the large iron gates. 'I want to get underway immediately.'

'Of course, sir,' replied Rollins. 'We will head towards the facility as one column, until we are two miles away. Once there, you will lead the main attack force and I will take the second group to outflank them, so we attack at the same time from the north.'

'Excellent. Iain, I trust you will look after things in my absence?' Hill enquired of his old friend. Iain was to remain in charge while the General led this latest mission. He wasn't the best rider due to his size, nor the best fighter either, and he was the only person Hill trusted to act in his best interests.

'Of course, General. There's plenty to be getting on with whilst you are away. Once I hear of your success, I will send our lectric people to you to start fixing the whole system. They can use the prisoners you take as well, of course.'

'Indeed. Then let's be on our way.' Hill was anxiously tapping his whip against his leg.

Hill and Rollins checked their chronos, agreeing each other's showed the same time. Satisfied, they mounted their horses. As soon as Hill placed his feet in the stirrups, he waved his hand above his head and shouted for the Army to move out.

It was expected that they would be travelling for most of the day, arriving by evening time. The plan was to rest throughout the night and attack at first light the next day. They hoped to make good time, as they weren't taking any of their heavy equipment. Just men, horses and weapons. Travelling light, the Army soon left Chilmark behind.

||||||||||||||||||||||||||||||||||||||||||||||||||||||||||||||||||

The Kernow scout lay fully hidden by a covering of grass, with a large fallen fir tree branch laid out on top. He was one of many placed strategically around the old home of the Bowles family since yesterday morning. They had been told to wait and watch for what could be up to three days if necessary. But he had some food and was comfortable, so was fully prepared.

The ground beneath him felt damp to the touch; everywhere was shrouded in mist. After stretching his limbs, he took out some protein biscuits to eat for breakfast. Content, for now, he prepared for what could be a long watch. He had an excellent view of the highway, slightly above the level of the road, and desperately hoped that he would be the one to catch the Army leaving.

After less than an hour he heard noises coming from down the highway. He could see a large number of horses approaching. Withdrawing into his shelter, he made sure he was fully covered. He watched as the convoy made its way past, horses first, followed by armed men jogging behind to keep up. Breathing out slowly, he tried to calm himself. Once they had left his view, he relaxed.

He was keen to get back to report what he had seen, but all the scouts had been told to wait for a while if they saw the Army – just in case there were any secondary followers. He waited, impatiently, for another half hour, before he crawled backwards out of his shelter. Now he had to run as fast as he could to the camouflaged communications point a few miles south, to get the news to headquarters. Proud that he would be the one to bring the news back, he set off as fast as he could.

|||||||||||||||||||||||||||||||||||||||||||||||||||||||||||||||||||||||||||||||

Hill led at a steady pace, using one of the ancient highways for some time, allowing his troops on foot to keep up with their leader. Riding at the front with his officers surrounding him, he was keen to get to their destination. He hoped to reach a waypoint near one of the watercourses along the route before long.

By the time they reached the slow-moving water, the sun was almost overhead. He signalled for the Army to halt, extravagantly raising his arm as the signal, stopping his horse before turning to face his men. 'We will rest here – thirty minutes, no more. Eat and rest, men.'

The soldiers, one by one, dropped to the floor to rest. Each took the food they had been given out of their pack. A few of the younger soldiers were tasked with ferrying flasks of water throughout the men. Not many spoke, eating and resting the only things on their mind.

Hill and Rollins discussed the remaining route to their destination. Soon they would have to turn off the highway, making their way along lesser roads and tracks. But they were on schedule and should be there before nightfall.

|||||||||||||||||||||||||||||||||||||||||||||||||||||||||||||||||||||||||||

Tom had spent the time since breakfast distractedly looking through reports from a pile in front of him. He had re-read the current one about five times. Rubbing his eyes, he put the report back on the pile and leant back in his chair.

A few rapid knocks on his door made him sit up. He called out for whoever it was to enter and the Kernow communications woman rushed in.

'It looks like they've taken the bait, sir. We've just had confirmation of a large number of soldiers heading west from Chilmark.' She spoke quickly, trying to catch her breath.

Tom stood, grabbing his tunic as he thanked her. 'Let me know any more news as soon as we have it. I'll gather the leadership and come down to you as soon as we're together.'

The young woman nodded as Tom hurried past her. She followed him out of the room before heading back to the communications area.

Tom saw two young messengers just next to the hallway. He told the first of them to get his sister and Josh. The other was sent to find Matthew. He waited outside his office, pacing up and down in anticipation.

It didn't take long for Leila and Josh to arrive. Matthew soon followed with Cador. Tom enthusiastically told them of the message they had received.

After the initial relief of hearing that their gambit might pay off, thoughts turned to actually carrying it out. They hurried to the newly installed comms room that now took up most of one of the smaller storehouses to the rear of the manor. The operator detailed what the messenger had reported.

'It sounds like they've gone all in, then,' Leila said.

'With fifty horses and over one hundred soldiers on foot, it sounds like it. From what Josh and Eddie have told us, that leaves them with what, a hundred or so at most defending the complex? It's our best shot.' Matthew radiated calmness. He looked over at Cador. 'Get our militia ready. We ride as soon as we can.' He glanced at Tom. 'Ready to avenge your father's death?'

'I am. Let's do this.'

The Kernow and the rangers were all waiting to go once the word got around. Within thirty minutes of the order being sent out they waited eagerly to leave.

Although they had a similar distance to travel as the New English Army, there was one major advantage on their side. All of the joint force would be riding on their journey. The Army could only go as fast as its slowest member, and with one hundred on foot they would be considerably slower. Even with their own planned route taking longer by sweeping south-eastwards first before coming back north, the Kernow and the rangers were still much faster than their opponents.

Everyone able to fight had joined the remaining Bowles rangers; alongside the Kernow, they made a formidable fighting team. They had left no one of fighting age behind. This was their one attempt to retake their home.

Irving remained, to organise anything that would be needed at the last minute.

With Tom and Matthew at the front, Leila just behind, they were ready. Matthew gestured his agreement for Tom to give the order, which he did with much appreciation.

Lifting his arm into the air, he pointed towards home. 'Rangers, people of Kernow, we go to wipe this damnable army away from our rightful home. We will not go back to older, more violent times. We do this for our families, for our children, and for the brave men and women who have died because of what they did.' He looked at the faces around him, people ready to die for what was right. 'Let's go.'

They moved off, slowly at first as they made their way through Somerton, but soon they were riding along the rolling, open countryside. The fields allowed them to canter, at many times the speed of a jogging soldier.

Josh and Anne rode alongside Alva, who was still visibly troubled by events with Nolan. Josh had talked about wanting to keep an eye on her to make sure she did nothing senseless during the attack, while understanding she had her own demons to overcome.

Before they left, Tom had sent an order to the workers still at the solar farm. They were to leave in the afternoon, heading north to a loyal farmstead for safety. If the General did have scouts watching the area, hopefully it would only look like they were finishing for the day and not rouse any suspicions. If all went well, by the time the Army arrived no one would be put at risk.

The ambitious plan had a large number of variables, many of which simply couldn't be known right now. All they could do was hope for the best and trust their instincts. For now, they needed to hurry, that much was clear.

With evening approaching and the sun sliding towards the skyline in front of them, they were only two miles away from their target. The travelling had been hard but satisfactory. Calling a halt, the General told his officers to let the men rest.

Before he dismounted, he called over one of his more trusted scouts, telling him to go and find the one watching the solar facility. He wanted an update on the situation before making the next decision. Although they had planned to camp here for the night before attacking, he was speculating on launching the attack tonight.

As the sky was clear, with no sign of rain on the horizon, they hadn't started to put up any tents or canvases yet. Some of the men were sent out to hunt for game; some were tasked with gathering wood for fires.

Rollins called for the General to join him under a large oak tree, where assistants were setting up a table. He was issuing a few instructions but there wasn't much to do till the final order was given. 'We made excellent time, sir.'

'As I knew we would. How are the men doing?' Hill asked as he surveyed the troops relaxing around him.

'Tired but good. A good night's rest will have them ready for the assault.'

Hill thought for a moment before discussing his idea with his strategist. 'I've been thinking about that. I wonder if it would be a better decision to have a short break then launch the attack this evening. The dark would provide more cover for the men.'

Rollins hesitated before he answered. 'In an ideal world, having the cover of night is a bonus, but our men are pretty tired after such a long journey. I still think letting them rest before is the best way to go about this.'

Hill looked at the soldiers scattered around him. Although he understood Rollins' concern, he was impatient to get on with the encounter.

'It's also the Kernow,' Rollins continued. 'We know very little about them at the moment. And while we are surely more than a match for them, we need to make sure they don't have any unexpected ways of fighting we don't know about. Especially in the dark.'

Hill grunted at the comment. From what he'd heard, the Kernow were just a bunch of brutes, strong, yes, but nowhere near as finessed as his men were at fighting. 'Let's wait for our scout to bring some information back before we make the final decision.'

He wandered off towards the soldiers, chatting briefly to ones he recognised. The soldiers appeared to appreciate his relaxed attitude before the attack.

The hunters soon returned with pheasants and a couple of small boars. The game was quickly butchered and prepared for cooking; the camp soon filled with the smell of meat roasting over the open fire. Hill was served first with the choicest cut, followed by his officers.

Eating, the General saw his scout return. Beckoning him over, he told him to report his findings.

'Sir. It appears that the workforce has finished for the day,' he began. 'The place is quiet now, just some sentries every now and then. We believe the workforce sleeps a little way away. We're not sure where the Kernow men are stationed. We haven't been too near to find out exactly where, as we don't want to give our position away.'

'Of course. Did our boy say when they normally return to work?'

'Always at sunrise, sir. They start work early, then the mounted Kernow begin their rounds a little afterwards.'

'Good. Go and get some food. You've done well.'

With a firm salute the scout headed quickly off to the fire.

Hill tilted his head a little in Rollins' direction. 'I think it may be prudent to wait until morning after all. If we leave here an hour before sunrise, then we can be ready to spring our assault just as they arrive in the morning. We can take the area, then finish off the Kernow filth.'

Rollins saluted. 'Yes, sir. I'll organise watches through the night and make sure we are up and ready to attack first thing.'

|||||||||||||||||||||||||||||||||||||||||||||||||||||||||||||||||||||||||||||||

Reaching the southern outskirts of their hometown chastened everyone who had been forced to leave here so recently. The rangers knew the fields well, yet it felt alien to them as they covered the ground. They stopped a mile away, in a large field next to an old abandoned church. After dismounting their horses, they removed the saddles, leaving the horses to recover from the hard ride of the day.

Heading into the decrepit building for one final briefing, everyone kept quiet. There was nothing inside the building, nowhere to sit, so both rangers and Kernow mingled together on the floor. Matthew and Tom headed to the end of the empty space, to an old stone font. As had happened to so many of the now defunct ancient places of worship, everything had been stripped away many years ago. This one was quite unusual to still have some remnants of its roof still attached.

In the fading light, Tom explained once again to the Kernow the layout of the town, describing the routes which criss-crossed the centre. He drew chalk lines on the wall behind him to give an overview of the town. With the numbers known about the Army, it was presumed this would be where some of them had been housed. Matthew was to lead the four teams of ten which were to approach the town from different directions, then go door to door clearing out any of the soldiers. Hopefully they wouldn't get much trouble from the workers, but they understood that they had to be merciless if any of them tried to get in their way.

Tom would take the larger squad, along with Cador as his number two, to the complex. They would go to the west side, just up the road from the complex, while giving Matthew an hour to complete his task.

Cador explained that they wouldn't be able to rid themselves of everyone in the town; it would be pandemonium in the dark once they started killing the soldiers. It was expected that some would make it back to the complex, raising the alarm and bringing out the majority of the remaining troops. Once these headed into Chilmark, they would have them in a pincer movement, ready to attack from both sides.

Not everything they planned for would go the way they wanted, so the leadership tried to cover all the alternatives that may happen along the way.

Finally, the time for talking was over; they were ready to act. Making sure everyone had the same time on their chronos, they organised the groupings, heading out to their positions.

THIRTY-TWO

Arriving at their positions, they settled down to wait till midnight. Finally, at the agreed time, Matthew started to lead the attack into the town of Chilmark.

They split into the four teams, fanning out to begin their approach from separate positions, moving silently as they watched the dying fires inside the buildings. Where they flickered in the windows signalled where their attacks would start.

With a piercing cry from Matthew, doors were kicked in and the yelling began. Their ploy was to not enter any of the buildings, but to draw out any soldiers who were inside. They were also counting on that the workers wouldn't be the ones rushing out to fight.

With stones being thrown through windows and a loud racket being caused, it wasn't long until the first soldiers started to emerge. They weren't equipped in any way for a concerted attack. The first men to come outside to see what was happening were quickly despatched.

Seeing their fellow soldiers killed, however, brought the remainder quickly to their senses. After the initial hurry to rush outside, no more followed.

Matthew was determined not to let the soldiers have any time to become too organised. A shrill whistle sounded around the town, causing the attackers to withdraw slightly as well as fall completely silent.

Faces appeared at the windows around the town. Downstairs, the soldiers peered out cautiously. Upstairs, faces crammed at each one.

By now, Matthew and his team had made their way to the town square. Once the initial strike, and the yelling, stopped, he stepped out of the shadows. Shouting at the top of his voice, he made his initial gambit.

'People held by the New English Army, we are here to destroy them and free you from their control. Fight with us now – drive them to us, if you can. Pick up anything to use against them. This is your chance.'

He repeated himself once more. As soon as he had finished, more shouting started as the Kernow militia and the rangers saw a group of soldiers coming out of the inn together. The defenders charged and soon the square was a mass of swords clashing. Suddenly, from the side of the fight came another group, yelling at the tops of their voices as they charged.

This group running at the fight were the workers, dirtily dressed and armed with not much more than lengths of wood, pans or occasionally a knife. They were rising up, as Matthew had begged them to.

The now bewildered soldiers, who were just about holding their own, looked horrified at the men charging them from one side. A few hesitated at the sight, giving the attackers a small amount of momentum; it was all they needed.

Some of the workers had grabbed a soldier, pulling him to one side, and were kicking and screaming at him on the floor. His face was slowly becoming a bloody mess and he soon lost consciousness under the blows. The freed workers carried on kicking him, long after he died, before turning to repeat the attack on another nearby.

As the combined force of the Kernow and the rangers pushed on, it became clear that there was nowhere near the number of soldiers in the town that would be needed to put up a defence against them. Especially with the rampaging workers now joining them.

Running out of one of the large production shops, one of the larger workers grabbed a nearby soldier by the neck, pushing him to the floor before punching his face repeatedly with both fists, one after the other. Teeth mixed into blood and saliva were dripping out of the dying man's mouth as he groaned loudly. As he stopped moving, his assailant hunched over his lifeless body, weeping.

The inn was now the soldiers' main retreat. With barely any soldiers remaining, the four groups merged back into one. They were ready to enter the inn, eager to clear the remaining soldiers out.

As the mass readied themselves, they heard a crash of glass above them. Everyone looked up, watching as one of the soldiers tumbled out of an upstairs window. He crashed onto the ground, arm bent at an unusual angle, not moving. Before anyone could react, two women came out from the front doors. Covered in blood, they grimaced as they gazed around.

One of the rangers gave out a cry, before rushing up the steps to the shocked women. He threw his arms around the nearest; she took a while to recognise him before falling into his embrace. Another ranger did the same to the second. They were the captured female rangers.

Others ran in to check the inn was clear. There were bodies lying on the floor inside. They rushed upstairs to assess the rest of the rooms. It was the same scene.

Matthew called everyone to him; they gathered round outside. Within half an hour of Matthew giving the order, they had subdued the town. They could see no more of the Army anywhere, just the throng of workers nervously milling around in the moonlight. Some were bloodied, others were only just poking their heads round the doors and window frames for the first time. Matthew ordered half his troops to check the buildings further. Time to spread the word.

It didn't take long. Workers in each building were more than happy to confirm there were no soldiers amongst them.

The Kernow and rangers came together in the town square. They had lost eighteen of their own in the operation, with a number of wounded as well. It was an excellent return for taking the town, but Matthew was still chastened by the loss.

A hush fell across the square as a wretched sight emerged from the inn – some of the captive women. The one leading the group was one of the rangers who helped in their own escape. She marched over to Matthew, who was in deep discussion with two of the more senior rangers. She held herself defiantly, despite the bruises on her face and all over her body.

She stopped next to the now silent rescuers. 'Mary Howey, Bowles ranger. We have some seriously injured women here who need help.'

'And you'll have it, immediately,' replied Matthew, motioning for assistance to be given.

A mix of the female rangers and Kernow women rushed to offer any assistance they could. Mary stood there, not showing any embarrassment at her own state of dress.

Her voice started to waver. 'Thank you. And thank you for coming to our aid. Has the Army been routed? Are we free?'

'Not yet, no. This is just the first part. We're going to attack the complex next, half the Army's still there.'

Mary's eyes opened wide at the news. 'Then I will be with you when we go.' It wasn't a request and Matthew understood completely.

'Excellent,' he replied. 'Let's get you more suitably attired. I will be proud to have you with us.'

One of the rangers led Mary away, trying to explain the events that had led to where they were now.

A messenger ran up to Matthew. 'Sir, there's no sign of anyone coming out of the complex to defend the town. We don't know if they know what's happened or not, but they're staying put for now.'

Matthew paused for a moment. 'It looks like we've got to launch an assault on the complex. Either they don't know what happened down here or don't want to come out.'

He called out once again to the watching workers. 'Look around you. This is only the first part of ridding ourselves of this general and his so-called army. You're all free now – go if you want to, with our blessing. But we're heading to take back the Bowles home. If anyone wants to join us and help, we'd be proud to have you.'

Many of the workers looked at each other; they seemed to be unsure of what exactly was happening.

One of the older men walked forwards, cautiously. 'I'll join you. I might not be much use, but I want to make them pay for what they've done to us.'

After that first one, many others stepped forwards. Matthew watched as within minutes around thirty men stood there. As he walked amongst them, looking them up and down, a tired-looking man raised his hand.

'Speak your mind. No need to ask permission here,' Matthew told him.

'Sir, thank you, thank you. But I'm no fighter, nor would I be of any use to you.' He looked around, waving his hand at the others still partially hiding to the sides. 'If we don't want to fight, can we just leave? Walk away with no penalty?'

Matthew smiled, placing his hand on the man's shoulder. 'Indeed, my friend. If you want to go, go. But when we have wiped this army out, the Kernow or Bowles family will always need workers, paid workers to live free. Whatever you choose, that is now your right. Go, stay or fight. We'll not make you do anything you don't want to.'

The man hesitated. 'Then if it's all right with you, I'm leaving. I've family in the east, and I want to see them again.' He bowed, then turned away. Many of the others went with him.

Matthew sent a messenger to update Tom, arranging to meet him just outside the complex's boundary. This would be harder than they had thought.

He gave the order to arm as many workers as they could before they made their way to meet up with the others.

When they arrived, the others were eagerly waiting for them. The news they had cleared out the town had energised them no end. Tom shook Matthew's hand firmly, before looking at the assembly of people around them.

Josh, Leila and Anne were discussing the news with Cador, who was standing close to Alva.

After quickly updating the leadership, Matthew laid their position out. 'We need to go in and take the complex by force, I'm afraid. You know the place better than anyone, Tom. What's the plan?'

'Most should be in the barracks, not in the main house. So that's where our main thrust should be.'

Anne agreed. 'Some of us can come in from the rear. If we use about a third of us to attack from the front, we might be able to draw them out for you. Then once we have dealt with them, that group can then head to the house to flush that out.'

'It will be quick, and it will be bloody, for both sides,' Cador added. 'But let's get this done.'

They quickly split up. Matthew led the attack to the rear. Anne organised the frontal team, ready to rush the gates.

Wasting no time, they began. The noise from the charge was bound to leave no soldier unsure as to what was happening. Suddenly lights came on, inside and outside, flooding the area in bright white light, and armed men appeared.

As Cador had predicted, it became very intense very quickly. The barracks rapidly emptied of its remaining soldiers, who started to offer plenty of stern resistance. Some of the freed workers ran headfirst at their captors but were despatched without much thought, before the main body reached the fight. A pitched battle started, the soldiers with their backs to the wall fighting for their lives. But although the Army men were seasoned fighters, it wasn't long before the numbers against them began to tell.

The group led by Tom and Josh had breached the gates and arrived outside the main house but there wasn't much opposition stationed around. They only found a few tired soldiers on guard, who they dealt with easily. After seeing the house was locked up, with no one heading out to face them, they ran to the barracks to help their colleagues before making the final assault.

Reaching the fighting, with the defending soldiers' numbers already dwindling fast, the extra help they brought ended the slaughter almost immediately. Cador led a team into the barracks to make sure there were no soldiers remaining behind. It didn't take them long to return, a thumbs up showing it was clear.

Everyone was catching their breath as Tom spoke up. 'The house looks like it's locked up tight. They aren't going to come to us, by the looks of it. We're going to have to go in and clear them out.'

'Agreed. Is there an easy way in?' Matthew asked.

Leila stepped forwards. 'The council chamber – one whole side is glass. We break it and enter that way.'

Matthew wore a thin smile on his face. 'It's over to you now, Tom. We will back you up with what you need, but you're now in charge. Go and take your home back.'

Tom turned to Josh and Anne. 'Right, let's do this. I will lead the attack. My team will move into the hall to clear the way. Josh, you take a team and clear out upstairs, go up the servants' staircase. Anne, you head to the stores and kitchen. Leila, with me, but be careful.'

Everyone followed around the building. They could see faces looking out of the windows upstairs. The lights were all on, clearly showing those inside.

'You know, I don't reckon there's many inside,' Josh said as they made their way to the windows of the council chamber.

Cador, who had caught up, laughed. 'You might be right. But best still be careful.'

'Absolutely. You're with me, Cador.' Josh grinned back. 'You'll make a great shield with me behind you.'

The remark broke some of the tension amongst the men and women about to head into an unknown situation. They had achieved a great success in the last hour, but they still had more to do tonight. And the main body of the Army was yet to return.

Reaching the council chamber, they grabbed large stones to break the glass. There was no one in the room waiting for them. On Tom's signal they all threw at once, causing a huge crash as the windows smashed to the floor. They climbed through quickly but gingerly; the end of the chamber was soon full.

Tom led his team through the main door to the grand entrance hall of his home. On the other side of the door, waiting behind some hastily upturned tables, were the rest of the soldiers. These were the officers who had stayed behind. They would not be as easy to beat as their juniors. The two groups watched each other for a moment. Suddenly, Tom raised his sword and screamed. The next fight had begun.

With their greater numbers almost assuring victory, Josh headed upstairs, followed by Cador, Alva and the rest of his team. On the galleried landing they fanned out, three to each of the first few doors. On his signal, they kicked the doors open and ran inside each room.

The initial rooms they entered were all empty, a quick check confirming that most of the occupants were probably downstairs amongst the throng. Each team then began to move to the next closed room. One by one they checked every room on the floor. All empty. Josh and Cador arrived at the final room at the end of the corridor. Alva and Anne led the rest up the side stairs to check the few rooms of the second floor.

Josh nodded to Cador, inviting him to break the door to this last room. Cador lifted his large boot and pummelled the door twice. It gave way on the second kick. Rushing in immediately, sword above his head, Josh stopped in his tracks barely three feet into the bedroom. Sitting by the window, as relaxed as someone with no cares in the world, was Iain Bates.

He smiled crookedly as they slowly walked towards him. He held his hands up, albeit sarcastically. 'I surrender. Never was one for hand-to-hand fighting, you know.'

Cador rushed to him, pulling the smirking fool onto the floor. In one smooth motion he grabbed his arms and began to tie them behind his back. He roughly pulled him up to his knees once secure and stepped back to where Josh was still watching.

'You will pay for what you have done,' Josh breathed at Bates.

'Oh, I'm sure. And yet here I am, still alive.' He was chuckling to himself.

As they were watching each other, a cry was heard from inside the house, then everything went silent. Josh motioned for Cador to see what had happened, while he stood staring at their captive. It wasn't long before he returned.

Cador gently placed his hand on Josh's shoulder. 'The complex is ours.'

Josh sighed, his head sagging slightly at the news. 'Then let's take this piece of scum downstairs.'

They pulled Bates to his feet, strong-arming him down the hallway. Making their way down the stairs, they saw the carnage emerging in front of them. Their fallen comrades were being gathered to one side of the entrance area. The bodies of the Army officers were all being bundled outside, with noticeably more care than they would have shown in return.

Reaching the wet red floor, they threw Bates to his knees in front of Tom.

'This is General Hill's second in command,' Josh told him. 'He's as guilty as anyone involved.'

'Pleased to meet you,' Bates said quickly. 'You seem to be better at this than your father was. Last time I saw him, he was dangling on the end of a rope.' He started laughing at his own words. Spotting Leila, he leered in her direction.

Tom walked over to this cruel man, staring at him with pain and hatred in his eyes. He glanced over to Josh. He knew exactly what he was thinking. He gave a single quick nod. Tom leant down, level to Bates' face, staring into his eyes. Neither blinked.

Tom drew a small dagger from his belt, lifting it so Bates could understand what he intended to do. Seeing it, his eyes widened, and he opened his mouth to speak. Before any words could come out, Tom thrust the tip of the dagger up through his chin. He pushed as hard as he could, and the blade slipped into the brain of the Army's second in command.

Tom pulled back. He let the lifeless body collapse onto the floor.

Josh knelt down and put his arm around his oldest friend. 'Part one complete. Now let's get ready to finish this.'

There was plenty to do. No one yet knew when General Hill would return with the rest of his Army. They needed to prepare quickly and as best they could. Matthew gathered the messengers together, sending them to find out if any news had arrived during their assault on the complex; he needed information as soon as possible. Anne gathered the men and women outside to organise the defence of their home.

Tom, Leila and Josh took a little time to wander slowly through the house. It felt good to be back.

THIRTY-THREE

THE FIRST JOB, AFTER TAKING THE COMPLEX, WAS TO CLEAR away the dead, temporarily for now at least. Alva took charge of the grisly undertaking herself, organising teams of the ex-Army workers to ferry the bodies to the barracks. She surprised many of those helping her by her simple insistence that they treated the soldiers' bodies with a certain amount of care.

The soldiers' weapons were also quickly gathered together in a pile outside the house, allowing Anne to arm those who needed one for the coming fight. The Army may have been many things, but they were well equipped. Cador gathered the newly armed workers together, trying to teach them a little of his fighting knowledge in the short time allowed.

Cador repeatedly stressed to all of those listening that they would not be on the front lines of the coming battle. Although they were keen to avenge their captivity, they were not strong enough, nor nearly experienced enough, to be at the forefront of taking the fight to the Army.

Less than an hour after their victory, one of the messengers Matthew had sent out returned with news. He relayed how the Army appeared to be camping down for the night, just outside of Somerton.

Hardly believing their good fortune and sending the messenger back with updates for the scouts, Matthew went to tell the news to Tom and Leila, collecting Josh along the way.

'Tom, Leila, it appears the General is waiting till tomorrow for his attack on the solar facility.'

Leila was unable to stop herself smiling. 'That gives us a lot more time to get ready, then, doesn't it?'

'Looks that way,' Matthew answered. 'And it does give us some time to rest as well.'

'We need to convince them that the complex is still under the Army's control when they arrive back,' Josh said. 'If only for a short time. Then we can rush them, catching them off guard.'

Matthew looked at the grand ceiling, head tilted slightly at the thought. 'An element of surprise is always useful. If we can get a good proportion inside the gates without realising, as they dismount we could spring a trap.'

'It's worth thinking it out more. At some stage there's going to be a fight – why not start it off on our terms?' Tom added.

Leila agreed. 'We need to make this place look exactly as it did when we arrived, then. There's not much we can do about the broken windows to the side of the house, but that's not easily visible from the front. We can put a wagon at the corner to give it some cover. Let's get the outside cleaned up as best we can.'

'Maybe we can dress some of our guys in their uniforms, to give an impression of normality,' suggested Anne, who had arrived halfway through but caught on to the plan immediately. 'Especially at the gates. That's where we need some to make it appear as if nothing has happened.'

'I'll do that,' said Josh firmly. 'I know what the leaders look like and how to address them. Hopefully that will start the pretence enough.'

Anne clapped her hands loudly. 'Let's get this done, then. We've got lots to organise.'

It was dark as General Hill walked amongst his soldiers, after a long hour of sitting, staring up at the stars. Adrenaline surged through his body, making him feel invincible, incapable of rest. It made the scars on his neck ache, though. A small price to pay, he thought.

As he weaved his way through the troops, he considered the endless possibilities ahead of him. Ultimate power was finally within his reach; his destiny would be assured.

He came to Rollins.

Rollins looked up; he had been dozing but he groggily got to his feet. 'Sir, how may I help?'

'Something isn't right.' The General turned, looking away from the camp. 'Why aren't there more of those Kernow guarding this facility? Didn't they have a larger team here?'

'Arrogance, probably. They don't think it's an issue,' Rollins offered.

'But where are they all? Send some men there immediately. I want to know how many there are.'

Rollins rushed off. Within minutes Jarek and five men were running towards the facility. The General walked to the edge of the field they were camped in, looking into the distance. Why weren't these Kernow men where they should be?

He waited there until Jarek returned. The man slowed as he reached his leader, catching his breath before giving his report.

'Sir, there's no one there at all. No guards, no fighters, no one.' As he spoke, two other returnees reached them.

Hill shouted at the top of his voice. 'Is this right? There's no one there?'

They nodded their heads quickly, looking at the ground as they did.

Jarek continued with the troubling news. 'Sir, I looked at some of the stores. If I had to guess, I'd say they have bailed out. It doesn't look like they were planning on returning soon. Everything seems to be cleared out or shut down rather than paused for an overnight break.'

Hill quickly ran through the possibilities in his mind. 'They knew we were coming and left it to us. Is that it?'

'This wasn't the rump of the Bowles lot, leaving like they did before.' Jarek rubbed his chin. 'The Kernow had it now. Why would they leave? With their numbers they would have been confident of defending this place. What would have been the point of coming all this way to take it, then deciding to leave it? Surely it was worth a fight to them.'

Rollins caught his breath. 'Unless they wanted us to bring the Army here. Splitting us up and leaving the new headquarters weakened. We brought the most experienced fighters here. The ones we left are bolstered by the newly promoted workers as well.' He left the implication of that last statement to hang in the air.

'They think they can attack us?' yelled Hill with disgust. 'Is that what they are doing?'

Jarek agreed with Rollins. 'If they are, then we need to get back to home immediately.'

'Call the men together,' Hill bellowed. They ran off as he commanded, leaving him alone.

The General smoothed his hair back, trying to calm himself as best he could. He rubbed his scars harder than normal; they ached as badly as they ever did right now. He couldn't believe that he had fallen for some form of trap, especially not one by the uneducated Kernow. Maybe they were overthinking this, maybe the people working here had simply heard of them coming and fled for their lives. But the Kernow ... they had made their play for this land. They surely wouldn't just have withdrawn without a fight.

The more he thought, the more he came to understand the possibility that a trap had been sprung against them. If it hadn't, he would lose a day travelling and they would prepare better when they left next time to take this infernal place.

But if it had... He just didn't want to contemplate that yet.

His soldiers started to arrive around him; the horses were being brought to one side and made ready. He looked at the waiting faces; he didn't want to speak to them right now. He called Rollins to him.

'Give the order to head back to headquarters. Those riding shall hurry back with me. If there is any problem there, then speed is of the essence. Those on foot shall double time back.'

'Should we split up our forces, sir?' Rollins asked, caution in his voice. 'Wouldn't it be better to arrive as one?'

'If I thought that, then I would have ordered it. Understand?'

Rollins saluted stiffly, before turning to issue the order as given.

Hill stormed to his horse, followed by the other mounted troops. He climbed on quickly and pulled hard on the reins. In less than a minute, they were hurrying back.

Working late into the night, planning how to use the rangers and the Kernow militia in the defence of the complex tomorrow, Josh watched Tom, Leila and Matthew working together. It was good to see the two territories' leaderships getting along so well. It boded well for the future. Everyone else was getting some well-earned sleep, wherever they could.

'We can station small groups of fighters outside the buildings, hidden as best they can,' Matthew said. 'The remainder will be behind the barracks. These will arrive just as the initial attack begins. Hopefully, we can take as many of them as we can before they realise what's happening.'

Cador sat down, rubbing his red eyes. 'Keep the rescued workers to the rear as best you can. They're weak after living with the Army.'

'Agreed,' said Tom. 'We've got a few hours till we expect them back. Let's all get some rest.'

Hill led the charge back to the headquarters, the horses strung out as they raced through the countryside. He was an excellent rider, controlling his horse beautifully over the ground. Rollins just about kept up with him.

By the time they reached the outskirts of Chilmark, the slowest riders were still minutes behind the leaders. Halting at the agreed destination, Hill dismounted and began to pace up and down, watching as the riders joined them one at a time, glaring at each one in turn.

'Send a scout up to the headquarters, with orders to immediately come back if they see anything out of the ordinary,' Rollins ordered one of the other officers. They quickly scuttled off, and within seconds one of the younger horsemen was racing towards the complex.

Hill spent the time impatiently walking up and down, a few metres away from the main body of men. Jarek and Rollins stood aside, discussing a few minor points. It wasn't long before the scout was back.

He jumped off his horse and approached Rollins. 'There's no guard, sir. Gates are closed, but not locked.'

Hill slapped his whip against his leg. 'Dammit, what is going on here? Everyone, let's get back and try to sort this mess out.' He stormed to his horse, ready to head home.

Everyone followed his lead, mounting up before making the short trip back. They trotted their way in silence.

One of the soldiers hurried up to open the gates wide, saluting Hill as he finished.

Hill nodded distractedly, before turning his attention to the complex. He urged his horse forwards; he was followed by the rest of the riders. Stopping on the lawn to the front of the complex, he dismounted. Rollins, Jarek and the other officers joined him, as the remaining men headed to one side.

Although it was very dark, the place seemed too quiet. Hill looked up at the house; there were no guards standing duty there. The mood he was in, he was about to give Iain the biggest dressing down of his life.

A young girl woke Matthew roughly. 'Message from the comms team, sir.'

He sat up in bed, motioning for her to read it out to him.

'There's been a sighting of the Army heading back, sir. Our scout saw the troops are running at a fast pace.'

Matthew was out of bed instantly. 'Dammit, something's changed their mind, then. Wake the barracks, will you?'

He hurriedly started dressing as she ran out of the room. As he did, he walked past the window. What he saw outside sent a shiver down his spine. He sprinted to the next-door room, saw Josh asleep. He grabbed him, shaking him awake. 'They're here.'

||||||||||||||||||||||||||||||||||||||||||||||||||||||||||||||||||||||||||||

Josh blearily looked up as he processed the words. He jumped out of bed and understood as soon as he glanced out of the window. 'Get the others.'

He grabbed his sword and ran to the top of the staircase. Luckily for him, he hadn't bothered getting undressed as he'd been too tired. He saw the front door open, the General walking inside and turning the house lights on with a wave of his hand. He pulled back, carefully so he couldn't be seen. Returning to the end of the passageway, he heard the others coming out of their rooms. Urgently motioning for silence, he called Leila over.

'It's the General. He's downstairs,' he whispered.

Leila put her hand to her mouth. 'How?'

Josh shook his head. 'Get everyone to the barracks the back way. Go, go.' He ushered her and the others down the servants' stairs, leading to the kitchens.

As the last of them were heading down, Josh heard someone coming up the stairs. Surely they would be heard? He dashed into the nearest bedroom and hid behind the door, listening intently. He heard footsteps moving from room to room, a voice calling out at each door.

When the voice reached his room, Josh took a deep breath. As the man leant in, Josh pulled him forwards violently, thrusting his blade into the man's back as he staggered.

The man fell to his knees in shock then toppled forwards, slamming his head on the way down. He would be dead in moments. Josh had to force himself to look away, to focus.

He rushed to the top of the main stairs, stopped and looked behind him. As loud as he could, he shouted down the stairs, 'We'll be down in a minute. Hang on.'

He raced down the servants' stairs and out through the back of the house.

When he reached the barracks, everyone was awake, although nowhere near ready for fighting yet. Cador and Alva were organising everyone as quickly as they could.

Matthew and Tom stood by the entrance; they couldn't see anything near the house in the dark. Tom saw Josh reach them and hurried him inside.

'Is that it? Is everyone out?' Tom asked.

'Yeah.' Josh was watching to see if anyone had followed. 'How the hell are they back here?'

'I just got a message saying they were on their way back,' Matthew told them. 'But they shouldn't be here yet.'

'Then it looks like this is where we make our stand,' Tom told them both. 'As soon as everyone's ready, we do this. Let's split into two. Matthew, you go around the back of the house, I'll head straight up. Let's try and come at them from both sides.'

The men and women of the combined Bowles and Kernow territories filed out of the barracks, keeping low and quiet. Josh watched as Matthew led his fighters up behind the house. Once they had gone, he walked side by side with Tom as they headed to the house.

Hill waited in the hallway, his mood getting worse by the minute. What was taking them so long? The voice said they were coming straight down. He stormed upstairs, fed up with waiting. Looking into the first few rooms, he was confused; they were empty. Where the hell had Iain gone? The beds looked slept in but there was no one inside. He headed back downstairs, to his waiting officers. He had expected to wake the whole household up, with an enormous dressing down to Iain about the importance of maintaining the guard. Without the release of that energy, he felt the stress inside his body.

Outside, joining the waiting horsemen, he looked around. His troops waited for his orders.

THIRTY-FOUR

From Hill's right, a huge roar erupted. He looked over to see a group of men and women rushing at them, armed with swords raised above their heads.

Seconds later, a new roar came from his left, from behind the main building.

The soldiers looked back and forth at the rushing people, startled by the noise and the sight. Drawing their own weapons from their packs still on the horses, they gathered together to form a defensive square. They quickly formed lines to both sides, with the General taking his place in the centre of one, ready for the coming battle.

A brutal fight to the death.

In the seconds it took for the attackers to reach them and engage, everything went eerily quiet. The rumble of running feet but nothing more, right up until the first engagement.

Then all hell broke loose. Swords clashed, shouting started and the fighting began.

Josh was next to Cador and Tom. All three began swinging hard at their opponents, who returned their blows with equal force. It was

Cador who cleared his man first, a huge great thrust of his sword cleanly piercing his torso. Pulling out his sword with both hands, he gave a loud cry before turning to help Josh with his own fight. Josh was more than glad of the help, vowing to stay near to Cador for the rest of the battle.

Josh's adversary looked dismayed as the huge man turned to face him, horror in his eyes when he saw the hulk of a man prepare to strike. The moment of hesitation was enough. Josh slashed at the man's neck, cutting deeply through. He fell to his knees, blood gushing out. His fight was done.

Josh pushed hard towards the now disorderly battle ranks. Out of the corner of his eye he saw Cador turn the other way; he cursed at not having him next to him anymore.

He engaged the next soldier, one who had already despatched several rangers and Kernow fighters. The man was an excellent swordsman, someone Josh would have difficulty defeating in a one-on-one fight. But because the Army's numbers were dwindling quicker than theirs, there were now more than enough combined fighters to take the Army men on two to one. A Kernow woman stepped up to the side of Josh and immediately the odds for the soldier fell drastically. With the superior numbers showing more and more throughout, the battle would surely not take much longer to win.

Josh feinted away from his adversary, allowing the soldier to concentrate on his other attacker. As soon as he saw his attention shift, Josh chopped hard at his shoulder, cutting to the bone. Dropping his sword as he screamed, the soldier watched plaintively as the Kernow fighter lunged, driving her blade straight into his heart. The man died instantly.

Looking around, Josh saw Tom staggering over to him. His right shoulder was bleeding profusely, and it was clear he was struggling to breathe. Josh rushed to his old friend, using his arm to steady him. He called the nearest ranger over.

'Here, look after Tom. He's hurt, get him to Leila,' he yelled.

Tom was pale; he was losing a lot of blood. 'It was Godfrey, bloody Godfrey Martgen. I only just took him down,' he muttered to Josh, before the ranger helped him, making their way to Leila who was setting up a medical area near the barracks.

As Josh turned his attention back to the fight, he knew the Army would not last much longer. There was only a small, tight group still fighting in the centre of the battleground. Seeing Matthew near, taking a breath, he ran over to him.

Matthew was bending over, tired but ready to rejoin the fight. Seeing Josh approach, he stood upright and grinned through his blood-spattered face. The two of them looked at each other grimly and moved in once more. The remaining soldiers were putting up a fierce defence, even with the overwhelming odds against them.

His hilt wet with blood, thankfully not his own, Josh gripped with both hands as he fought against a stocky bald man. He recognised him as a senior officer in the Army. Jarek, he remembered. He instantly regretted picking this particular fight, knowing his adversary's skill and strength was much greater than his own. He only just parried a frenzied attack, holding his sword just above his head as the blows rained down, one by one sapping his resistance. Losing his footing slightly, slipping backwards, he was once again eternally grateful for the assistance of Cador.

Cador had seen the mismatch, managing to make his way over to interrupt. Swinging their swords wildly, the two of them rained blows down on each other. Josh stepped back, not wanting to get anywhere near either of their blades. He saw many of those left fighting also pausing briefly, seeing these two master fighters at work. It felt like this was symbolically the last stand for the Army.

Both warriors stood their ground, feet firmly planted, taking turns to attack and defend. Neither willing to give an inch to the other. It was only after a full minute of attack after attack that Cador began to wear his adversary down, such was the force of his blows. Jarek moved backwards slowly, fear finally showing through his bloodied face for the first time. Cador increased the power in each swing. With a huge grunt, he swung hard. Their two swords came together for the final time. Jarek watched as his blade fell out of his hands, before turning his attention back to Cador. Almost instantly, the Kernow man's blade sliced deep through Jarek's neck, almost decapitating him, causing Jarek to slowly slide forwards with a last look of bewilderment showing on his face. Cador dropped to his knees, utterly exhausted.

Josh turned his attention to the remaining soldiers. Only three were now standing in front of them, General Hill included. With an exhausted but forceful voice, Matthew suddenly called out for everyone to pull back, leaving the three Army men standing there alone.

General Hill stood upright, looking around at the scene unbelievingly. Of the two men behind, one immediately threw his sword down at his feet, slowly followed by the other. Hill watched this gesture of surrender with a sneer, before sheathing his sword ostentatiously.

Josh walked over to the General, his weapon pointed at his face. 'Sword on the floor, if you don't mind.'

Hill just stood there, unmoving. He stared at Josh. Mechanically he undid his belt buckle, allowing it to fall to the floor. As soon as it touched the ground three men ran up behind him, pushing him to his knees and tying his hands behind his back.

Matthew stared at Hill, tilting his head slightly. 'So, you're General Hill, then?'

Hill glowered back, almost snarling in reply.

Leila and Anne ran over, stopping right in front of Hill. Leila approached cautiously, before slapping him across his cheek. Hill reeled slightly, before grinning back at her, showing his bloody teeth.

'It's done, over, you lost.' She spat out the words at him. 'And you will pay for it now.' She turned to Josh and Matthew. 'Thank God we've won this part, but what about the other returning soldiers?'

'Let's try and finish it without any more blood being spilt,' Josh told her. 'The ones on their way back aren't the hardcore officers, just the lower ranks. We need to let them know that whatever it was they were fighting for is over. Once they know that, I don't think they'll have much fight in them.'

Matthew nodded. 'Agreed. We need to make sure they know there's no point carrying on with this futile fight.'

'Then let's make it clear to them,' Josh said. 'A show of force when they arrive, everyone armed and ready. And a demonstration that their Army is over.'

'How?' asked Leila.

Josh pointed to the defeated Hill, kneeling in front of them. 'A repayment for what he did to your father. Hang him just outside the gates. Let the others see for themselves that the Army is no more.'

Hill's eyes went wide. 'You fools! I can rebuild this country to its rightful place. No one else here is willing to do what it takes! You all think so small—' A swinging bludgeon knocked him to the floor.

Alva stood above him. 'No one wants to listen to your insane ramblings anymore.' She looked over at Josh, eyes burning with hatred. 'Let's get this over with.'

Leila motioned for Hill to be brought to the gates, at the same time giving orders to pile all of the dead soldiers in lines outside the complex.

Anne caught Josh's arm as everyone hurried to carry out the execution. 'Are you okay?'

He put one arm around her waist. 'Tired but good, you?'

Anne bent in, kissing him quickly. 'Yeah, okay. I can't believe we've almost done it.'

'Almost, that's the word.' He hugged her tightly.

They slowly made their way down to the gates and onto the road. The soldiers' bodies were arranged in lines on either side of the road. Hill was kneeling again; this time next to a group of rangers preparing his fate, with the rope already hanging above him from a sturdy branch over the road. Alva stood behind him, watching.

Josh approached Leila and Matthew. Leila kissed him on each cheek before looking into his eyes.

'You can finally avenge your father.' Josh spoke directly to her, but his voice was loud enough for everyone to hear. 'But I don't take any pleasure in seeing this man die. Everything that has happened has just brought death, for no other reason than one man's twisted desires.'

Leila looked at the kneeling General. 'Let his death be a lesson to everyone. When good people come together, they can overcome anything evil can throw at them.' She looked directly into Hill's eyes. 'He doesn't deserve any more words. Hang him.'

Alva stood to one side. Two men slipped a noose over the General's neck. With no fanfare or further words, he was brutally hoisted into the air, six foot off the ground, before the rope was tied off to the side. Everyone watched as his body twitched and writhed, his face reddening and swollen, till it finally hung there lifeless.

Josh turned to the waiting people. 'Listen, we still need to deal with the remainder of the Army. They will be here soon, so let's get ready. We can lay out the rest of the dead soldiers underneath Hill as a warning to the rest.'

The tired men and women started rushing back to the complex. More bodies were brought down and laid neatly on the road, just under their leader, as he swung there gently.

Once all the dead had been laid out, there was a little time for everyone to rest their muscles, if not their minds. Matthew had gathered the Kernow together, thanking them and urging them on one more time. Leila and Josh were doing the same with their people. But once the speeches were over, it was noticeable how the two groups mingled together freely this time. The battle had made them one, cementing lifelong friendships.

They formed line after line of fighters, just behind the dead soldiers, waiting for what was to come.

Not knowing exactly when the remainder would arrive, it was hard to gauge whether to relax or stay on their guard. Josh opted to sit with most of them, keeping his attention firmly on the road ahead. In the end it was little over an hour, but no one afterwards could recall how long it was.

At the end of the road, just coming around the long bend onto the straight, jogged the foot soldiers of the New English Army. Suddenly, one of the lead men looked up, stumbling at what he saw. The soldiers next to him caught him, then saw the same thing, stopping and shouting to the men behind to do the same.

The soldiers all tried to see what was happening in front of them, faces peering through their disorganised ranks to get a better look.

Seeing them stop fifty yards away, Leila walked forwards with Josh at her side. They stepped through the bodies carefully, walking a few paces beyond.

'It's over. Your Army is dead,' Leila shouted, before motioning with her arm to the swinging body of Hill. 'And there is your master.' She paused. 'If you want to join them, then so be it.'

Behind her, the rangers, the Kernow and the ex-workers from the Army had stood and started screaming at the top of their voices. Josh was startled by the noise. God knows what the soldiers themselves were feeling.

He stepped forwards. 'Or you can surrender now, and I swear that none of you'll be harmed. You'll be disarmed and sent on your way. We know none of you are the senior leadership of this army, so we will be compassionate to you today. You will leave this territory at once and never come back.'

Immediately, about half of the soldiers hurried forwards, throwing their weapons to the ground and putting their hands over their heads. It was clear that these were conscripts who had no desire to die for a lost cause. Josh urged them forwards, then ordered them to get to their knees on the side of the road once they were close enough. Some ran off into the woods, as fast as they could.

At the sight of their treacherous brothers in arms, the remaining rump of the New English Army closed ranks. These were the older, longer-serving members. Thirty men stood together.

Josh shouted once more. 'Don't be stupid. Give in now and we will disarm you and let you go. You don't have to die today.'

'Go to hell,' was the only response that came back.

The soldiers drew their weapons, ready to attack. Suddenly, from both sides, the final strike came. Cador led the way on the right-hand side, followed by the now intermingled fighters screaming at the top of their lungs. At the same time Alva led her team from the left, charging at full tilt at the horrified soldiers.

Within seconds the three groups joined together, the fighting seeming more frantic than ever before. Blades flashed down onto the Army men with such a force it was all they could do to defend with all their will. The rangers in the attack were fighting with everything they had and more.

Watching the sides clash, Josh ran forwards, followed by another twenty men and women. By the time they reached the fight, the tired soldiers were being pummelled into submission, although death was the only certain thing now for them. Some rangers and Kernow had also fallen, but it was almost over.

It didn't last much longer. The last few remaining soldiers were being slaughtered quickly.

When there were only three remaining kneeling on the floor, Cador stepped in to stop them being beaten to within an inch of their lives by a group of blood-covered fighters. One man was pounding a soldier's head again and again with his fist.

'Enough.' His voice boomed to the blood-lusting man beating the soldier. 'They have lost, and we will not stoop to their level by doing this. We may have to fight and kill, but we are not like them. Kill them and be done with it.'

Swiftly, each was despatched by a single stroke from a blade, till no more soldiers remained alive willing to fight for the New English Army.

Josh walked up to Cador, shaking the huge man's hand with all he could give. Cador threw his arms around the smaller man, enveloping him with a giant bear hug.

Everyone made their way to the prisoners, kneeling, guarded menacingly by those workers they had once used.

Leila called Anne over, thanking her yet again for her commitment to their cause. 'Take these prisoners, find out who they are and why they were in the Army.' She ordered to those guarding them, 'I'm sure many were there against their will but be careful just in case. The workers will help you with that task, I'm sure.' She looked at Josh and Cador. 'Let's go home. There's lots to do.'

THIRTY-FIVE

THEY MADE THEIR WAY TO THEIR REGAINED HOME, EXHAUSTED at this bittersweet moment. William's death had been avenged, the territory regained, the Army destroyed. But with such a loss of life, it all seemed so futile.

Leila and Josh headed down to the barracks to check on Tom, to give him the news that it was over. As they reached the door, one of the girls walked straight into them.

'Oh, Leila. I'm sorry, I'm so sorry.' The girl sobbed.

Leila burst past, followed by Josh. They ran inside, seeing Tom lying there, unmoving. Leila knelt down, looking at his motionless face.

Josh joined her, looking at his oldest friend. He pushed some hair away from Tom's face, smoothing it back carefully. Reaching over, he took Leila's hand, holding it tight as she started to sob.

'Oh, Leila, I'm so sorry. This isn't right. He should be with us right now.' He brushed his own tears away. He watched her lower her forehead to Tom's chest. He could only imagine the pain she was experiencing – first her father, now her brother.

Anne came rushing into the room, stopping as she saw the lifeless body on the cot. 'Oh my God!' She put her hands over her mouth.

Josh rubbed Leila's back tenderly, before taking Anne to one side, speaking quietly. 'I'm going to stay here with Leila for a bit, but we need to secure the complex, and maybe the town. I don't think there's anyone left, but after everything that's happened, I want to make sure we aren't caught unawares again. Can you organise patrols?'

'That won't be a problem, everyone will help out.' She looked over Josh's shoulder at Leila and Tom. 'I'll let everyone know what needs doing. How are you?'

Josh shook his head. 'I can't believe it, he's gone.' He closed his eyes as Anne put her arms around him.

Leila lifted her head, eyes red and puffy. 'I need to get medical attention for the wounded and food organised for everyone.'

'We can do that. You stay here a while,' Anne told her.

'No.' She stood up, brushing her clothes down. 'I'm in charge now, I need to do this.' She bowed her head to Tom, saying a quiet prayer before turning to Josh and Anne. 'So, let's get this done.'

They followed Leila outside and headed up to the house. Leila told everyone what she wanted. Josh wasn't surprised by how many volunteered to join the patrols. After getting their gear together, they soon formed teams to patrol the area and headed out.

Josh and Anne watched with pride as the people left.

'We did it,' Josh said quietly. 'It cost so much, but we did it.'

'We did. We did.'

||||||||||||||||||||||||||||||||||||||||||||||||||||||||||||||||||||||||||||

Josh concentrated for the rest of the day on organising the ex-Army workers into work details, pleased at how many were so keen to show their appreciation for their rescue. He used Eddie to help with the task; he was trusted by them for being one of their own. Eddie also confirmed there were no soldiers hiding amongst the workers, trying to save their own skins.

Messages were sent back to Somerton, requests for essential maintenance workers to return, to help restore the complex and the town to its previous state, although once everyone heard the news it was hoped that many more would want to return as well. Irving was heading back, to help Leila with the repairs of the complex and the management of the people. The Kernow assisted where they could, working easily with their new allies.

One of the first orders Leila issued was to find Henry Martgen and bring him to the complex.

For the rest of the day and into the following morning, the immediate attention was spent caring for the wounded. Josh and Anne helped as much as they could, but sadly many succumbed to their wounds.

After a hasty lunch, Josh wandered outside with a steaming hot cup of tea. Wanting to have a few moments to himself before heading back, he sat on the damp grass. He stared over at the cornfield, where he and Nolan had watched events unfold during their escape. Knowing he would never see him again made him angry, such a waste of a good man.

Hearing a noise to his right, he glanced over to see Leila. 'Morning, get some sleep?'

'A little, you?' she replied, looking at the gently swaying corn in front of her as she sat.

'Same.'

They stayed in silence for a while. Leila rested her head on Josh's shoulder as he put his arm around her. The sun rose a little higher, the wind a little faster.

'Any news?' said Josh, breaking the silence.

'The patrols keep returning. It looks like there's no members of the Army left around.'

'That's a start, at least. It's not going to be easy. We've lost so many. With most of the rangers gone, there's only so much we can defend against for the time being.' Josh leant back, a tear forming in his eye. 'I'm so sorry about Tom. I still can't believe it.'

'I know. I don't think I appreciated him properly, not until he's not here. He was always the one who knew he would lead the territory after Dad wasn't here anymore. I don't know how I'll manage.'

'You'll have a lot of help, from all of us.'

Leila looked at him. 'Thank you.'

'So, what's next?'

'We carry on, get everything running again. Just as Dad would have done. I was discussing it with Anne last night and we agree that rebuilding the rangers is a priority. We can't allow us to be unprepared again.'

Josh understood how important that would be. 'I know. We thought things like this were over. Years of peace have made us forget what lessons our great-grandparents learnt after the Chaos.'

'It looks like it, doesn't it? We must never make that mistake again.' Leila turned her head at the sound of a carriage heading through the gates. She nudged him before standing and brushing herself down. 'Let's go see who it is.'

They both hurried to the front of the building. As soon as the carriage stopped, Irving jumped down and rushed over. He and Leila hugged each other.

Josh smiled at the sight, shaking hands firmly when Irving was free. 'Good to have you back, Irv. You've got a lot to do, you know.'

Irving looked the calmest Josh had seen him since William's death. 'It will be an honour to work for the Bowles family once more.'

Leila grabbed his hand firmly, before pulling him towards the house. 'Well, let's get to it, then. God, I'm glad to have you back, Irv. I need your help more than ever now.'

Josh remained standing, watching wagons flowing past the gates heading back into Chilmark, people returning to rebuild their lives after the events of the New English Army. Some harsh shouting caught his attention. Two men and a woman were pulling a man up the driveway, hands tightly tied in front of him, with some bystanders jeering at the sight. It was Henry Martgen, and since Leila had given the order last night to bring him in, people had heard of what he had done. As the most senior representative of Bowles Mercantile nearby, Josh pushed through the gathering throng, stopping as the guard pulled Henry to a halt in front of him. The crowd around fell silent.

'Henry Martgen, traitor to William Bowles.' Josh kept his voice monotone as he spoke. 'I welcome you back to his home, his before you contributed to his death.'

Henry was shaking, trying to hold his head high. 'This is outrageous. How dare you accuse me of such a crime? Taking me away from my home in the middle of the night! I demand to have my rights respected.'

Josh leant in, so only Henry could hear. 'We know about your son Godfrey in that damn Army. He's dead by the way.' He pulled away, so everyone could hear again. 'William was like a father to me and I shall see you hang before the end of the day.'

Josh watched the blood drain from Henry's face. Henry stammered a few sounds but said nothing further.

'Take him inside to Leila's office.' Josh looked at the three guarding the traitor. 'I want you to be with him at all times. He is not to be left alone, understand?'

The three nodded immediately, before bundling the forlorn figure towards the house. Josh watched until they had entered the house then followed them, taking the cheers and thanks from the returned people all around.

By the time he had arrived at the house everyone was heading towards Leila's office. He had to jostle his way through to reach the room. Leila and Irving were already there, and he was soon joined by Anne. Leila kept the door open, letting the watching eyes see everything.

'Why, Henry?' she asked plaintively. 'Why would you do this?'

Henry stood in front of the desk, shaking. 'It wasn't my idea, Leila, I had no choice. The General threatened my family. I didn't want to, but I had my family to protect.'

'Your family? Wasn't your son an officer in his Army?' she spat out.

'Against his will. He would never have joined such a vicious gang.'

Irving jumped to his feet. 'For God's sake, Henry, have some honour and own up to your crime. Instead of trying to make out you're a damn victim here.'

Henry stared at the two of them, his accusers. Realisation spread across his face that he was found out. He took a deep breath. 'I'm sorry. I'm so sorry.'

'So, you admit it?' Josh demanded.

Henry nodded.

Leila stood, putting her clenched fists on the table. She spoke in a distant, quiet voice. 'Take him outside and hang him. I don't want to be there to give him any satisfaction that he deserves an audience. And confiscate his assets and land from his remaining family. They are not to be hurt but banished from our territory.'

Two guards grasped Henry's arms, pulling him out of the office and through the crowd as the other guard cleared the way.

Josh went over to Leila. 'The right decision, Leila, the right decision.'

'Would you make sure he is dealt with, please? Take him round the west side of the house.'

'Of course.' Josh left the room to catch up with the hanging party.

Outside, a large group of people was nearby. He hurried over to them, raising his arms in the air. 'People, people, Leila has ordered this man be hung for treachery.' He paused briefly until the cheer subsided. 'She also ordered it to be unwatched. She doesn't want this man to have an audience for his death. It will be done, but it will be done with no fanfare. No stories will be told about it.'

There was a general murmuring of disagreement amongst those gathered around, but Josh showed his determination to carry out Leila's wishes. He stood there firmly, staring at the crowd until they understood he meant it, and started to disperse. Once they were alone, he walked with Henry's guards round the side of the house.

Another woman hurriedly joined them and threw the rope she had brought over a thick branch of a large yew tree. She tied the end into a noose and placed it over Henry's head. Henry looked resigned to his fate, breathing heavily.

Josh placed a wooden crate under the noose, telling Henry to stand on it, which he did slowly. The woman tied the other end of the rope to another branch, lower than the first, making sure the rope was taut. They were ready.

Josh bowed his head, saying a short prayer for the small group to hear. Just as he was about to carry out Leila's final order, he heard a series of taps from behind him. Everyone looked round, then up, to see Leila at one of the windows on the first floor. She nodded once at Josh to start.

Josh turned to look Henry in the eye. The condemned man was about to open his mouth. Not allowing Henry to speak anymore, Josh kicked the crate from under him and stepped back as he kicked and twitched on the rope. Once Henry was motionless, Josh looked up to the window again, but this time it was empty.

He bowed his head briefly before thanking those who had helped. 'Cut him down and bury him. I don't care where. Just nowhere near here.'

Over the following week the remaining rangers, helped by the Kernow, toured the countryside, searching for signs of any remaining pieces of the Army. Although people relaxed slightly as each day passed with no news, no one wanted to let down their guard too much, so scarred were they by what Hill had done.

A steady flow of residents continued to return to their homes and farms. Although wary, people were determined to return to their lives.

The worst time was when they buried the dead rangers from the battlefield. Over one hundred locals volunteered to help, overwhelming Leila with their generosity. William was brought back, buried alongside his wife in the family's burial plot. The rangers were laid to rest in a large area next to the battlefield, a place where Leila planned to erect a monument to their bravery.

Alva sympathetically tended to Nolan's body before his own burial, having a ceremony attended by the whole of the leadership. Leila offered him a space in the family's plot, a reminder that without the people's support the family were nothing.

The solar facility was being brought back on-line; with the Kernow help, it would soon be back to its full capacity. Irving made the decision to waive the tax on the lectric for the next few months, a move gratefully received by everyone.

At the end of the week, a drizzly Sunday morning, Leila gathered those who had fought so closely with them. Calling a council meeting, she invited the Kernow leadership as well.

Josh had woken early, still struggling to sleep well after all the slaughter. He was sitting in the council chamber, waiting for the others. The smashed glass had been removed and replaced with wooden boards.

Leila was the first to enter, carrying a large bundle of papers stacked neatly under her arm. She smiled as she looked across to Josh. 'Thought you hated these meetings? What are you doing here so early?'

'I thought it's time I took a bit more interest in them, a way of honouring your father, let's say. He always wanted me in these things, so I might as well find out why.'

Leila chuckled as she placed the papers on the desk in front of her. 'I'll bet you get bored halfway through.'

Josh rolled his head from side to side. 'That's a distinct possibility!'

Anne and Irving were the next to join them, deep in conversation as they had been for the last few days. Anne grinned at Josh from across the room; in their spare time they were inseparable now.

As the remaining members of the council came in, Josh waved cheerily to each of them. It was a great achievement to have anyone back around the table. Suddenly, the room fell quiet and he looked over to the door where he saw Matthew and Cador walking in. Then the whole room burst spontaneously into a round of loud applause. The two, slightly bemused, Kernow men didn't know where to look. Josh grinned as he watched Cador's face turning a bright shade of red. Both of them hurried to the nearest chairs, thanking people as they went.

Alva was right behind them, anxiously smiling at everyone, relaxing when she noticed Cador just as nervous as herself.

Leila stood at the head of the table, tapping her fingers on it for quiet. 'Friends, welcome. Thank you all for coming. I'd like to open this Bowles Mercantile council meeting. But before we get down to the business of repairing and running the territory, I want to extend our most grateful thanks to the Kernow, who saved us in our hour of need.'

Everyone stood, once again applauding the two men sat amongst them. Matthew bowed his head as he looked at everyone stood around him; Cador put a hand up reluctantly to accept the applause.

As the applause died down, she continued. 'We can never fully repay them for all they have done, but I propose that we offer a full alliance between our two territories. We have already started sharing our food production knowledge, we will now offer you full disclosure of its manufacturing techniques as well.'

The Bowles council agreed wholeheartedly, with not one against the proposition.

Matthew gave them all a deep bow. 'Thank you, thank you, we are extremely grateful for the offer. Our people will benefit considerably from such an offer. We will accept an alliance between the two territories. Having your ability to produce food plentifully through the winter months will be a huge boon to us. In return we will increase our sharing of lectrics with yourselves. We are also working on reviving more technology from before the Chaos. We have people working on many things deep in the south of our territory – hopefully, we can introduce you to some of that as well.'

'Thank you, Matthew, we accept your kind offer. Sharing each other's skills and technologies will be a huge step between our two peoples. We will both benefit greatly from such an agreement.'

Matthew now stood before the council. 'We are proud of all the advances we have achieved here, but we also hope that our territory has made its first step back into integrating itself with the wider country as well. We know how we are perceived by those around us, for actions our forefathers took, but we also know it is time now to move on. Thank you again for welcoming us into your hearts.'

'We've also agreed to have an ambassador live amongst us, and our own ambassador amongst the Kernow,' Leila told the listening council. 'As such, Matthew's nephew, Cador, has agreed to act in that role, acting as liaison with their own collective.' She smiled at Cador. 'And we will send one of our own back with Matthew to act on our behalf.'

Alva, sitting at the other end of the room, beamed with a broad smile at the news.

Irving leant forwards. 'May I ask for a vote from the council on our proposals.'

As ever, one by one the council members cast their vote. It was the quickest vote ever conducted, and no one was surprised by the unanimous verdict.

'Although I have to report fully to our collective, I have already discussed some of these matters with them and I can assure you my consent with these agreements will not be challenged,' Matthew told the watching people. 'We shall return home tonight, but I will leave forty of our best militia, just in case any remnants of the Army are still around. I know that you will not rebuild your rangers quickly, so if you need us for anything we shall return as soon as we can to your aid.'

'Thank you again, Matthew,' said Leila. 'Now, I propose that we allow our visitors to leave with our thanks, so they can organise the return of their brave men and women to their homes.'

Matthew and Cador stood, taking their leave from the appreciative council. As they left, Leila took the opportunity to break up the meeting for an hour while they bid farewell.

Josh stood outside waiting for Matthew and his team to leave. They would collect their militia on the way, sending the ones who were to stay here as soon as they could. Anne rested her head on his shoulder, his arm gripping her tightly to him. Leila came out of the house, heading straight for them.

'Right, you two, back to work,' Leila told them. 'Haven't got time to waste, plenty to do.'

Anne looked a little put out that she wouldn't be able to say farewell to the Kernow, but Josh stood his ground. Luckily for Anne, Leila laughed a moment later.

'Sorry, couldn't help it,' she said as she composed herself. 'Josh, I've been talking to Anne and we have a proposition for you.'

Josh looked curiously at the both of them, sensing a catch. 'Okay, what is it?'

'We know you cared for Dad as much as anyone and saw him as a father in more ways than one. And believe me, he looked on you as a son, everyone knew it. So, we want you to have the farmstead and lands of the Martgens. The rest of them have already left, God knows to where and frankly I don't care. But it needs an owner. We think Dad would approve of you taking it over.'

Josh was staggered by the offer. 'I couldn't possibly take it on – it's too much, it really is.'

'Nonsense, you're more than capable. And it's about time you grew up and took some responsibility on for the family. You're a part of us, and we need those lands producing for us.' Leila glanced at Anne. 'Besides, you can't settle down and start a family without a home, can you?'

Josh felt his face flush. Anne was grinning beside him. She patted his arm, winking at Leila as she did.

'Good. I'm glad that's settled then.' Leila laughed. 'Now, let's say goodbye to Matthew.'

They walked towards their new friends, ready to say goodbye for now.

GLOSSARY

Bowles Mercantile: From Gloucester to the Isle of Wight to the old city of London, the Bowles company holds sway over all matters of business and security. Based in their main complex at Chilmark, Bowles has grown over the last few decades to be the richest and most influential power in the region. The company is governed by their council in all matters, with quarterly board meetings to assess the state of the company and set its direction. The board (consisting of approximately twenty members from the territory) votes according to share ownership or privileges, meaning this can change quite quickly depending on the success or failure in business of the various board members. Currently, the Bowles family own, or control, sixty-five percent of the voting rights and so retain ultimate control of the company.

The Chaos: The name given to the events of the collapse of civilisation and when plague almost wiped out humanity. Commonly dated to start in 2057.

Firestones: Chemically manufactured stones, which when struck together spark into fire, hot enough for a few minutes to burn without any wood. They are imported from the Welsh valleys, and it is a highly guarded secret how they are made.

France: Reports from the occasional fishing ship and merchants who have small dealings with the French across the Channel show that the north of France is governed from just outside the remains of Paris. They appear to have the same level of living standards as the territories in England, with reports of the southern part of the country being completely uninhabitable, for unknown reasons.

Kernow Collective: Area consisting of what used to be Devon and Cornwall in the south of England. An executive system which imbues their leader with total power. It is made up of representatives from large towns and production centres, as well as fishing groups and mining cooperatives. Currently led by Matthew Taylor, head of the family that owns many copper mines and most of the solar pane industry, Kernow's main export. Currently, it is the only major technological territory known about. They have for decades operated a fairly strict isolationist policy; trading is welcomed but they keep themselves to themselves. They have a good relationship with Bowles Mercantile, and have a fairly relaxed border system between the two.

Plazt: Ultra-strong material. Plastic mixed with carbon fibre which could be extruded into shapes or sheets. Building was revolutionised by its invention, but the manufacturing technique has been lost since the Chaos. People became good at reusing the durable material for modern life.

Solar Power: The main export of the Kernow Collective. With the re-opening of the tin and copper mines, combined with their glass industry, they restarted the production of solar panes to collect the sun's energy.

With power still only needed at a fairly low level (or for quite specific areas of industry), they are the sole makers of the products and as such retain strict control of who uses it and what for.

Water/Algae Farming: Originally developed out of the seaweed farming industry, the techniques were developed into a huge industry pre-Chaos to help alleviate the world's food shortage. It was forgotten during the post-Chaos decades. The Bowles family restarted production to help during winters after poor harvests. It also greatly improves health, hugely important in these days of basic medicine. The main processing plant at Somerton turns the farmed algae into edible protein products.

Weapons: The main weapon of choice is the short sword, approximately two feet in length. Most territories teach blade swordsmanship from an early age. The most highly skilled swordsmen are the ruling classes, having been trained since childhood. Most people are, however, fairly proficient due to the necessity of current life.